The Bastard of Saddle Isle

Daniel Barr

AOS Publishing, 2025
Copyright © 2025 Daniel Barr

ISBN: 978-1-998662-42-5

Cover Design: Meredith Lindsay

Visit AOS Publishing's website:
www.aospublishing.com

*The Bastard of Saddle Isle is dedicated to my family,
especially to my father*

The Patricians of Saddle Isle - 1096:

House Northorpe:

Lord Bruk, son of Betra, (b. 1080)

Lord Robt, son of Betra, (b. 1081)

Lord Neman, son of Betra, (b. 1082)

Lord Suln, son of Ferma, (b. 1085)

Lady Breck, daughter of Ferma, (b. 1090)

House Matfen:

Lady Daid, daughter of Rean, (b. 1083)

Lord Angull, son of Limo, (b. 1086)

Lord Maxim, son of Limo, (b. 1086)

Lady Oline, daughter of Mar, (b. 1090)

House Wharram:

Lord Eli, son of Manty, (b. 1076)

Lady Kezi, daughter of Coe, (b. 1078)

Lady Bennk, daughter of Stanp, (b. 1079)

Lord Kinby, son of Stanp, (b. 1081)

Lord Bris, son of Coe, (b. 1081)

Lady Wonin, daughter of Manty, (b. 1082)

House Pearson:

Lady Catar, daughter of Nea, (b. 1083)

Lord Shay, son of Nea, (b. 1087)

Lord Barrat, son of Nea, (b. 1090)

House Hepston:

Lady Anto, daughter of Elan, (b. 1091)

Lady Aott, daughter of Elan, (b. 1095)

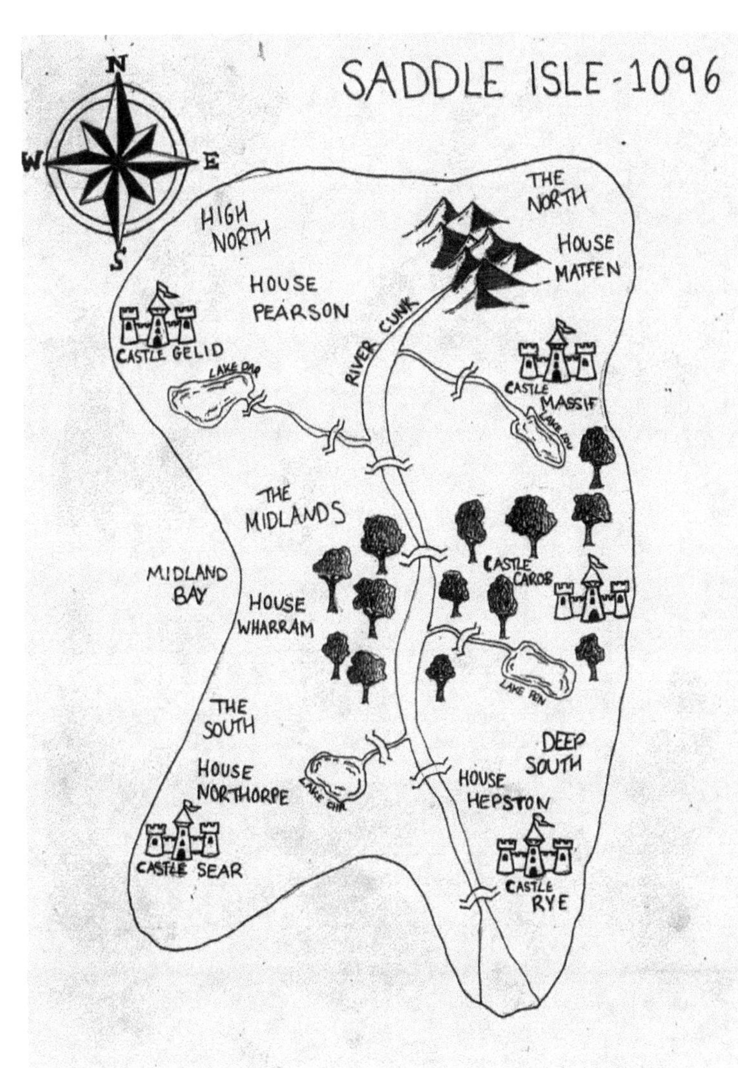

SADDLE ISLE - 1096
N
W E
S
HIGH NORTH
THE NORTH
HOUSE PEARSON
HOUSE MATFEN
CASTLE GELID
LAKE DAR
RIVER CLUNK
CASTLE MASSIF
LAKE IDU
THE MIDLANDS
CASTLE CAROB
MIDLAND BAY
HOUSE WHARRAM
LAKE PEN
THE SOUTH
DEEP SOUTH
HOUSE NORTHORPE
LAKE CHR
HOUSE HEPSTON
CASTLE SEAR
CASTLE RYE

The Great Voyage of 1096

Who am I, who deems himself important enough to request your attention for such an arduous account of a history that you know nothing of prior to my telling? Lord Barrat, son of Nea, of House Pearson - that's who I am. Yes, that ridiculous amalgamation of words is what my name became once nobility was thrust upon my lap. I prefer the simplicity of Barrat alone, although most were forced by law to call me by my full title. I say forced because, if given the choice, they wouldn't even bother to call me Barrat. Some would call me the Bastard of Saddle Isle. Others who lived long enough to know it would call me the Fleeing Bastard. At least those names, cruel as they were, are far easier to remember than: Lord Barrat, son of Nea, of House Pearson. What a ludicrous task for anyone, being implored to remember twenty titles as long as mine. I am a lord by law, and the people never had the power to change that. I have been a lord as such since I was of six years, give or take. You see, I am the bastard son of King William II, who himself was the son of King William I, better known as William the Bastard or even more commonly known as William the Conqueror. But being a bastard meant that I was worthless in regard to nobility in the eyes of the Catholic English population, as were the nineteen other bastards he fathered.

King William II was a figure shrouded in rumour and mystery. Of course, my knowledge on the matter has only been formed from the tales of others who speculated about my father's actions. The religious people of the land were ashamed of their king as he often engaged in scandalous sexual activity, which of course resulted in his bastard children, myself included. People even speculated that he not only enjoyed the pleasures of women, but also the pleasures of men. What people did not give my father credit for was his care. Although my family was poor in our little village, Pearson, the king always ensured that we were safe and not struggling for food. Many labelled the king as a drunk and a whore lover, and he may well have spent many a night on the ale and paying for pleasure, but I believe that the king built genuine connections with the people that he lay with. Take my mother, Nea, for example. They called my mother a whore for mothering the king's bastards, yet she bore three children to the king. Why would my father often return to my mother's side when visiting Pearson if there were no feelings there? People who were acquainted with my father have always suggested that, although he never married or settled down, it was never because he did not care for people. If anything it was the opposite. My father loved too many and could never choose just one to give his love to. Of course I resented him for not being around. I resented him for never being a father to me but just a name I would hear every once in a while. I wanted a father to teach me how to be a man. I craved his knowledge and his affection, however I was constantly kept from him because of the world we lived in. To most, I was an abomination and so was unworthy of any love.

My father may not have been the best of kings but in our time of need he saved us from what could have been disastrous for all tarnished with the bastard title, and I possess enough humility to admit his good deed towards us. The year was 1096 and my father was worried for his life. His brother, Henry, despised my father's disinterest in his own power and so many rumours arose that he was planning regicide to take the throne. Henry had always hated the tarnish of 'bastard' towards his father's name and so he despised all bastards of England, and this worried my father. The powerful often lack logic, and if Henry was to become king then all bastards in England were in danger of perishing under his rule, including myself and my bastard siblings. My father never did produce a legitimate heir and so the throne was Henry's for the taking, and that is the reason why Saddle Isle was given to the bastards. He shipped us off to an island within England's control, along with as many other bastards of England that could be saved without Henry discovering the king's actions. Very few knew of this island because it was in a rather inconvenient geographical position and hadn't been inhabited for centuries. It came as a surprise that our father knew of it. I am led to believe that the king read about its history in some ancient pieces found by a scholar friend of his, and so sent his most trusted men to see if the land truly did exist. They found that it not only existed but was perfectly inhabitable too. We sailed for two seasons across the rough seas, sailing past France and Spain towards lands untouched, and were acquainted with the other noble bastards for the first time. Brothers and sisters of many names and places all under one sail, united through our father's seed alone. Twenty children who ranged between the ages of one and nineteen, all not knowing what was happening but knowing that they would never see their mother again.

*** * * ***

I was of six years when we set sail, seven upon arrival. This meant I was at an age where I could only remember glimpses of my own mother, but too young to understand why I had to leave. But I still do remember those glimpses, even now. I remember her green eyes and her soft smile. How she would cradle me in her arms when the snow fell and keep me warm when the nights grew coldest. She would sing me off to sleep in the sweetest of voices with an Anglo-Saxon lullaby that her mother sang to her:

> Hush, the wind blows wildly,
> And all the stars shine low,
> But I will be beside ye',
> From now until I go.
> Let all the earthly wonder,
> Close ye' eyes so wide,
> To let ye' see and ponder,
> What lurks on the other side.

In truth, all the nighttime songs my mother sang were bleak. Perhaps she was trying to make dreaming seem an improvement on reality. When she sang those words to me I would drift right off to sleep and wake again in the morrow as if no time had passed at all. I haven't slept soundly ever since I was dragged out of her arms by my sister. I don't think I'll ever sleep soundly again, if truth be told. I have everything now that I could ever wish for and yet I still cannot drift off into the sleepy lands that my mother transported me to through her song all those years ago. But that's beside the point - I must apologise for that. I have a rather active mind, you see. It's the only reason that I'm still alive to write this historical tale of Saddle Isle today, so I cannot quibble about my mind's wonderment all too much. I was telling you of the ship on which we travelled to our new promised-land. A land in which being a bastard meant nothing as all men and women were. A land in which all twenty bastards went from being the lowest of the low to lords and ladies of the provinces, with each house being given their own freedoms and responsibilities alike. The land sounded great from all accounts. As I said, I was too young to fully comprehend for myself the vastness of the opportunity that lay ahead for us all. My sister, Lady Catar, however, was more than pleased with our voyage. She saw this as an opportunity for her own greatness. My sister taught both my brother, Lord Shay, and I what she considered to be the values of what it meant to be a patrician of House Pearson. This notion was supported by our nursemaid, Miss Norma: a small lady with short greying hair that was always tied neatly, and a slightly worn face that was only lifted by the kindness in her bright blue eyes. She was responsible for our care and education and was very capable of it, but she was too intelligent to contradict the wishes of her provincial leader. As you probably may have derived for yourself, my sister was named Head of House for the Pearsons, and neither my brother nor I were too perturbed about that, at least not upon our arrival. Despite the lessons that Lady Catar tried to teach me, we never did fully agree on what was best for our people. Perhaps that is why there was so much animosity between us.

But the boat - yes, the boat. The ship, I should say. It was a grand vessel named The Conqueror, presumably after my grandfather. The new lords and ladies sailed on the same vessel in an attempt to acquaint us all. It was thought that this would secure peace, and so we met our brothers and sisters from other villages for the first time whilst on board. The other bastards soon followed in their thousands upon ships less grand than ours but pleasant enough nonetheless. There were, of course, the bastards that were sent years prior to our arrival to construct villages, develop farmlands, and oversee the growing of crops - which I'm sure was an idea that didn't directly descend from my father but a good decision either way. They were also tasked with amending three pre-existing castles, presumably from an unknown history, as well as to completely construct two further ones in the South and the Deep South. It was three years after our arrival that the pre-existing castles were fully restored back to their former glory, and a further three years to complete the construction of the two newly built castles. It was a miracle that they were in a good enough condition for us to have a home on arrival, although all patricians had been used to the customary timber housing with thatched straw roofs whilst in England, and so wouldn't have minded residing in homes not too dissimilar on the isle, despite those builds not necessarily coinciding with our newly found nobility.

Back to the ship. The Conqueror was constructed from oak, the traditional wood for construction and one that the lands of England had a copious amount of. Twenty cabins, but not one for each bastard. Each house had one cabin between them, apart from House Wharram who had two as they were the biggest house, with six to their name. The other cabins were for a crew that included sailors, cooks (most of whom remained with us on the isle to serve the bastards of the king), and the captain. It was the captain's job to teach the self-elected heads of the houses the protocol of the island. This included telling them of their lands and what they are most useful for. He also taught all patricians their basic expectations to aid their Head of House in protecting all citizens of the isle. We were split into five houses based on the small villages in which our mother's resided. These houses all had names: House Pearson, House Matfen, House Wharram, House Northorpe and House Hepston. I am a member of House Pearson. I have already mentioned how my sister - Lady Catar, daughter of Nea, of House Pearson - was our Head of House but there were four others for you to be introduced to, and you shall learn of the other provincial leaders soon enough, I assure you.

*** * * ***

The ship was a rather dull experience for a child. Everyone's names were too pompous or damn stupid for me to remember, and all were on their best behaviour in order to remain amicable with those who were to be their greatest allies when docking. I was all too young to be bothered about amicability. I was not the youngest, though. No, the youngest was Lady Aott, daughter of Elan, of House Hepston. She was barely of one year when we set sail. Her sister: Lady Anto, daughter of Elan, of House Hepston, was merely of five years and was already their Head of House as they were the only two noble bastards from their province. It's scary the power placed into the hands of those only noble by the contents of their blood and not by their valour or their intellectual abilities. Having said that, Lady Anto became a fantastic leader, so maybe I am too quick to judge. Either way, having a ruler who is only of five years seemed foolish and so she was assisted by a trusted elder, who was an acquaintance of our father, until she bled and became a woman. There were others of five, but even they were too young to entertain me. My own brother: Lord Shay, son of Nea, of House Pearson, was of eight years and so was expected to roam about the place pretending like he wasn't a fool. I was rather alone.

That was until I was introduced to another of six years: Lady Breck, daughter of Ferma, of House Northorpe, who had been ill for the first season of our voyage. Northorpe was a landlocked province of England, you see, and so she had never seen the sea before, let alone sailed. The strange movement in the night made her incredibly sick but she eventually adapted to her new oceanic normality. Once she emerged from her cabin to meet us all for the first time, we became friends instantly. She had the same cheeky wit as me, although nowhere near to the same extent. We would strut the decks as if they were halls of our very own castle. We would be at each other's side for the duration of the day and would spend the nights eager to be at each other's side once more. Her deep, brown eyes were mine to look into and mine alone. We belonged to each other, best friends despite the barriers of opposing house names. After weeks of our precious routine we were all told that our docking day was just a few weeks ahead.

"I can't wait to get there, to the isle." Lady Breck said in her soft voice. She was always optimistic about what was to follow, which I liked.

"Me too. Think of all the adventures we'll have and all the land we can explore!" She was so excited that words ceased to exit her mouth.

"I'm so happy that we met," she eventually replied.

"Me too."

I always knew that we would be connected, somehow.

****

Our plans for adventure were a tad premature, I must admit. We hadn't considered the vast land that would separate us from each other. We were made to live within the provinces of the isle allocated to our houses, and our respective provinces were located on opposite sides of the land. Here is how Saddle Isle was divided:

- ❖ Being from the north of England ourselves, those of House Pearson, along with roughly 600 bastards for us to rule over, settled in the High North in a small castle named Gelid.
- ❖ Next to us in the North were those of House Matfen, who were granted Castle Massif to live within. The castle was located just below the mountains, where the source of the River Cunk was located. They were provided with around 1,000 bastards.
- ❖ In the centre of the isle known as the Midlands, which was the biggest span of land, were those of House Wharram at Castle Carob. They were granted roughly 1,500 bastards, some of whom enjoyed living in the woodland areas of the province and so took up little village space.
- ❖ My best friend and her new family of House Northorpe settled in the South, where they were tasked with mining the caves along their beaches for metal to weld into tools and precautionary weapons. They resided in Castle Sear and had a healthy 1,200 bastards to their name.
- ❖ Finally, the two young girls of House Hepston took up the Deep South, where the mouth of River Cunk met the sea. They were predominantly in charge of crops and so were granted 700 bastards to work the fields, which was a great amount considering that they possessed the smallest province. Their castle was named Rye after the crops that they grew.

This meant that the twenty bastards were tasked to control between five and six thousand bastards, despite none of us ever having even a scent of power in our lives. Obviously, not all the bastards of England at risk of destruction could be saved by Saddle Isle, and so many were left behind. The vast majority of the bastards that did make the journey were of twenty years up to being of twenty-five years. There were exceptions of older and younger bastards, but this age range made up the vast majority, which was beneficial as reproduction would be needed for sustainability. What I will say is that we were not expected to start a new civilization from scratch, it was more that we were expected to maintain the functioning civilization that they had spent a few years laying for us. It was ensured that each house had their own source of natural water and enough land to cater to their new people. They were also provided with livestock to feed them that were acquired from lands in closer proximity to the isle, with breeding being a priority on their arrival. The two most northern provinces were granted only sheep and pigs, whereas the other provinces also possessed cows. That being said, the northern waters were full of fish that we would trade with the south for beef when it suited. Being fair was deemed the key to peace, and peace was paramount for our survival, so it was difficult to argue against what was given. Of course, I didn't care all that much about the fairness of the provinces - not when I was so young. I didn't care that the people had enough to eat or that they were blessed by the Leonist gods so that Lake Dar (the lake within the High North) would be full enough to provide all with water for the season. I just wanted to see Lady Breck. I just wanted to see my friend.

The Patricians and The Houses

I have taught you the names and properties of the provinces and have invited you into my family history to meet my brother and sister. What I haven't done, however, is teach you of the houses that are not my own. I shall do you that honour now, beginning with those of House Hepston. Now, I shall remind you that the two young girls were named: Lady Anto, daughter of Elan; and Lady Aott, daughter of Elan. The expectation was for all in the same house to treat each other as if they were siblings whether they shared the same mother or not. In this case, the girls did share the same mother and so were considered blood siblings. The Saddle Isle project was a thorough and well thought out ordeal but was far from perfect on many counts. The biggest contradiction that always puzzled me was the mentality towards fathers on the Isle. The elders, who helped the naive patricians to establish laws and order, decided that the patriarch of each bastard was disregarded on the basis that they were irresponsible and mostly absent. Of course, this contradicted the forming of the patricians of Saddle Isle, as we were chosen because of our connection to our father, King William II. It was decided that, because the king had designed a safe and effective process for fearful bastards to leave England, his wish for his bastard sons and daughters to rule as patricians should be respected. However, by law, his parentage was disregarded in favour of our mothers, and so (unless we shared the same mother as each other) we were not all considered brother and sister.

Back in England, Lady Anto and Lady Aott lived within the comfort of the south amongst farmers of the land. This was partially the reason for their position upon Saddle Isle. Their mother, Elan, once sewed clothes for the workers of Hepston, an honest living. Although the king always ensured that they had enough, Miss Elan was a woman of great pride and so wanted to contribute to her daughter's stability directly. Of course, Lady Aott was only a babe when she boarded The Conqueror and so her mother never got the chance to provide for her. During the Prosperity Era of our land, which lasted until the year 1108, the two girls grew to be both strong-willed and kind, often rewarding the men of the fields and the women of the river mouth with grand feasts and celebrations of their work. That is more that can be said about some other provinces. I often wonder how some got it so wrong in the treatment of their people, especially as we were once exactly like them. Lady Anto was rather small, even as a woman, but held mighty power through her intelligence and fairness. It probably helped that she was also rather beautiful and so was sought after by many patricians and commoners alike. Her large, hazel eyes were a cause for attraction and her hair altered in colour with the seasons, being a darker brown in the winter but light once the sun shone. Lady Aott never was considered across the land to be as beautiful as her older sister, but that did not mean that she didn't have her admirers. Her lighter blonde hair made it easier to differentiate between the two of them, especially considering that Lady Aott's eyes were just as striking as Lady Anto's. Although she was moderately taller in height, Lady Aott had struggles with the transition into womanhood, causing her quite a bit of anxiety. Because of this, she never held the same authority in conversation that her sister was so brilliant with, but she was always a kind soul who had much love to give. I would often ride to the Deep South to visit the two ladies. At one point I was given responsibility to ensure that each province received an appropriate quota of crops each season and, as the Deep South was the only province that possessed the right soil and climate for such mass growth, I saw them more often than most. Well, other than those of House Northorpe, but that was very rarely a business visit.

The isle was not excessively large. In fact, I would say it was the perfect size for us to cater for all of our refugees as well as allowing for us to grow and develop as a prospective country. Despite the comparably small size of our land, the journey between the High North and the Deep South lasted longer than a day's travel. This was because crossing between borders was somewhat infeasible at nightfall, not if one wanted to avoid danger. This was most prominent through the Midlands, more of which you will discover later. I had travelled through nightfall on rare occasions during my time but it was certainly not suggestable for one to attempt, and was a rather fearsome experience for the most part. In contrast, travel from the High North to the South could be managed on horseback within daylight hours, but one would have to travel a short stretch through slight darkness during the colder seasons, which was inconvenient but perfectly feasible. This meant that to travel from the High North to the Deep South, whether in the winter or summer, one would be required to set a suitable camp to ensure protection through the night. I never did mind the long journey, however, as on each occasion that I made that long trip to the Deep South I was always treated well. It was almost as if they were happy to see me, which I know wasn't true. It was a real inconvenience for them to give crops away. It was hard enough feeding the mouths of their own as it was. I shall never forget their kindness.

*** * * ***

Those of House Matfen were rather different. Matfen was located on the Eastside of England and so was inhabited by many Nordic ladies looking for some money to fill her pocket. Unlike Elan of Hepston, the Nordic women weren't so keen on working for the village. Rather, they would sell themselves to passing soldiers, including the most noble of them all: my father, the king. It was because of their Nordic mothers that they were placed in the mountainous province of Saddle Isle. House Matfen was composed of four: Lady Daid, daughter of Rean; Twins, lords Maxim and Angull, sons of Limo; and the youngest and most beautiful of all: Lady Oline, daughter of Mar. Unlike House Hepston and House Pearson, the patricians of House Matfen had differing mothers. Lady Daid and Lady Oline were not considered siblings because all fathers were disregarded by law and they did not share the same mother. However, because they resided in the same house, they were expected to act as siblings and create a family dynamic together with the other members of House Matfen. You'd have thought that the differing mothers would cause inner house conflict, but that would be incorrect. Power for one meant power for all and so sticking together was beneficial. Besides, their mothers were gone so what good was loyalty to them?

Lady Daid was elected Head of House, which was quite the shock. Unlike my own sister, Lady Daid hadn't yet bled and so was not considered a woman. Nonetheless, she was still the eldest of her house and so took up the position of head. Lady Daid was an innocent enough girl, but throughout the Prosperity Era she grew to be a brutish woman, towering over six feet tall with freakish strength and unexpected speed. More often than not, she wore her shoulder-length black hair tied up as if she was anticipating conflict at any moment. I only ever saw her with her hair down once, and that was during an impromptu visit to her chamber. She was a warrior, that was for sure, as were her two younger brothers, although they never reached her height and ferocity. Lady Oline, however, was the polar opposite. She was small, almost fragile, and possessed long, flowing, ginger hair that never looked bedraggled or untidy. She certainly appeared more regal and dignified than her siblings, which was understandable considering the differing strength and stature between Lady Oline and the others. She was, by all regard, the most beautiful woman in the entire land and many, including my own brother, wanted her hand in marriage when we all reached adulthood. However, Lady Daid refused any proposals for her to marry before her eighteenth year despite that she bled five years prior, and so she remained unmarried for the entirety of the Prosperity Era.

Despite those of House Matfen living closer to me than most, I very rarely visited Castle Massif, the main reason being that the house rarely broke trading protocol and so my presence was scarcely needed. However, whenever I did go, I was always wary. I never did trust Lady Daid. There was violence within her and her desire for power meant that there was little certainty about her alliance, no matter how guaranteed it seemed. I always feared that her ruling in the North would lead to an isle-wide conflict. It is fair to say that, when that conflict came, she played her part.

****

The Midlands, in which those of House Wharram resided, was the largest of the provinces, but the house was the largest noble family so it was difficult to argue against the logic behind them ruling there. They were a house derived from nature, to put it kindly, having lived in the woodlands in England before the voyage and being keen to get back to some sort of normality when we docked. As you can imagine, they weren't as civilised as the other houses and would often abandon their castle walls to roam the woodlands at night to hunt the wildlife within their borders. They were entitled to do this, of course. As I said, they were a rather large house with six to their name. Their Head of House was Lord Eli, son of Manty, of House Wharram. He was a brutish individual, in a similar fashion to the aforementioned Lady Daid. His shaven head, which was down to the scalp and often painted with splotches of blood either from himself after a shave or his enemies after a battle, was accompanied by a bushy beard that was always dirty and straggly. The scars across his face and torso were worn with great pride and his muscular physique was either admired or feared by all across the isle.

As the Head, he led his house siblings: Lady Bennk, daughter of Stanp (whom he was said to have relations with); Lady

Wonin, daughter of Manty; Lord Bris, son of Coe; Lady Kezi, daughter of Coe; and finally, Lord Kinby, son of Stanp. None were particularly dignified or attractive, other than Lady Wonin, who seemed rather out of place amongst her siblings. They had heart, though, and a real sense of freedom. Perhaps we should've seen societal restraint as an issue from the beginning. It is only when listing the members of such a large house that I truly realise the ridiculousness of the titles that the captain of The Conqueror gave to us on our voyage. But one should not complain. It was but a small inconvenience for those who were set to rule despite our inexperience in that department. I mentioned the woodland before and shall mention it again, as the woodland was the staple of the Midlands. The main tree of the isle was oak, however the carob tree was also an inhabitant of Saddle Isle. Oak was used to construct our necessities, such as ships, but carob was also used to create ornaments and was considered to be a high value wood. It was the job of the Midland folk to provide wood for construction. It was also their job to construct the nine bridges across the kingdom to allow for passage across the River Cunk as well as streams that led to the four lakes: Lake Dar in the High North, Lake Lou in the North, Lake Fen in the Midlands, and Lake Chr in the South. The Deep South didn't have a lake but they did live alongside the river's mouth so there was plenty of fresh water for them.

My personal interactions with the Wharram House during the Prosperity Era were usually rather pleasant. Well, not pleasant, but more pleasant than one may expect considering their nature. I wouldn't have to visit all too often, which was good for me. I was rather intimidated by them, if truth be told. It was mostly my friend, Miss Frith, that dealt with them when that was necessary, but I visited to discuss more unconventional trades every once in a while and that never went awfully. I attribute that to the fact Lady Wonin was often the patrician I would converse with as her fellow house members often spent days on end in the woodlands. She became a trustworthy friend of mine over time. I never anticipated a pursuit of power from those of House Wharram at any point. They seemed too free to crave politics. However, their actions within their own province were frowned upon by other houses and so they were under the threat of being controlled. That was never going to go down well.

****

The inhabitants of the South were always my favourite to visit during the Prosperity Era, as I'm sure you'd have guessed. My beloved friend, Lady Breck, resided there with the rest of those of House Northorpe. They were originally from the south of England and were used to their position on Saddle Isle, which brought me great comfort despite preventing me from seeing Lady Breck as regularly as we had hoped. Those of the South were tasked with welding and metalwork. They were responsible for making fishing tools, supports for the bridges, and the forging of weapons that would be vital in case of an attack from Henry, which was unlikely but not impossible. They also possessed yielding land like the Deep South, but the South utilised the soil to grow vineyards as the climate allowed for it. Subsequently, the South made the land's wine, resulting in those of House Northorpe being rather affluent.

Along with Lady Breck, daughter of Ferma, of House Northorpe, there were four other members, or siblings by association, of the house. There was Lord Bruk, son of Betra, who was the Head of House. There were also three other men: Lord Robt, son of Betra; Lord Neman, son of Betra; and my friend's blood brother, Lord Suln, son of Ferma, with whom I was rather good friends at a time. I had many good, personal experiences with those of House Northorpe and would go as far to say that the relationship developed between myself and their family was often key to my own survival. Of course, I spent most of my time with Lady Breck, whom I only grew to love more and more on each visit. Her joyous attitude to life and her ability to make even the most dull of affairs enjoyable made every second I spent with her worthwhile. I did, however, gain the respect and admiration of her brothers, who all would be gladdened by my visits. I was particularly appreciative of Lord Bruk's affection for me as it meant a lot to have the approval of the Head of House. I always admired how demonstrative he was, and his appearance only enhanced his approachable nature. He was of medium build with consistently short brown hair and demanded respect due to his calm nature and his kindness. His warm smile always made me feel welcome with his family, bringing Lady Breck and myself much comfort over the years. Whenever the Council of Heads met in the High North, Lord Bruk would make an effort to see me and would teach me what it truly meant to be a leader - something that my sister seemed to deem unimportant for me to know.

"You'll make a great leader one day, Barrat," Lord Bruk would say. He was wrong, but I adored him and his family possibly more than my own.

The Prosperity Era

I won't undermine your intelligence by explaining the meaning of prosperity to you, but I will tell you how we came to the conclusion that our first years on Saddle Isle were prosperous. The first Council of Heads agreed to dedicate copious hours of labour and devotion to maintaining the work done by those who sailed before us. Of course, it was the common folk that did most of the work. It was important that the fields were worked, and it was even more important that the workers were paid for their service fairly. In the High North, that was the job of my brother, Lord Shay. He was the people's favourite, afterall.

Lord Shay was a truly great man. He certainly felt more like family to me than Lady Catar ever did, but it would always frustrate me how he would never call her out. He was closer in age to her, so maybe if he supported my arguments against our sister then we might have avoided some of her mistakes. But I could never be mad at Lord Shay. He had a kindness like no one else. I have spoken of the kindness of the likes of Lady Anto and Lord Bruk, who I admired greatly, however neither of their kindness was as unpolitical or natural as Lord Shay's. His kindness was as pure as he was. That's why everyone in the High North loved him. He, like myself, was a small man with long, flaxen hair that he often left freely hanging whilst I sported mine in a top knot on most days. However, unlike me, he was strong and practical. He was fascinated by fishing and working on the ships and he spent as much time as he could throughout our childhood down at the dock, enhancing his strength and physique over time. The most annoying thing for me, though, was his beard. It was so thick and prominent - not a patch in sight. I could never grow a beard like that, no matter how many times I tried.

Lady Catar was never really liked by our people. She wasn't particularly liked by me, and I was her own blood. These people were under our rule because they were told to be, that was all. It was important that there was one of us that they could respect, at least. I couldn't tell you what the common folk of the High North thought of me. I was rather popular when I was a child, but patrician children were always adored by the people. Once I grew, I spent most of my time moving about, never free to be the people's favourite patrician of House Pearson. But my brother had to serve some sort of purpose, I suppose. I joke, of course, he was a great asset to the province.

* * * *

The Prosperity Era lasted from our docking in 1096 up until the year 1108, when I was of nineteen years. That was when peace no longer lasted in the land and the twenty bastards became the twelve. The era of prosperity was the greatest in the history of the Saddle Isle. It was the time in which the crops grew strongest and the animals bred well to provide plenty of meat for all. It was at a time when all five provinces were united, and when all five provinces were led by all five houses. It was a time in which I fell in love with Lady Breck and a time in which her entire family respected me. Some of their respect remained past the threshold of prosperity, but some is never as great as all. All seemed fair as all was fair. That's the only way to share power, through keeping things fair. The second one has more power than any other... no, that isn't strong enough. The second one simply craves having more power than any other, then all camaraderie falls apart. Fairness is a pillar of peace, but fairness was lost. I saw it coming. You may not necessarily believe me, but I did. I saw the violence within Lady Daid. I saw those of House Wharram attempt to break free from restraints. I saw my own sister lose a sense of logic over the prospect of power. How could we remain fair when so many wanted everything? I would give anything to have the Prosperity Era restored. Well, perhaps not everything.

The Council of Heads

Whilst explaining the various houses of Saddle Isle, I mentioned the Council of Heads on a few occasions and so I shall explain it properly. The council was comprised of the five Heads of House: Lady Catar, daughter of Nea, of House Pearson; Lord Eli, son of Manty, of House Wharram; Lady Anto, daughter of Elan, of House Hepston; Lord Bruk, son of Berta, of House Northorpe; and Lady Daid, daughter of Rean, of House Matfen. The council would meet at the change of every season and the location of each meeting would alter on rotation. Each Head would take turns to host their fellow leaders and each meeting would be led by the ruler of the province in which it took place, which proved a logical way to fairly dictate matters within the land in an order that maintained peace and mutuality. For years, I never got anywhere near a council meeting. Whenever meetings took place in the High North, Lord Bruk would bring along his sister, who was always as keen to see me as I was to see her.

"She pesters me all the time to let her see your brother, you know," Lord Bruk would tell Lady Catar, who would laugh and tell him that I was the same, which was the truth.

Similarly, when the meetings were held in the South, my sister would allow me to travel with her, which would always please me. Lady Catar would often comment on how irritating I was due to my excitement on our journey down. I would constantly talk of Lady Breck and tell her of what my friend and I had planned for our few days together. There were also times when Lord Shay would take me to see her, and when her brother, Lord Suln, would bring her up to the High North, but the privacy we got when the council met made those times the greatest. Once we both grew older, we were given responsibilities of our own within our provinces. From the year 1104, when I was in my fourteenth year, my sister attempted to name me the tradesman for the High

North, which would have made me the only patrician to possess that role in the land. The rest chose loyal common folk, who I grew to know rather well as I often conversed and held meetings with them. This was met with slight confusion from Lady Catar's fellow Heads of House, and ultimately led to a reshaping of the trading system in our land, resulting in me taking up the newly formed role of Head of Trade - an event that I will explain in due course.

Lady Breck was given the responsibility to act as a public figure within her province, the job that Lord Shay manned for the High North. Lord Bruk was always rather busy making sure everything was in order and the presence of a woman with such beauty and purity brought great comfort to the people of the South. Our new responsibilities meant that we saw less and less of each other, which was rather upsetting considering how rarely it was that we met up previously. However, I did make sure to visit her often whenever I was needed in the South, making the journey very much worth its time. Sometimes I would fabricate false trading issues within the South unnecessarily, as selfish and unprofessional as that was, just so I could see her face again. Despite the hardship of not seeing Lady Breck for long periods of time, I did rather enjoy being involved in some meetings of the council. I can't say that my sister was too pleased with my regular appearances, especially once my friendship with Lord Bruk was formed. She believed that Lord Bruk was preparing me to take over from her, but that was far from the truth. Either way, Lady Catar wanted me nowhere near the meetings, which was rather strange considering that it was her who paved the way for me to become Saddle Isle's Head of Trade.

I cannot provide a record of the first meeting but I can tell of the first meeting that I was allowed to attend.

*** * * ***

My first meeting was on the far side of the isle in the Deep South with Lady Anto, daughter of Elan, of House Hepston leading. She was only of thirteen years and yet led with much wisdom. Her first bleed had occurred in her eleventh year so she was now fully in control of her province, to the delight of the commoners who resided there. She was, by my reckoning, which is by far the most well informed throughout the entire land, a rather remarkable woman. Castle Rye had only been fully completed for two years so the bricks were still in fantastic condition. It was only a small castle, but there were only two patricians who resided there and the land was home to a copious amount of people considering its similarly small nature, so this made logistical sense. Despite this, the keep was a rather impressive sight as we rode through the villages, which were much closer to the castle than in the High North.

All the provinces had villages that were set out rather similarly. There were often hundreds of small villages of around ten to sixteen houses that were set out in circular structures so that each house faced into a small shared space, where the children would often entertain themselves as the parents got on with their work. I say all the villages but that is actually incorrect, as the Midlands was rather different; although some more traditional Midlanders set up villages in this way, away from the woodland. In the Deep South, the field workers and women of the river mouth often lived in villages close to the River Cunk, which is where the fields were located due to the need for plenty of water. I had already been impressed by the cleanliness and regal-nature of the stone floors that lined the corridors, so my reaction to the meeting room in which we discussed matters must have been a sight to see. In the centre of the room was a large oval table constructed from oak from the Midlands. The chairs were made in similar fashion, but the carvings on the furniture were almost as remarkable as the provincial leader who owned them. There were depictions of the Great Voyage of 1096, as well as beautiful images of people working the fields, children chasing each other in the villages, and the growth of the two patricians.

"These carvings are exquisite," I remarked to Lady Anto as we settled.

"They truly are, aren't they! We have some rather talented woodworkers here in the Deep South. They came and asked if they could carve these images to thank us for our leadership."

"That's very kind of them." I must admit, I was rather jealous of how much more amicable the Deep South was compared to the High North.

"Indeed. We are very lucky down here."

****

After we settled upon the ornate seating in the room, which was illuminated due to the copious amounts of windows, my first ever attended Council of Heads meeting began.

"Thank you for travelling all this way. I know it can be very inconvenient for the most northern of you to come so far," were Lady Anto's words of welcome.

"Thank you for your great hospitality," Lord Bruk answered.

As I've described, the Southern provincial leader was very kind, rather like his sister. He had respect for his fellow leaders and for his fellow bastard brothers and sisters. That was more that could be said for the Head of House Wharram.

"Can we get on with it? I have animals to slaughter," Lord Eli snapped.

He spoke with such disinterest for the cause. Men like him never did understand the importance of order.

"A rather cruel pastime, don't you think?" I couldn't help but chime in.

"Excuse my brother. He does not know of respect."

Lady Catar never let me have my fun. To add to her boring nature, she was also wrong. I knew of respect, I just didn't give it out without merit. Lord Eli was a poor ruler who let the strongest of his people grow stronger and the weakest weaken. I refused to respect those that only are respected because of their father. We all shared the same father anyway, so his one claim to respect was null and void in my eyes.

"Now, I'm sure he was just being humorous," Lord Bruk commented, defending me. At least someone understood.

"Well, the boy can keep his comments to himself," Lord Eli snapped back.

I didn't appreciate the brute calling me boy, but I wasn't foolish enough to stand up to the Midland's leader.

"The boy is just as much a lord as you are, Lord Eli," spattered Lady Daid, who was not as reserved as myself, clearly.

Her defence of me was halted quickly by my sister who was eager to get rid of me from the meeting.

"Shall we proceed in sorting out the necessary trading requests. That way my brother can sort them as quickly as possible ahead of the forthcoming winter?"

"Good idea. Who would like to start?" Lady Anto did well to regain control.

"I would, if you don't mind, My Lady," I quickly jumped in.

I thought it best for me to set a few ground rules under my leadership. That was the only way to get the respect that I needed.

"Yes, Lord Barrat, do proceed."

"Thank you, Lady Anto."

I continued, "We expect that the quotas necessary for the natural flow of trade will be met by each province. I, of course, predominantly refer to the grain of the Deep South that acts as the staple for so many common folk of the five provinces."

"Yes, Lord Barrat. The grain is poised for prosperity for the coming year."

"What a relief it is to hear, Lady Anto. I'm sure that everyone agrees. The coin necessary from the four trading provinces shall be provided upon the trade."

She nodded her head in approval.

I continued again, "I assume that the regular trading of beef for fish is still acceptable for all?"

I was glad to hear of the wish to continue that trade. I did enjoy a good piece of beef every once in a while. Cursed, I was, to be chained to one of only two provinces without the permission to farm cows.

"Lord Barrat, I would like to make a request in terms of trading," Lady Daid spoke up.

She was not as polite as Lady Anto or Lord Bruk, but at least she didn't completely look down on me - well, figuratively anyway.

"Of course, Lady Daid."

"I request that the South provide the North with appropriate weapons to hunt."

This caused a stir within the room. Those of House Wharram were the only ones known for hunting animals within their province. Of course, both the North and High North fished, but that was different. This request raised many questions, especially from Lord Eli.

"I know that part of our woodland scratches onto your province, but hunting is not a sport associated with your people."

I had never heard the leader of the Midlands to be so concerned. It was quite nice, in truth, to know that even someone so stern could care about something.

"Please, Lord Eli, grant me the respect of implementing my title when you address me, as you would to Lord Bruk."

I never fully trusted her, as I have said, but I did admire her rightful insistence that she was to be respected.

She continued to explain, "We do not wish to hunt in the woodland, and we do not wish to hunt merely for sport. Our province has far less means for trading than others. Yes, we fish, but we don't acquire the same numbers as those in the High North."

"That is true," I seconded, knowing she hadn't finished but needing a break from her accent.

"We have spotted goats in the mountains and would like to hunt them. We could farm them like our pigs and sheep and breed them for meat."

"I don't think that is wise, Lady Daid!" Lord Bruk piped up. "Goats are the animals of the gods. We cannot hunt or kill them for meat, you know that."

"Do tell me, Lord Bruk, what have the gods ever done for us?"

"They gave us this chance, Lady Daid! This cannot be done," Lord Bruk answered, correctly in my opinion.

We were all fortunate to be alive, nevermind lords and ladies of our own isle. We were lucky.

It was not like my sister to remain this quiet, so I was not shocked when she joined the argument, "With all due respect, Lord Bruk, since when was the goings on of our land your sole decision to make? I personally would quite like to taste the meat of the gods at some point."

"Lady Catar is right. We shall vote," said the democratic Lady Anto. "I vote against."

Lord Bruk agreed. With the Head of House Northorpe's vote cast, it was two to none, but that was not enough. As expected, the two brutes of differing provinces voted to allow for the hunting of goats, and my sister shortly followed. Lord Eli, despite being the most religious of the provincial leaders, was convinced that the goats must hold great power if they were sacred and so was keen to consume such a godly meat. Lady Anto concluded the vote.

"Then it's settled. You shall be allowed to hunt the mountain goats as you please."

****

"You shouldn't have done that."

Despite my sister's best efforts, the results of the council meeting meant that I had very little to attend to in the Deep South.

I had completed my jobs before the meeting was adjourned, meaning that I could travel to the High North in her company. This comforted me as an overnight camp was required, something I wished not to do alone. In normal circumstances, Miss Frith would accompany us on our travels, however she was recovering from an unsuccessful attack by a Midland Savage - an occurrence that was becoming all too frequent for all on the isle, not just patricians and their associates.

"Little brother, you don't know what should and shouldn't be done."

She always felt that she was better than me. For a time she was, but that was only due to my age. I was older now and far wiser than she, which caused her to fear me in some ways.Despite this, she still felt as though her opinions outweighed mine.

"I know a hell of a lot more than you, sister." My bitterness caused her to scorn me. I can still remember the look.

"You venture over our borders only four times a year. I venture across various borders forty times a season. I have seen the people of each province, both the noble and the common, and I have befriended many of them. Do you know what so many folk have in common, sister?"

She remained rather disinterested.

"No, but I'm sure you'll enlighten me, brother."

"They all pray to the gods."

In an attempt to gain any form of authority on the matter, I gestured for my horse to gallop forward and turned to face her properly.

I continued, "I know that you are sceptical of Leonism, and I am too, but if you want to keep as much peace with the common folk as possible then you shouldn't do anything that would upset their gods. That way, if something were to go wrong, they would have less reason to blame us."

"You think you know so much, brother. I can assure you that nothing bad is going to happen because we killed some goats, Barrat."

She clearly didn't listen properly, but she never did. I would have been a fool to think that I could convince her that what she did was wrong. She was far too stubborn for that. I just had to hope that, if the time came, the blame didn't fall onto me.

Lord Suln, son of Ferma, of House Northorpe

I am fully aware that our voyage to Saddle Isle, as arranged by my father, saved thousands of lives, and for that I am very grateful indeed. But that doesn't diminish from the reality that we needed to be saved in the first place. There was enough hatred aimed our way to force us to flee away from our homes and away from our mothers. It's scary to think that fear and hatred can force someone to sacrifice that which they love so much. I was of six years when we fled and it was an incredibly distressing experience. I didn't want to leave my mother, Nea, behind, but I didn't get to make that choice. I'm sure that there are events more traumatising than being saved, but that doesn't take away from the fact that I was scarred by what happened to me. In my experience of what the people of this world are capable of, there hasn't been an event in my life that was more unexpected than being dragged away from my mother. I have seen and heard of many a brutal act in my time: I have seen an arrow take a man's life in seconds. I have seen a spear pierce straight through a spine, and I have heard of a man being pounded to death on the floor of his own home. But I deemed all those events to be somewhat expected, mainly because I had learnt quickly how cruel humanity could be. An unexpected event is much more traumatising, and traumatising events result in a real lack of trust. It's not nice for me to reminisce on such a horrific memory, but I need you to understand exactly how distrustful I was in order to fully appreciate how great of a man Lord Suln, son of Frima, of House Northorpe, truly was. I owe him great gratitude and so I have made it a priority of mine to present him in the most accurate light possible. He was an incredibly kind man who was vitally important during my childhood, not just in regard to my relationship with Lady Breck but in my development as a person too.

He was a handsome man, Lord Suln. I remember overhearing Miss Norma converse with Miss Celie, a young servant girl who resided in the servant villages outside of Castle Gelid in the High North, where she swooned over him as he visited with Lady Breck one winter. He had a clean face - no stubble at all, with a sharp jaw-line and a perfectly straight smile. His hair was a dark brown, always slicked back with water to maintain a debonair look and, although he wasn't particularly muscular, he was rather animated and energetic with his movement. I'm sure by now that you have derived that Lord Suln was the blood brother of Lady Breck, so that perhaps played a slight part in my admiration for the man. But that doesn't guarantee that their relationship was the reason why I held him in such high esteem. Lady Catar and Lord Shay were both blood siblings of mine and, although she and Lord Shay got on rather well, Lady Breck never did grow close with my sister. To be fair to Lady Breck, not many did. Either way, Lord Suln was a great man who did many great things for Lady Breck and myself.

It shouldn't go unnoticed that my own brother, Lord Shay, played a rather similar part in my childhood to Lord Suln. There were occasions where Lord Suln would travel with Lady Breck in order for us to be together, but there were just as many occasions when my brother would do the same with me - more so, if anything. I suppose this asks a rather difficult question of me: what was it that set Lord Suln so ahead of my own brother? That's slightly unfair. The fact that Lord Shay was my brother definitely played an almost paradoxical part in my further appreciation for Lord Suln. I suppose when it's your own brother, who you love so much anyway, it's hard for a greater appreciation to evolve. Plus I sort of expected it from Lord Shay. He had been there for me my whole life and I was accustomed to his love and support. Lord Suln was a stranger to me, a man who I had not known for a long time at all, and yet he was bringing my beloved to me. That was the best gift he could ever give. Despite what I've said, I do understand that Lord Suln was Lady Breck's brother and so the situation was exactly the same. It's just one of those things, I suppose. You always appreciate the acts that you aren't necessarily accustomed to and sometimes that makes you take the normalities of your life, that are really blessings and moments of kindness, for granted. I certainly took Lord Shay for granted and I hate myself for that. But still, I was appreciative for Lord Suln and I know that Lady Breck was appreciative towards Lord Shay, so it did somewhat work out in the end. That's what I tell myself, anyway.

****

A particularly fond memory I have of Lord Suln took place midway through the spring season of 1100, when Lady Breck and I were both of ten years. It had only been four years since we met but that felt such a lifetime ago. I remember it was during that winter that I had my first night's sleep without dreaming of my mother. When I awoke, I cried more than I had ever done when she regularly haunted the alternate world that resided in my head, for when she disappeared from my dreams I felt like she was truly lost. Lady Breck had planned to visit around that time as she hadn't experienced the High North during the cold season. It was never the best place to be when the cold sets in, but she begged to come anyway. Those plans were aborted, however, as the land experienced the harshest winter in our history. We all lost many friends to the frost that year. This meant that our visit was postponed slightly, but that was okay as the calmness of spring allowed us to do more enjoyable activities rather than freeze in a castle.

On seeing my approach, Lady Breck quickly jumped from her horse and ran in my direction, thrusting herself into my arms when she eventually reached me.

"It's great to see you again. I've missed you," my friend excitedly said.

She let go of me, examined the smile on my face, then hugged me once more, even tighter this time.

"I've missed you too."

I smiled before kissing her on the cheek, which brought a slight chuckle from her brother, who lagged ever so slightly behind.

"I hope you have one of those for me," Lord Suln joked as he dismounted his horse. "It's good to see you, my friend."

He ruffled my hair, which I neither appreciated nor made a fuss about, before embracing me.

"It's good to see you too. How was the journey?"

"Breck was as annoying as ever. She does get ever so excited at the thought of seeing you." He looked over to his sister, smugly smirking.

"Suln!"

His words embarrassed her so much so that she ran up and hit him on the arm, which only caused him to laugh.

"What? I think it's rather sweet."

We all mounted our horses and began to ride through the fields, going deeper into my province. We rode slowly though, to allow for us to converse with one another as we journeyed. Lady Breck took place in the middle of Lord Suln and myself as we all rode side-by-side. He spoke to me over his sister's head, which bobbed up and down with the movement of her horse.

"So, Little Lord, you are of ten years now, if I'm correct. You must have started fighting. Which did you choose: a sword or an axe?"

I looked down at my horse momentarily, ashamed to answer. "Neither."

"A mace then? That's a rather unusual choice at your age."

"No, not a mace."

"Ah, do we have an archer in our midst?" His excitement at the thought suggested that archery was a passion of his.

"I'm sorry, I don't know what you mean." I replied, looking at him with shame still plastered across my face.

He smiled at me reassuringly.

"One should never apologise for not yet knowing something, Little Lord. An archer fires arrows with a bow."

"We don't have any archers in the High North."

"Then what are you training in?"

"Nothing. Catar has forbidden me from training. She says that she doesn't trust me enough to put a sword in my hand."

The siblings turned their heads to me, shocked to hear this.

"You are rather clumsy," commented Lady Breck, who was struggling to get her words out due to her laughter.

"I am not!" I wasn't going to accept being called incompetent, not even from my dearest friend.

"Yes you are! You trip over all the time."

It annoyed me that her giggles brought such joy that they prevented me from being mad at her. I could never be mad at my Lady Breck. I attempted to defend myself as she attempted to stop giggling.

"That's only in the South. All the paths are stupidly designed down there."

"The cobbles can be rather uneven, I'll give you that," Lord Suln agreed. "But being clumsy is no reason to stop a boy from training. She may be Head of House Pearson but she has no authority to take that right away from you."

"Well, she has."

We carried on ahead, silent for a short while.

"Right, stop here," Lord Suln commanded.

Lady Breck and I did as he said. We stopped and dismounted our horses once more.

"What have we stopped for, brother?"

Lady Breck was an impatient child, and so stopping without 'reason' wasn't something that she was just going to accept without question.

"Because there's a tree."

"There are a lot of trees everywhere, all across the isle. What's so special about this one? Is it because it's all on its own?"

Despite her initial taunts, she suddenly became in awe of the notion that this tree was special and examined it closely. Lord Suln was amused by her stupidity but his laughter made her sulk, which he wasn't in the mood for.

"There's nothing special about the tree, sister. Don't sulk, Breck. Come on."

She walked over to me and wriggled under my arm into a hug, digging her face into my chest to hide her annoyance.

"He can be really mean, sometimes."

Lord Suln called over to us once more.

"Once you two are quite done, come over here."

We did as he said and rejoined him by the tree. He took his bow, which was attached to his horse's saddle, and pulled six arrows from its accompanying quiver. Placing one arrow on the string, he drew back and then released so that the arrow hit the tree directly in its centre. Lord Suln fired one more arrow at the tree as he began to speak to me, which pierced the bark directly below the arrow already there.

"I may not know how to swing a sword, or throw an axe, but I am the best archer in my province and I think that you could be the best in yours."

"I would be the only archer in the High North."

"Then being the best should be rather easy!"

He passed the bow to my left hand, and then placed an arrow in my right hand and started to talk me through the process.

"You want to stand with your feet shoulder width apart," he began.

I looked down to my feet and placed them in the right position.

"Side on, Little Lord. I thought that would be obvious. Now loosen that grip. Don't be scared of your bow but be at one with it. You are the bow and the bow is you."

"That sounds ridiculous," remarked Lady Breck, who had decided to sit down once she knew we'd be stopping there a while.

"That, sister, is not helping." Lord Suln shot her an unimpressed look, then reached around me and guided the arrow into place on the bow. "Did you see how I did that?"

I nodded to confirm as he stepped back from me.

"You'll need to remember that. Now, look at my hand. You see what my fingers are doing?"

He split his index finger from the two below.

"That's how to hold the string. The arrow goes in that little gap between your index finger and the middle. Now, draw back the string using your back muscles."

I drew the string back.

"No, Barrat. I said to use your back muscles. You are using your arm there."

I adjusted and started to use my back muscles, as instructed.

"That's better. You want your index finger under your chin, and the string to lightly brush your nose and lips. That's it! Now, when you're ready, I want you to aim for the highest arrow. Relax the grip and slip your fingers backwards to release."

I took my time. Eventually, I released the pressure on the string. The arrow missed the tree, flying straight past it, making Lady Breck laugh.

"That was rubbish!" she jeered.

"That was a good start," Lord Suln insisted, reassuringly. "Unlucky, Little Lord. Try again."

He glared over to his sister disapprovingly before turning his attention back to me. After a few more attempts, and a few trips to collect the arrows, I eventually hit the target. After that, I hit the tree twice more in five tries. I was rather proud, I must admit.

"Can I have a go?" queried Lady Breck, who was looking rather bored.

I did feel bad for my friend. As much as I appreciated Lord Suln for doing what my sister wouldn't, the visit was intended for Lady Breck and I to spend time together. So far she had spent most of the day watching me miss a tree with some arrows at a safe enough distance so that my clumsiness didn't cause her any harm.

"Bruk specifically said that you weren't to fight and he's the head of our house."

She pulled a disapproving face as if something didn't add up.

"You said that Lady Catar was wrong not to let Barrat learn."

He bent his knees to meet her height, putting his hand on her shoulder.

"I did. And I stand by that, but our brother said no and I'm loyal to him. I'm not loyal to Lady Catar."

"But Lady Catar gets to fight!"

"That's because Lady Catar doesn't have older brothers who love her too much to let her fight."

She started to sulk again.

"Bruk says she's quite good at it," Lady Breck eventually continued, refusing to give up. I couldn't help but smile at her fierceness.

"Well, Bruk also says that you are not to train!"

His snap embarrassed him enough to make him momentarily pause. He looked at his sulky sister, feeling sorry for her.

"But we are not in the South, so I suppose you could have a go."

He ushered for me to hand him the bow, which I did. Lord Suln gestured to talk her through the process as he had done for me, but she refused to let him.

"I've seen you shoot an arrow enough times to know how to do it, Suln!"

She took the bow, moved forward into position and fired an arrow at the tree. It didn't land precisely in the centre like the shots from Lord Suln, but she pierced through the bark on her first attempt.

"Very good! You're a natural, as is your friend here."

Lord Suln was so impressed that he applauded his sister. She skipped back to where we were standing, smiling.

"Do you suppose Bruk will let me train if he sees that I am a natural, as you said?" she asked, her deep, brown eyes gleaming with so much optimism.

Lord Suln paused to think about his response as he took the bow from her hands.

"That man loves you more than you could ever know, so I highly doubt it. You may be his sister but he sees you as his own child, Breck. He wants to shield you away from any scenario where you could get killed. I would let you train if I was Head of House, I truly would. You certainly are capable of it. But I'm not in charge, so I'm afraid you're not going to win this one, little sister. I'm sorry."

She took it pretty well - far better than I expected, actually. She seemed to appreciate how precious she was in the eyes of her eldest brother, which I can understand. I have always craved my sister's love, despite how wicked I thought she was. We decided that we had trained enough for one day and so rode deeper into the province, heading for Castle Gelid. Despite her acceptance, Lady Breck did insist on riding slightly ahead in order to fully calm down.

"Lord Suln, next time I'm in the South, will you gift me a bow and some arrows?"

"Absolutely not."

It was safe to say that I was disappointed by this.

"The next time you come to the South, I will teach you how to make your own bow and how to forge arrows as well."

"Why can't you just make it for him?" Lady Breck enquired, eavesdropping on the conversation.

"Tell me, sister, who benefits more from the fish in this province, the patricians or the fishermen?"

"The patricians, obviously! We're the ones who get to eat the fish."

"Do you not think that the fishermen also eat the fish?" Lord Suln countered.

Lady Breck hadn't considered this and so her confidence dissipated, causing her to remain quiet as she pondered.

"You see, those fishermen benefit from the fish most because they not only have fish for themselves but can also sell fish to the rest of the province for coin. If I were to make Barrat his bow and arrows, he would always need to rely on me for his weapons. I'm not going to be around forever, you know. In this scenario, you should want to be like the fisherman - able to provide for yourselves. Perhaps, with the knowledge he will acquire through his practice, the Little Lord could teach people in the High North to shoot too."

"Thank you, Lord Suln. It means a lot to have your support," I smiled at him. "You know, I don't really like fish."

"But you live in the fishing province, Barrat."

"I know, but they're too salty and they smell like my sister's feet."

I screwed up my face in disgust at the thought of it. He laughed as we continued the ride to my home.

The Summer of 1102

In her twelfth year, Lady Breck bled for the first time. It was custom in our society that the first bleed initiated the blossoming from childhood into womanhood - a great cause for celebration within the South. When asked what gift she was to be given in aid of this momentous milestone in her life, she said that there was only one thing that she wanted: to spend the entire summer season with me in the High North. I had gained the admiration of Lord Bruk, son of Betra, of House Northorpe, and he had gained mine. He was my hero when I was a boy. He showed me that leaders can be kind whilst maintaining their power, something that I had to venture far from home to learn. Despite that he held me in high esteem, he was wary of sending his little sister all the way to the High North to spend an extended period of time under the watch of my very own sister. It was fair to say that my sister wasn't one to try and squirm her way into the hearts of her fellow leaders. She had a power-driven mind and wasn't afraid to speak it. Lord Bruk loved his sister more than anyone else in the world. She had been under his protection since she was of six years and he worried that her illness would cause him to lose her to the long voyage. Once she thankfully recovered, he promised to himself that he would do what was in her best interest, always. He wasn't too sure that this trip of hers met that promise.

"I just don't know if it's the best idea, sister."

Lady Breck was a stubborn child, and so the added independence that womanhood brought made her feel all the more entitled to what she thought was right than ever before.

"You said that I could have whatever I wanted," she moaned.

"I said you could have whatever you wanted, within reason."

As stubborn as Lady Breck was, Lord Bruk was not a man who would back down easily.

"I fail to see how my request is beyond reason," she snapped, unimpressed. "I am a woman now, brother, and so I can make choices for myself. I know that you think Lord Barrat to be a good man, which he certainly is. I can't see what doubt there is to have."

He beamed in pride at her fierceness, but couldn't budge.

"Sister, Lord Barrat has my admiration, as you know, but he is still very much a boy. Lady Catar holds the power in the High North and she is a woman who I simply cannot trust."

He ushered her to sit upon the seat next to his own, but she refused his offer and remained standing with a bitter expression on her face. Lord Bruk ignored her countenance.

"I am responsible for your safety, whether you are a woman or not. Staying with Lady Catar for the duration of an entire season is dangerous. What if she gets bored of having you there? She would order you to come home, alone. I refuse to leave you to trudge home through the land that belongs to the Midland Savages. Only the gods know what they'd do to a beautiful, young woman like yourself."

She looked on in disgust at the thought, but she knew me better than that. She knew that I would never allow my sister, no matter if she was Head of House or a mere commoner, to treat my love in that way.

"Barrat would not allow it."

"I can't guarantee that Barrat would be able to stop her," he persisted.

I would have. He paused for a moment, poured some wine, and sipped at it.

"And if I can't guarantee that then I can't guarantee your safety."

"Well, I'm going whether you like it or not. I have already asked Suln to take me and he has agreed to."

Lord Bruk slumped, as he uncharacteristically accepted defeat.

"Fine," he sighed. "Although I would appreciate it if you ran these things past me first."

"If I had run it past you first then I wouldn't be going."

She smiled smugly at him and he couldn't help but smile back. Regretting her tone, she attempted to comfort her brother slightly.

"You know, Lady Catar is not as bad as you make her out to be."

"Oh, really?"

"Yes, really. I actually think she quite likes me. She's not like any other woman I have met. She is strong."

"I know many strong women, sister."

"Well, yes, but very few of them are as assured as Lady Catar. She knows what she wants and will do anything to get it."

"And what does she want?"

She poured herself a glass of water and sipped it before continuing.

"Respect, and to maintain her power. She says that, because she's a woman, the men in her province are less likely to respect her and that's why she has to be so stern. But she is rather nice, really."

Lord Bruk sat forward, now interested in what she was saying.

"You seem to have become great friends."

"Lady Catar insists that I know her better than Barrat does. See, I love him more than I love anyone else and I want to marry him, when the time is right. But even I can admit that he is very proud and very stubborn."

"You sound just like his sister."

"They are her words, brother. Barrat knows that he is very capable and so does Lady Catar. She fears that he'll try to take her place as head and so she has to be stern with him. You know, to show him that her position is not for the taking."

She paused momentarily, then told her brother of some news.

"She says that she is going to make Barrat the trader for the province, soon."

"But that's a commoner's job."

She looked down for a moment, as if upset by what was to come for me.

"I know it is, but I understand why she's doing it. He can't have power anywhere else, not if Lady Catar is to remain as Head of House Pearson. This is the only power he'll ever get. She hopes that it will be enough to make him feel like he's doing something."

"And what of Miss Frith? I do hope that nothing bad has happened to the good woman."

"I cannot be too sure. I do speculate that Miss Frith is in perfectly good condition. I assume that she will simply be replaced by Barrat and become a guard, or something similar."

Lord Bruk disapproved of this decision. He knew how capable I was, and how well I'd do in the role for that matter, but he also knew how humiliating it could be for a lord to take on a commoner's role. Besides, Miss Frith, who had been the tradeswoman for the High North since trade began, was a good woman who always did well to keep Lady Catar realistic about what she could demand. Perhaps that was why my sister was so keen to replace her, not that I would allow her to have her way without reason. But there wasn't much that Lord Bruk could do, though that would not stop him in his quest to find an alternative solution.

"I'm sure he'll do a fantastic job," was Lord Bruk's way of remaining optimistic.

"Yes, I'm sure he will," she agreed with assurance.

"Well, I should get ready for my departure." Lady Breck announced. "It's a truly beautiful place in the summer, brother. You should come visit, at some point."

"Perhaps I will," he provocatively said, knowing that her offer wasn't sincere.

He smiled to reassure her that he was joking but in reality was still cautious, despite all she'd said, for his sister's wellbeing.

"I shall see you when the summer ends," Lady Breck remarked, confirming that he wasn't to visit at any point. "The next Council of Heads meeting is in the High North so I shall travel back with you when you depart from there."

"You have it all figured out."

"Of course."

"My sister! Now a woman! It's quite hard to believe. Do have a safe journey, and remember that you don't have to do anything that you don't want to."

She rolled her eyes as she hugged him.

"I know, brother. I'm a woman now, I know these things."

*** * * ***

After a day-long journey with Lord Suln, Lady Breck had arrived safely to the High North, to the disgust of my sister, and had settled well in her chamber. We had decided to walk through the fields, for it was a beautiful day and the High North flowers were in full bloom, which brought great delight to my beloved. It was from these fields where Castle Gelid looked at its best. The High North was flat and unadorned compared to the other provinces. The North had their majestic mountainous backdrop, and the Midlands were blessed with the natural spectacle of the woodlands. The South had the precision of the vineyards, and the Deep South had their rolling fields of yield. For us, Castle Gelid was the only monument of the province and it truly did look spectacular as one crossed the border, especially due to its four tower structure and its height. However, once you got up close, the effect of the castle lost its lustre. It was, if you remember, one of the pre-existing castles on the isle so it could possibly be excused for having such inconsistent brick work, with many of the bricks being worn and eroded by the many years (presumably, based on the state of them) that the castle had stood for. However, when compared to the other castles, my home was certainly fatigued. Perhaps that played into my sister's constant pursuit of more power.

"I'm so glad that I could come," Lady Breck said in a semi-nervous chuckle.

"I'm so glad of it, too."

I couldn't help but look at her face. The freckles that ventured out from her nose onto her cheeks, that only appeared in the summer when the sun got to them, never failed to make me smile. In the winter they were only visible on her nose, which was still a beautiful sight. I adored her deep, brown eyes that were so full of wonder, and her smile - oh, what a smile! - that scrunched up her cheekbones and accentuated her winsome dimples. It was a smile destined to bring much comfort and joy to the people of Saddle Isle for years.

"Did you have to roll out the lies about my sister?"

We had been planning this season together for the last few times we'd seen each other. Our brothers, Lord Suln and Lord Shay, had been kind by taking us on many occasions to see each other. But they always teased, as all big brothers do. We both wanted some time - proper time - to spend alone with each other. We were growing older, and with age came responsibility. We did not know how free we would be to do such a thing in the future. It had to be now. In our infinite wisdom, we had anticipated that Lord Bruk would be cautious. He was right to distrust my sister. Lady Catar seemed to hate the fact that I loved someone from the South so deeply. She had hoped, I presume, that I would court a woman from our own province in a similar vein to Lord Shay, who had begun to pursue a local farmer's daughter. Because of the law stating the disregard of the father's blood, it was never forbidden for patricians to marry each other as long as they did not share the same mother. However, it was a factor that didn't sit too well with my prideful sister. Because of this distrust, we devised a plan to convince Lord Bruk to allow for my sister to care for Lady Breck by highlighting some of her more loveable qualities, which didn't actually exist but would act as a good persuasive device.

Lady Breck reached out for my hand as we walked.

"I didn't think I would need to. I was holding my own with him, I truly was! He accepted that I was going but was rather concerned. So, in the end, I did tell him just to make sure that he let me come."

"Good. You look beautiful today."

She did look extremely pretty. Her flaxen hair was tied back partially, letting the length of the back free to blow in the slight breeze that accompanied us on our walk. Her beauty and grace was only emphasised by the flowers that the cook's daughter, Miss Celie, a small ginger girl with a bucket load of enthusiasm, had decorated Lady Breck's hair with.

"Thank you, Barrat. That is very kind."

We continued on, Lady Breck now blushing. I led her in the direction of Lake Dar, which was always surrounded by much wildlife during the spring and summer seasons.

"I really love it up here, you know."

You could tell by the way her eyes locked on to anything she found beauty in, such as flowers, birds, and the occasional butterfly, that she truly did have an admiration for the land.

"Don't get me wrong, I do like the South but it is nowhere near as beautiful as the other provinces."

I picked a lilac flower, which reminded me of the thin woollen dress that my mother was wearing when I last saw her. I added it to the plethora already in her hair.

"You're right," I proudly said. "I hated this place when I first got here. It is nothing like my village in England and I have never really liked the taste of fish, which is inconvenient."

She laughed.

"I decided that I hated it before I gave it a chance, really. But it is a truly beautiful place."

"I know you don't like fish, but do you know how to catch them?" she asked, looking on intently.

She really did find me fascinating, as I did her.

"Yes, of course. Before he took on a public role, once Catar realised that no one actually likes her, Shay would insist that he wanted to be a fisherman and so he was allowed to try it. He would take me out and show me how to cast a net. I still know most of his former crew quite well."

"Can you take me, do you think?"

"Well, the fishing crews go out for weeks and it can get quite scary out there. Besides, have you forgotten the state the waves left you in during the voyage?"

Lady Breck shot me a look which suggested that she was, now, offended.

"You think that I can't handle scary? I can shoot an arrow better than you, you know. And in regards to the voyage, I was only a child then. I am a woman now!"

I loved her fierceness so I took no offence to that comment.

"Okay then, I'll ask them if we can go on their next trip. I'm sure the sea will be at its kindest, since it's summer."

"Oh, Barrat, I can't wait!"

✳ ✳ ✳ ✳

After a while continuing on the pathway to the lake, Lady Breck briefly let go of my hand to examine a frog that was hopping down the path in the opposite direction to ourselves. It climbed onto her offered hand and sat on her palm.

"I remember these creatures from back home! I can't remember the name."

I stroked its slimy back as I spoke, playfully threatening to wipe the mucus into her hair, which made her scream and giggle.

"These are frogs, Breck. My sister wants to get rid of them."

"Why would she want to do that?"

The thought of all the frogs dying upset her, understandably. I placed my hand on the bottom of hers and pulled it gently to the floor to allow the frog to depart her palm and be on its way.

"They live in Lake Dar, which is where we get our drinking water from. Some of the children are getting sick and her advisors blame the frogs. If she would have built the wells, like my brother suggested, then it wouldn't be such an issue."

"I don't like your sister, if you don't mind me saying."

I took her hand in mine again. Luckily, she didn't mind the mucus.

"You're not the only one, don't worry. I wish that Shay would stand up to her. When I'm a man, I won't let her do all of her silly and cruel things. I will do anything to try to stop her."

She smiled and kissed me quickly on the cheek, as if she wasn't meant to do it.

"I love you."

"I love you too, My Lady."

"I'm not your lady," she corrected me, smiling wider than before. "But soon I will be, hopefully, once we get married."

"I can't wait for that day."

She came up close, closed her eyes, and kissed me on my lips. It was the first time that anyone had done that to me before. I kissed her soft lips back, and with that I knew: I shall be hers and she shall be mine, and no one else in our cruel world will matter in that moment, or in any other moment after that.

****

Over that summer of 1102, we only grew closer together. Despite my sister's attempts to put a dampener on our enjoyment, the summer was truly a perfect one. It was possibly the most perfect summer that Saddle Isle had ever seen. We connected in a way that we had never connected before, and neither of us ever wanted to connect in that way with anyone besides each other again - not ever. I was sad to see her leave with Lord Bruk once the summer had ended and autumn had arrived. Of course I was upset, I loved her more than anyone or anything else. But it was okay. I had something to look forward to, the day in which we would marry. A day that would mean that all summers - no, all seasons - would be as perfect as the summer of 1102.

The Head of Trade

The Head of Trade position was one that didn't exist before 1104, mainly because it had never been a necessary role until around that time. Each province assigned a loyal commoner to deal with matters of trade across the land. Each provincial trader would have a meeting with their respective provincial leader, the Head of House for each province, and would report back on details of how the seasonal trade had gone. This included tracking quantities of produce, as well as reporting back on how successful the Deep South harvest had been and what that meant for the winter months ahead. Admittedly, as the provinces began to develop further, the job of provincial trader became increasingly difficult. Initially, it was only food that was traded. This meant that there wasn't a necessity for all five provincial traders to interact with each other. For example, the Southern and Midland traders never interacted with each other as their realms each farmed pigs, cattle and sheep. Similarly, Miss Frith, the provincial trader for the High North, never interacted with the trader for the North as both realms farmed pigs, sheep, and fish. Once I became Head of Trade, the North started to hunt goats from the mountains and so trading between themselves and the High North increased.

The only provincial trader who had to interact with all traders was Miss Worrall, who was the trader for the Deep South. This was, obviously, because the Deep South was the only province with suitable soil to harvest grain, which was a necessity for those of every province of the land. Miss Worrall was a very personable woman and, when I got involved in the trading system, it was her that made me feel most at ease when discussing matters. For the first six years on the isle, tools, wood and stone weren't a means for trade but instead were expected to be given without question. If we, in the High North, needed new fishing supplies, like hooks, rods and spears, we would simply send word to the South to request an order for them to weld. Soon enough, they would be delivered without an expectation for anything in return. However, in 1102, The Council of Heads decided to alter the system by introducing supplies into the trading scope.

This was a fair decision. If we were to develop as a functioning 'country' then we needed to respect the value of our communities. By adding supplies to trade, welders, lumberjacks and builders could make more coin for themselves, which only made our land more prosperous than it previously was as they could then buy more produce from other villagers, such as blankets, clothes and candles. However, this meant that the role of provincial trader quickly altered, becoming much more difficult. Traders now had to interact with all provinces and so were forced to travel across the isle more frequently. As well as this, the traders had more demands from their provincial leaders or any other patricians, which led to even more travelling. Matters were complicated further as workers and patricians began to negotiate on trade. The provincial traders weren't accustomed to negotiation and debate and so fair trades were few and far between, causing some conflict between provinces.

Some changes were made in 1103 in an attempt to improve the flow of trade, and those did make somewhat of a positive impact. The provincial traders would have meetings, similar to those of the Council of Heads, to discuss price ranges and price caps for certain trades. It was also agreed that at least one provincial trader would be present for each Council of Heads meeting, with that being the trader from the province in which the meeting was taking place, in order to discuss the events of that season's trade. These changes resulted in slight improvement, although there were still issues to grapple with. Despite there being better communication between the provincial traders and leaders, the traders still weren't suited to negotiation and debate. The simpler trade deals often went smoothly, as you would expect. However, any tension or disagreement resulted in a failed trade, elongating negotiations unnecessarily, ultimately having consequences across the land. It was also found that, when patricians interacted with traders from other provinces, there was a lack of respect based on the disparity between the noble and the common folk, and that too caused many issues.

There were countless discussions in council meetings about possible solutions, but the Heads of House seemed to be stuck without options. So, when Lady Catar announced that she planned on replacing Miss Frith with myself as provincial trader, it presented the other heads with a fresh opportunity to re-examine the trade situation. Lord Bruk was particularly confused by my sister's decision and wanted to save my dignity as well as the job of Miss Frith. He suggested that the council utilise my acceptance of an involvement in trading to fix existing problems regarding negotiation and respect. He proposed that I be named Head of Trade and would spend my time in consistent discussion with all of the provincial traders. This would mean that, in any instances where conflict breaks out during negotiation, it would be my job as the Head of Trade to intervene and reach a solution. It would also fall to me to attend Council of Heads meetings whenever I deemed it necessary, as well as be the one to directly deal with trade pleas made by patricians that weren't regular trade requests (i.e, food, tool or wood related). The council rightly thought that I would demand more respect and authority and I was certainly more keen on this proposal than my sister's, which offended me slightly considering my status, as narcissistic as that may seem. This was a win-win scenario. I agreed to the redesigned role and the provincial traders seemed much more encouraged by the appointment after our first meeting together. We quickly began what was a relatively peaceful and successful four year period, which would have likely lasted longer had the isle's situation fallen more favourably. It was arranged that I would always have protection on my travels across the land, which was a priority considering that my sister had prevented me from learning how to wield a sword and so I was incapable of defending myself on the road. That protection sometimes came from whichever High Northern guard was around at the time, but for the most part I was protected by Miss Frith. In fact, for the first two seasons after my appointment, I shadowed her as she continued trading in order to learn more about my new job.

****

All five provincial traders could look after themselves and were trained in wielding a sword. It was necessary for them to do so, especially with the Midland Savages roaming around the central province of the land, which obviously needed to be passed through to make it from the isle's northern provinces to the south. But it was Miss Frith who was the most impressive of the five. She wasn't particularly large or muscular, but her ability to swiftly control the blade made her one of the most talented one-on-one fighters the High North, or the isle, had to offer. You could see the evidence of experience in her appearance through a scar that ran from adjacent to her left eye all the way down to her top lip, distracting from her otherwise soft features. When I first met the woman, her long, dark hair swooped across her face in an attempt to cover the wound, but by the time she had become my trading tutor she had begun to consistently tie her hair in a messy chignon. Her kind eyes and warm smile were a better reflection of her respectful personality, and her calm approach to teaching made my learning process much easier than if she had been impatient. I appreciated how she always showed me respect, despite the fact that I was only of fourteen years when she mentored me.

Coincidentally, Miss Frith was of fourteen years when she made the voyage to Saddle Isle. I do not remember much of her from our time in Pearson. Of course, I was only of six years at the time and very rarely was accepted to play with the older children. However, Lady Catar was good friends with Miss Frith back in England. They used to spend days together in the sea, swimming down and retrieving pebbles from the seafloor and using them to create images in the sand of whatever came to mind. I suppose it was a real shame when my sister was thrust into responsibility, as their relationship decayed from one of friendship to transactional. Miss Frith would act as the trader for the High North in exchange for Lady Catar to refrain from punishing her for her crimes. See, when we lived in Pearson no one was too fussed when Miss Frith killed her father, and I still find it rather strange that this opinion had to change when power came our way.

Miss Frith's father was a tradesman himself back in England. He often attempted to purchase nights with the women of Pearson, or any English village that he passed through, but most in our village refused his service. Miss Frith's mother, Dymphna, was one of the women who refused his offer of money in exchange for a night in her bed. However, Miss Dymphna was also the most beautiful woman in Pearson and had been weak due to illness. Under the disguise of night, the tradesman broke into her home and forced himself onto her. Nine months and a very cold winter later, Miss Frith was born. Her mother remained ill after the birth and so many women of the village cared for both Miss Dymphna and Miss Frith until the child was old enough to care for her mother on her own. No wonder Miss Frith took the breakdown of her friendship with my sister so personally - those days by the sea were the only days when the poor girl was allowed to be a child. One evening, when Miss Frith was of eleven years, her tradesman father passed through the village again, now much older but still demanding a bed that night to share with one of the women. On getting nowhere once more, he decided to reenact the horrors he induced years before. However, when he broke into the house on this occasion and found Miss Dymphna, he had barely taken down his trousers before Miss Frith had pierced his neck with the knife she was using to prepare tomorrow's soup.

The village mothers helped to clear the body from their home. It was burnt on a bonfire in the middle of the town and later buried in the woods by some of the farm boys. It was agreed that Miss Frith's actions were heroic rather than evil as she protected her sweet, innocent mother from her abuser, so all vowed to protect Miss Frith and keep her safe if the body was ever discovered. Harsh winter after harsh winter came and went, the final England winter taking Miss Dymphna with it to everyone's dismay. I suppose it was lucky then that the voyage to Saddle Isle was devised - a new start for Miss Frith alongside her now noble friend. However, Lady Catar took her rise to power very seriously and considered the actions of Miss Frith to warrant punishment. Typically, death is punishable by death, however Miss Frith had too much to offer physically and intelligently to see her die for an act that did not occur in the High North itself. After much deliberation, it was deemed suitable for Miss Frith to develop her survival instincts further with combat training so she could take up the arduous and dangerous role of trader for the province - a role that she took in her stride and worked endlessly to prepare for. Miss Frith became lethal in combat and an asset to the province, yet my sister never did loosen the tight clasp of Miss Frith's past actions. She was always to be at my sister's will.

＊＊＊＊

"My Lord, it is a true honour to have been chosen to assist you in your new role."

As I said, I had encountered Miss Frith on many occasions before becoming Head of Trade, both in Saddle Isle and out of it, but I had never interacted with her for any lengthy period of time. It was always my sister who dealt with trade. Lord Shay and I were never invited to get involved in those discussions.

"Thank you for agreeing to it," I responded, politely. "I know that your job is hard enough without having to play the role of teacher simultaneously."

"I'm sure you will be a great help to me in these forthcoming seasons and, of course, for many years to come, once you've fully settled into your new role. I have to say, I can't think of a better patrician for the job, My Lord."

"That is very kind, ma'am. Thank you."

I knew from that interaction that I was in good hands. She clearly knew how to address people with respect and seemed to be rather keen to shape me into the best Head of Trade that I could be, which was a great necessity for my own reputation as well as for the entire isle. I was always eager to learn new skills, even as a child, and so I truly believed that this combination would work quite well. And it did. She taught me about the lawful price caps on various different items, which I learnt by heart rather quickly. She also allowed me to lead negotiations for some trades for the High North to ensure that I understood the role from the provincial traders' perspective. This helped me tenfold when I took up the Head of Trade role properly as I could sympathise with the complaints and suggestions that came my way. I also learnt how to view isle-wide matters from the perspective of the common folk. I hadn't had the opportunity for much interaction with the commoners before this role, especially not those of other provinces. It was an impactful, eye-opening experience for me to travel across the land and meet so many incredible citizens of Saddle Isle. This helped me to understand why people felt entitled to more coin for their involvement in trade, and so I learnt how to handle those situations with empathy.

But it wasn't just the aspects of trade that Miss Frith taught me. Throughout our time together, I was always in awe of her sword skills. Whenever we stopped to rest or set up camp, or even when we were waiting for a trader to meet us, she would practise with her blade at any opportunity. Just watching her swiftness and control made me wish that I could do the same, but that never came to be. Every day I would ask her to teach me, but she would always say no for three reasons. Firstly, I was five years behind in development and so it would be harder to teach me the techniques needed to be competent. Ideally, I would have had to start learning when I was of ten years, but my sister never allowed it. Secondly, Miss Frith was too wise to go against Lady Catar's wishes. My sister had made it very clear that I was not to be taught to fight under any circumstances. Lady Catar had discovered Lord Suln's lessons in archery and was rather aggrieved, to the point where she had a rather vicious conversation with Lord Bruk about the matter. She couldn't stop me from shooting my arrows but she could prevent me from using a sword, and so she did. Miss Frith knew that my sister had control over her life. Lady Catar had already threatened to replace her as provincial trader before, and who knows what the consequences would be if the trader wasn't offering anything in return for her former friend's mercy. I have told you of my sister's plans to appoint me in Miss Frith's role in 1102. Had it not been for the difficult alterations to the trade system, that replacement probably would have gone ahead. In the end, the replacement was postponed as my sister felt it wise to hold on to Miss Frith's experience during the complicated transition, a notion I agreed with. Either way, Miss Frith did everything she could to stay on my sister's good side after that, which was fair but it meant that I was never destined to learn.

"My Lord, the worst thing I ever did was learn to swing a sword. I understand that protecting yourself is important. I understand why wielding such a striking representation of power and control excites a young man like you. But as soon as you possess the ability to kill it becomes a reason for you to do so. Peace is the most prosperous of personal states and I see so much peace in you, My Lord. It would be irresponsible of me to corrupt that."

I was eager to spark some concern about my safety.

"But what if someone attacks me?"

"You are a patrician of the isle, My Lord. You will always have people who will give their lives to protect you."

"But what if they fail?"

"My Lord, if you maintain the respect for your citizens that you currently possess by being kind and fair, then you will always be surrounded by the best protection in the land. You cannot expect people to give their lives for someone who has no respect for them, whether they are a patrician or not. I mean no offence, of course, but being a patrician does not make you better than anyone else. You are just people, like the rest of us. When a patrician acts as though they are above their citizens by showing a lack of respect then they lose respect for themselves. That is when you become at risk from poor protection."

I always tried to treat the people of Saddle Isle as an equal. Of course I had more privilege and a higher quality of lifestyle, but I understood that I was just like them. Some of the people in the High North were our neighbours in England, where we lived alongside them in identical housing and lived identical lives. We were given power through some sort of luck, not from merit. It was down to us to show the people that we could handle that power and that we deserved their cooperation.

I was convinced by her argument, but that didn't stop me from wanting to feel like a man.

"It would still be useful for me to be able to protect myself. I feel so useless when I see children, four years younger, who are much more capable than I am."

"Those children don't have the luxury of being Lord Barrat, son of Nea, of House Pearson. You have talents that I've never seen in any individual before, especially for your age. Your ability to think your way around situations is genuinely impressive and is incredibly valuable. Prosperous persuasion is always more powerful than physical prowess, so you are well equipped for survival, My Lord. You just need to make sure that you maintain dignity."

I cannot say whether it was the flurry of compliments or the power of her argument, but my friend was very convincing, to the point where I didn't believe that this woman could ever struggle in negotiations. I accepted this as a competent enough reason for me to avoid wielding a sword and so I dropped my constant pestering for lessons, to the delight of my tutor.

****

As the first season of my training came to a close, I experienced my first taste of the dangers of the job. We were travelling across the Midlands in the direction of the Deep South to discuss the prosperity of the season's grain. It was only during my travels with Miss Frith that I fully absorbed the natural beauty of the Midlands. When visiting Lady Breck, we would only travel down the west coast of the isle to avoid Midland Savages, so being able to travel through the woodland was a new experience for me and one that never got old. Before our arrival on the isle, the bastards that travelled to prepare the land for our arrival found that the majority of the Midlands, as well as parts of the North, was completely wooded. As beautiful as it was, there needed to be land for the farming of pigs, cattle and sheep to ensure that resources for each province were fair. Half the woodland was cut down to make room for fields, which were located on the west side of the province. Despite the copious space, the majority of the Midland citizens opted to build their houses in and amongst the woodland to adhere to their wish to hunt the wild animals that lived there. This meant that the villages had a very different layout to those of other provinces, as more citizens lived in isolated houses rather than a bunched layout, although some did live in round communities if that was their preference. The most savage of Midlanders didn't reside in houses at all, but lived in the trees, whether on constructed platforms or simply resting on the branches. The fear that ensued forced the most vulnerable in the province to live away from the woodland, which would've been fine if the water source wasn't on the opposite side of the woods, making it difficult for the vulnerable to get to without facing danger.

Castle Carob was also rather different in appearance, despite being one of three pre-existing castles on the isle. Although House Wharram had the highest number of patricians, the castle was the shortest in height. Instead, the required space was distributed through width. This meant that the impressive build sneaked up on you as you passed it, especially considering that the walls didn't celebrate the expensive brickwork as they were covered from top to bottom with ivy. All the castles were located on the coast, and Castle Carob was no different. It was located in the east and was equally positioned between Lake Fen and the woodland, so was in a suitable position for the patricians to reside in. But it was the fact that it didn't act as a monument for the province that made Castle Carob so special. It suggested a comradery, respect and understanding between the patricians and the people, despite their philosophy being unconventional. I mean in the sense that 'respect', as such, was more centred around an ability to showcase power rather than peace, something that was missing from other provinces in the land. I used to love catching Castle Carob peaking through the trees, hiding from oncoming traffic, but this occasion tarnished that experience for me.

I was always under the impression that the Midland Savages were more likely to avoid patricians in their violent hooliganism, but it soon became obvious that my assumption wasn't the case at all. They wanted to show that they were powerful and dominant, and if they could dominate the most powerful people in the land then they would happily do it. I was just glad that it was me that was met with this threat and that I wasn't alone. We were walking through the woodland when a Midland Savage dropped down from an overhanging tree and appeared on the path in front of us. His bare chest was covered in dirt and what looked like dried blood. His shaven head was smothered with sweat, and his teeth were sharp like daggers as he growled at us to indicate he wanted trouble. I was forced to freeze on the spot by the sight of this monstrous man. I only moved once Miss Frith pushed me to stand behind her back as she simultaneously removed the sword from her scabbard. She bent her knees to squat slightly, getting her body low as she secured her sword with two hands. They scuttled in a circle, not breaking eye contact once.

"This doesn't have to be like this," she calmly stated. "This is your chance to walk away."

The savage didn't respond but simply continued to sneer at my protector.

"I see. My Lord, get behind that tree."

She didn't look at the tree, but I could tell which one she meant. I ran for protection and watched on from the safe distance that I was now, thankfully, at. They continued to circle each other for a few moments more, again maintaining eye contact at all times. It was then that the savage pounced. I was shocked to see how quick he was, considering his size, but I was further shocked by the agility on show from Miss Frith. She managed to duck under a swing from the Savage and rotate her body around to slice his shoulder with the blade. But the Savage seemed unfazed, shaking it off as if it were merely a graze before continuing to slash at my protector with a curved sword of his own. Each time the Savage struck out, Miss Frith met it with a block, but she was nowhere near as physically strong as her Midland opponent. After a few more strikes, Miss Frith was forced to the ground. I closed my eyes. I didn't want to see a woman who had become my friend get slashed to pieces so I refused to watch. My fear was halted, however, by the returning sound of swords clanging against each other. She had managed to recover by sliding through the spread legs of the Savage, who had swung his sword down for the kill. To give credit to my friend's opponent, he managed to turn quickly enough to block what would have been a fatal blow.

It was so difficult to tell who would be victorious. I knew that if Miss Frith was to die then I would follow her to the grave, so my anxiety only increased. They matched each other blow for blow. I was worried that Miss Frith would either be out-strengthened again or run out of stamina, as it seemed as though the savage would never tire. The combat seemed to last for hours but it was always going to have a conclusion. All my friend needed was a lapse in judgement to take the victory. In a swift change of fortune, the Savage, on getting fed up of being matched with the swords, decided to take a swing with his leg in an attempt to get Miss Frith back to the ground. This left him exposed. As the Midlander swiped with his foot, she jumped over the swinging leg whilst simultaneously slashing her sword at the Savage's neck, making use of the Midlander's inability to block due to his unbalance. Miss Frith's swing made contact and the Savage fell to the ground with a thump, his blood pouring down his chest from his sliced throat.

I ran over to my friend to thank her. She too had fallen to the ground out of fatigue. Despite how impressively she had fought, you could still see the look of disappointment in her eyes. Not necessarily disappointment in her performance, but because she couldn't convince the Savage to back down. The fight was unnecessary and so the death of one of our fellow citizens was unnecessary too, but that was the way of the Midland Savages and there was nothing that Miss Frith could have done to stop him. After showing my gratitude for her protection, I helped her to her feet and handed her a waterskin to drink from, which she thanked me for. She leant against the tree that I hid behind for a while, asking for some time alone to reflect on the event, before eventually returning to where I had sat down as I waited for her. She silently handed me a dagger from her belt and began to dig a grave with her sword, prompting me to help with the less than ideal apparatus provided. We dug until the sun began to set and placed the corpse in the shallow grave. After saying a prayer to the Leonist god of grace, we continued our walk until it fell dark, as if the conflict had never happened at all. I knew then that I was always going to be safe as long as I had someone like Miss Frith at my side. I just needed to ensure that someone always felt respected enough to die for me.

The Midland Savages

There was a very fine line between peace and conflict within the limits caused by the environment of the isle. The isle was set up to allow for each family to have the freedom to live in whatever way made them feel comfortable. I know that the idea of everyone being happy and comfortable sounds great, but it was more complicated than those who devised the isle (whomever they were) seemed to think it would be. The bizarre reason for our issues was that we were neither completely similar or completely different from each other. If we were all similar, then it would obviously be easier for peace to prevail. But, similarly, if we were all completely different from each other, we would have been more susceptible to accept our differences and to allow for independence. The problem that we had was that four of the five houses were (relatively) similar to each other, with only one being completely different. This meant that no one was particularly happy to allow that single, differing house to do what they pleased, as the majority believed that their own system was the correct way to lead. This differing house was, as you may already have worked out, House Wharram, which was led by the brutish man: Lord Eli, son of Manty.

Lord Eli didn't implement many restrictions in the Midlands, which ended up causing quite the stir across the provinces. In the other four provinces, some sort of crime and punishment system was put in place in order to maintain order, but those of House Wharram believed that everyone should be allowed to do as they pleased. That would then cause the strongest of their people to thrive, making the future offspring of the province set to be the strongest in all the land. His lack of restrictions meant that chaos unfurled throughout the province. Lord Eli's people were free to kill whoever they pleased, in whatever manner they chose. They were free to steal from each other, rape one another, and torture those who they deemed to deserve it. This became a particularly unamicable issue when those passing through the Midlands from other provinces became victims of this uncivilised way of life - something that myself and Miss Frith experienced firsthand. The families and patricians of the victims' province could get no justice as Lord Eli always stood by the fact that these rules, or lack of them, were known throughout the land.

The uncivilised nature of the Midlands caused the rest of the land to refer to the people as the Midland Savages, a title that Lord Eli was rather proud of. He was a man who was infatuated by power, but not the same power that was craved by most other patricians. He wanted to be the strongest physically and would train to develop his strength every day. This obsession of his meant that he was always rather useless at the more political side of his role as Head of House. The meetings that took place in the Midlands were "hardly worth the effort", according to my sister. I would have to say that, on the very few occasions on which I was honoured with his company, I can see why that may have been the case. I was just glad that I got to spend most of my time with the more sane Lady Wonin, who was good friends with the province's primary trader and a trustworthy friend of mine, when visiting the Midlands as part of my trader role. After a few years (I cannot believe it took them this long), the other Heads of House decided that a change must be made. Too many innocent people who were placed in the protection of House Wharram, out of chance rather than choice, were under attack unnecessarily. And so, at a council meeting conveniently located outside of the Midlands itself, Lord Eli was encouraged to take more moral responsibility towards the matter.

****

Despite that I was (as I have moaned about many times) not the Head of House Pearson, I was always invited to attend the Council of Heads meetings due to my role as Head of Trade.

Typically, I wasn't allowed to contribute to discussions separate from trade, but considering that my team of provincial traders often dealt with the fear that accompanied crossing over the Midland borders, my sister thought that it would be suitable for me to pitch in and so I was glad to contribute to the debate wherever I could.

"Last month, fourteen of our people were brutally murdered in your land and we could do absolutely nothing about it," Lady Daid complained.

The Head of House Matfen was a selfish woman and so you shouldn't be fooled by the care she had for her people. She knew very well that, if an opportunity to seize more control and power arose, it was her people that she would have to rely on to achieve it. Either way, it's better to have a leader who selfishly cares than one who selfishly didn't.

"They know the risk," Lord Eli stated with an eerie nonchalance.

He clearly didn't see the problem within her complaint.

"They shouldn't have to be at risk when simply crossing the land."

"If they don't want to face the risks then they shouldn't pass through."

Only Lord Eli could fail to be intimidated by Lady Daid.

"In all fairness, Lord Eli," Lord Bruk chimed in. "The Midlands act as a barrier between the northern and southern provinces. It's hardly as though passing through can be avoided."

"That's not my fault. I won't change our way of life because it inconveniences you!"

"Those people - my people - were taking goat meat down to the southern provinces. They were, by law, entitled to do that."

Lady Daid was enraged by Lord Eli's arrogance, to the point where I feared she would start a brawl with her fellow brute. Of course, she would not win a one-on-one combat against him.

She continued, "In fact, the trade was sanctioned by Lord Barrat here, which means that they were in the protection of the land."

What she said was true. As Head of Trade for the land, any trade deal that I sanctioned meant that, technically, any harm caused to those transporting produce or finalising the trade would have to face the Head of the province in which the crime was committed. Of course, with this being in the Midlands, Lord Eli waved the case off as a non-issue. This infuriated Lady Daid, as you can imagine.

Lord Eli was not stirred at all by her passion.

"I dealt with the case. My law states that, in my province, this so-called crime is not a crime at all. My law is designed to make our people stronger and so I will not alter it for anyone."

As scared as I was, I couldn't help but be intrigued at his way of thinking.

"I hope you do not mind my intrusion but I must ask, do you believe that the killing and raping is beneficial for your people?"

He didn't take a single second to think.

"Yes, it only makes our people stronger."

"Because only the strongest survive."

"Exactly."

I wanted to get him to imagine what it was like to not be the strongest, which was rather difficult considering he was the most physically able man in the land. I did have the fortune of knowing how important family was to those of the Midlands, however, and hoped that tapping into those emotions would make him change his mind. I continued, trying to be purposefully blunt.

"Your brother, Lord Kinby. He isn't very strong, from what I've heard."

He didn't seem too pleased at this, perhaps because it came from myself. I was rather plump, especially for a young man. Being an honoured guest of the different provinces meant a lot of fine food was passed on to my plate.

"He is capable," was Lord Eli's attempt at keeping a calm head, which I appreciated.

"But not as capable as most of the men of your province."

Lord Bruk, who was standing next to me, interrupted as he whispered his concern into my ear. "Be careful. You don't want to annoy such a brutish man, Barrat."

"Just trust me," I whispered back before resuming my point. "Lord Eli, I know that, despite your impressive exterior and the pride you take in your scars and physical condition, you love your brother very much. I know that you wouldn't want anyone to harm him. But, even so, one could quite easily harm him and face no consequences at all, if they so wish. I also know that your sisters, Ladies Wonin, Kezi and Bennk, as strong as they are, wouldn't always be able to hold off a Savage if one was to, say, try and rape them."

"I would stop them!"

He was upset, which was good. It meant that my plan was working. I was encouraged as I could see my sister smile slightly from the corner of my eye.

"You can't stop all of them. And, even if you did, you are the strongest man in all the land. If you killed all those who were weaker than you, there would be no people in the Midlands at all."

He seemed confused, so Lady Catar jumped in. I didn't appreciate her interruption, but it wasn't often that we could work in tandem so I let her have this one.

"I think my brother is trying to say that your rules are destined to put your family at risk, Lord Eli. Yes, no one has dared to hurt your family just yet, but nobody is arrogant enough to think that they could outstrength you. One day, someone will come along who thinks they are stronger and your family will get hurt because of that."

Lord Eli paused to think, which took a while. It seemed like he hadn't considered the danger for his own family at all prior to this instance. It was sort of nice to see such a brute of a man be so sensitive in regard to the people who he loved the most.

"How do I stop them?"

I remained silent. Despite being given permission to partake, I began to think that my elongated interruption was so far past ordinary protocol that I was going to get a bollocking from my sister once everyone had left. To my surprise, no one chipped in with an answer to Lord Eli's question. Instead, they turned to me. In truth, I hadn't thought that far ahead but I gave it a shot. I took a second to think.

"Oh, okay. Well, it seems simple to me. All you need to do is change the law. State that no patrician, or person of another province at all, shall be harmed in any way by your people."

"Thank you," Lady Daid remarked in a rather condescending manner towards her patrician peers. "Someone with sense."

Lord Eli was less on board than I would have hoped.

"My people won't like that."

"Do you think that our people like everything that we put in place?" Lady Anto asked, sternly.

You know of my admiration for the Head of House Hepston already, but I must express how happy I was for someone to back me up.

She continued, "If you try to please everyone, then you are not a true leader. You would be letting them lead instead of doing what you feel to be right. You have to do what is best for the most."

I jumped back in.

"Exactly. We, as patricians, were tasked with protecting the people of our provinces and the people of the land in its entirety. In order to protect everyone, we have to keep peace with each other. That requires you to do what is best for the most. I know that you are a strong province, but you are not stronger than the other four provinces combined. To protect your people you must stop them from causing harm to ours. We are all allies now, but that status is not set in stone. Your people will get used to this development."

Lord Eli paused again, and eventually agreed to make a change.

"I will do as you say."

"There we have it," Lady Catar, as the Head officiating the meeting, confirmed. "So, from now on, no patrician or any citizen of the land who does not reside in the Midlands shall be harmed without punishment. Do we all agree?"

"Aye," they said, in unison.

With that, the law had been changed and was announced to all, with mixed response, on Lord Eli's return to his province.

****

"That was a good win today," Lord Bruk commented.

After the meeting adjourned, the Head of House Northorpe and I took a walk across the High North fields to catch up properly. I was happy to see him. He seemed pretty happy to see me too, and was pleased with my contribution at the meeting.

He continued, "I always said that you'd be a good leader."

"I'm not a leader, Lord Bruk."

He put his arm proudly around my back.

"Yes you are. You don't need to be Head of House to be a leader. What you did today has prevented the killing of many innocent people."

"But not all the innocent people."

I was disappointed in myself, in all honesty. I was so focused on making a good impression to all those powerful people that I played it safe. Because of that, the new law still didn't protect those people of the Midlands who don't want to be forced to fight for their lives.

"I know, but the man is difficult. Even a little win is a good one, and this win is a big one in its own right."

I appreciated his praise. It made me feel better about what I considered to be a failure. But I was not comfortable with stopping at getting safety for only some of our people. Lord Bruk clearly could see that I still wasn't satisfied and that I wouldn't change my mind on the matter.

"We'll keep pushing for a change in his province, of course. But we've been trying for so long with no luck at all. But what you did when you related our experience to his family, that made him budge. With this win today, we should be able to help all those who are trapped in the Midland's system soon enough."

"I hope so."

"We'll need you to take the lead when we try."

"I'm not sure my sister would appreciate that."

"She was proud of you today. She may not say it, but I could tell. She knows how talented you are, as do I."

"I just wish that she'd show it every once in a while."

We disagreed a lot, and I never felt that I ever truly gained her respect, but I always wanted her to love me. Lord Bruk told me that she did, but it was hard to believe him. I never felt it. Despite this, everything I did was to try to impress her. I wanted her to see that I was useful and intelligent, and that I was there to help, but she always seemed to think that I was against her. That I was her enemy from within. I never wanted that.

Lord Bruk's words interrupted my thoughts.

"Maybe one day she will, but until then, you just have to keep going. You're a good kid, and a smart man. You'll find a way to win her over eventually. I know it."

I loved my sister, but she never gave me the push I needed to be great. Sometimes I thought that I was born into the wrong family, and served under the wrong house.

A War of Words

Lord Bruk described the Midland brute as a "difficult man" and he certainly was. We had managed to get through to him in regard to altering his laws to protect those of other provinces, and he implemented the new laws quickly, in fairness. The only problem was that this change came with its own repercussions, which we had worried about but had very little control over. The Savages had no justification for acting out. It didn't take much to provoke violence and, more often than not, the violence that they perpetrated was a means of sport and entertainment rather than what they deemed necessary, which was often debateable in itself. Our yearly estimates of population figures and distributions suggested that the Savages had murdered roughly 146 citizens of provinces not including the Midlands that year, a serious increase from the previous year and a real cause for concern, especially considering our improved yet low population. The new laws now prevented those deaths from happening, which was a real victory for our respective provinces. Obviously there were still occasional murders that were met with punishment, but the numbers decreased significantly.

The repercussions, however, were rather distressing. Unfortunately, the number of attacks did not decrease but were just displaced. More and more innocent people of the Midlands became victims of this violence, something that played on my mind after the decision to change the law was made. On our arrival to the isle, we were tasked with protecting all citizens, no matter their personal province. We were failing miserably. The main issue with this was the deaths of the innocent, obviously. However, I was more concerned with the second issue, which was the tension caused between the leaders. Lord Eli's mistreatment of his own people was seen as offensive by his fellow Heads of House, and this caused a real disliking towards the man. It was understood that he had grown up differently to everyone else. He was the eldest patrician and so it felt almost justified for him to do as he pleased, but the amount of violence and death was so unnecessary and dangerous for the land that it was vital for it to be stopped. After a few seasons of unsuccessfully trying to further the justice system of the Midlands, Lord Eli's stubbornness became a source of real frustration. This accumulation of vexation eventually caused the other Heads of House to discuss ways in which he could be stopped. Despite it going against protocol, the next council meeting, located in the Deep South, was focused purely on coming to some sort of arrangement between all provinces in an attempt to stop the violence.

＊＊＊＊

"You are completely incompetent!" Lady Daid shouted in Lord Eli's direction.

Her approach to creating change was a strange one to me. I was typically present at meetings due to my role, and had recently been even more important in regard to the issues caused by Lord Eli. However, on this occasion, I had been called urgently with regard to a disagreement in trade in the North and so asked to be excused from this one, unaware of the intention of the meeting. Reluctantly, I was allowed to go. Despite not being there myself, hearing from my sister of how things were handled caused me great concern. Of course, I can only speculate based on what I had heard, but I knew these patricians and their ways rather well and so have a sound idea of how these events would have unfolded. Having said that, I had always thought that the Head of House Matfen was a somewhat sensible leader, yet my sister's account contradicted my previous opinion. Composure is needed in scenarios like this one and, on this occasion, Lady Daid seemed to have all the composure of a blind hawk.

Lady Anto attempted to calm things down, rightfully so,

"My Lords and Ladies, please! Let's not be so rash with our words. Comments like that don't get us anywhere."

"I've tried to be nice to Lord Eli, but he doesn't ever listen."

I understand Lady Daid's point of view. I too found it incredibly frustrating that he refused to protect his vulnerable, despite that I also understood that his mindset differed from everyone else's. But he was the most dangerous man in the land, and not a man to aggravate. This was foolish.

Surprisingly, Lord Eli remained calmer than one may have expected.

"Why should I change my way of life for you? I have changed our outlook to coincide with your wishes before, and I accepted that the killing of people from other provinces shouldn't happen, but I will not alter our traditions any further."

"But can you see why we find it so disconcerting?" asked a concerned Lord Bruk.

The Head of House Northorpe had been somewhat quiet in the preceding meetings, which was a shame considering that he was probably the most likely to get a result.

"No, not really," Lord Elli replied, nonchalantly.

I didn't like much about the man, but I did appreciate his honesty... at times. It was unlike Lord Bruk to get frustrated, but Lady Catar's account suggested that he was rather flustered.

"How can you sleep knowing that you are responsible for the rapes and deaths of innocent women and children?"

"With comfort," was the rather shockingly blunt response that was met with great disapproval from his peers.

It was nice for my sister to finally pitch in, "Disgusting! Their lives are your responsibility to protect! You agreed to protect our people whilst on The Conqueror all those years ago, but your way of running the Midlands is completely contradicting that agreement."

Lady Catar was right. He agreed to the terms of his reign in the Midlands but had failed to meet those terms based on his traditions.

"Exactly," Lord Bruk continued. "I appreciate that you want your land to be strong, but you don't get to have what you want. The weakest of your people are still your people, and you let them live in fear for their lives. You are not fit to lead."

Lord Eli took this attack on himself rather personally and became defensive.

"I would like to see any of you try to stop me from ruling the Midlands."

No matter how strong he was, threats as poorly considered as that one were dangerous to make. Again, Lady Anto was left as the main voice of reason.

"Please, let's not get overly emotional here. We don't want anyone to say something that they don't truly mean."

Getting overemotional was, indeed, the downfall of the council system. I was quite surprised that the Council of Heads lasted as long as it did, in all honesty. The amount of power-complexes and disagreements could never blend well together. It was never going to end well.

"I mean what I said! I never come here to be attacked!"

"Oh, your presence is immaterial," Lady Daid responded, frustrated by his philosophy. "You don't contribute at all, and you are the cause of most of our problems."

"She's right, Lord Eli," added Lord Bruk. "You don't have the right to talk to us like that when you are failing to do your job."

"I am the eldest patrician...."

"... That means nothing," Lady Daid quickly interrupted.

"Don't interrupt me!"

"If you don't want to be interrupted then don't be such a shrew!"

Lord Eli, on hearing her further slander, lunged for her across the table in a truly savage - perhaps Savage - fashion. Of course, the fellow Heads of House attempted to intervene in their brawling, but it was rather difficult considering that the brawling brutes were the two physically strongest leaders. After requesting help from some nearby farmers who were delivering meat to Castle Rye, they were eventually split up.

"The sooner we extinguish your power, the better," muttered a rather bitter Lady Daid, whose head was now bleeding.

"I agree. You're clearly not fit to lead a province," Lady Catar added.

"It would appear that you're right," Lord Bruk, who was rather bashed after the altercation, seconded my sister's opinion.

Lord Bruk's agreement, which certainly wasn't contested by Lady Anto, seemed to solidify that there was simply no trust or faith remaining whatsoever in Lord Eli's leadership ability in the Midlands. Unfortunately, there was no real authority for the other Heads of House to abolish Lord Eli as a leader, and so there was a sense of uncertainty about the room.

"I neither need nor care about your judgement!" Lord Eli bellowed. "I am the leader of the Midlands and I will do whatever I deem best, whether that means that your people die or not. I would rather do what's best for my people than take such discriminative criticism from you!"

As I said, I wasn't there myself, but I imagine that Lord Eli's shouting was rather intimidating. With that, he left. He gathered his people and returned to the Midlands with the intention to change the altered laws back to their original state, discarding the work I had instigated. From then on, he disassociated himself with the Council of Heads completely.

＊＊＊＊

"What are we going to do about him?" asked a concerned Lady Anto.

With his departure, it came to the remaining four leaders to plan the takeover of the Midlands. Too many people would die under his rule, so many already had, and now that he had left the Council of Heads there was nothing to prevent him from doing whatever he wanted.

Lady Daid, who was still attending to her wounds, was rather eager to see him gone completely.

"We need to take his land. He is a danger to us all."

My sister could smell an expansion of our land and so was keen for this plan to unfold.

"I agree. If he refuses to adhere to our ways then he shouldn't be in a position of power."

"Taking control over the Midlands would be a much harder task than you're all making it sound," was the opinion of Lady Anto.

She had a point. Yes, a combined army from the other four provinces would be effective, but my sister and Lady Daid seemed to believe that a victory would be comfortable, which was far from the truth. No others in the land fought with speed and force like the Savages. The volunteers for the armies were brave people, but not trained fighters by any means. It would be a tough battle, even with the advantage in numbers.

"We can take them," claimed Lady Catar, with confidence.

"I know we can take them, but it won't be easy. I think we should think this through more thoroughly before making rash decisions."

"I appreciate the sentiment there, Lady Anto," Lord Bruk voiced his thoughts. "But I worry that he will deteriorate rather quickly. The longer we wait, the more people die - innocent people who don't deserve to."

He seemed to be the only one to respect the etiquette that was, despite that it often felt ridiculous to adhere to, always useful when maintaining a respectful environment.

"Do innocent people not die in battle, Lord Bruk?"

"Of course. But at least those innocent people volunteered to risk their lives for a cause, rather than being slaughtered in the most humiliating of ways."

****

The debates over the moral implications of taking the Midlands was never actually resolved, as the debate transferred to who exactly would acquire the Midlands after the land was taken. Personally, I would have given the land to those of House Hepston. They had the smallest province, so an expansion was due. Plus, Lady Anto was the only one who didn't ask for it, and that should've counted for something in my opinion.

Lord Bruk began by making his argument, which was actually quite a fair one.

"It makes sense for the South to take the Midlands. We have the most patricians so we won't be too stretched with the extra responsibility."

My sister, who had never been satisfied with what she had at any point in her life, was not going to give up the opportunity for more power that easily.

"The South is big enough as it is. The High North is the second smallest province in the land, and the Deep South only has two patricians. I mean no offence, Lady Anto, but I hardly see Lady Aott being able to cope with such an expansion. She still, after all, has not yet bled. We have the best solution. Who in the land would we trust more as a replacement for Eli than my brother, Lord Barrat?"

It was nice to get some recognition from my sister, although I suspected it was only a ploy for her to get more control for herself.

"I would feel comfortable with him as leader," confessed Lord Bruk.

Unfortunately, Lady Daid could see through my sister's manipulation.

"I agree that he would be a good leader, but he would still be under your control. I don't trust you to do what is best for all."

"Are you calling me incompetent?"

Lady Catar didn't take well to the Northern brute's comments, so much so that she stood with intent. Lady Daid followed suit by standing too, tucking her chair under the table to suggest that she wouldn't back down.

"I'm calling you untrustworthy."

Physically, my sister couldn't handle Lady Daid, but she did have enough pride to continue fighting against her.

"I'm no more untrustworthy than you," my sister shouted, as if that was a notable argument.

She moved closer to the brutish woman from the North, knocking her chair down as she did, causing a beautifully carved image of the five provincial leaders to crack on the stone floor.

Lady Catar continued, "You're the one who always flies off the handle. It was your behaviour today that pissed Eli off enough to leave!"

"That's unfair! He's in the wrong and you know it."

"It takes two to have a fight, Lady Daid."

On seeing that they were now mere inches away from each other, Lady Anto and Lord Bruk moved to stand in between the two, which I thought was quite brave of them considering the tempers of their fellow Heads.

"You know, maybe the North should take control of the Midlands. And then, maybe the High North should take control from you," my sister snapped.

Lady Anto tried to intervene, turning to my sister.

"Ladies, please calm down. Lady Catar, you cannot mean this?"

I can almost picture the angered look on my sister's face as she continued to insult.

"Oh, I mean it. This narcissistic shrew gets an awful lot of leeway considering her incompetence. She can't even look after her own people!"

"Watch your mouth! Don't make threats that you know you won't go through with."

"Who says I won't?" Lady Catar asked, unfazed. "Sharing the land was nice for a while, but I think it's time for one house to take all."

Lady Catar headed for the door in a similar fashion to Lord Eli. Lady Daid, now more ferocious than before, pushed past Lord Bruk to confront my sister more closely.

"I agree. I can't wait to see your pathetic little army crumble."

"You'll have to watch from within your castle walls as I burn your family alive."

With that, the two left with only one thing on their minds: dominance. As it goes, they never did go head to head on a battlefield, sometimes fate is more effective than rationale. They did, however, start a war - one which no one was guaranteed to win, but my sister was guaranteed to lose.

The Terms of War

After the calamity of the previous Council of Heads meeting, which ended up being the last official meeting of that format of council altogether, war was declared and was set to take place imminently. The war was inevitable. There were far too many in the land who were plagued with power and very few who could cope with that responsibility. Too much distrust and too many narcissistic leaders created an uncomfortable environment that felt extremely forced. If the council was ever going to work then the members needed to want to be there, which they never really did, especially towards the end. Although the war made the atmosphere across the land rather tense, it was agreed by all provincial leaders, including a Lord Eli who had been less than keen to cooperate in the past, that the war was to be treated as a civil one for the benefit of the people. I personally believed that no war at all would be for the benefit of the people, and anything less than that doesn't benefit the people at all, but my opinion hasn't always seemed to matter.

The Prosperity Era, as the name suggests, was a lucrative time for Saddle Isle regarding trade and agriculture. This not only maintained a fairly reasonable standard of living for people but it also provided a comfortable enough situation to promote population growth. The original population of the island, which was estimated to lie between five and six-thousand (although I am led to believe by the estimations made across the year that the original population leant more towards the five-thousand mark opposed to six), was not enough to maintain sustainable living on a long term basis. Due to this, we encouraged people to procreate, and this scheme was very successful. This meant that by 1108 our population sat much healthier, between 7,000 and 7,500 across the isle. Unfortunately, this meant that even more lives were placed in the hands of patricians blinded by their own craving for power. If this war wasn't done in a sensible manner - if any war could be done sensibly - then almost 7,500 people could die. In the context of the mistakes that had already been made, a civil war was the most necessary solution.

Because of this decision, it was necessary for the leaders to meet to agree on the terms of war. It was decided that the South was the place to do this, mainly due to the fact that the Midlands, despite being the most logical location geographically, was not considered a sensible option. Each province headed to Castle Sear with the promise of good behaviour, along with their entire household. I was furious that this was happening at all, of course. It seemed so irrational to go to war with each other. Then there was the issue of my sister. I knew that she wanted power, but I also knew that we didn't have the resources to achieve her ridiculous ambition. But that wasn't the only thing on my mind. After the terms were agreed, I was prevented from seeing Lady Breck for the war's duration. There was a chance that I would die before seeing her again and that was a thought that I wasn't strong enough to endure.

****

It was unclear exactly how the terms of war were going to be drafted. Obviously, this had never happened before and the leaders of the land hadn't shown any ability of negotiating whilst part of the council, so this seemed an impossible task. Luckily, if you could call any of it lucky, Lady Anto provided a rather suitable solution to the problem at hand, as she often did.

"I would like to make it clear that the people of the Deep South do not wish to be a part of this. We do not have the resources and, even if we did, I would always refuse to advocate the needless killing of our own people. It has been a difficult decision, but my sister and I are willing to sacrifice our power to whomever becomes the first monarch in order to maintain peace for our province and trust that we will be treated with kindness because of this cooperation."

Lady Daid seemed a little unimpressed by Lady Anto's decision, but their mindsets were always going to contradict.

"I know that you disapprove of the war, which I respect, but would you perhaps consider leading the war discussions. It is only fair that a non-biased patrician takes charge, now that there is one."

Despite her initial reluctance, Lady Anto eventually decided that, in the awful circumstances, it was probably the most efficient and sensible way to sort the inevitable out. She took a quill and parchment and began dictating the terms.

"What exactly would these terms consist of?"

A very valid question that no one had seemed to have thought about before travelling south. We had never had a war before and our lack of understanding towards how one would work made that as clear as day. I thought that I should start suggestions, considering no one else would.

"The priority needs to be the protection of the people. This is a war caused by us, not them. No one deserves to die unnecessarily because of our little quarrels."

"I agree," Lord Bruk seconded. "The brave people in our armies signed up of their own accord and so know the risks. Innocent people, who choose not to risk dying in battle, deserve to have their choices respected by us."

Lady Daid agreed with the sentiment but couldn't envision the solution.

"How are we going to ensure that, though?"

Of course, Lady Anto was the one to provide the solution that was missing.

"Well, considering that this war is a civil one, it shall be stated in the terms that all planned attacks should be as such, planned. Each leader should give at least an eight hour notice of an attack in order to give time for the defending province to ensure safety for those who need it, and battles shall be given specific locations and times."

"That's a terrible idea!" moaned Lord Eli.

It was no surprise that the Head of House Wharram wasn't too keen on our kind approach to war, if any approach to war could ever be described as kind.

"How is it a terrible idea?" Lady Daid asked, unimpressed.

She certainly maintained her grudge against the Midland brute.

"It ruins tactics," was his eloquent response.

"Or maybe it promotes intelligent thinking."

She often did hit back with condescending quips that never went down well with those plagued by pride. Lady Anto, like everyone else, was keen for the two of them to calm down.

"Let's not have another brawl now. I am adding 'a period of daylight's notice before an attack' to the terms, and these letters shall be sent by the Head of House directly. I am also stating that all battles need an agreed location and both a start and end time. That is, if an end time is necessary for a day's fighting..."

".... Quillian Day needs to be respected," requested an interrupting Lord Eli.

Lady Anto didn't even put it up to debate with it being an isle-wide day for the Leonist gods.

"Of course! Right, I believe we also need to address surrender terms in order to move forward."

Lady Catar was evidently keen to get involved.

"Yes," my sister chimed in. "It should be stated that you can surrender in three ways. The first way is to not partake in the first place, like yourself, Lady Anto. Then, the second way being a submitted alliance in order to save your own province in battle. The third being the death of a Head of House on the battlefield."

The general consensus seemed to support two of her suggestions, however some disagreed with the third. The argument against it was predominantly led by Lord Maxim, son of Limo, of

House Matfen, who presumably would become Head of House if Lady Daid was to perish. The twins were identical. Both men were relatively muscular in physique and certainly would have looked more intimidating had they been stood next to me, for example, rather than their brutish sister. They wore their dark brown hair in the same way, medium length with a central parting allowing them to see past their relatively long fringes. The only real difference was in their general expressions, with Lord Maxim adopting a rather consistent stern look upon his face, and the more humorous Lord Angull often wearing a cheeky smile that made him look quite smug.

"It should be the decision of the remaining patricians to call a retreat if they deem that to be the most suitable option, not the death of the Head of House," was Lord Maxim's argument.

"I actually agree."

I knew that agreeing with Lord Maxim would annoy my sister, not that I worried too much about doing that, but I genuinely thought that it was a better solution. The death of a head would damage the attack but wouldn't necessarily derail the attack completely.

"I also agree," added Lord Robt, son of Betra, of House Northorpe. "There are five people in our house and if my brother was to fall, gods forbid, we would still stand a chance at victory. Although, it should be the decision of the highest ranking patrician to call a retreat, not just anyone."

As annoyed as she was, Lady Catar was an intelligent woman and so saw the logic in what was being said.

"Fine. That makes sense, I suppose."

Lady Anto added the agreed terms to the parchment.

"Let me reiterate. In summary, one can surrender by withdrawal, making a forced alliance in battle, or when the highest ranking patrician calls a yielding retreat. Is there anything else?"

"The reward for victory should be stated," said Lord Eli, brimming with confidence.

"Yes, of course," Lady Anto continued to write reluctantly. "Well, it seems simple. The last province to surrender will be victorious, and the highest ranked patrician of that victorious province shall become the first monarch and so will decide who becomes the new leader of each individual province. The first capital shall be the province that originally belonged to the victors."

The leaders decided that the terms were fair, and so signed the document to confirm the beginning of the Great Packsaddle War. With that, everyone dispersed to prepare for the imminent catastrophe that was to follow.

****

The meeting was an awful experience. It was horrible to see such hatred and feel such tension, but that wasn't what ruined it. The worst part of it was that I didn't get to say goodbye to Lady Breck. I didn't get to speak to her at all. At least she seemed to take our lack of interaction rather hard too, if that can even be considered a positive. After what was a rather tough day, Lord Bruk decided to check on his sister, who didn't seem herself. She lay on her bed cuddling a pillow and crying.

"What's the matter, little sister?" he asked, softly.

"I'm fine, honestly."

Lord Bruk sat down next to her on her bed.

"I know when you're lying, Breck. Now what's the matter?"

"I don't want to talk about it!" she insisted, turning away from her brother.

"Is this about Lord Barrat?"

Lord Bruk had spent years watching Lady Breck sulk because she missed me and so he was rather competent when it came to picking up on her sadness.

"I didn't even get to say goodbye! This is all so foolish, Bruk. Why did this have to happen?"

She began to cry harder, as her brother rubbed her back in an attempt to comfort her. Lord Bruk started to well up a bit too. He hated seeing her upset but there wasn't much he could do.

"I know, I know. Unfortunately, some people are too selfish to maintain peace."

"Then they shouldn't have power."

Lord Bruk chuckled at her observation.

"If only everyone was more like you. I know it's unfair, but we have no control. I tried to prevent it, I really did. It's just one of those things. I'm so sorry."

She sat up and cuddled up to him.

"I know it's not your fault, brother. I know that you are a good man. I bet you would make a brilliant king."

"That's very kind of you," he humbly said as he kissed her head. "Do you know who'd also make a decent king?"

"Who?"

"Barrat. He's a good man too."

"Please don't do that."

Her tears, which had slowed down slightly, picked up pace again.

"Do what?" Lord Bruk asked, confused at what she was so upset about.

"Talk about him."

"Sometimes talking about what makes you sad can really help."

Lady Breck shot him a dirty look.

"Please don't talk to me like I'm a child!"

"I'm sorry. I forget that you're no longer that little girl that I met all those years ago."

Her brother's reminiscing caused her to smile, briefly.

"Talking about it might help," she eventually confessed, after a brief pause.

"Please do," he encouraged.

She snuggled in closer to him as she prepared to bear all.

"It's not even that I won't get to see him. I've spent most of my life missing him. I'm just so scared that I'll never see him again. There is no chance that the High North will win a battle. I've spent so much time there over the years and they are nowhere near as battle-ready as the other provinces. I mean, the Midlands would rip them apart in minutes."

"But Barrat would have the sense to surrender."

"The only way he could do that is if his siblings died first," she correctly pointed out. "There's no guarantee that he'll survive. Lady Catar banned him from combat training when he was of age. The only training he's ever had was taught to him by Suln and I've never seen him be convincing with a bow."

Despite the aim being to raise her hopes, Lord Bruk seemed to only grow more concerned for my wellbeing himself.

"I'm sure Lady Catar will protect him."

"Oh, please! She's been trying to get rid of him for years. Why do you think she tried to shame him with that common trading job?"

He had to admit that my sister wasn't my biggest fan.

"I know, but look what he did there. He didn't sulk or moan. Instead, he took it in his stride and reshaped the trade system successfully. He is seen throughout the land as a brilliantly talented man."

"That's not going to help him in battle, though."

He shifted position to look at his sister more directly.

"That's not the point. He always finds a way to pull through. You need to have more faith in him, Breck."

"I suppose. I just wish I could have him here."

"I know."

She paused, getting choked up again.

"You know, it has been so long since I've had him close to me. I wish he could've stayed here. I wish I could just watch him sleep. I wish I could run my hands through his soft hair and chuckle to myself when he lightly snores, or shifts position. If I knew that the last time might have actually been the last time then I would never have allowed him to leave. I love him so much and I love thinking about what our future will hold. That is, if the gods allow us to have a future. I love thinking about our wedding and our family. Oh, he's going to be such a great father, I just know it. I love thinking about growing old with him, walking along the Southern beaches with our children - and maybe even grandchildren, who'll run along the sand and laugh as they splash in the waves. And yet, a part of me wishes that I could just freeze a moment with him forever. A moment when he is simply asleep next to me. When I can know that I will have him to watch and to love for eternity, and know that he will always be safe here with me."

Lord Bruk began to choke up too.

"I hope that you will have a thousand moments where you are safe together," he added. "But for now, you need to be brave and pray that the gods allow you to have the happiness that you both deserve."

Lord Bruk let his words linger for a bit before starting to shift away from her.

"I think you should get some rest. Hopefully you'll feel more optimistic in the morning."

He stood up to leave.

"Thank you for this, brother," she smiled at him. "I love you, you know."

He gave her a smile in return.

"I know. I love you too, my dear sister."

The Underdogs

For the first time in the history of Saddle Isle, the provinces were at war. However, it was rather hard to tell that by my surroundings. Since the war was declared, I had been confined to the High North, understandably. No province wanted to be seen supporting another in their bid for the Crown, so the role of a trader was pretty much made redundant. After many years of having the freedom to travel across the whole land, I expected that this imprisonment would be a difficult change, but in actuality I rather enjoyed it. Looking out upon the land and sea from my window brought a bizarre sense of peace during such a turbulent time. There was a short period where we were at war but no one seemed to make any vast moves for the throne. As I've said, the Deep South expressed no interest in the throne at all and so they were expected to continue with their labour in the fields as if nothing was happening elsewhere. But the inactive nature of the other provinces was a concern of mine. My sister has always craved power. Growing up, she would never let Lord Shay or I take up any aspect of responsibility or leadership, whether that was in games or in more serious occasions, such as the running of our province. This resulted in Lord Shay taking a rather reserved role in the family and became subservient to Lady Catar, which was ideal for her. I, on the other hand, was keen to improve my leadership skills under Lord Bruk's guidance and encouragement. As great as that was, and as competent as I became politically, Lady Catar didn't take too well to my abilities and didn't show me much respect. I say this because I saw what was to come. With no other province making moves, presumably because they were preparing for upcoming battles properly rather than just assuming that a win was guaranteed, my sister fell into their trap. She was a relatively competent warrior, to give her credit, but she was not patient enough to be a good commander. She didn't see the lack of action as a means for concern but as an opportunity to attack whilst the enemy wasn't looking. That seems like a sensible move on parchment, but our attacking forces were significantly smaller than that of the other provinces. In terms of population, our province was one of the smallest and so we were never going to win. It was as simple as that.

****

Lady Catar called my brother and I to a meeting, which was worrying.

"Brothers, take a seat," she demanded, sounding optimistic.

The meeting room in Castle Gelid couldn't hold a candle to the one located in the Deep South. I loved the detailing in that room. One needed many candles to displace the darkness in our room. There was only a single window, as was the case in many of the chambers in the castle, and so darkness was the most prevailing feature. I have previously mentioned the weathered brickwork on the outside of the castle, and the inside wasn't much better. It smelt damp and often felt cold, even in the springtime. Lord Shay and I took our seats on the battered chairs that had been carelessly assembled from some old ship decking that needed replacing. The slate table we leant upon, which at one time would have looked so bold in the room, was no better either. The chips and broken edges made it appear rather pathetic. It was a grim place to debate any matter within, but discussing our impending doom in such a room was simply depressing. Lady Catar continued after we'd reluctantly sat down.

"The war has begun, as you know, and we need to make the first move."

Despite her slightly intimidating nature, I couldn't allow her to doom us all.

"No! We haven't got the numbers to attack first."

She shot a look of scorn, which wasn't uncommon.

"We have plenty of warriors."

"And every other province has plenty more. We do not have the capacity to win, under any circumstances. Any attack from us would result in the massacring of our people."

"Perhaps on a battlefield, yes, but we have something that very few do."

"And what is that?"

"Ships, brother. An entire fleet! We have more ships than all the other provinces combined."

Despite her baseless pride, she was correct. We were the fishing province and so we were the only ones to possess a fleet of ships, if that's what you'd call it. Our ship count was only increased by the North's abandonment of their fishing duty in exchange for hunting the wild goats of the mountains, of which there were copious amounts. This, of course, was held over me by my sister, whose vote was the deciding one to allow for the goat hunting in the first place despite my advising against it.

"And what do we plan on doing with these ships?" asked my brother.

It was nice to see Lord Shay after such a long time, but I knew that he was to be my downfall today. There was little chance that he would argue against my sister. I was always destined to be outvoted.

"We sail down past Midland Bay, of course, and make an attack on the South."

Saddle Isle is shaped rather like a tooth, with a wide top and two prongs at the south end of the island. This meant that, to the west, there was a rather large groove in the land that formed Midland Bay. Although sailing wouldn't save us much time on the journey, it would save us energy, which an army as small as ours would need to even survive such an ill-advised battle. It was a rather bold move from my sister and, if our army was a larger one, a rather well thought out strategic move. To reach the South, we would have to pass through the Midlands. Those of House Wharram had the most men, as well as a savagery that other's failed to possess. Avoiding passing through the Midlands was a wise move.

"By sailing past the Midlands and attacking from both land and sea, we will have the advantage of surrounding those of the South from multiple sides. Even the South will struggle to cope with such an attack," Lady Catar explained. "Not only that, but those of the Midlands won't know that we are there until it's too late. After we take the South, we can sail half our remaining men back north and ambush the Savages from both north and south."

Her ambition was to be admired, but something that would cause death for many a High Northerner.

"Even if we attack the South from multiple sides, which I would rather we didn't do to my friends, they would still have a vast numerical advantage on us. Besides, they have archers in the South. I know because they have taught me. They could easily burn our ships from the land before we even make it to shore. That would truly be a pathetic attempt at victory, even for an army so small. It cannot be done. We have so few warriors that we will not be able to defend our land if the battle comes to us. I understand that. But surely we would be better off waiting for other battles to occur and then make our move. I have had word from a friend in the Midlands, who I assure you is trustworthy even in times of war. She says that those of House Wharram are preparing to attack the North. That is a battle destined to be full of bloodshed. Whoever wins that battle will be heavily weakened and there for the taking, even for an army as small as ours. If we have control of the High North, the North and the Midlands too, then the South will surrender - I know it."

I hated the prospect of attacking my friends in the South but I was more worried for the safety of our people. We could not afford, in any way, to attack first. If we did, we would surely be defeated. We were always set to argue, we were as stubborn as each other.

Lady Catar continued the debate.

"But, brother, I cannot trust the words of one from another province. If we don't attack then we'll be attacked. I understand your reservations - I do. I understand that you love that girl from the South, but this is war. There is no room for love or friendship on the battlefield. You say we are a small army - you're right. But that means that we must be the ones to move forward. We can't defend our land - you're right about that too - but we might have the chance to take land from another, if we play our cards right."

I only grew in frustration. I knew she was listening, but she was not taking my advice into real consideration.

"We don't have a hand to play, sister. You have it wrong. If we can't defend our own land then we certainly can't take the land of another. That's the harsh reality of our position."

"I would disagree."

I knew by the fact that she maintained her eye contact that she was not going to back down. This wasn't a case of her hanging onto a hopeless dream to rule, she genuinely believed that she could win and so she was going to do all she could to get what she wanted.

"Please listen to me! Our army is half the size of those of other provinces. Even those of House Hepston have a bigger army than us and they pledged for peace because they knew they couldn't win. The only way that we are going to maintain any fragment of power is if we make alliances with other provinces."

"But then I wouldn't be queen," she said with disappointment in her tone.

The sadness in her eyes made me bizarrely feel sympathy for her, but I had to continue. "There is no reality in which you become queen, sister. We have not got the resources to achieve that goal. Taking that into consideration, I know that I would rather see you live without a crown on your head than die hopelessly trying to get it. I refuse to see men and women of our province die fighting for a hopeless cause."

"I don't see it as a hopeless cause."

Her opinion didn't shock me, in all honesty. Of course she didn't see it the way I did. She saw herself sitting on a throne with a crown on her head.

She continued, "But let's say you're right. What should we do then, if you're so smart?"

"You're not going to like it."

I knew she'd say no, but I had to tell her.

"I say we declare peace, like those of House Hepston. We don't have the numbers to win this war so we should do what's best for our people."

Lady Catar was visibly disgusted by that thought. My proposal meant that she would be forced to give all power up to whoever won the war and I knew that was something she was far too proud to do.

"Those are the words of a coward!"

"And those are the words of a fool!"

She stood from her battered seat in anger.

"You're too set on staying friends with those of House Northorpe so that you can marry Lady Breck. If anything, you're the one fighting for a hopeless cause, brother. We are at war and so all of our enemies must die. It's as simple as that."

"You have quickly forgotten that these enemies of yours were your friends and colleagues less than a season ago. It is over-emotional language such as this that has put us in this ridiculous situation in the first place. And regarding your accusations on my allegiances, I assure you that I am simply set on keeping us all alive, Catar. The South would defeat us. They'll wait for us to sail close enough and then they'll burn our fleet. Even if we somehow do make it to shore, they outnumber us on the battlefield. We'll all die."

"So be it! We'll either win in glory or die in glory. We sail at first light, and I will hear no more of it, Barrat."

Those words from our sister caused Lord Shay to look at me with great fear in his eyes.

She stood and made her way to the door, followed by my reluctant brother shortly after, who looked pale with fear at what was to follow in the days to come. I remained seated, staring out of a window on the far wall of the room.

"What was the last thing that Mother said to you?" I asked in a last ditch attempt to change her mind.

My question caused her to stop in her tracks. She paused for a moment before turning back.

"What did you say?"

"What was the last thing that Mother said to you?" I repeated.

"I don't remember," she lied.

"Then I'll remind you. She made you promise that you would put the safety of Shay and I above everything else, always."

She remained silent.

I continued, "And now you lead us off to die, like farmers leading their sheep to be slaughtered. I hope you're proud of yourself. Mother certainly wouldn't be."

I waited for her to change her mind. I waited for my sister to realise that she was being overly greedy and that she had no chance of winning this war. I waited for her to feel the weight of responsibility that Mother placed upon her shoulders - responsibility that she had always craved so much. I waited for that weight to drag her to the ground.

"I said that I would hear no more of it," my sister repeated, sternly.

She turned away once more and headed back towards the door.

"At least promise me that Lady Breck will see no harm," I requested, desperate to ensure her safety as much as I could.

"I cannot make such promises."

Her response made my heart momentarily sink.

She thankfully continued, "But I will advise the people not to harm her. Whether they do or not is up to them from there."

That was as good as I was going to get and I was grateful for it.

"I suppose I'll send words of war to the South then," I regretfully stated as I reached out for parchment and a quill.

It was supposed to be the Head of House that sent words of war to an opponent, but she was half way out the door.

"No," she said with an authoritative tone.

Her pause gave me hope, but that hope was cruel and subsequently shattered almost as quickly as it had developed.

"We're not sending word. As you said, brother, we are outnumbered. We need the element of surprise if we're going to win."

With that she left the room, shortly followed by Lord Shay.

I remained, continuing to look out of the window. Setting sail at first light would mean that we would arrive in the South by that same day's sunset, if the winds were kind. Many would be in their homes, and none would be in our way. I am a man of peace, but peace wasn't an option anymore. It was my duty to follow my sister's orders, as horrific and foolish as they were, but I could not. As a man who deems himself noble, failing to send word of the attack would have ended all hope for me. I know it sounds rather foolish to tell an enemy of your imminent arrival but this was a civil war. We had our own people, but the people of the entire isle were placed into the hands of the twenty and so it was our duty to protect them no matter which province they resided in. Sending a pigeon with words of war would give them a day to prepare for battle. It would allow for those of the South to provide shelter for the pacifists of the land, as well as the children and elderly. It was always a tragedy to lose warriors on the battlefield, especially those from your own province, but those warriors volunteered to fight. They knew that death was a possibility, if not a probability. But those pacifists, children and elders did not sign up to die and so should have their decision respected. I did my duty to my sister. I vowed to march into battle by her side, as poor of a fighter as I was. But I refused to let innocents die in their homes at the hands of my family. We had worked hard to make House Pearson a house of honour and I intended to keep it that way.

*** * * ***

Those of House Northorpe were feasting when my letter arrived. They sat together, as a family who truly cared for one another and ate fine beef and drank fine wine that all came from the fields of their land.

"My Lords, My Lady," Mister Rufus, a loyal guard and servant, interrupted.

Mister Rufus looked almost as rundown as our meeting room. He was missing two fingers on his right hand after an altercation with a prisoner only a few months after our initial arrival. His face was weathered and wrinkled and there was no evidence of the previous thick black locks that used to spread across his scalp, only the thinning grey disparage on what previously thrived. His eyes had very little life left in them and his smile was missing a few teeth. I say this because he is quite possibly the most noble man I ever had the pleasure to meet and none of these aspects of him, as clear as he may be in your mind, have any relevance whatsoever. He had numerous qualities to him that every individual should strive to possess: wit, charm, intelligence, kindness, ability, loyalty - the list could be endless. Those qualities are more important than appearance and that will never change. You could tell by Lord Bruk's face that he knew what was coming.

"What is it, good sir?" asked the Head of House Northorpe. "I assume that you bring me words of war."

"Yes, My Lord. I'm afraid I do."

Fear is one thing that cannot be separated by status, as shown by the shared terror in the eyes of both the servant and his lord. The Head of House stood from his seat and walked towards Mister Rufus.

"Who from? I suspect it's from Lord Eli."

"No, My Lord. It's from Lord Barrat, on behalf of Lady Catar."

All eyes turned to my beloved, who looked to the ground.

"Are you sure, good sir? This must be some sort of mistake. He wouldn't."

Lady Breck looked up to meet the noble servant's eyes as he answered.

"It is definitely from him, My Lady, but I'm sure it's out of reluctance."

"Yes, I'm sure of it too," Lord Bruk seconded as he poured himself some wine. "But that doesn't matter now. We have to prepare for an attack. Good sir, please begin preparations to find safety for the vulnerable of our province. The keep should do fine."

Mister Rufus' response shocked the lord, but pleasantly.

"We already have, My Lord, as suggested by the man who sent this letter."

"Well then, you were right, Rufus. It is definitely from Lord Barrat. He's the only man I know who would inform me in this way. Brothers, we must prepare for battle. We must protect our province and our people. Expect ships coming in from the Midland Bay. She may be a horrid woman, but Lady Catar is not a fool. She will utilise her most powerful asset, and her most powerful asset is her fleet. We must prepare the archers so we can stop as many ships from coming ashore as we can. And if you see Lord Barrat, spare his life and capture him instead."

Lord Robt was confused and angered by this statement.

"Capture him? He is of House Pearson, who have just declared to battle against us. I respect him as much as the rest of you but we are at war. He is our enemy now."

Lord Bruk momentarily ignored his brother's rage and turned to his servant.

"Good sir, do hand my brother the letter."

He did as he was commanded.

"Who is it from, brother?" Lord Bruk provokingly asked, pouring himself another cup. "Do read it aloud."

Lord Robt announced the letter's writer to the group.

"Lord Barrat, son of Nea, of House Pearson, on behalf of Lady Catar, daughter of Nea, of House Pearson."

"That, brother, is why we shall spare him his life on the battlefield."

Lord Bruk was met with confused looks from his brothers, yet he sipped his wine before he continued with his explanation, as if he had all the time in the world.

"If Lady Catar intended for this letter to be sent, she would have sent it herself. That was the agreed system set by the neutral Lady Anto, daughter of Elan, of House Hepston, when the terms of war were set."

"I don't get what you mean," admitted Lord Neman.

Lord Bruk continued to explain as he sat next to his sister and allowed her to cuddle into him, as she was visibly shaken by the conflict between my house and hers.

"Lord Barrat sent us those words of war of his own accord. He will have gone against the wishes of his sister today, all to save hundreds of innocent lives within our province. In doing so, he has risked the lives of his own army to maintain nobility, as all patricians should. He deserves our gratitude."

Lord Robt smiled at his sister.

"I suppose he does deserve our mercy."

"Robt, Neman, Suln, go and prepare for the battle tomorrow."

They all stood at Lord Bruk's command.

He continued, "Suln, I want you to take charge of the archers. As soon as all the ships have either been sunk or have docked, make your way to the villages to give us swordsmen support. Formations will be difficult considering the ambush. Lady Catar's decision to break the terms of war mean that there is no battlefield to fight upon, only the space around the homes of our people. We will all be alone out there and so will need as many warriors as possible.”

“Of course, brother,” was Lord Suln’s loyal answer.

“Now, get some sleep, all of you. We don’t know when they shall arrive so we need to be prepared from dusk till dawn. A big day awaits us tomorrow, brothers, and we must be sharp. She may have lost dignity today but the woman can fight.”

With that, the three brothers left, leaving Lord Bruk alone with Lady Breck.

“It’ll all be okay, sister. You know, you’ve fallen in love with a good man. I hope, for both of you, that the gods are kind to good men tomorrow. Now, go get some rest yourself. You can stay in your own bed tonight but you’ll need to be up bright and early to make your way to the keep. The innocent will need to see their lady to maintain hope of making it through the fighting.”

“Yes, brother,” she complied. “Please look out for him, won’t you.”

“Of course. He is just as much my brother as Robt, Neman and Suln. I will do what I can to keep all of my brothers alive tomorrow.”

The Battle of Midland Bay, 1108

The sound of birds singing outside my window indicated to me that the time had come to depart. The day was calm and the winds were low, which would result in a slightly slower journey to the South than Lady Catar may have hoped for. In different circumstances, I would have been happy to wake up to a day like this one. The view of the High North from my window was beautiful, with its flowery fields and glistening sea, and there tended to be a pleasant atmosphere about the province on days when the sun was prominent. Everyone much preferred the warm weather than our harsh winters. It was a rather paradoxical experience to be alarmed by the beautiful sound of nature when the day was set to be full of such bloodshed and violence. The birds indicated the break of dawn but didn't wake me from any form of slumber. I hadn't slept at all due to the anxiety that I was feeling towards the day ahead. I had so much to lose because I loved so many who were poised to die.

My reluctance towards going into battle against the South was seemingly unrequited by the rest of the province. The people were optimistic and prepared for what was to come. I wonder if that was down to ignorance or simply credited to my sister's baseless narcissism in her approach to caution, and her flawed belief that if she can imagine things going well then they will. I was also reluctant about the day because I went against my sister's orders. Of course, the principle of trying to save lives, or at least trying to give people a chance to save their own, meant that it was also my duty to tell Lady Catar that those of House Northorpe knew that we were attacking. For some reason, that was harder to do. Writing a letter to Lord Bruk meant going against my own house, but that was for the good of the people. I was worried about my sister's reaction to the news because I knew that she, despite having enough goodness in her heart to understand my rationale eventually, would rashly become enraged with me. Despite my concern, I had to tell her so that we didn't blindly head to the South expecting to catch them unaware, for them to be prepared for our arrival.

＊＊＊＊

Lady Catar stood in total disbelief as we stood on the dock moments from sailing away.

"How could you? You have ruined my entire strategy! How evil must one be to speak as an ally but act as an enemy?"

I refused to lose the dignity of our house over Lady Catar's crazed ambition.

"I am evil enough to have saved thousands of innocent lives! The people of the South are our people just as much as anyone else. If you were to become queen in that manner, every single one of your subjects would blame you for taking away their innocent wives, elders and children! And that wouldn't be temporary. They would hate you from the second you took your seat upon that throne and would only stop when it was no longer yours to sit on."

"You should have consulted me," she said, bitterly.

I was equally as bitter.

"I tried, remember? But your mind is too set on seeing a crown on your head for you to realise what that crown truly means."

"I shall deal with you, brother, after our victory."

She paused, seething as she paced up and down the dock. After a few minutes, she turned her focus away from me and addressed our army.

"Men and women, brave soldiers of our province, I speak to you now as a fellow warrior. Thanks to my brother's love for a southern whore, we face a harder task than we first thought. But is it not the challenges we face that increase our legacy? Is it not the challenges we face that makes victory taste all the more sweet? We have been challenged by destiny today and we will face that challenge with might, bravery and strength! We still have the advantage of ships! We still can attack from multiple sides! We still have the chance to change the shape of history, and we will take that chance with the beating pride of the High North thumping in our chests! We will take that chance with the flowing dignity of the High North coursing through our veins! We have been overlooked for too long. They have called us mere fishermen, cooped up in the far corner of the isle with only the purpose of improving other provinces and not our own. Well today, that stops! Today, we solidify the High North as the highest province: lifted by our honour, bravery and strength - qualities that I know lie within the hearts of each and every one of us! They have the numbers but we have the grit and determination to take what we deserve!"

"For the honour of the High North!" was the shout from thousands, who roared as they boarded ships that had already been stashed with weapons and armour.

The sound of a familiar voice arose from behind me. It was my old friend, Miss Frith.

"My Lord, I must say that I am glad of what you did. I told you that you had a special form of peace inside."

"Thank you, kind friend. Although, you must say it quietly. I wouldn't want you getting struck by my sister before we've even set sail. I imagine we will face many a strike today."

"We certainly will. Many of these brave warriors won't be making the return trip."

"I do wish you had taught me how to use a sword, now," I half-joked, knowing that I genuinely meant it but also knowing that it would make her smile.

"I will admit that the skill would be of great use today, but I would much rather be in your shoes than mine, My Lord. I imagine that the kindness shown towards those of the South places you in a much more favourable position when it comes to mercy.

We both know that victory for us would be a miracle. I just hope that you survive whatever lies ahead."

"I can only hope the same for you, my friend," I said, giving her a hug that she seemed to genuinely appreciate.

"May the gods look down on you!"

"And may they look down on you also."

That was the last time I ever saw my friend. I cannot even say how she died, mainly as I do not know for certain but also because of the pain the thought causes me. She was a good person who gave everything for our province. If anything, I deserved to die in her place. Soon after Lady Catar's speech, the ships had been filled with our warriors. And so, before I could even request that my sister reconsider her plan with the new knowledge of the South's preparedness, we embarked on our passage to Midland Bay. With Lady Catar still seething, I appreciated that I was stationed on a ship with Lord Shay rather than her. I hoped that our separation would allow for her to cool down, or at least forget about our disagreement. There was a good chance, siblings or not, that my sister would have killed me on the voyage if we were in close proximity to each other.

*** * * ***

Down in the South, Lord Bruk and his army were already awaiting our arrival. They were tasked with keeping the fighting as far away from the villages as possible, but that would be a struggle considering the close proximity between Castle Sear, the villages and the coast. This was made all the more difficult as Lady Catar had split the army in half. To combat this, Lord Suln was manned on the castle walls, preparing archers to burn our ships before we could make it towards land. There wasn't much necessity for Lord Suln to lead the archers, as such. He knew very well that each archer had specific skill and experience, and so he was more than willing to allow his archers to fire at their own pace to get the best out of them. Of course, Lord Suln was the most skilled and so made sure to clarify that no one should needlessly attempt to keep up with his pace. Before our arrival, Lord Bruk went to ensure that all was well with the archers. He met with Lord Suln, who was rather concerned about his sister's well-being.

"You shouldn't have been so optimistic to Breck. She's just going to get hurt."

"What do you mean?"

"She said that you've promised to protect Barrat, but he could be on any one of the ships that come in."

Despite Lord Suln's affection for me, he was right to question this logic.

"I know that, but..."

"... But nothing, Bruk. Breck is a wonderful young woman and I love how much you care for her, but you can't keep shielding her from the reality of this life. This battle is going to be hard enough to win. I know we have the numbers but they have blind hope. You shouldn't have made those promises to her. She'll start to distrust us and make foolish decisions, and you know how strong-willed she is already. It is too hard to focus on winning this battle and keeping Barrat alive. Of course, look out for him, but you cannot put his safety above our people."

"He did that for us," Lord Bruk responded, still trying to fight for me.

"I know, and I am grateful for that. But that was different. This is a battle now and Barrat's life can't be a priority. Do you understand?"

"I understand."

*** * * ***

"We'll earn our coin today, Ritche."

We were getting close and the tension on our ship was rising, which I'm sure was the case throughout the fleet. The journey wasn't a long one, less than a day due to favourable winds that had picked up since the morning, and the initial adrenaline had faded due to the looming reality of bloodshed and death. And so, as you can imagine, the soldiers began to get anxious. This anxiety caused some nervous conversation to break out between them. Some of the soldiers were saying quite bizarre things, such as this exchange, which was held in my vicinity.

"We don't get paid for this, Basek."

"What do you mean we don't get paid for this?"

Basek's annoyance at this reality made Ritche chuckle slightly.

"Well, exactly that. We don't get paid for this."

There was a brief pause in which the wind slightly picked up. But soon enough the sound of the sails blowing was interrupted again.

"Then why are we even doing this?" Basek asked.

A fair question. In reality, these soldiers had nothing to gain from this battle. If we won the war, Lady Catar would become queen and they would go back to fishing and farming.

Ritche's response was equally fair. He pushed out his chest as he spoke.

"For pride! It's a great honour to fight for our province."

"But it doesn't mean enough for us to get paid?"

"Well, no, but we volunteered so pay was never to be expected."

"So it's like charity?" asked Basek.

Their conversation was interrupted by the fleet arriving at the south end of Midland Bay, which was where half the soldiers would dock to attack on foot. It was decided that Lady Catar, who was accompanied by Miss Frith, would lead the attack from land. It was meant to be me but she changed her mind after my actions, meaning that Lord Shay and myself would be headed for the castle, which I hated the idea of. We sailed for a further hour before Castle Sear came into sight. I had been to the castle many times, the love of my life had lived in that castle for the last six years, and yet it was only when I was on that ship that I appreciated the genuine phenomenon that was Castle Sear. It was a gargantuan feat of architectural genius that caused so much fear to course through my body. Of course the modern brickwork was stunning. Of course the symmetry between the six towers added an extra level of grandeur. But the utter size of the castle under the light of the setting sun emphasised the sheer magnitude of the task ahead of us. Back on land, my sister did a good job of staying in sight of our ships and giving us a formation to stick to. At that moment, I cleared my mind from the vastness of the castle and focused on what we had in our favour. As I did, I felt as though we might actually have a chance. Maybe I had overestimated the South and underestimated my sister. That hope, however, was shattered as I looked back towards my beloved's home to be greeted by the sight of hundreds of flaming arrows falling towards our ships, like a sky full of stars falling from the gods.

"Incoming!" was the shout from someone unidentifiable.

"Barrat, get out!"

Lord Shay, who was standing at my side, shouted as he pushed me with such force that I fell overboard and smacked the water with a harsh impact.

The contrast between the residual heat from the incoming arrows and the sharp coldness of the sea threw me into a state of shock. I sank quite deep and opened my eyes to see arrows darting into the sea with some vigour. This made me cautious to come to the surface, but I needed to breathe. It got to the point where my body wouldn't allow me to stay underwater for any longer. I burst through the surface level of the water and was thankful for the gift of air. After calming down slightly, I looked towards the inferno in front of me. The smell of burning flesh made me retch and I vomited into the surrounding water. I composed myself, trying to ignore the smell and the cold. I turned to my left and saw my bow, which had come away from my body as I hit the surface. I grabbed it and started fishing around for as many arrows I could find, as my quiver had been emptied. Once I felt equipped, I turned my attention to my brother.

"Shay!" I called out, trying to tread water. "Shay! Shay! Answer me!"

I twisted around to face the land. It seemed miles away despite only being a few hundred yards from me.

"Please Shay! This isn't funny anymore!"

"Barrat! Is that you?"

I turned at the sound of my name, dipping under the water slightly as the weight of my armour made staying afloat rather difficult. I saw a woman, who I didn't recognise at first, swimming towards me.

"Yes, yes! It's me, it's me!"

My answer caused me to lose my rhythm and drop under again before bobbing back up with some difficulty.

"Get to the land, you idiot! We need to keep the fight going."

It was Lady Catar, who had swum out to me after seeing the ships burst into flames.

"But, we need to get Shay."

Lady Catar sighed, which wasn't a good sign.

"Shay is gone. We just need to continue, okay?"

"He gave his life for me," I said, devastated. "He died because of me!"

"Barrat, come on!"

It was only at this moment when, perhaps for the first time, I truly looked at my sister. It was the first time that I saw the beauty on her face. It was the first time that I noticed how much she looked like our mother. It was her eyes, green like emeralds, that had the sparkle of hope in them that Mother always had. The hope that Mother had in her eyes every night that something would change. A hope that we wouldn't struggle for food, or a hope that she wouldn't have to worry about all of us surviving. It was just a shame that I couldn't concur with Lady Catar's hopes. My thoughts were interrupted by her continued shouting.

"Brother, I really need you to come now! If you can't do it for me, do it for Shay."

She was right. I needed to snap out of my shock, despite how traumatising it was, and get my focus back towards the battle that had much more duration to come. By the time that we had made it back to the land, Lord Bruk, Lord Suln, and their archers had made it to the ground to assist the already dominant swordsmen that had been stationed under the joint command of Lord Robt and Lord Neman. Our people had a lot of fight, and I was impressed with what I was seeing from them, but it would take a miracle for us to win - that was clear.

"We could call this off now, you know. All you need to do is give the signal and all this stops."

"Whose side are you on?" she asked, pushing me away in frustration. "Look around. These people are giving their all and that's all we need! Now get out there and do something!"

She ran onto the battlefield and I followed her, keen to get into a good rhythm. It was important for me to develop a rhythm of removing, nocking, and firing my arrow with speed. If I didn't then I would die. Luckily, I got going pretty quickly. I hit a few good shots and was starting to gain confidence in myself. I had somehow managed to set the initial pain and panic of my mourning aside and hit thirty or so more shots. Once again, I started to feel as if victory was possible. I saw a relatively large huddle of High Northerners over to my left. They were being picked off one by one by an archer who was perched behind a village hut not too far away. Our soldiers couldn't seem to work out where the arrows were coming from due to the speed of each shot. I saw a chance to take the archer out, as their head kept popping slightly around the round walls of the house every time they took a shot. I followed their position by perching behind a dead horse that was nearby. I took my time, took my aim, and waited for them to nock their next arrow before shooting them in the back of head. My shot attracted the attention of a few nearby soldiers from the South, who headed my way. I tried to quickly nock another arrow for myself but found that my quiver was empty - something that I had feared for some time. I had accepted my death when a few soldiers from the group I had saved came to my rescue. Their reciprocating rescue gave me a moment to breathe for the first time since I had made it to the ground. I took a moment to rest against the bony back of the dead horse, which effectively hid me from the sight of the opponent, and looked around at the violence on show.

These people were butchers and bakers, mothers and fathers, farmers and fishermen, and now they were armed with swords, maces, axes, bows and shields, tearing each other limb from limb. We were told to protect these people. We were given authority and power to assist each and every individual and to make their lives better than they ever could have been on mainland England. Saddle Isle was a place where we could live without the branding of 'bastard' hanging over us like a sword on a string. We had the possibility to create a well-functioning, peaceful land that was miles ahead of England, simply because of its nature. And here we were, allowing people to die for us, all because we inexplicably couldn't be satisfied with the great opportunity that we had been given. I could describe a hundred different cases of travesty from that day and you would vividly understand how truly selfish the patricians of Saddle Isle were. But I will only give you one. Whilst I rested behind the protection of that horse, completely devoid of arrows and unable to wield anything else, I watched a boy die.

He must have been no older than twelve years. I know, because I recognised him from the High North. He was the butcher's boy. For years, I had watched the butcher and his son from my window in Castle Gelid. I was always jealous of their loving relationship - something that I never experienced with my own father. The butcher would teach his boy how to wield a sword and they would practise twice a week. You should have heard the pride in his father's voice every time the boy made an impressive block, or when he managed to strike his father in one of their many training fights. Now I watched that boy, with tears running down his cheek and a seething snarl plastered over his face, stand over his dead father's body and fight for retribution against the Southern farmer who had killed him. In that moment, that boy wasn't fighting for his province but rather out of pure rage. He was fighting because of a rage that was formed by grief and anger - a fate that would never have been sealed if it weren't for us. He put every last ounce of his energy into his swings. His world had just been damaged permanently, so what did he really have to lose? He got close a few times, but his lack of experience meant that on just one occasion he overswung. He was sliced down. There he lay, one hand on his wound, the other on his dead father's body. In a matter of minutes, they lay dead together. How dare we, the undeserving few chosen to lead these people, truly believe that we were worthy of our position when those same people we were tasked with protecting were dying all around us? Thousands of loving, brilliant people, who shaped our community into the prospering place it had been for over a decade, all died because of the quarrels of a few. They came with us to escape slaughter and instead were foolishly led straight into death's peril. That will stay with me until I die.

It was only the sight of an arrow landing in the flesh of the horse inches away from my face that broke my state of reflection and sprung me back into action. I quickly shuffled from behind the corpse and scuttled in the direction of the dead archer, trying to stay as low and inconspicuous as possible. I thought that I would find at least some arrows to refill my quiver, perhaps enough to tide me over until I found a new place of refuge. The body lay face down on the ground and there were thirty or so arrows for me to take. I was lucky. As I removed the arrow, the weight of the body shifted, causing the face of my victim to be revealed. To my horror, it was one that I recognised: the blood-brother of my beloved and a man I called my friend, Lord Suln, son of Ferma, of House Northorpe. I dropped to my knees and screamed, furious at myself for what I had done. At that moment, I didn't care that I could die. All I could do was hold Lord Suln's body in my arms and weep for him.

My weeping was interrupted by a man on foot, wielding a sword too grand to be that of a commoner. I looked up. Through my teary eyes I saw that it was Lord Robt, distraught at the sight of his dead brother.

"What have you done?" he bellowed, fuelled by his pain. "What have you done?"

"Robt, I didn't know! I didn't know!"

"He called you brother!"

He lifted his sword above his head and swung it down in my direction with some force.

I shut my eyes, waiting for death, when death himself was silenced by the sound of clanging swords. My eyes opened again and there was Lady Catar to block Lord Robt's swing. Before I could move, my sister kicked me away with her left boot. This caused my knee to slice against an abandoned sword, making any movement rather difficult and painful. She continued to match Lord Robt blow for blow. The loud clatter of metal on metal echoed around the vicinity. I watched on, helpless. She opted for three swift swings that Lord Robt blocked each time, but the force caused him to lose his footing. Lady Catar was able to knock Lord Robt down to the ground and forced him to drop his sword. She was seconds away from slicing his neck when she was suddenly bundled to the ground with great impact. It was Lord Bruk coming to his brother's rescue. I got to my feet with the aim to stop his attack, but couldn't hobble over in time to stop his onslaught. He met Lady Catar's sword - which she was capable with, even from the ground - with fierce strikes time after time. Eventually, her grip was lost and her sword fell to the ground, giving Lord Bruk the chance to slice through her side.

"No!" I wailed.

Lord Bruk heard my cry and turned to see me hobbling over to her. A Southern soldier came from behind me with sword at the ready, but Lord Bruk rushed and pushed him away. He looked at my distraught face and helped me over to my sister, lowering me down to her side. I held her dying body in my arms. I tried to fight back my tears in a feeble attempt to comfort her.

"Oh, Catar! It's me. It's okay, Catar, it's okay."

"Mother," she called out. "Is that you?"

On her fall to the ground she had hit her head on the surface. She wasn't quite sure where she was or what was happening.

"Barrat, I'm sorry," Lord Bruk interrupted. "It had to be done to protect my own."

"Just let me be with her. Just leave me to be with her as she dies."

"Of course."

He stepped back and checked on his brother as I turned to my sister. I decided that she would rather it was Mother than me. I rested her head on my thigh as I sat slumped on the floor beside her.

"Catar, my darling. Yes, it's me. Your mother is here and it's all going to be alright now. I'm here."

"It hurts, Mother."

"I know, my love, I know. It's alright, it's safe. Drift off to sleep now, darling. You've made your mother so proud today, but it's time to sleep now."

I stroked her blood-matted hair.

"Please, Mother. Please sing our song."

For a moment, I was stumped. I started to panic as I desperately wanted to comfort her yet didn't know what she meant. But then it came to me: she referred to the lullaby that Mother sang to us when we were children.

"Okay, my love. If it will help you to find peace."

I cleared my choked up throat and sang to the best of my ability:

> "Hush, the wind blows wildly,
> And all the stars shine low,
> But I will be beside ye',
> From now until I go.
> Let all the earthly wonder,
> Close ye' eyes so wide,
> To let ye' see and ponder,
> What lurks on the other side."

She smiled before peacefully dying in my arms. Lord Bruk knelt down beside me, as Lord Robt finally got back to his feet.

"You killed Suln!"

Lord Bruk intervened, holding his arm out to indicate for his brother to stop moving.

"Robt! Just leave it."

The battle was, despite all this, still occurring. In fact, had it not been for the separation caused by the many houses in the many villages, we all would have likely been killed had this same event occurred on a proper battlefield. At least Lady Catar's foolishness gave us this last loving moment together.

It was only the signal given by the patrician who was in charge of their respective army, which was now me in the case of the High North, that could call an end to the slaughter.

"Barrat, look at me," Lord Bruk commanded.

He pulled my face to look at his as I refused to take my eyes away from the sister that remained in my arms.

"Where is Shay? He can end all this and you can live. Where is Shay, Barrat?"

"He's dead," I cried out after a selfish pause. "He burned alive on the ship, and you killed Catar, and now I am alone."

"Are you sure he is dead?"

"What kind of question is that?"

Lord Bruk shook me in an attempt to make me see the severity of the situation.

"Barrat, it is now down to you. Do you yield?"

I ignored him for a while, so he tried again.

"Barrat, people are dying! Do you yield?"

"Yes, I yield!" I eventually proclaimed. "I never wanted this to happen in the first place!"

"I know, Barrat, I know."

Lord Bruk, aware of my distress, comforted me. Despite my state, he rightfully prioritised giving the signal to stop the fighting as soon as possible.

"Robt, send the signal, spread the word. The battle is done."

Lord Robt went off and did as his brother told him. The unified sound of swords, maces, axes, shields, bows and quivers being dropped echoed across the field, as many also dropped to the floor in exhaustion. People from opposing provinces began to see to any injured soldiers around them, before taking a moment for themselves to rest and to thank the gods for their lives. After he gave the signal, Lord Robt returned to the site of my sister's death. He was keen to know what was to be done with me, the person responsible for the arrow in Lord Suln's head.

"That bastard killed Suln and lost the battle," Lord Robt shouted at his brother. "I love you, brother, but if you don't send him to the dungeon, I will wash my hands of you."

Lord Bruk understood, but hoped that this reaction from Lord Robt was only caused by the freshness of the travesty. Either way, that freshness wasn't going to fade on the battlefield. The decision was made and I was pulled away from my sister's corpse and led to the dungeons of Castle Sear.

The Battle of the Brutes, 1108 - I

I mentioned before that I had received word from an old friend from the Midlands that Lord Eli planned on making his move against his bitter rival Lady Daid, and that was indeed the case. Those of House Wharram correctly declared their intentions of battle through a letter adhering to the words of war, as stated in the terms set out by Lady Anto. This meant that the battle was set out in a more orthodox manner, with both armies setting up camp. This involved a multitude of tents for the soldiers, as well as tactical bases, on opposite sides of an agreed battlefield. It says a lot about our decision to attempt to attack the South secretly when the most savage of people in the land managed to follow the terms. Of course, being right never felt as good after Lady Catar's death. On arrival at the agreed battleground, both armies prepared for what was to come. They waited to begin the battle at an arranged time and set an agreed cut off point for the day, which was just after sunset. After a night of camping, in which I imagine not many got any decent sleep, the two armies stood at either side of the chosen battlefield and waited for someone to make the first move. I am glad to say that I never had to stand opposite a Savage army, with every soldier wearing the mandatory shaven head, bearing their muscles, scars and grimaces as they prepared to charge.

It was clear from the outset that Lord Eli was going to go after Lady Daid first. There had always been a real bitterness between the two of them, perhaps because they were, arguably, the most similar. They were both renowned for their strength, but also their stubbornness - a quality that seems to have negative connotations but actually can show a real sense of drive. I would say that Lady Daid's stubbornness was more of a blessing than Lord Eli's, but that is only because I found her way of thinking to be sound on the whole. But on reflection, I suppose Lord Eli's stubbornness also had its merits. It's very easy to look at situations and events from only your own perspective and that was the case with Lord Eli. We never agreed with his philosophy and so we always saw him as a danger, but a significant number of Midland citizens saw their provincial leader as a hero and as someone to admire. I suppose even the worst people have some strengths, otherwise they never would have gained enough power to be deemed the worst.

****

Lady Daid was a very talented fighter. She had the technical ability to beat anyone in one on one combat, no matter how strong they were. Lord Eli was always going to be the favourite, though. He was the most feared man in the land and was physically the strongest. It would have been interesting, and rather gory, to see Lady Daid and Lord Eli fight one on one when both were allowed to be at full strength. I say this because they had grappled before, but Lady Daid had never had the opportunity to be armed in a fight with the Head of House Wharram. Their one on one combat never did happen though, as Lady Daid took up the position of commander - something that she was equally talented at despite it only involving her joining the action as a last resort. Lord Eli was not so keen on the tactical side of battle and probably would have been quickly defeated if he hadn't led an army made up of the most savage fighters in the land. It is scary, even now, to imagine what Lord Eli's Savage army would have looked like with the tactical faculties of Lady Daid, who was the only patrician to take a truly structured approach to battle during the entirety of The Great Packsaddle War. Without her planning, Lady Daid's army would not have stood a chance against the might of the Midland Savages. In all fairness, none of the armies of the land, including the Southern army that picked the High Northern army off with the ease that I anticipated, would have been able to defeat Lord Eli's warriors alone. This is what was said in the Council of Heads before ambition clouded judgement. They were holding their own, probably better than anyone else could, yet still Lady Daid and her army were losing and so something needed to be changed if the Head of House Matfen wanted to hold any chance of surviving.

*** * * ***

"My Lady," said a soldier with a bloody face and missing teeth.

He had run from the battlefield to Lady Daid, who was stationed just beyond her camp on a slight hill in order to gain a better vantage point of the carnage that was occurring below.

"We are holding our shape but they are just too strong. We need some time to regroup."

"Just hold your position," she commanded, sternly. "The sun is setting and so the cut off point for today's battle is only a few minutes away. Hold for now and then we can regroup tomorrow."

I have mentioned that, despite the majority of the patricians not having these beliefs, the commoners were very religious people. It had become tradition that the first full moon of the season was to be followed by a day of reflection and care, which was known as Quillian Day. Although the Midland Savages were brutal in combat, they were possibly the most adhering to the sacred rules. They believed that the Leonist god of strength gave them the power to kill and so they were allowed to use it to develop the race. It intrigues me that no other province interpreted the gods in this way. I should note that it was the elders of the provinces who became the religious figures and they were entitled to teach in any way that they deemed to be suitable and true, and so I suppose that could be the reason for the religious disparity throughout the isle. In England, the religion practised was, and I assume still is, Roman Catholicism, which originated on mainland Europe. Of course, those old enough to know the teachings of this religion were expected to abide by what the holy text states, and this became a problem for people like myself. I say "old enough" because I personally have no recollection of these teachings. I am led to believe that this religion in England scorned those born out of wedlock, labelling us as bastards and illegitimate, lesser people. As you can imagine, this had an influential part to play in Saddle Isle's rejection of the faith and creation of our own religion: Leonism - derived from the proud lion and the strength of the pack. I would engage in a deep, insightful analysis of the similarities and differences between Catholicism and Leonism, but my knowledge and patience for both ideologies are suitably low. What I do know is that, unlike Catholicism, there were many Leonist gods who represented various notions regarding which aspects of oneself should be prioritised. For example, the Midland Savages tended to focus more on the lion's strength and might rather than other qualities such as patience, community or grace.

I don't know whether it was out of stupidity or sheer arrogance, not that the two necessarily need to be separated, but this particular season's Quillian Day fell the day after the Battle of the Brutes took place. If the battle was to end without victory on its opening day, then it would not resume until after the day of reflection had passed. This, of course, was stated in the discussions between Lord Eli and Lady Daid before the battle commenced.

"What if they don't stop, Lady Daid?" he asked, shaking slightly in fear of his opponents.

"They will. I know they are Savages but they have pride. They'll want to win fairly to prove a point."

"I hope you're right."

She looked on intently, scanning for any weaknesses in her opponents, but their frantic approach to the battle made it difficult for her to see a direct route to victory. Her soldiers were falling fast and Lord Eli's warriors were refusing to die, no matter how hard you hit them.

"It doesn't look good, sister," Lord Angull pointed out, to Lady Daid's annoyance.

Lord Angull had been fighting, but was forced to stop after a rather nasty knock to the head. Luckily, some soldiers managed to drag him back to camp for treatment. He was their patrician afterall and the mantle of leader would have passed on to him if Lady Daid were to fall. Well, either him or his twin brother, Lord Maxim.

"I can see that, brother. Perhaps if you were still out there we wouldn't be so porous."

"I don't see any blood on you, sister," he bit back.

"We only need to hold off for a few more minutes. We can regroup from there and go in with a rebuilt formation overmorrow."

They continued to hold their position and made it to the cut off point for the day. Like Lady Daid had predicted, Lord Eli did stick to the rules. That was perhaps due to his own pride rather than respect for his opponent, or maybe even due to his own request for Quillian Day being respected. Either way the rules were obeyed. Despite the free day for extra preparation ahead of the battle's recommence, it was deemed suitable by the Head of House for a meeting to be held that night. Lord Angull joined Lady Daid and a few of the province's most capable soldiers in the tactical tent once the other soldiers had all retreated to their respective spaces.

"Where is Lord Maxim?" she asked, eager to get started.

The soldiers looked to one another, which told her all she needed to know. She turned to her brother, who was distraught by his twin's passing, and nodded to inform him that he didn't need to stay. He took that opportunity and left to take his frustrations out on a few innocent bales of hay in a nearby field. Her most trusted soldier stepped forward.

"My Lady, we have lost Mister Marn too. He, like your brother, was taken by Eli himself."

"I see. Then go to the keep and do what we discussed."

"And Lady Oline?"

She took the time to deliberate this decision.

"No. If the people see her go then they will panic. It is her duty to bring them comfort, so that is what she shall do."

The man headed for the keep, leaving his provincial leader to sit in silence for a while, contemplating on what to do. Rumours had spread about Lord Bruk's victory in the South and were later confirmed by letter. This news plagued the brute's mind. She could never gain the throne if she was dead, so perhaps waiting it out would give her a better chance at glory.

"Which one of you has the fastest bird?" she asked. "We cannot win this battle alone and I refuse to see any more death for our people. Get me a bird! I am sending an official request for assistance to the South."

"But, My Lady, if you do that then you'll give the land to Lord Bruk. He will be king and you will have nothing."

"Which is precisely why I'm asking," she admitted, looking to the ground. "We have been somewhat blessed with an extra day. I know they will be fatigued after a battle of their own, but perhaps they will be more willing to accept my request due to the elongated time for rest and, of course, the opponent. I know I'll give up my power but I'd rather Lord Bruk was king than Eli. I can't leave my people under the rule of a Savage."

The journey from the South to the North could be done in a spring's daylight, but one must be well rested and eager for such a trip. Lady Daid was right in her thinking. The added security of an extra day's rest will ensure that even the most tired of soldiers could make it before overmorrow and still be rested enough for a decent performance on the battlefield. That only increased the already high chance of an alliance with Lord Bruk and the South. The letter was written, the bird had been sent, and the Head of House Matfen could finally attempt to get some sleep.

But as she lay in her bed, all she could think about was the possibility of Lord Bruk denying them his aid. She had done all she could. It was up to the South now.

****

"My Lord, a letter. It's from Lady Daid in the North," Mister Rufus spoke in his usual respectful tone.

The guard had been mildly injured in the Battle of Midland Bay and so was forced to hobble around the Great Hall of Castle Sear to find Lord Bruk. The hall was being used as a recuperation area for those injured in battle, no matter what side a person was on. Lord Bruk took the letter from the brave man, opened it, and read it quickly. He immediately called for Lord Robt and Lord Neman to join him, which they did with the required haste.

"Brothers, we may have just found our pathway to peace," he announced, with an optimistic smile. "Lady Daid has requested our official assistance in the North, as her troops are struggling against the Midland Savages."

Lord Robt was glad to have a momentary distraction from the grieving for his fallen brother.

"The fool! If we accept and win, she must forfeit her power to you."

"This is our chance to end this all! Round up anyone who is able to fight, whether they be from the South or the High North, and tell them this: 'Overmorrow, we have a chance to be rid of the Midland Brute once and for all, so prepare to give your everything to the cause!' No one wants Eli to rule and so all will be eager to serve. We ride as soon as the sun rises tomorrow, and will go at a pace that suits all practising the traditions of Quillian Day. We could saunter to the North and still make it before the battle resumes, and so we shall. We will be victorious, I can assure you of that! Go, find me the noblest of soldiers."

So, with the added High Northerners to their ranks, and the fact that we made such little impact in our battle, the Southern army was almost restored to its original number. All of them rode or marched for the North with the united aim to put an end to Lord Eli. The Battle of the Brutes was not yet over, but now the odds were stacked in Lady Daid's favour.

The Dungeon

Each of the five castles of the land were built with underground dungeons capable of holding 100 prisoners - 150 if you're willing to let a few dozen get crushed to death for their crimes. Each province was allowed, as voted by the Council of Heads, to decide what punishment was suitable for certain crimes. As expected, the provinces that were ruled by competent leaders, such as the South and the Deep South, saw very low crime rates. Both Lord Bruk, son of Betra, of House Northorpe and Lady Anto, daughter of Elan, of House Hepston imprisoned felons within their dungeon and held fair trials for them in front of patricians and trusted advisors. After the trial, the persecuted either remained in cells for a period of time or were forced to serve time as unpaid servants in their respective castles. The other three provinces acted differently. The heads of the two Northern provinces: Lady Daid, daughter of Rean, of House Matfen; and the late Lady Catar, daughter of Nea, of House Pearson, both implemented similar eye for an eye approaches to justice. If a farmer killed another after an argument, that farmer was put to death. If one was to steal from another, then their possessions were taken from them and given to the victim of the crime. If one was to rape a person, well, they would be castrated and shamed. It seems a fair system for the little things, but this system does not work when more serious matters need dealing with. I often pointed this out to my sister and was subsequently told to "know my place". But an eye for an eye approach doesn't take emotions into account. If a farmer murders another, there would have been a reason for it, such as rage within the moment. If we kill a man under the premise of an eye for an eye then we kill without emotion, just out of so called justice. That sets the wrong precedent to our people and shows how little mercy my sister had. Sometimes I wished she would just look to the South for answers, but she was too proud for that. Lord Eli, son of

Manty, of House Wharram, had a completely different approach still. Leaders have a duty to do what is right for their people. Actions have consequences, and so the consequences that a leader implements as punishment for their peoples' actions are vital for forming a coherent and united province. It was Lord Eli's lack of responsibility that made all those with a functioning brain and mercy in their hearts know that all chances of civilisation would go up in flames if he became king. If we were clever, we would have attempted to unite the North and South in aid of ripping him to shreds to ensure that he never rules, but no one is as clever as they think.

Once the Battle of Midland Bay had been won by the South, I was escorted to the dungeons after being beaten and dragged down the steps by two rather enthusiastic guards, who I presume had been defending the keep during the battle. I had never actually been to a dungeon before as we didn't tend to use ours up in the High North. It was quite the unusual place. It was much darker than any other room in the castle and there was a strange smell to it too. A sort of damp smell that lingered constantly. Bizarrely, it reminded me of home, which I didn't want at that time. I noticed how there was no one else around. I knew that crime was low in the South but I had expected to be surrounded by a few criminals. On contemplating my surroundings, I came to the conclusion that all crimes were pardoned if prisoners fought in battle and so the dungeon was now empty. I tried ever so hard to devise these sorts of questions and queries to distract myself from the haunting thoughts of what I had done. It wasn't much use. Every single momentary lapse of thought meant that my mind honed in on the image of Lord Suln, my poor friend, with blood pouring down the back of his neck as he died painfully alone. I couldn't help but cry. Tears streamed from my eyes, mimicking the blood that streamed from his head, as if my own body was mocking me for my crimes. My face was wet with tears, but my lips remained dry from the salt. I imagined how the salty taste in my mouth would have been one of iron for Suln as his mouth, forced open by the hands of mortality, filled with his own blood. How was I supposed to live with what I had done? I didn't deserve to live, in all honesty. If it weren't for Lady Breck, I would have happily given up my life as punishment for taking his.

*** * * ***

"I don't care what my brother said," were the words that broke the painful silence.

Somehow, I had managed to fall asleep for a short while. I suppose it was a mixture of exhaustion after a day of battle and my deep regret. I was awoken by a stir from the top of the steps that I had been dragged down just a day before. It was Lady Breck's voice that I could hear.

"My Lady, Lord Bruk specifically said no, and he is Head of House."

The guard sounded rightfully intimidated by her. She had a kind heart, but she got what she wanted more often than not.

"Perhaps I'm growing tired of Lord Bruk controlling my every action," she snapped. "I am going to see him."

I couldn't see her but I knew the look that she would have had on her face: one of boredom for the discussion, as she already knew that it was pointless for this man to argue against her.

"He killed your brother, My Lady," was the guard's desperate attempt to convince her to follow Lord Bruk's orders.

My brief contentment from hearing my beloved fight to see me was shattered by those words. That was it for me, now. I was always going to be the bastard that killed his beloved's brother, despite all that her family had done for him.

"I know that, but I shall see him regardless."

They argued for quite some time, to the point where I was certain that she was never going to appear down those stairs. But she never gave up and eventually descended. She sat down on the dirty floor and reached between the bars for my hands.

"Thank the gods that you're alright," she exclaimed as she rushed to my cell.

I wanted to see her face. I wanted to look into her eyes again and run my hand across her cheek. I wanted to kiss her freckled nose and hold her until we could not hold each other for any longer. But my tears prevented my sight, and my shame wouldn't allow me to speak.

"I thought that you would die, Barrat. I thought I was going to lose you."

"You have lost me," I wailed.

I don't know how, but she understood me despite my hysterical distress.

"How have I lost you? You're right here in front of me."

I wiped my puffy eyes on my dirty sleeve in an attempt to gain some resemblance of composure.

"How can you bear to look at me after what I've done? I have betrayed you."

I caught a glimpse of her for the first time. Her eyes were as red as blood. She had been crying for Lord Suln, as she should have been. He was a great man who I had killed in the aid of a horrid woman. She pulled my hands to usher me to scoot forward and get closer to her.

"You haven't betrayed anyone. It was your duty to fight alongside your sister, and that's what you did."

"But what about Suln? He was my friend, your brother. I loved him so much and now he's gone because of me."

She started to cry more aggressively now. She pulled our hands to her lips as she spoke, maintaining her sweet, soft tone.

"I loved him too, more than any of my family. I am going to miss him so much, you know that. But you cannot blame yourself for what happened. Yes, you fired the arrow, but every man and woman in that battle knew what they were getting into. When you play with swords and arrows, people die. That is a part of the game. If we weren't at war, you would never have killed him, and so how can I blame you for this?"

There had been many moments since I had met Lady Breck that made me know that I loved her with all my heart. The feeling that I got every time I saw her face assured me that what we had was real. But it was this moment, after I had hurt her more than ever before, that I knew we belonged together. She shielded me from my pain, despite all I had done, out of her love for me. I was selfish here - I know it - but I was also shown we were made for each other. Something out in the universe had chosen the two of us to be connected, always, and ensured that we would have the strongest love. From when those words left her mouth, I promised that I would never do anything to hurt her again, no matter what.

"I love you, Breck."

I kissed her through the bars, which hurt my scratched cheek, but it was worth feeling her warmth again. It was something I really needed.

"I love you too."

We sat in silence for a while. I couldn't really tell how she was. I assumed that she was being brave for me, which she shouldn't have had to do considering what I had done to her. I could tell, however, that she was thinking of him. But so was I. I had listened to what she had said, and she was right. I would never have done anything to hurt him in the normal world. But the battlefield defies what one knows. It brings out the savage in you, which made me fear the Midland Savages even more. It doesn't matter what happens on the battlefield, one way or another, you die. You may get an arrow to your face or a sword through your heart, and that would introduce you to death, but even if you walk away without a scratch a part of you dies anyway.

"I brought you this. I know how stingy the guards can be."

She passed a waterskin through the bars, along with a solitary piece of beef that she knew to be my favourite.

"Thank you," I said, smiling at her kindness.

I was starving after the battle and so was very grateful to her. I shovelled the meat down my throat, then sipped at the flask. I looked at her as I did and saw, again, the pain in her once innocent eyes.

"How do you feel?" I asked as I ate.

I needed to stop thinking about Lord Suln - as hard as that was - but, more importantly, I needed to start thinking about her.

"A tad empty," she bluntly answered. "But I'm glad that I didn't lose too much."

She stared forward for a while, not blinking.

"Well, you won, so it could be worse."

"We didn't win. We just didn't lose as badly as you. Do you know what happened to your family?"

I spoke in a tone that didn't match my sadness, which shocked us both. It was my turn to stare at nothingness.

"I held my sister in my arms as she died, and Shay burned on the same fishing ship that he used to occupy."

"I'm sorry."

There's a real helplessness with death. It's upsetting to talk about, and just as upsetting to hear about too, but it's the awkwardness that gets to you the most. The fact that you can't do anything about it. You can't bring people back and you can't make mourners feel any better. You can only sit and watch the pain.

"It's like you said, it's part of the game."

Once more, we sat in a melancholy silence.

"You know that I'll die for what I did, right?" I asked, breaking the void of silence.

It was a harsh reality, knowing your own fate. Lady Breck seemed so relieved to see me alive, but I was not going to stay alive for long. Her brothers wanted me dead and so that was what was ahead for me.

"No you won't! Not as long as I'm around."

"I don't think you'll get a say."

"Bruk tried to stop me from seeing you, yet I'm here aren't I?"

She was so passionate. Here I was, defeated and deflated. I'd accepted my death before I'd been given the sentence, and yet she was still fighting for me.

"I killed a patrician, Breck. I killed your brother." I needlessly reminded her.

I pulled her closer. We both placed our heads on the bars so that, if they were to disappear, we would be resting on each other.

"Whether it was in battle or not, your brothers will want my head for that."

"They killed patricians too," she pointed out. "I'm sorry to say it, but it was Bruk who killed your siblings, my love."

I already knew that, yet it still hurt to think about a man who I loved and trusted killing my own family. But then he must have felt the same about me.

"But he was on the defensive and he was on the winning side - or 'less losing,' as you say."

She paused and started to cry again. It seemed like I had convinced her that she was going to lose me. Then, suddenly, she stopped crying.

"They're not here!" she blurted, getting rather excited at that prospect. "They've headed north to assist Lady Daid against Lord Eli."

I struggled to see how their possible deaths could cause such excitement, but she continued too quickly for me to chime in.

"With them gone, we could escape. There are barely any guards and the people here love you, Barrat."

"I doubt they will now."

"Well, they love me. They'll help us to escape."

"And where would we go?"

I hated to burst her bubble but there weren't many places for a criminal lord, who was known all across the land, to hide.

"There are still some ships standing. I've seen them! We could sail to a new land and start afresh. Just you and me, like we've always wanted it to be."

I smiled and kissed her hand once more.

"That sounds perfect. But if we get caught then I'm certain to die and you are certain to be punished for helping me. I've already caused the death of one Northorpe, I refuse to cause the death of you. I love you too much for that."

"And I love you too much to watch them cut off your head! It's either we escape or you die, and I won't see you die, Barrat."

Her shouting worried me as the dungeon guards were not too far away. As I tried to calm her down, I realised that not all hope was lost for me. I hadn't thought about Lord Bruk before this moment. He was a kind man, who loved me. I'm sure there was a way for me to survive if he became king. I paused to fully think it through.

"Perhaps not. I assume that, if they are heading north, one more victory would make Lord Bruk the king. He is a merciful man, Breck - you know it. Robt and Neman will hate me for what I did, but Bruk is more likely to understand - particularly as he killed my brother, who was just as innocent in all this as yours. If Bruk is king, then it doesn't matter what your other brothers want because they'll have to abide by the king's orders. I have a better chance of living if I stay here and hope for Bruk's mercy."

Lady Breck paused and absorbed what I'd said, not giving anything away regarding her thoughts towards the matter.

"Okay, I hope you're right."

She kissed my lips, as painful as it was on the bars, one last time before standing up and wiping her dirty, woollen dress down.

The Battle of the Brutes, 1108 - II

Just as Lady Daid had hoped, Lord Bruk and his reinforcements arrived in plenty of time before the second day of battling was to commence. They successfully made their way around Lord Eli's camp and had enough time to be instructed by Lady Daid on what the best route forward may be. She expressed her desire to stick to her formation strategy, but Lord Bruk was not too keen on the idea considering there was a mixture of three different armies present. That made sense considering that they had all previously followed differing strategies, or no strategy at all in the case of the High Northerners. This caused some tension, a rather unhelpful addition considering that this battle was still going to be tough for all and was completely necessary to win for the overall benefit of the land. After going back and forth for a while, they eventually decided that a compromise would have to be made. This resulted in a new tactical development consisting of Lady Daid's army creating a strong formation in the centre, and Lord Bruk's newly revamped army attacking from the outside areas of the battlefield in an attempt to crowd the Savages in. This was a particularly strong idea considering that Lord Eli's warriors had found much success when attacking from the sides. This was accompanied by what was a small group of remaining archers, who stood on the hilltop with their commander. Despite being effective when attacking ships, the archers, who were nowhere near to the standard of Lord Suln or even myself, were mostly inferior to the sword dwellers when in one-on-one combat. They did fight one-on-one during the Battle of Midland Bay, but that was forced due to the action taking place through the village rather than on a battlefield.

"Lady Daid, I know that you have many great assets when commanding, but I do believe that having you assist us on the wider attacks would increase our chances of victory. These soldiers are brave but they are also tired. Your freshness and sheer ability will ensure a great advantage towards our aim."

Lord Bruk knew of the importance of a win and was fully aware of her abilities. He was keen to convince Lady Daid to make the alteration, although she wasn't too keen on this idea and was annoyed that he was trying to make even more adjustments this close to the battle reconvening.

"The maintenance of the formation is key to the wide attacks being possible. If we break at the centre then all chaos breaks loose with it. Chaos is where the Savages thrive. This must be avoided."

"I understand that risk but I am certain that there are people capable of keeping the formation in shape. How about your brother? I know he is too wounded to fight but perhaps he could still play a part yet."

Lady Daid paused in consideration before giving her opinion. She was fully aware of her brother's own high level of ability.

"In different circumstances, I would be inclined to give Lord Angull the chance to command, but he has just lost his twin - the closest person he had. I'm just not sure that he would be in the right mental state to take up such an important job."

Lord Angull, who had been invited to the tactical tent, managed to arrive just in time to overhear Lord Bruk's suggestion.

"I can do it! I would give anything to be able to rip Eli's throat out for what he did to Maxim, but I know that I physically can't fight. If I can help in bringing him down, in any way, then I'm more than willing to do it."

"Are you sure?" Lady Daid asked, rather apprehensively.

"Of course. For Maxim."

"Okay. For Maxim."

****

After procuring her helmet, which she didn't wear as commander for the benefit of improved sight, Lady Daid picked up her mace and mounted her horse. She trotted to stand beside Lord Bruk and his soldiers and patiently waited for her brother's signal to move against the common enemy. Even from afar, the Savages seemed just as energised and bloodthirsty as they were before the first day of fighting.

"See you on the other side, My Lady," Lord Bruk said to the Head of House Matfen.

"I'll see you when you're king, My Lord."

After a few more beats, which felt like minutes, the torturous anxiety of the standoff was broken as Lord Eli's army charged full speed towards his now much larger opposition. As they moved, Lord Angull called for places to be taken. This consisted of the centre body marching forward and creating their barrier formation with shields and spears at the ready, as the outside runners waited for the main body of Lord Eli's army to bundle in towards the centre. Only then could they create the necessary width to completely surround them.

To Lord Bruk's shock, the patricians of the Midlands didn't lead the charge but instead remained at the back, waiting for their savage warriors to create chinks in the formation. This meant that it would be the savage patricians who Lord Bruk of the South and Lady Daid of the North would meet first as they circled around. When the time came, Lord Angull gave the shout and Lord Bruk led his men to curve around the left hand side of the centre formation. Simultaneously, Lord Robt and Lord Neman led an identical pattern on the opposite side. Soon enough, their spears, which those of House Northorpe had rightfully opted for as opposed to their preferred swords as they were fighting on horseback on this occasion, were finding the bare bodies of the savage fighters and the battle was swaying in their direction. Lady Daid, who felt quite the excitement of being engulfed in the action, was also having quite a hefty amount of success. That was until her horse was slashed by the curved sword of a savage on foot, causing her to fall down to the ground. I should note that the Savages mostly rode on horseback too, but some chose to charge on foot, which normally would've been a crazed decision but their sheer agility made them rather effective. Lord Bruk, who was part of the consistent circular flow created by the soldiers operating the wide attack, saw that Lady Daid was in some trouble and so removed himself to assist her.

"Daid, fall back! You can crawl in under the formation."

The Head of House Matfen would have followed those instructions had she not been preoccupied by an onslaught of Savages attacking on foot, which Lord Bruk eventually saw and assisted in her defence. Lady Daid managed to hold some off, bashing their exposed skulls with her mace as Lord Bruk supported her with his spear, giving him a great advantage due to his distance from the opponents. As Lady Daid went to speak, she was interrupted as Lord Bruk was faced with a charging Lady Bennk, daughter of Stanp, of House Wharram. Luckily, he had noticed her charge and managed to block her spear with his, but being in a standing position made him momentarily lose balance. If it weren't for Lady Bennk's momentum taking her horse a fair distance away, Lord Bruk would have most likely fallen that day. Lady Bennk sported the shaven scalp and was equally as intimidating as any other savage on the battlefield. Her lack of hair accentuated her prominent cheekbones but they were overshadowed by her bashed nose, which had clearly been broken on multiple occasions. She, like her eldest brother, wore her scars with great pride, including one that ran right along her collarbone that was exposed even during the battle. Lady Bennk managed to combat the momentum and slowed her horse down enough to be able to swing back around to face her enemies, but Lord Bruk, having regained his balance and composure, had already whipped his horse to demand the gain of speed in the opposite direction before swinging back around himself to face Lady Bennk. This resulted in a scenario resembling a joust that would be hard to predict the outcome of. Lord Bruk had the advantage of armour, which in most situations would be such an insurmountable advantage that it wouldn't be worth me describing the proceeding events, however Lady Bennk was the best rider from her province and so could quite possibly have pulled off a shock victory.

The two charged at each other in the open field. There was a greater risk on the open field of the horses colliding. This meant that both riders had to focus even more on the steering of their horse, as well as attempting to defeat their opponent, which favoured Lady Bennk. On the first charge, both Lord Bruk and Lady Bennk missed each other with their spears. Once swinging back around, they charged once more. This time, Lord Bruk got a relatively solid connection on Lady Bennk's shoulder, but didn't pierce her. Instead, he simply knocked her off the top of her horse. Somehow, she managed to hold onto its mane and quite quickly used her impressive upper body strength to remount the creature. However, by the time she swung back around, Lord Bruk was already just metres away from her. He pierced her through the shoulder, flinging her completely off her horse where she landed with a thud onto the ground. She scrambled for a nearby sword before trying to quickly get back on her feet to defend herself against Lady Daid, who was running towards her with the ambition to finish the job. As Lady Bennk reemerged and readied herself, Lord Bruk charged at her a final time, trampling her down with the overbearing force of his horse. Before Lady Daid could reach her, Lady Bennk was already dead.

Lord Bruk dismounted his horse to converse properly with Lady Daid. Once he had steadied himself on the ground, he turned to see Lady Kezi, daughter of Coe, of House Wharram, who had begun on horseback but had lost her horse just a few moments before, approaching him from a distance. She, too, had a shaved head, but all attention had to go to the nasty scar over her right eye that caused the organ to be permanently damaged.

Despite this disadvantage, her impressive muscular physique ensured that no intimidation was depleted whatsoever. Lord Bruk composed himself after the fearful altercation with Lady Bennk.

"You've been fighting on foot for too long. You can barely breathe, Daid. You need to crawl through the formation and get some rest."

"You've been fighting for longer than me, Bruk. I only commanded on the first day. I have plenty of fight left yet. You, however, have had a day of battle already."

"You want me to drop out?"

She took a break from the conversation to bash a Savage woman's head in with her mace.

"I think it's for the best," she answered back. "You've done enough already."

"Fine," Lord Bruk submitted. "Take my horse and get back in the circle. It's safer to be riding in the pack than being out here."

"Thank you. Will you ensure that my brother is okay?"

From their position on the wrong side of the formation, there was too much going on to see Lord Angull, the commander, on his hill. This caused Daid some distress, especially as the archers had stopped firing their arrows. She desperately hoped she hadn't lost another brother. Once he crawled through the formation, he would only have to get through the circling horses to make it back to where Lord Angull was standing.

Lord Bruk swapped his spear for a curved sword from the corpse of a Savage as Lady Daid swiftly rode her way back into the running, leaving him alone on the field to battle Lady Kezi. She had now made it to where her sister was trampled by the Head of House Northorpe, armed with an identical curved sword, which was customary for those of the Midlands, and nothing else. The patrician from the Midlands wasted little time in her attack, forcefully throwing swings with her sword at Lord Bruk, who blocked them each time. Lady Kezi was a good swordswoman but was at a slight disadvantage due to her damaged sight. Despite his fatigue, Lord Bruk knew that the most efficient tactic would be to constantly scuttle to his left in the hope to slip into her blind spot, which is what he did. He struggled at first as Lady Kezi was too quick with her attacks to allow him any time to make significant moves. However, with each aggressive clanging of their swords, Lady Kezi squandered precious energy. This meant that, eventually, her power was depleting and her consistent onslaught became more and more infrequent. Lord Bruk, who had also tired due to the power needed to block her fierce shots, had bided his time effectively to preserve just enough of his energy to pick up speed in his movement. After countless shuffles, he managed to maintain a position in his enemy's blind spot long enough to force her into aimless, desperate swings. Those swings exposed her, leaving Lord Bruk an opportunity to end the battle - an opportunity that he gratefully took. He saw her exposed stomach and slashed across it, piercing the blade deep into her flesh. She fell to her knees, leaving her neck at a height too irresistible for Lord Bruk to leave. He ended her life with a slice to the lady's long neck.

Lord Bruk took no time to admire his work. He quickly headed towards the nearby shielded formation and was allowed to crawl through, taking a few bashes to the head from clumsy feet that caused nothing more than bleeding. He then took a breather before making the dangerous cross from one side of the barrier of horses to the other. However, once he made it across he didn't rest but decided to find himself a fresh spear and a rested horse instead. He checked that Lord Angull was managing before rejoining the other riders, who were still running in their circular motion.

****

The only patrician in the battle to fight on foot was Lord Bris, son of Coe, of House Wharram. He was by no means the strongest but he was the tallest and had a particularly impressive reach. For that reason, he too opted for a spear. Like his older brother, he wore a scraggly beard which, by this point, was matted with the blood of his victims. He had been tearing holes through Lady Daid's formation with ease and didn't seem to be slowing down. This was noticed by the onlooking Lord Angull.

Lord Neman's horse had been clipped slightly on the front left thigh, causing the animal to slow down so much that the patrician's position in the circle was becoming a hindrance. For that reason, Lord Neman made his way to the far outside and headed back to the camp. He soon found a replacement horse and was ready to slip back into the circle when he was stopped by Lord Angull. By this point, the Northern patrician had made the decision to abandon the archers as they were hitting more of their own than the enemy. He commanded them to stop firing and gave them swords, despite probable lack of experience using them, and ordered them to reinforce the formation in the centre of the battlefield.

"Lord Neman. Taking a break, I see."

The Southern lord looked intently out over the battle. It was clear that he wasn't too happy to be taking orders from a younger man,

"This better be important, boy. I'm not done yet."

Lord Neman was a proud warrior. He prided himself in being the most physically gifted member of his house. He didn't have the same intelligence or charm as his Head of House, Lord Bruk. His nose was broken and his smile was slightly wonky, but he did have the height advantage on the two of his remaining brothers and his added muscle gave him the confidence that he believed was necessary to be a successful patrician.

"Neman, do you see Bris out there? He's the tall man that's killing everyone."

Lord Neman has admitted many times to me that he often found the younger patricians, which I assume includes myself, rather irritating, with this occasion being no exception.

"I know who he is, and of course I can see him."

"Do you think you could take him out?" Lord Angull asked, purposefully sounding rather sceptical of his fellow patricians's abilities to entice him into saying yes.

"Of course I can! I'm the best fighter in my province."

Lord Neman rode off and, after a few circuits around the circle, made his way to the enclosed area at the battlefield's centre. There, he immediately caught the eye of Lord Bris, who was eager to prove his worth to his province.

"That one's mine!" he shouted, shifting his spear to his dominant right hand and making his way towards Lord Neman, who had remained on horseback.

Lord Bris moved quickly around the horse, who was unable to rotate its four legs with the same agility as the Savage. Lord Neman got a few nicks to his armour courtesy of Lord Bris' impressive reach, but was fully aware that, because of his advantage of height due to the horse, it was his fight to lose. Eventually, after monitoring Lord Bris' motions for a short while, Lord Neman started making jabs of his own but found that his opponent had too much time to see where his spear was headed due to the distance between the pair. Lord Neman held his ground. He was in control and knew he must be patient enough to wait for Lord Bris to make a mistake, which he did. Getting frustrated at his lack of opportunities to strike, Lord Bris decided that he would stand a better chance if Lord Neman was also on foot and so went for the horse instead. Lord Neman blocked a few attempts but Lord Bris eventually stabbed his spear's point into the horse's thigh with great force, flinging Lord Neman from its back and causing him to hit the ground relatively heavily. Lord Bris saw his chance and yanked at his spear, but it was lodged. The force of his stab sent the spear too deep into the horse's thigh muscle. Lord Neman, who was still on the ground, turned and saw his enemy grappling with his weapon and, more importantly, looking towards the horse and not at him. Lord Neman grabbed the spear that had fallen just metres away and rushed towards Lord Bris, who still had both hands on his weapon as he attempted to dislodge it. The sound of Lord Neman approaching made Lord Bris turn to face him, but it was too late. Before Lord Bris could get his hands away from the horse and into a blocking position, Lord Neman had pierced the spear of his own straight through the patrician's throat. As blood spewed from Lord Bris' mouth, Lord Neman picked up a fallen mace and fought through the crowd of warriors fiercely to keep his own life - a right he had earned after his victory.

****

The horses were beginning to seriously tire as the day went on and it seemed that more of them were dying than actual soldiers. Because of this, Lord Angull made the call for the circle to break and for those whose horses were done to retreat to camp and reinforce the formation, which had many gaps by that point. The remaining patricians remained on their horses, along with a few more. The exception was Lord Neman, who was no longer trapped by the circle of running horses but was still, like many others, horseless himself. The majority of soldiers joined the formation, with the Savage army now being significantly smaller than it had been before. The combination of Lady Daid's tactics and her reinforced army meant that the Savages began to tire as the numbers were so significantly out of their favour. It was estimated that on the second day of battle there were three soldiers on Lady Daid's side for every one soldier on Lord Eli's, which was a similar statistic to the Battle of Midland Bay. Along with this, the Savages had strength but not the luxury of armour. They chose to flaunt their physique with bare chests, regardless of gender, and they wore no helmets, meaning they were easier targets when horses were introduced.

All this meant that Lord Eli was now doomed. Some Savages saw that the war was lost and started to retreat. Others carried on the fight, but were soon dealt with relatively easily due to their fatigue. Either way, Lord Eli was left alone soon enough. He could have backed down. He could have given the signal and accepted that Lord Bruk was the new king, which would've allowed him to return to live amongst the people in the Midlands. But of course, he didn't. The man had too much pride for his own good and decided that he was to become king or die trying. A few soldiers ran at him, presumably for some personal glory, but were also dealt with rather swiftly. In the end, it came to the three patricians on horseback. After being given some rope by a nearby soldier, Lord Robt and Lady Daid circled Lord Eli and tied him up so that he could cause no harm to Lord Bruk, who rode over to his enemy.

"I am a man of mercy. I will give you one last chance to yield."

"Never!" was Lord Eli's cry.

"So be it."

Lord Bruk dismounted his horse and was handed his custom-made sword.

"On behalf of the innocent people of the Midlands."

He pierced Lord Eli straight through the gut.

Finally, after twelve years of misused power and a lack of consideration for the benefit of his people, Lord Eli breathed his last. With that last breath, he crowned Lord Bruk the first king of Saddle Isle.

An Alliance of Words

"A sea of bodies. Some from the South, some from the North, and most from the Midlands in the end - all dead for the quarrels of a few." That was how, many years later, Lord Bruk described the scene that remained once those of the Midlands had surrendered and retreated at the conclusion of the Battle of the Brutes, as it was later coined. It was a sore sight to behold but one that was ameliorated by a new sense of hope as well as the inevitable tarnish of regret. The war was over, although technically it was unofficial at that point, and that was a cause for celebration no matter what side you were on. As I had suggested, the war was indeed a mistake that many after acknowledged as such. I had feared the detriment that would accompany this war in regard to the efforts made throughout the Prosperity Era to increase the population of our isle. Unfortunately, we estimated that the population of Saddle Isle had taken a devastating decrease because of this war. The Prosperity Era saw the population rise to a high of roughly 7,500. After the war ended we derived that, thanks to the selfishness of certain patricians, the population had dropped by almost a thousand. This travesty and loss of life was unforgivable on the part of the patricians - who ourselves were now the twelve rather than the twenty. It was well regarded throughout the Autocrasy Era that the patrician duty to the people was to make amends for the war in any way that was suitable and achievable as penance for our disastrous and deadly squabbling. It upsets me to disclose that the Autocrasy Era never did see the population rise above 7,000 again, despite our best efforts to improve the figure and return to the former glory of the Prosperity Era. What actually happened was the population plateaued because of the increase in deaths due to a decreased living standard post-war.

Of course, the end of the war did not end all threats for the isle. With the retreat of Lord Kinby and the remaining Midland Savages, there remained fear in the kingdom. I presume that Lord Kinby made a swift return to the Midlands to procure Lady Wonin, who was the only Wharram patrician not to fight, before they both went into hiding. No matter what those of House Wharram did after the battle, they couldn't help that the requirements for victory had been met by Lord Bruk, son of Betra, of House Northorpe, and so he was to be the inaugural monarch of Saddle Isle. Now, for the first time in its history, the isle was officially a kingdom.

In contrast to the Battle of Midland Bay, the formalities of battle had been adhered to. This meant that the opportunity was presented for Lord Bruk, who had a rather bloody head that needed seeing to, and his remaining brothers to discuss with those of House Matfen in the privacy of a tent before heading back to the isle's new capital province, the South. This discussion was in regard to Lady Daid's decision to request assistance from Lord Bruk and therefore submit the power within her province to him. It seems like a relatively simple topic of conversation considering that Lady Daid had no leg to stand on, which may be an insensitive choice of diction on my part considering the location of their meeting and that many a detached limb could be found dotted around the battlefield. I apologise for that, yet refuse to remove the phrase as it is a perfectly useful idiom. As I was saying, the conversation seemed relatively straightforward to both Lord Neman and Lord Robt, but Lord Bruk knew of its complications. The South now had control of the North, along with every other province, but Lady Daid's decision to create an alliance of words with those of House Northorpe presented the future king with a rather favourable opportunity - one which any wise one wouldn't pass up.

****

"How's that head of yours, brother? You've been in here for some time," asked Lord Robt to his new king.

After giving Lord Bruk some space to get some treatment from a Northern nurse, his two remaining brothers entered the tent. Lord Robt was rather different to his brothers. Don't get me wrong, he was just as skilled a fighter as either of them but he was certainly lacking in height compared to even Lord Bruk, but especially Lord Neman. He was also lacking the short, brown hair that his brothers shared, with his hair being of a ginger tinge and a curly nature instead. He did have bulging, expressive eyes though, and pre-war I found him to be rather jovial with his cheeky smile and deafening laugh. Of course, our relationship drastically changed after the Battle of Midland Bay and so that side of him was very rarely shown around me. Lord Bruk guided the nurse out of the tent and gave his brothers an embrace.

"Shut up, Robt. I needed it! I pulled my weight much more than you on that battlefield."

"You must be commended for your performance out there," Lord Neman admitted. "But we did our fair share too and so I wouldn't mind a visit from a pretty nurse like that one."

"You don't have a scratch on you, brother," Lord Robt pointed out, laughing as he did.

"The mark of a truly great warrior!"

They all laughed. Lord Bruk calmed them down.

"Now, we do have some important discussions to have before we head off home. I'm sure the pretty nurses can wait a while longer, Neman. I am now the king, and even the wisest of kings need assistance. Will you do me that honour, my brothers?"

With great pride, they agreed.

"Our first port of call must be to decide who shall take the places of the Heads of House as the new leaders of the provinces. Of course, my siblings will each preside over a province. It is the least that the two of you deserve after displaying such loyalty and bravery. Do you have any preferences?"

Lord Neman was very quick to step in.

"My brother and My King, the honour of leading any province is a great one, but I must admit that the Deep South is most favourable to me. It is not too far away from home and I have always been an admirer of the work they do."

"What a load of twaddle! You just want the Deep South because there is no need for a rebuild. Plus, we all know your desire for a certain lady who may reside there."

"Shut it, Robt!"

"Well, I was intending on placing our little sister there so that she wasn't pushed too far away from home," Lord Bruk said, provocatively. "But I suppose Breck won't be too pleased about our dealing with Barrat, so a bit of distance might do us some good, at least whilst things blow over. Fine! The Deep South is yours. Although, I'm not too sure Lady Anto will be too keen on your affection after you kick both her and her sister out of their home."

Lord Neman, who hadn't considered this, shot a concerned look that was ignored by his brothers.

"Robt, my dear brother, as the second oldest, I propose that you preside over the Midlands. The land is big and the people are challenging, but I am sure that you will thrive in this new position of power."

"Thank you, My King."

Lord Robt bowed to him in the process, to which Lord Bruk pushed him down to one knee.

"That is how you address a king, Robt."

Lord Bruk helped his brother back up after becoming afraid that he had been too rough, especially after the two battles that they had previously endured.

The future king continued, "That leaves Breck with the High North. She has always been affiliated with the place and the people love her dearly. That should make a good match."

"I'm not sure she'll feel strongly about the place once we remove Barrat's head," commented Lord Robt, with a slightly sadistic chuckle.

It seemed that he had already determined my fate.

"She is not that shallow, my brother. I am sure she'll do a great job."

"Yes, I'm sure."

"She is of House Northorpe! Of course she will! So, that just leaves the North."

"Yes, brother. I think I have an idea for this province," said a rather smug Lord Robt.

"Go on, tell me."

"We should alter the split of the land to only have four provinces. If we add some more land to the High North, that could become the North. Then, we could add the remaining land from the current North to the Midlands to maintain its size. Finally, we could take land from the bottom of the Midlands in order to expand both the South and the Deep South."

Lord Bruk took some time to consider this proposal and almost changed his mind on what he had decided to do with the North before his brother's suggestion. However, he knew that peace was key and so stuck to his original plan.

"I like that proposal, Robt. I really do. But I think we have to utilise this vacancy to our future advantage. I have great admiration for those of House Hepston. They are both incredible young women who deserve respect for their views on violence, yet I must admit that I do not see them as a threat in the slightest. Lady Daid and the rest of House Matfen, however, worry me. They could become a threat in the future and so I have deemed it suitable to continue on from our current bonding by rewarding them for their alliance and allowing them to remain, as a house, in leadership of the North."

"As a free province?" asked Lord Neman, concerned about the proposal.

Lord Bruk was offended that his brother thought he was foolish enough to allow Lady Daid any real power.

"Absolutely not! Any decision made in the capital will be implemented in the North, as with all provinces. They would simply be able to remain in their home and feel as though they have been respected, in some capacity, for their cooperation."

"And you feel as though those of House Hepston will be fine with this?" Lord Neman asked.

"Not fine, as such, but I doubt that they will feel in a position to complain. It is, of course, a shame for House Hepston but we cannot please everyone. I would rather please a big threat than a non-entity. I'm sure you'd agree."

"That, my brother, is fine thinking. Would you like me to inform Lady Daid of your great nobility and kindness?"

"If you would please, Neman. That would be great."

Lord Bruk smiled at his brother as he left the tent to find Lady Daid.

"Robt, dear brother, I am glad that I get this time to speak with you alone. I have much respect for you. I know that you will be loyal to me, and respect my decisions and authority."

"Of course, brother."

"I also know that you will speak up when you deem my proposals to be ill-advised."

"If I deem it necessary. I have never been shy to point out your flaws, brother."

"Indeed. That is why I have chosen you as my chief advisor. I haven't worked out exactly what that entails of yet but I know that, whatever I throw at you, you will prosper."

Lord Robt gleamed with pride as he shook his future king's hand.

"Thank you, brother. I won't let you down."

"I am sure of it. Now, go and ensure that our horses are prepared for departure. I'm sure our poor sister is worried. We should get back home to her as soon as possible."

****

On normal occasions, Lord Bruk and his brothers may have been expected to remain in the North for the night, especially considering that the surviving Midland Savages would still be riled up and ready to kill any man who passes, future king or not. However, the worry for Lady Breck's well being, coupled with the longing for their own beds, meant that the decision was made to ride on through early sunset in order to return to the new capital as soon as possible. There were a few men that fell that night, a shame considering that the war was over. It was an added misery that, despite Lord Eli no longer enforcing his backward ideology, the new leaders of the provinces had not yet been announced or implemented and so there was very little that could be done in terms of justice for those killed on the journey home. Either way, they made it to Castle Sear and were greeted by Lady Breck, who hadn't slept a single minute since her brothers headed to aid Lady Daid, despite her exhaustion. Of course, her brothers weren't the only cause of that reality. Uncertain about the proper conduct considering that her brother was now set to be king, she decided that it was still suitable for her to run to her brothers with the view to hug them, leaving Lord Bruk till last.

"I'm so glad you're safe. I was so scared for you."

Lord Bruk refused to let her go, mainly in the knowledge that his brothers' contempt for me would most likely result in my death, something that Lord Bruk didn't want to break to his little sister.

"Thank you, dear Breck. You look more worse for wear than ourselves!"

"I do love your compliments."

After being released by Lord Bruk, she joined her brothers for a meal that had been prepared by the castle cook. The meal consisted of fine cuts of beef, potatoes and a generous helping of red wine. It was over this dinner, after more jovial conversation had taken place, that the family turned matters to the elephant in the room - or should I say the lord in the dungeons. The obvious wishes of Lady Breck were already creating a sense of tension.

"Now that the war has been won, will you please release my beloved from his cell."

Despite not being addressed, it was Lord Robt who felt it suitable to answer.

"Absolutely not! That traitor's head shall hang on our walls for all to see. He killed our brother - your brother by blood! It is almost treacherous itself for you to fight for his release!"

Lord Bruk intervened, frustrated by his approach.

"Robt! Can we please deal with this matter in a more civilised manner? Or, failing that, a more dignified volume."

"I'm sorry, My King, but the girl is mad to think that he should go free."

Lady Breck, who had briefly frozen in shock after thinking of the prospect of having to view my head on the walls of her home, rejoined the room.

"You cannot be serious, Bruk. I know that the loss of our poor Suln has hit us all hard, and I am in great mourning for him. But killing Barrat is most certainly not a valid action! You said that Barrat is like a brother to you before the battles commenced. Would you, Bruk, kill your own brother?"

Lord Bruk understood the importance of keeping things calm.

"I know that you love him, sister. The love that you share has brought me great joy over the years. And yes, Barrat has been like a brother to me. I love him as one and have done since I took him under my wing all those years ago. But do you seriously think that I can spare him his life? If Robt was to kill Neman, his fellow brother, this instant, do you think that I wouldn't condemn Robt to death purely based on the reality that he is my brother? A crime is a crime and so should be punished, especially considering it was Suln who was prematurely taken to the gods."

"That is unfair!"

"Don't raise your voice, Breck," Lord Bruk requested, to no success.

"You give me no choice, brother!" she snapped. "If Robt were to kill Neman in this instant then I would understand the decision to punish him, but my Barrat's situation differs greatly. Suln's death is a tragedy and is an event that has caused Barrat as much pain as it has us, but it is not a murder that should be punished. My beloved killed our brother under the premise of war. By the laws of our land and his loyalty to his house, Barrat was an opponent in battle. He was simply tasked to fight for his province, something that one must do with honour, no matter the circumstances! Suln signed up for war and he knew the risks. Do you think, if they both sat here in this instant, a fantasy that I would give anything to make reality, that Barrat would put an arrow through our beloved Suln's head? Of course not! It was a consequence of war, and so he should be freed. You must think of the context."

Lord Robt stood and, to everyone's surprise, went to strike his sister. He was only prevented from doing so by Lord Neman, who pulled him back. Lord Bruk intervened.

"Robt! If you cannot compose yourself then exit this room immediately!"

"But she speaks with no sympathy for our brother."

He didn't leave like Lord Bruk suggested but instead sat down in a sulk.

"I know that Breck's argument seems somewhat insensitive to our brother's death," Lord Bruk began.

This comment upset Lady Breck, as she did truly mourn for Lord Suln. Despite her emotion, she remained silent.

The future king continued, "But she is correct. Technically, Barrat's actions were a result of war and he has never done anything to suggest that his killing of Suln was for any reason otherwise. We must remember that, if it weren't for Barrat, many of our innocent people would have been ruthlessly murdered and we may have been killed in the ambush also. Having said that, we are the prominent house of this kingdom. We are the ones who won the war and so we are the only ones who can see the death of our fallen patrician as an injustice. I know, sister, that it may not seem fair but sometimes life isn't as fair as it should be. It is clear that, despite the points you have made, there is still anger towards Barrat from our family. And as the family with all the power in the kingdom, we have the right to do as we please."

Lady Breck's initial relief was then replaced with a gasp of shock as she suspected that, despite being correct, her argument was, in fact, for nothing.

"As a leader, it is important to implement compromise. I have no wish for the lad to die. As you know, I have a great affiliation with him. However, I do note that my brothers feel that there is justice to be had and so I must consider that. I also note that you, Breck, have put forth a valid argument in his defence, an event that has given me great optimism for your future as the leader in the High North. I must consider that also."

Lady Breck barely took note of her imminent relocation to my presumably former home, as she hung on Lord Bruk's every last word, to the point where she grew impatient of his extended speech.

He concluded, "I have therefore come to the conclusion that Barrat is to serve the rest of his days here, in the capital, as a servant to the Crown and our family."

Typically, murder was punished by death in all provinces, excluding the Midlands, but the murder of Suln was under the auspices of war. If the law had been followed correctly in regard to my case then I would have been set free from my cell immediately, but Lord Bruk knew that allowing me to leave would cause too much conflict with his brothers and so punishing me to a life of serving was the compromise he came to.

Lord Robt remembered the permission that Lord Bruk handed him to express his disagreement.

"I am not happy, My King, but I respect your authority."

With that, he left for the Great Hall where there was to be a celebration with the Southern people. He was shortly followed by Lord Neman, who claimed he also wanted me dead but was not as perturbed by the decision to keep me alive. Lady Breck waited for her brothers to leave before standing.

"You have done Lord Barrat a disservice here, My King. I am happy for your safety and your victory and will respect you with my presence for the remainder of the evening, but I shall be leaving early in the morning."

"Breck, come on," Lord Bruk pleaded. "If I would have freed Lord Barrat, your brothers would have killed him themselves, and you know that."

He was frustrated at her behaviour but understood her disappointment.

"Don't pretend like you did this for him! You're just scared to rule without our brothers' support. That's why you did it. Clearly my assistance means nothing to you."

She started to cry, something that she desperately wanted to avoid doing in front of any one of her brothers. She headed for the door but stopped once being addressed.

"Where will you go, Breck?"

"To my new province, of course. At least there I'll be surrounded by people who have the guts to do what's right."

She thought that, since she had failed to suppress her emotions, she might as well use her tears against Lord Bruk. Despite her threats, she actually remained in the capital until after the coronation. This was partly down to the fact that she would not officially be the leader of the High North until after Lord Bruk was crowned king, but was mainly to ensure that no decisions were overturned in regard to my life, which would have been a high possibility if Lady Breck wasn't there to fight in my corner.

She left, leaving Lord Bruk alone in the dining room. He sighed, poured out the remaining wine into his cup, drank it, then put on a brave face as he prepared to greet his people.

153

Long Live The King

Despite the fact that my beloved Lady Breck had fought to save my life and had managed to convince her brother to let me keep my head in exchange for my services, I remained in the dungeon for the weeks between the official end of the war and the coronation of the inaugural monarch of what was now the Kingdom of Saddle Isle. I expected to remain there for the duration of the coronation ceremony and so was quite shocked when, on that day, I was dragged from my cell, cleaned up, and placed in servant robes. I was shown to my new chamber, which was a significantly smaller room than I had ever seen before. It was laid out in a box shape, with a bed seemingly designed for half a person and a small hole in the corner for obvious purposes. I suppose privilege is just another form of ignorance, in many ways. Even though my circumstances were far from, and certainly a downgrade from, the norm, I was relieved to be out of the dungeon and into somewhere a little more comfortable. The room was certainly more comfortable than the floor I had been sleeping on for what seemed to be sometime between one night and a full season. Every day had blurred into one and so even a season felt like a never ending day. But the comfort in my clothing, cleanliness, and slight good fortune was nothing in comparison to the discomfort of my mind. Guilt still plagued me and the permanence of my siblings' absence, both of house and of heart, in the case of Lord Suln, kept me in constant wonderment of whether my mind would ever return to the stillness and contentment that I was formerly blessed with. I was also cursed with pining for Lady Breck, who had been a staple of my thoughts for months. This was only magnified by the lack of distraction in my cell and the fact that she hadn't been allowed to visit, which was expected but still painful for me.

****

I was contemplating my mistakes and losses as I sat on a bed that needed a fresh supply of straw, which I wasn't foolish enough to request, when there was a short knock on my door that was quickly followed by the unpermitted entrance of a servant girl.

"What was the use of knocking if you were to be too impatient to wait for me to grant you a consensual entrance?"

Although I was genuinely annoyed by her action, I did instantly regret my response.

"I'm ever so sorry, mister. I didn't mean to offend."

She pushed her loose, greasy hair away from her face, revealing her button nose and slender cheeks to be equally as dirty as her presumably blonde hair.

"No, I'm sorry. It's been a tough day."

"Oh, you must be the new addition!"

Her nonchalant attitude towards the matter was slightly disconcerting. 'New addition' made it seem like I was some sort of apprentice rather than a criminal.

"I suppose you could say that."

"Well, I'm Miss Aton," she announced, extending her hand for me to shake. "And who are you, mister?"

That was an interesting question. I suppose I was still Lord Barrat, son of Nea, of House Pearson, but I didn't feel like him anymore. I decided to err on the side of caution and to adopt a different name from my own. It might as well have been mine either way.

"Oh, well, my name is Mister Anwir."

"Well, Mister Anwir, the pleasure is mine. I'm sure you get this an awful lot, Mister Anwir, but I must say it anyway. You look rather like one of those fancy men from up north. Lord Barrat is the one I mean."

Despite all that had happened, I still managed to feel a sense of disappointment that all my hard work over the years had only resulted in me being 'a fancy man from up north.' She didn't even address me by my province.

"I believe he's from the High North, to be precise."

"Oh, look at you," she mocked, condescendingly. "What's a man with your superior knowledge doing as a mere servant then?"

"I killed... someone."

I thought it wiser to abstain from telling the people of the South that I had killed one of the more popular figures of their province. Surprisingly, this was met with a laugh from my new colleague.

"No, you can't have, my friend! I am no fool, you know! Everyone knows that if you kill someone you get punished by death. It was one of the first things I was taught even back on the mainland."

I stopped to consider whether continuing down this truthful path, in parts, was wise but I determined that I hadn't very much left to lose.

"Yes, I know. Maybe my head will go still."

"I doubt it. They don't bring them lot down here, the ones to be beheaded, Mister Anwir. They just leave 'em to rot in a cell."

Miss Aton spoke with much confidence, as though she was the expert of crime and punishment. She rather cheekily took a seat opposite me on my bed and was seriously beginning to irritate me.

"I have been rotting in a cell since the war ended."

"Oh, so you're a war criminal then! I thought they let them people off, on account of it being war an' all. You must have done somethin' proper bad to end up down here with the rest of us scum, if it was a war crime you committed, that is."

I didn't respond to her attempt to get me to speak of my crime. Instead, I just looked hopelessly towards the door, wishing for anyone to walk in. What I would have given for Lady Breck to enter and tell me that things were going to be okay.

"I won't judge, you know. I mean, I'm here for stealing, myself."

"Oh, right. What happened there then, exactly?"

I saw this as an opportunity to steer the conversation away from me. Miss Aton adjusted her position to have her legs crossed on the bed. The sheer dirtiness of her bare feet made her face and hair look clean.

"Oh, let me tell you, Mister Anwir, the war criminal! It was an average day and my sister was moaning, as she often did. She wanted to make her little kid, my niece, her favourite meal but that meant acquiring some pork that we just couldn't afford. I had been working on a farm shovelling this an' that, but they told me to leave after one of the farmer's lads tried it on with me. I am quite the looker, when I've had a wash that is! Anyway, I was the one to blame, apparently. Called me a whore he did, the farmer that is. 'Get away from my boy you filthy whore.' Not the nicest of men but few of them are, I suppose. I hadn't the heart to tell my poor sister that the money was tight. She's a worrier you see and she was going through enough stress as it were with her husband killed by those Midland Savages a few years back. So, I went out in the aid of pleading for a chance to get my old work back. After I was told a firm no, I saw a chance to nick a piglet on my way out. I got half way home before they caught me. They were on horseback, you see. I'm quick but I can't outrun a horse, now! Definitely not with a little porker in my hand, I tell ya'!"

It certainly was an injustice for a poor girl to be punished for the advancements of a farm lad.

"That all sounds terrible. How long have you been a servant here?"

"Just the five seasons, so far that is. Lord Bruk, or should I say our new king, was relatively fair with me. He only sentenced me to three years as a servant. Could've been a lot worse. Hey, if those in the North caught me I would have lost everything to that farmer, as their rules go that way. That doesn't seem all fair to me."

She picked dirt from her fingernails when she spoke, leaving the resulting mud to coat my sheets.

"Well, I'm sorry for your misfortune."

I imagined that my sentence was not going to be as short as my new friend's, although my sentence would still remain more fair than hers. I was about to enquire what I would have to do as part of my servant role when she spoke again.

"It's a real shame what happened to that poor Lady Breck, don't you think?"

Immediately, my heart sank. What had they done? Why was it a shame? It didn't even cross my mind that my beloved was much loved by her brothers and that they would never purposefully cause her harm. I was in such a panic that all reasonable logic escaped me.

"What happened to her?" What have they done?"

"Oh, you haven't heard?"

I didn't appreciate her provocative approach to conversation.

She eventually explained, "Well, the topic of our prior conversation, Lord Barrat, had been sentenced to have his big head chopped off for killing our beloved Lord Suln."

The sound of that didn't sit well with me. Had my heart not already been in my stomach it would have retired there due to that thought.

"It was all agreed until Lady Breck came bounding in, pleading for her brothers to have mercy. You see, our fair lady has been doting on that lord for many a year. I imagine that she was hoping to marry him, had this whole 'killing her brother' thing not come about."

Again, her nonchalant attitude to trauma was incredibly distressing.

"Anyway, her pleading got so desperate and pathetic that she went a bit too far. She said, and I paraphrase as I was not on duty at the time, that she 'couldn't bear to live without him' and that they should take her head instead. Lord Robt, being quite the stern man that he is, saw this as a betrayal from their sister and thought that Lord Barrat would suffer more knowing he was the cause of his beloved's death. They agreed to her taking his place on the chopping block."

I gasped out in shock as a sharp pain stretched from my chest all the way up to my head, which I placed on the bed in my pity.

"Do tell me it's not true!"

"Of course it's not bloody true!"

Her tone switched as she lifted my head up to look at me as she bellowed with an outburst of laughter.

She continued, "You don't think I know a lord of our land when I see one? Mister Anwir my arse! You do make me laugh, Lord Barrat."

I was furious with her tricks.

"Why would you do that? Lying like that is incredibly cruel."

"Oh, you cannae try to teach me the morals about lying when you lied to me first. Besides, I had to lie. If I were to ask outright then you'd just deny it. This way, I had undeniable evidence."

She did, annoyingly, have a point.

"You still took it too far."

"I know, I will admit that. Although, it was quite funny to watch your sad little face get all angry, I can tell ya'. Look, I am willing to let bygones be bygones if you would do me one honour."

"What exactly would that entail?"

She could tell that I was getting tetchy but still resorted to her cheeky approach to conversation.

"Well, My Lordship," Miss Aton said, sarcastically. "When you eventually get let out of this little situation of yours - which I am pretty certain you will, by the way, based on how much our new king talks about you - will you please bless my family some support. They could be dead, for all I know. I never did see them in the keep when your sister led that attack of hers. But, if they are still breathin', they need all the help they can get."

I sighed, but understood that it must be done. She clearly cared about her family and was, despite her tendencies, a kind soul who was harshly treated.

"If I ever get out of here, I will do all I can."

*** * * ***

A few minutes after our conversation had closed, I was left alone with my thoughts once more. Luckily, not long after, all servants were called to the pits of the Great Hall as the coronation ceremony was to begin. They would watch from floor level, mainly to hear the address of the king as it was wrongly estimated that he would comment on law changes throughout his new kingdom. As everyone else was led to the pits, I was taken aside by a guard who would later be presented to me as the same Mister Rufus, son of Brant, who I have introduced already. He took me on a different path that led to me being guarded at the far side of the throne, not to be seen by the guests but close enough for an efficiently swift action to drag me in front of the king when I was needed. This was, despite the circumstances being rather bleak, the first time that I had seen my beautiful Lady Breck since the war, when she took advantage of her brothers' absence and visited me in the dungeon. That was an event that brought brief, yet much needed, love and peace into my otherwise turbulent heart. She looked stunning but anxious, and didn't once look in my direction. Despite this, I could tell that she was safe, which was the main thing.

Before I could even absorb my surroundings, the ceremony began.

"All rise!" a rather loud voice from over the way from me announced. "All rise for the king!"

With his command, the thousands in attendance that spanned from the Great Hall to the streets of the South all stood, if they weren't already standing, to greet their new king. The Great Hall in Castle Sear was a sight to behold. I have never seen a room so big and it seemed to enlarge even more when packed full of excited citizens. Of course, it was proportionate with the size of the castle but it was still baffling how such a room could be produced. The ceiling seemed never ending and there were a series of stone pillars, so clean and smooth, that aligned the walls. The floor was similar to that of Castle Rye but seemed to have an even more polished finish. If any room in the isle was set to be the room of a king, this would be the only one suitable for such an honour. In any other circumstance, I would have found this day a great one. In fact, even despite the circumstances, I still held pride for my friend and knew that he was the best man to lead the kingdom into a new era of success. It was just a shame that he had to start his new adventure without my support.

"Please be seated," the loud voice broadcasted once more.

After walking through the crowd, Lord Bruk took a seat on the throne. It was a newly constructed seat with a perfectly intricate design for the purpose for which it served. Before making his coronation speech, Lord Bruk was made to swear before the Leonist gods that he would serve the land and that he would rule with a just and fair hand. If any other possible monarch, and I include my sister in that, was to swear the same thing I wouldn't have believed them. But with Lord Bruk, it was different. He didn't want to lead and yet was willing when he was called to, making him the greatest choice. After he made his vow, the now King Bruk gave his first address. He stood to speak, holding himself with grace and honour.

"Good people of the Kingdom of Saddle Isle. Thank you all for coming to what is a very special occasion for myself and my family. I am grateful that we can all be here together to celebrate what is bigger than a coronation. I am thankful that we can all be here together to celebrate what is bigger than the beginning of a new era. Most of all, I have the utmost appreciation that we can all be here together to celebrate the day that marks the official end of the Great Packsaddle War."

This was met with a great ovation that King Bruk paused to appreciate before continuing.

"Of course, we must never forget those who lost their lives fighting bravely for their provinces. Whether fighting on behalf of myself and my family or for our opponents in the war, their sacrifices showed honour and loyalty that can only be remembered fondly. We, as a developing kingdom, must adopt their favourable qualities of loyalty and honour and apply them to ourselves as we move forward. As we regroup after such a turbulent and troublesome time, it is important to remember that not all will be perfect straight away. But, if we stick together, we will soon be back to our prosperous state, I assure you."

This was met by another cheer.

"As part of our aim to return to a prosperous state, I have decided to maintain the isle's former system, which worked well for many years. The only difference, of course, is that the leaders of the provinces will now have a much stronger relationship with each other. This is due to my brothers and my sister taking up leadership roles across the kingdom, an honour that they are all well prepared for due to my mentoring over the years. Lord Robt, son of Betra, of House Northorpe shall be residing in the Midlands. Lord Neman, son of Betra, of House Northorpe shall be residing in the Deep South. My beautiful sister: Lady Breck, daughter of Ferma, of House Northorpe shall be residing in the High North. As a result of their cooperation and the alliance that was formed between our two houses during the turbulent times of war, those of House Matfen shall remain in the North. I haven't had any confirmation as of yet but I assume that Lady Daid, daughter of Rean, of House Matfen shall continue to lead their noble house. I have great faith that she will continue to help the North to prosper as she has successfully done for many years. On top of this, I will also continue to hold council meetings here in the capital. As there is much to do, and much to fix, I have decided to decrease the former size of the council in order to increase the number of meetings that can be held. The council will consist of myself, Lord Robt, and Lord Neman, at least until our kingdom is in a position of stability once more."

This made sense, even though Lord Robt and Lord Neman were both practically useless, in spite of their slight kindness towards me in the past. Of course, Lady Daid wasn't too pleased to have been removed from the council.

King Bruk continued, "My people, in 1096 we were forcibly removed from our homes. We were separated from our mothers and shipped away to the isle, all because of the label that was placed upon us by society. But we are more than our former bastard state, as we have proven with our past prosperity. We are not bastards here, but instead are all respected and valuable members of our kingdom and that shall not change. Our former home wants us to be shamed with the bastard name yet we no longer are plagued by that label. There is, however, one man who deserves the name of bastard for he has corrupted the nobility and trust of my family. Mister Rufus, please bring forth the one formerly known as Lord Barrat."

As instructed, Mister Rufus brought me before the king. I was met with jeers from the crowd, which I thought was rather undignified and unnecessary. The king addressed me, not looking at my face but to the floor instead.

"Lord Barrat, I have shown my mercy as king to spare your life, despite that murder is typically to be met with death in return. I have granted you this mercy due to your previous commitment to our kingdom. You will, however, be a servant for the rest of your days here in this very castle. As well as this, I hereby strip you of your titles. You henceforth shall be known as 'The Bastard of Saddle Isle,' a name deemed fit by my brothers. Mister Rufus, please take him back to his chamber."

As ordered, Mister Rufus dragged me back to the pathetic chamber where I now resided. I had lost Lady Breck to my old home and now began to lose all hope.

The Strength of Words

King Bruk, son of Betra, of House Northorpe was a cursed man. I say this as he was cursed with unwanted power. The Great Packsaddle War was born from the greed of three Heads of House: Lord Eli, Lady Daid and Lady Catar, so I find it rather humorous, as funny as death can be, that King Bruk was the victor in the end. I know it is said that those who thrive in power are those who never seek it, but I personally believe that there has to be some sort of wish for power to inspire a job well done. Either way, Lord Bruk was now King Bruk, and so had a duty to serve. I was spared my life by the king, despite my crimes, to the disdain of the members of the new King's Council. I assumed that my survival was mainly down to the love shared between Lady Breck and myself, an added bonus of our relationship. I was truly grateful for my life, as obvious as that may seem. Having said that, if my head was removed from my body then the guilt that I felt, and still feel, for the death of my friend, Lord Suln, wouldn't have weighed so heavily on my mind. I may have been gifted my life but I wasn't gifted any freedom. I understood the punishment set for my crime - I did kill the king's brother - but I found it rather difficult to be confined within the walls of Castle Sear. I did, however, cease to find myself with nothing to do. They worked me hard and true, and squeezed every last hope out of me. They sent the love of my life to my old home to prevent her from seeing me. They took me from my patrician status and squashed me down until I was the lowest of the low. I went from being a patrician to the Bastard of Saddle Isle, but I knew that I deserved it. Maybe not technically, but I personally needed some punishment to ease my guilt. I struggled to change my nature, however, to match my new lowly status. I had spent four years travelling the isle as Head of Trade, making friends across all the provinces. On those travels, I developed personally as a man of politics and struggled to turn that off now that I was forced to complete the petty chores of an incompetent council. I was forced to sit and listen to the two foolish members of House Northorpe, Lord Robt and Lord Neman, dismantle any chance at maintaining peace, a crucial goal during an era of turbulence within the kingdom.

****

"Thank you both for travelling to the capital for this King's Council meeting," were the welcoming words of the king.

Despite his promotion, King Bruk maintained his noble stature and showed to his brothers the respect and gratitude that a leader should show to all, not that they paid much attention to his teachings. During this specific King's Council meeting, I was charged with clearing up a meal that the three brothers had shared with each other. I even managed to swipe a few scrap pieces of beef for myself as I did. The wheat on the isle was of great quality, and the Deep South workers had done themselves great honour in their labour for many years, but bread really does taste boring when you consume it for every meal. King Bruk started the meeting.

"I understand, lords of my house, that you have both devised some suggestions in aid of moving forward through this new era of our kingdom."

"Yes, My King," they both responded.

Out of all those of House Northorpe, I knew Lord Neman the least, but what I had heard suggested that he was not the most suitable man to sit on a council. He was much more valuable on the battlefield, as was Lord Robt. Lord Neman released a rather nervous sigh before presenting his case.

"I have a proposal for you, My King, from the advisory of the Deep South. A great king like yourself needs to show great valour and you did that by protecting your province and your house. In doing so, you brought down many capable warriors and five patricians who all betrayed your trust and threatened our family."

"Hear, hear," was a rather unnecessary interruption from Lord Robt, I thought.

"To honour your bravery on the battlefield, we have sanctioned the renaming of all five castles of the provinces."

As those foolish words left Lord Neman's mouth, I couldn't help but stop what I was doing to listen more carefully. I knew instantly that no advisor from the Deep South had ever suggested this action, especially not Lady Anto, daughter of Elan, of House Hepston.

Lord Neman continued, "This castle that we feast in today shall be renamed Castle Eli. The castle of the North, Castle Kezi. In the Midlands, which belongs to you, Lord Robt, the castle shall now be known as Castle Bennk. My castle shall be renamed Castle Shay. Castle Gelid in the High North, where our sister resides, shall now be Castle Catar in respect for the dead."

The two lords laughed at the remark, but King Bruk remained silent and looked over to me with sympathetic eyes.

"It shall be announced tomorrow at the royal address, My King," Lord Neman confirmed.

King Bruk paused. He knew that the decree had been made and that plans had already begun and so the castles would be renamed whether he liked it or not. I, as a man of much intelligence, knew of this fact as well but that didn't stop me from regretting the poor decision on behalf of the king. After a pause, King Bruk trudged on with the meeting.

"Lord Robt, what do you bring forth to me?"

Lord Robt gestured to me to bring him more wine, which I did. He sipped the fine juice before beginning his presentation.

"My King, I come to you with a concern. During the Great Packsaddle War, Lady Daid, daughter of Rean, of House Matfen requested our assistance in what commoners refer to as the Battle of the Brutes against those of House Wharram. We, in our wisdom, knew that Eli was not fit to rule due to his savage nature. We rode to Lady Daid's assistance and in return she swore to support you in your claim to the throne."

"That is all correct, brother, but I see no means for concern here."

It appeared that the king was rather bored of this recounting of events that occurred not too long prior.

"My King, my concern lies in the manner of this alliance. We gifted those of House Matfen with the North and have taken the word of Lady Daid to be sound and true. However, over the past few weeks I have been kept awake with the worry that her word alone is not enough. As long as those of House Matfen maintain their land, they are a threat. They have the means to block the river to cut off all sources of water, if they wish. They have support from their people, and there are those who would turn on the Crown in order to see anyone but you as their monarch."

This time it was the king himself who needed wine from me to help him through the meeting.

"Well, that is of concern. What do you suggest we do, my chief advisor?"

Lord Robt paused, as if a solution was unexpected of him.

"I suggest that we should attack," he stupidly proposed, eventually.

Obviously, I had no place to convey my opinion - that was made clear enough - but I couldn't help but shake my head in disapproval.

Lord Robt continued, "I know that we made our decision but the strongest men are those who can admit to their mistakes. We know that they are weak. We were needed for their own survival! Now would be the most prudent time."

"If they are weak then they aren't a threat," I spoke out.

I knew my place but I did not know how to maintain it. In all honesty, it was a miracle that I hadn't already spoken out against Lord Neman's foolishness in regard to the castles.

"You do not get to speak, bastard! Know your place."

Lord Neman turned and struck me down to the floor.

"That's enough!" King Bruk sternly, yet calmly, commanded. He stood to help me to my feet.

The king commented, "We shall not attack on the North, yet I see your point. There must be another way for us to strengthen without any more bloodshed. As I've said many times, we have all lost too much already."

"What other way is there, My King?"

Whatever way they would eventually fall upon, Lord Neman, who asked this question, was not the one destined to think of it.

"I suppose there is another way we could strengthen our hold on the throne, My King," Lord Robt chimed in. "You could take Lady Breck as your queen."

My heart sank, so much so that I dropped from my upright position and fell on one knee, to the amusement of Lord Robt.

"What, bastard? Did you think that she was still yours to love?"

I took a moment in an attempt to hold my tongue. I failed.

"No, of course not. I just thought that you wouldn't be such an imbecile. That's all, My Lord."

This understandably caused a stir within the new leader of the Midland province.

"You treacherous little bastard!"

He stood and marched towards me as I remained on the floor. He slammed his knee to my chest, forcing my body to curl up. I spent a while wheezing.

"I'm sorry, My Lord."

I wasn't.

I pleaded, "Please, can you allow me to say my piece?"

"No, bastard! You are only alive because of our mercy, yet you act as if I were as low as you."

I had to pause in my speech as I struggled to breathe.

"If you had... your way... I would be dead... already. Don't... lie to me... about... mercy."

Lord Robt scoffed and kicked me in the stomach.

"Enough!" intervened a somewhat agitated King Bruk. "I order you, Robt, to stop."

Lord Robt did as he was instructed and turned to face his king, looking in disbelief that King Bruk sided with me. The king continued, still disappointed.

"This meeting is adjourned. Thank you for your attendance, but you both can leave to your chambers. I want a word with the boy, alone."

*** * * ***

The king was patient with me. He allowed me to take my time in standing back to my feet, which I made the most of. Lord Robt's kick had knocked all the air from me and I needed all the time I could get. After a short while, he lost patience and walked over to help me up. He led me to the seat positioned opposite to his and sat down again. He paused to sip his wine, then spoke.

"I thought, of all people, you would be smarter than that," he eventually said, disappointedly.

I would have hated his disappointment in me if I wasn't so cautious of what was happening. I trusted him but assumed that he wouldn't trust me.

"I'm sorry, My King, but I cannot sit and listen to those fools ruin this kingdom."

"There it is again. You really should learn when to keep your mouth shut and when it is necessary to talk."

"My King, they talk of war, of violence, and of provoking those who you need to bring to your side. I..."

"... Do you seriously think that I support their foolish schemes? I am no fool, Barrat." he interrupted.

"I know that, My King."

He sipped more wine, as he sat back down.

"Do you know why you are still alive, boy?"

"Because of the love I share with Lady Breck, My King," I answered, truly believing that to be the case.

He laughed at my comment before standing to pace around the table.

"Perhaps you are more foolish than I thought. I love my little sister. I love her more than any of my brothers, for sure..."

"... That's good, considering you are to marry her," I sharply remarked.

"Don't interrupt me, boy!"

King Bruk remained composed but showed slight frustration.

He continued, "My sister begged for your life but it was not her that saved you, it was me. I saved you because I know that, despite your mistakes, you are a patrician of peace and patricians of peace are incredibly difficult to find. I have known you since you were a boy and I have cared for you since then, and still to this day. I see greatness in you, Barrat. I can see that you were born to lead and lead you shall, from whatever position you are in. You know what is best for the most and that is why you command respect."

He stopped and took more wine, offering me some. I knew it was rude to refuse him but I couldn't take it.

"No thank you, My King. Once I start I struggle to stop and I have many jobs to do."

"Fair enough."

He paused for a moment then started pacing once more.

"I was there when you attended the first Council of Heads meeting, back when the five Heads of House sat upon these seats. You were merely Head of Trade and yet you commanded the entire room. Lords and ladies, who were more respected throughout the land than yourself, were all forced to respect you because you were born to lead. Even from then I knew that you were just as capable as everyone else in that room, myself included. I don't know for sure, but I can take a wild guess about the advice you gave your sister prior to the Battle of Midland Bay. I would guess that you advised her against the battle because you are a man of peace, Barrat. Tell me, is this correct?"

"Yes, My King," I answered, respectfully.

He took the time to sip at his wine once more.

"And why exactly did you advise against the High North's attack on the South? Please, be specific with your reasoning."

I paused, worried that it might be a trick. He picked up on my concern.

"It's only me, Barrat. You can be honest," he assured me.

I paused still, as I remained unconvinced.

"Barrat, come on. You can tell me that it wasn't for my family's benefit because I already know it wasn't."

I examined the lowly position I was in and determined that I had nothing to lose.

"You're right, My King. It wasn't for the benefit of your family, as much as I adore you and your fallen brother - and your sister, of course, My King."

"Then why was it?"

"I advised against it because I knew we would lose. I saw what Lady Anto did for the people of the Deep South. She saved thousands by being noble enough to not seek power. We stood no chance and so thousands of our people were destined to die. I had to obey my sister's orders but I refused to venture south without at least trying to save them."

"But you were the one to send word of the attack, like any noble man would?"

"Yes, My King."

King Bruk smiled to himself as he sat back down.

"And there it is. That's all the proof I needed. You fought your sister in an attempt to save the people of the High North, a very noble thing to do. Then, you went against her wishes and subsequently saved the lives of many from the South. I have more respect for you than I have for most."

"You honour me greatly, My King."

He smiled, and ushered for me to stand, which I did. I began to move to get more wine but was haltered.

"Unlike you, Barrat, I know when to stop."

I smiled at his words and stood to his right hand side, awaiting his continuation.

"You understand, more than most, that peace is of great importance for any leader, even when one is a king. If I truly could have my own way, you would sit not just on my council but as my chief advisor. But I can't. Robt and Neman want your head to be presented on our castle wall and hate that I have spared you your life. They loved you, but they loved their own brother more and want so-called justice. You belong here, at this table, boy. But if you ever wish to take your seat, you need to show my brothers that you are more valuable as an ally than a servant."

"Yes, My King. I shan't let you down again."

I respected him as a king but smiled at him as a friend. He ushered me to leave.

"Go and prepare my bed for the night then go to your own chamber."

I knelt before him, as expected of me, then headed for the door.

"Oh, and Barrat," he called after me.

I stopped my movement and turned around.

"I'm sorry about the castles. I never intend to dishonour you, but you know what my brothers are like."

"Thank you, My King," I said as I left his presence to complete my duties.

The Patricians of Saddle Isle - 1108:

House Northorpe:

Lord Bruk, son of Betra, (b. 1080)

Lord Robt, son of Betra, (b. 1081)

Lord Neman, son of Betra, (b. 1082)

Lady Breck, daughter of Ferma, (b. 1090)

House Wharram:

Lord Kinby, son of Stanp, (b. 1081)

Lady Wonin, daughter of Manty, (b. 1082)

House Matfen:

Lady Daid, daughter of Rean, (b. 1083)

Lord Angull, son of Limo, (b. 1086)

Lady Oline, daughter of Mar, (b. 1090)

House Pearson:

Lord Barrat, son of Nea, (b. 1090)

House Hepston:

Lady Anto, daughter of Elan, (b. 1091)

Lady Aott, daughter of Elan, (b. 1095)

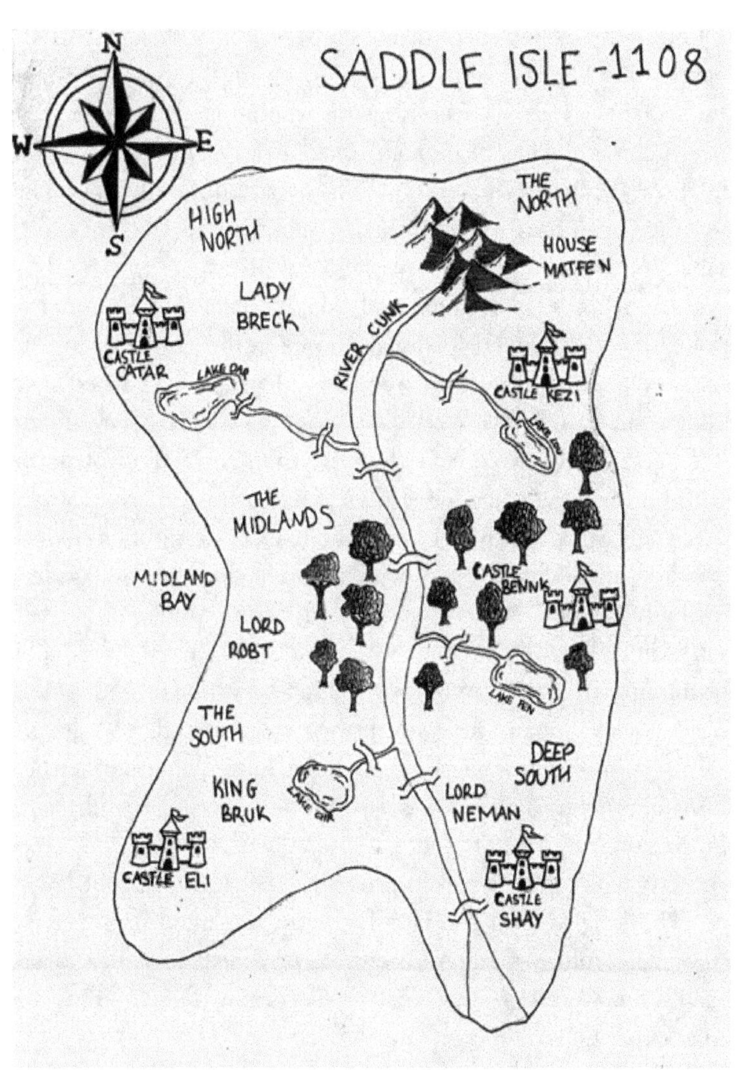

N
W
E
S
SADDLE ISLE - 1108
HIGH NORTH
THE NORTH
HOUSE MATFEN
LADY BRECK
RIVER CLUNK
CASTLE CATAR
LAKE DAO
CASTLE KEZI
LAKE IRU
THE MIDLANDS
CASTLE BENNK
MIDLAND BAY
LORD ROBT
LAKE FEN
THE SOUTH
DEEP SOUTH
KING BRUK
LAKE CHK
LORD NEMAN
CASTLE ELI
CASTLE SHAY

I Live To Serve

Following my rather encouraging conversation with King Bruk, I decided that he was right. I needed to be on the King's Council. Other than Lady Anto, who now was without land, I was the only one who was intelligent enough to stand a chance of preventing any more conflict, a situation that was paramount to the success of the king. In order to achieve this, I spent the proceeding weeks making amends for my actions and my disrespect towards both Lord Robt and Lord Neman. I sought them out in order to apologise and I worked for longer hours in the day to make sure that they too, like the king, were served properly. I hated it, of course. Those men deserved less praise than a child of seven years after successfully avoiding defecating in their bed through the night, but their egos needed stroking and so I was there to stroke. After a few weeks, Lady Breck arrived back to her home province, as invited by the king. It had been announced in the royal address that Lady Breck would be visiting under the negotiation to make her King Bruk's queen, which was perfectly reasonable considering that they were only siblings by house and not by blood. Despite many knowing prior to her arrival, she did not seem too knowledgeable as to why she made her return, which ultimately meant that she was all the more occupied with laying her eyes on me.

"My King, Lady Breck approaches," began Lord Robt.

The king's blood brothers had both remained in the capital rather than return to their respective provinces in order to talk their sister round to the idea of becoming queen. This was unnecessary due to their incompetence.

"Have Barrat escort our sister to her chamber," was King Bruk's order.

This command, although coming directly from their king, disgusted the two brothers of House Northorpe. They, despite growing to feel some respect towards me again, still mourned for their fallen brother and so wanted me nowhere near their sister, whom I famously loved. Lord Robt was particularly concerned.

"My King, are you sure that's suitable?"

"Yes, brother. I trust the boy."

"Can we trust you, boy?" Lord Neman directed at me, getting rather too close to my face for my liking.

"Yes, My Lords. Lady Breck is set to be queen and I only live to serve my monarch. I shall be nothing but respectful."

I hated playing their game but I was winning, so I had to continue sucking up to the fools.

"Say the words, bastard," Lord Robt demanded.

His smug face looked good enough to punch but it remained untouched.

"I know my place, Lord Robt," I reluctantly obliged.

With that, the grand doors were opened and I was allowed to trek down the steps to greet my beloved. She looked as beautiful as I remembered, perhaps even more. Her chamber was off to the east of the castle, something that she was accustomed to. I had been there before in different circumstances, yet this was the first time I hadn't felt completely ecstatic to pay the room a visit. She specifically requested to stay in the room that was once hers during the Prosperity Era, which now felt like a lifetime ago. This meant that venturing through the grand doors was unnecessary and so was to be avoided. I reached her cart and opened the door for her, offering my hand to assist her to the ground.

"Lady Breck, welcome home."

I tried to remain professional but I couldn't help but smile at seeing her again.

"Oh, Lord Barrat, I have been dying to see you ever since I left here."

Lady Breck hugged me tightly, to the disapproval of an onlooking Lord Robt. It was a look that forced me to gently push her away.

"Yes, same for you," I happily admitted. "But, may I humbly remind you, I am not Lord Barrat anymore, My Lady. I am to be called 'bastard' from now on."

Lady Breck, who knew of this change but never was one to hide her true feelings, looked over to her brother in disgust, fuming at this information.

"I know, but I refuse to call you that!"

"Thank you for your kindness, My Lady," was my rather compliant response.

I moved out of her way, giving her a chance to survey her old home.

"Would you like to see your brothers or would you like to rest? The king says that, if it be more suitable, you can wait until the morning before formally seeing him."

She looked at me with tears in her eyes.

"Yes, I would like to rest," she requested.

"As you wish, My Lady. I shall inform the king."

I ushered her in the direction of her chamber. She grabbed my arm as I turned and stopped me from leaving.

"No! My own servant shall inform the king and will take your place serving him until you are dismissed from my side, Barrat."

In overhearing this, Lord Robt rushed down the steps to put a stop to Lady Breck's alteration of order. He placed his hands on her shoulders and argued against her wish.

"My dear sister, this bastard is the king's personal servant."

She lifted Lord Robt's hands off of her.

"And I am King Bruk's personal guest. I'm sure he will respect my request."

With that, she led me off to her chamber and intended to converse with me as if I were still the lord that she fell in love with all those years ago. Of course, that was far beyond the realms of possibility considering my promise to King Bruk. I swore that I wouldn't touch her and that I would remain committed to my new position as a servant to the king.

****

"I hate this!"

Lady Breck sat gracefully, despite her anger, on her bed. I stood with my hands behind my back, waiting for further instruction.

"They have no right to treat you in this way, Barrat."

"My Lady, I am lucky to be alive. The king had every right to kill me after what I did to your poor brother, yet he spared me my life. Now, I live to serve."

She laughed at my performance, taking off her outer coat and throwing it to the floor.

"Well, you can stop that silly act immediately. We both know that you're not the subservient type, Barrat."

I looked down to the floor, ashamed.

"I'm a servant now, My Lady. It's not an act, it's a duty."

"Barrat..."

"... My Lady, listen, if you please. I must maintain my dignity as a servant if I am ever going to regain the trust of your brothers. The king has said that, once I prove my worth, I may be allowed to sit on the King's Council as an honorary advisor."

"That would be a good start," she smiled, optimistically, which made me smile in return.

"I believe that I am more suited to advising than sweeping floors. I'm certainly more skilled in the former, My Lady."

She stood and locked her eyes onto mine.

"Oh, Barrat, stop calling me 'My Lady,' and please remove your hands from behind your back! You look ridiculous."

"But, My Lady..."

"... That was an order," she interrupted, making me smile.

"Yes, of course."

"Now, if you're going to maintain this servant trope, then you will do as I command. I command you to kiss me, to love me, and to take me right here in this very room."

She rested her arms on my shoulder and put her lips to mine, but I had to pull away.

"Is something wrong?"

She glared at me in fear that I no longer looked at her with eyes full of love. I did, of course, but things had changed. I made a promise to the king - a king that I was already in much debt to. I should've been dead already and yet here I was, kissing my future queen.

"I promised..."

I paused, breaking down in tears, to the surprise of us both.

After a short while, I continued, "I promised I wouldn't touch you."

She reassured me by holding me in her arms, which was the first bit of comfort I'd felt since she kissed me goodbye those many months ago.

"It's okay, Barrat. I want you to. You don't have to be afraid, my love, because I want you to kiss me. I want you to touch me. I love you, Barrat. I have loved you since we were of six years and I will love you until my dying breath. You don't have to fear me."

"It's not you that I fear," I started to explain.

She brought me over to sit beside her on a bed that was much more comfortable than mine.

"The king made me promise not to touch you as you are to be his queen. And so, I can't."

She sat in shock. She did not want to be queen, not at all. She had fallen in love with the High North once more, as she did when she was a child, and she wanted to remain there. She loved her brother, but not in that way. She could only ever love me in that way.

"I won't be his queen," she said, sternly.

"I'm not sure you'll have a choice, My Lady."

"I am not your lady! I am your beloved, do you hear me? I love you..."

She did not mean to shout but she couldn't help herself.

"... And I love you," I interrupted, again. "I always have, I always will. But I am nothing. I have nothing. No title, no family, and no freedom. You cannot marry me, Breck. Your brother, the king, won't allow it. Not after what I did."

"I don't care about all that."

"But he does," I pointed out.

As risky as it was, I allowed her to rest her head on my shoulder and I kissed it softly before continuing.

"At least if you are queen, we can still be friends."

"I don't want to be your friend. I want to be yours."

She kissed me again. I can't say that I would've kept my promise to the king if we weren't interrupted by a rather loud knock on the door, causing Lady Breck to rather frustratedly sigh.

"Enter," she eventually demanded.

It was another servant who, despite that we were of the same lowly status, seemed to have great hatred for me. As he entered, I stood from the bed and placed my hands back behind my back. The servant smugly smirked, bearing his yellow-stained teeth.

"Bastard, the king has requested that you see him in his chamber."

"Yes, I will be there right away."

I turned to face Lady Breck, who looked back at me in return, her beautiful, deep brown eyes tainted with sadness.

"Rest well, Lady Breck."

"And you, Barrat. I hope to see you soon."

"As do I you, My Lady." With that, I left her alone.

*** * * ***

"My King, you wished to see me?"

I knelt down in front of him.

"Yes, Barrat. Stand before me," I did as he commanded and stood on the opposite side of the desk at which he was sitting. "I take it that my sister is well."

"Erm, yes, My King," I replied, lacking any real conviction.

I couldn't shake the thought that he, somehow, knew of our kiss.

"You don't sound too convinced, boy."

I apologised and looked to the floor but then, once realising who I was addressing, lifted my eyes straight back up.

"She just seems a little upset about my new status."

He took some time to sip his wine.

"Well, that was to be expected I suppose. She isn't the only one. As you know, I still regret your position. Hopefully it will soon be altered."

"Thank you, My King. You do me a great honour."

I couldn't help but smile. The king smiled too, before moving the conversation forward.

"Do you remember, not so long ago, when I told you of my wish to have you seated on my council?"

"Yes, My King," I answered.

It was all that I had thought about since he mentioned it. Well, that and Lady Breck, of course. She was constantly on my mind. He ushered for me to refill his cup, which I did carefully.

"I believe it is time for you to prove your worth," he announced. "I fear that peace isn't going to be maintained in the kingdom and my council have failed to enhance our position thus far. So, if you were in my shoes right now, what would you do?"

I paused, considering exactly what this opportunity could lead to.

"Well, My King, I would remove them, for they would be too big for feet as small as mine," I quipped.

He laughed, luckily, at my attempt to humour him.

I continued, "In all seriousness though, My King, if I were you I would reconsider the marriage to Lady Breck."

His eyebrows raised, which I didn't take as a good sign.

"And why would that be?"

"Please, My King, do hear me out."

I readjusted my rags so they sat more comfortably as I prepared to present my analysis on the situation, which I had thought about greatly.

"I know it may seem within my best interest to keep Lady Breck as far away from marriage as I can, and I would be lying if I said that I didn't love her more than anything else in this cruel world, but that is not why I would advise against it. You see, My King, the Great Packsaddle War may have won you the kingdom but it didn't wipe out all of your enemies. My many years as a trader of the provinces allowed me to meet many a friend, and through those very friends I have gained word of the situation in the Midlands, even whilst confined here."

"You must be much liked across the kingdom," King Bruk said with a smirk.

He sipped some more of his wine. I wasn't too pleased to be interrupted, but he was my king so I ignored it.

"I like to think so, My King. Many Midland Savages remain loyal to those of House Wharram, despite the fact that Lord Robt now resides in the province. I'm sure that Lord Neman's decision to rename three castles after their fallen patricians hasn't helped our cause with the Savages. They are not as forgiving as those in the High North, you see, but what's done is done. I've heard of two thousand Savages keen to charge alongside any patrician who is willing to remove the crown from your possession, with your head along with it. Marrying Lady Breck would enhance the Northorpe succession, that is for sure. But the Northorpe succession can be enhanced by any woman of noble birth in the kingdom. Lord Robt made a rather good observation, uncharacteristically I dare say, in regard to those of House Matfen, who still reside comfortably in the North. He said that an alliance of words alone is weak, which is true. He did somewhat ruin his point by suggesting a further war so soon after the last, which any man famed for his ability in battle would strive for, of course. You rightfully dismissed his ludicrous suggestion but then, with all due respect, made that the end of it."

"What are you suggesting?"

His intrigue would only work in my favour.

"If I were you, I would aim higher than your own sister in marriage, My King."

I could tell that my playful slandering of his family was beginning to overstep so I toned it down slightly.

"With only a simple alliance of words between yourself and Lady Daid, who expressed great desire to be queen during the Great Packsaddle War, I believe that you are in danger of a rebellion from your friends in the North. I am also led to believe, and do correct me if I'm wrong, that both Kinby and Wonin of House Wharram are still at large."

"That is correct," he confirmed.

"Thank you, My King. Your successes in battle and your subsequent rule have left two members of both House Wharram and House Hepston without a home. The Hepston girls strive only for peace and Lady Anto has my utmost respect, as I'm sure she has yours too, but if they see that another leader can achieve peace more effectively than yourself, they will back that horse without question. Let's not forget that they took no part in the previous war and so have plenty of men to spare if another was to break out. Lady Daid has granted you with her support but is scornful, as you know, due to her lack of seat on the King's Council. She is a bitter woman, My King. She won't have taken that lightly. Let's say that Lady Daid decides to challenge you for your crown, may the gods forbid it. If she could get the support of the vengeful Savages and those of House Hepston, which is certainly not out of reach, then House Northorpe stands no chance of winning. They'd take the High North with ease and both the South and Deep South would be doomed."

"That's a rather frightful thought, Barrat," King Bruk confessed.

He sat in his chair as pale as a ghost, which meant that I was getting through to him. I knew, even then, that it was of vast importance for the kingdom's hopes for peace that the king listened to my advice.

"Yes, it most certainly is."

I decided it was time to make my suggestion.

"So, My King, to answer your question: if I were in your position I would call off all plans to marry Lady Breck immediately. Lord Robt was right to think that marriage is the best way to strengthen your position, but there is only one true way of combating the horrific prospect of further bloodshed and marrying Lady Breck is not it, I can assure you."

"What is the way then, Barrat?"

As I spoke he looked on intently, hanging on my every word.

"The way forward is certainly one that won't be too much of a hindrance on your happiness, My King. You must further strengthen your alliance with the North by marrying the most beautiful girl in all the land: Lady Oline, daughter of Mar, of House Matfen. That way, the North will be committed to you by a sacred vow, which is much stronger than words alone, as you well know, My King."

He didn't confirm his opinions on the matter. Instead, he simply thanked me for my time and advice and instructed me to get some rest. Obviously, I did what he said and was happy to do so as I was rather tired. I wished him a good sleep and left for my chamber.

Sir Rufus, son of Brant

Over the many years I spent travelling across Saddle Isle, I was fortunate enough to meet a plethora of great people. Those people included many of my fellow patricians, some of whom I became relatively close with despite not necessarily seeing them properly. But even the kindest of patricians never had the natural likeability of some of the more common people of the land. Even Lady Anto and Lady Oline, who were both incredibly kind, more so than others, had been taught since childhood that it was their duty to be that way, especially to fellow patricians. I had grown up with the kindness of Miss Norma who looked after me as a child, teaching me how to read, write, and act with decorum and acclaim. I was also blessed with the friendship of the inspirational Miss Frith, whose death during the Battle of Midland Bay caused great despair. I have a lot of respect and admiration for both of them and have always considered them as maternal figures in my life, but it was Mister Rufus, son of Brant, who I had the deepest of friendships with in the end. I was, of course, introduced properly to him by my beloved after first encountering him when I was merely a prisoner in the South. He was the most loyal man I ever met. He had been a dedicated protector to King Bruk and his family, and I have spoken to Lady Breck about him on occasion and derived that she too was a great admirer of the man. He then went on to protect many others after the Great Packsaddle War, including myself and my very own daughter, eventually. All of his protection only accentuated his gentle nature and his wisdom.

*** * * ***

Mister Rufus grew up in a small village named Clapton in the south of England. He was the son of a farmer's daughter, who was impregnated by a knight from the local town whom she never married. From what he tells me, his father apparently died during the Battle of Hastings in 1066, fighting on the losing side for King Harold. His mother and himself were disowned by his grandfather who, despite knowing that Mister Rufus' father was a knight, saw his daughter's illegitimate pregnancy as a means for shame on his family. And so, Mister Rufus and his mother, Miss Brant, travelled to Northorpe in order to make a new start. Miss Brant had experience of farm life and so found it easy to find some work, but the good fortune for the two soon ran out. Miss Brant fell ill to the point where she lost her job. This meant that Mister Rufus was forced to beg as a child in order to get food for himself and his mother. More often than not, people showed kindness to the child and provided him with some bread. On some occasions he was even given some meat by generous folk, which was worth much coin. However, there were days when there was no food to spare and so they were forced to go hungry.

By the time Mister Rufus turned ten, his mother had unfortunately passed away and so he was left alone. He spent three months having to fend for himself before being taken in by a relatively old couple who had no children of their own. The old woman took care of him as if he was her son and taught him of the kindness and love that existed in the world. Eventually, when the old man could no longer cope with the strain of work, Mister Rufus took over his duty selling candles in the busiest part of the village. The old woman would make the candles in a small hut at the back of their home, then Mister Rufus would carry them into the village's centre square to sell. Eventually, they made enough coin to expand their candle manufacturing to the point where the purchase of a donkey and cart was feasible, which made a real difference to their sales. By 1094, two years before the voyage to Saddle Isle, a now aged Mister Rufus was left alone once again.

He carried on the candle making for a while but never had the same touch as his guardian of many years. He also struggled with taking on the responsibility of both making and selling and so, when the opportunity for a new start was presented to him through the voyage to Saddle Isle, he was rather excited about the prospect.

When he made it to the isle he was told that he would reside in the South, which made sense considering that he had lived in the same village as those of House Northorpe for the vast majority of his life. He took up the role of welder for a while but found the technical aspect of it quite difficult. He eventually decided that the option of serving in the castle was suitable for him, considering that he would have to live alone in a village but would get the communal experience of living with his fellow paid servants in Castle Sear. Spending years carrying large collations of candles built up his upper body strength, making him ideal to act as a guard for the patricians of House Northorpe. After spending all that time around the family, Mister Rufus grew rather affectionate for the young patricians, and that was strongly reciprocated. His wisdom and advice was greatly appreciated, especially by King Bruk, who initially found his leadership role to be quite a daunting prospect. This made the event of Mister Rufus being made the official chief guard for the king, a role that no one else had ever been deemed loyal enough to be honoured with, a rather special occasion for all in attendance.

****

King Bruk wanted the great man to have an event for this great honour, but its close proximity to the possible royal wedding meant that another big event in the kingdom wouldn't be financially feasible. Despite the large event being off the table, King Bruk wanted to make sure that the appointment was both dignified and respectful. In order to achieve this, King Bruk ordered for both members of the King's Council to be there. Lady

Breck was also in attendance as she was still in the capital under the impression that she was to become King Bruk's queen, despite her contempt for the idea. Of course, all three were delighted to attend the event and to honour their guard and servant. Mister Rufus was told to enter the room and was rather surprised to see all four of his most favourable patricians awaiting his arrival.

"My King. My Lords and Lady. Is everything okay?"

He dropped to one knee out of respect and, with a slight struggle, stood straight again.

"Everything is as great as it can be," King Bruk said to his old advisor. "Mister Rufus, please stand before me."

He moved directly in front of his king.

"Hello, Mister Rufus. How have you been?" Lady Breck interrupted.

She hadn't had the pleasure of seeing him since her arrival in the capital and was rather happy to see him after some time away.

"I have been just fine, thank you, My Lady. You look well, my dear."

"Thank you, Mister Rufus. It is so nice to see you."

"You too, My Lady."

King Bruk, who was slightly frustrated at his sister for her interruption, saw this as an opportunity to regain control. The king shot her a sly look.

"Well, now that you've been reacquainted, sister, may I proceed?"

Lady Breck, who realised her foolishness, was quite embarrassed.

"Yes, My King. Please continue."

"Mister Rufus, you have been a great servant to myself and my family for many a year now. It is safe to say that, without you, we would have really struggled to adapt to our new home and changing situations. We couldn't have been luckier than we have been."

"Oh, My King," he said, welling up with pride. "Those words are incredibly kind. It has been a truly great honour to have served such a loving and compassionate family. I only wish that Lord Suln, whom I had so much appreciation for, could be here too."

"We all do," commented Lord Robt.

I assume that was a relatively obvious show of contempt towards Lady Breck's remaining affiliation for me.

"Yes. I do hope that I am still of service to you all."

King Bruk, on realising that the intention of this meeting wasn't completely clear, made sure to clarify that his job was not at risk.

"Mister Rufus, I am personally grateful for your service for all these years. I trust you more than I would anyone else. Because of this, I would like to name you as my chief guard."

Mister Rufus immediately dropped down to one knee in respect.

"My King, this is a truly great honour."

King Bruk complimented the chief guard as he helped him back to his feet.

"A great honour that you deserve. From this day forth, you shall be Sir Rufus, son of Brant."

"My King, I shall thank you for this honour with my eternal protection."

They celebrated the event with plenty of wine, something that added to Sir Rufus's pride. He had loved the young patricians for many a year and so knowing that he had earned their respect meant the world to the old man.

The Lackey Lord

I had never before been allowed to attend a royal address. I had been present for some council meetings, as I have recounted, but that was only in the context of my position as the king's servant. The addresses were aimed primarily towards the most important citizens of the kingdom to keep people from across the land up to date with what was happening, so the fact that I had received an invite was a good sign. The address was the first time I'd seen Lady Breck in over a week and she looked as beautiful as ever. Leadership looked good on her. She had left the High North in a prosperous position before heading down to the South, which was a job made easier by the fact that everyone truly loved her. She brought a gentleness to the place that had been lacking under the leadership of my sister. Lady Catar's rule in the High North created much produce and certainly put us in a good trading position, but I'd be lying if I said that the people were happy. They needed time to spend with their families and to enjoy their lives, but over the twelve years that Catar controlled the province it was certainly more work and less play. Perhaps that contributed to the High North having the poorest population statistics across the isle. My beloved was destined to change this outlook. I'm sure that Lady Breck's long absence from my home saddened many throughout the province, which only ever made me proud of what she had managed to achieve in such a short amount of time. But, as it stood, it didn't really matter. She was about to be torn away from it all and handed the role of queen instead.

****

"Please stand for King Bruk, son of Betra, of House Northorpe," said the familiar loud voice of the announcer, whose name eludes me, I am ashamed to say.

The king made his way to his throne as the crowds called out to him. It was promising to see so many people supporting King Bruk. Despite the fact that I had been his prisoner since the Battle of Midland Bay, I still thought that he was the best man for the job. He had the respect of all in the land and he made sure that he granted his people respect in return.

"Please, be seated, if that opportunity finds you," began the king.

Most of the crowd did not have a seat to sit on, but those that did followed what he commanded.

"It is so lovely to, once again, see so many dedicated to the maintenance of our prosperous kingdom. I am truly honoured by your presence, especially those who have travelled from the furthest provinces. I shall hopefully make my address worth your journey."

His subjects appreciated the kindness that was conveyed through his words.

The king began properly, "Firstly, those of the High North will be wondering if they will ever see their leader back in their province. Well, you'll be pleased to know that Lady Breck, daughter of Ferma, of House Northorpe, is free to travel back. I can assure you that she adores the High North and has missed her new home whilst being here with her family. Similarly, those of the Midlands and the Deep South will be wondering about their leaders. Well, I can announce that Lord Neman, son of Betra, of House Northorpe shall be reporting back to his province as early as tomorrow; and Lord Robt, son of Betra, of House Northorpe shall do the same shortly after."

This, to my surprise, seemed to please the crowd.

"You have been told of the proposed marriage between myself and Lady Breck over the last few weeks, and I am sure that many of you have been excited about the prospect of a royal wedding. However, after much discussion with Lady Breck and many an advisor, we have decided that a marriage between the two of us would not be beneficial for the kingdom. I have instead been in discussions with Lady Daid, daughter of Rean, of House Matfen, who presides over the North as she did so well throughout the Prosperity Era, in regard to the proposed aligning of our two houses through a marriage between myself and the beautiful Lady Oline, daughter of Mar, of House Matfen. Lady Oline shall be invited, as Lady Breck was, to spend time in the capital and to make her decision as to whether or not she wishes to be your queen. I, as many of you will, hope that she accepts my proposal as I believe that she would make the finest queen for such a deserving kingdom."

This was met with a rather loud cheer, which brought me a weird sense of pride. Yes, it was the obvious alignment, but still, it was I who convinced the king to change his position on the matter despite being a mere servant at the time.

"When I was honoured with the crown, I promised to create a fair and just kingdom in which those who need rewarding are justly rewarded, and those who need punishment are fairly punished. As you know, at the beginning of my reign I decided that the Bastard of Saddle Isle, formerly known as Lord Barrat, son of Nea, of House Pearson, was to serve his king as punishment for his crimes against my house. As you can imagine, the reality of losing my brother: Lord Suln, son of Ferma, of House Northorpe, took a toll on my emotions and I acted rather hastily in my decision. Yes, Barrat was responsible for my brother's death, but was I not responsible for his brother's death also? Was his brother the one to storm to this province with a thirst for power? I knew Lord Shay, son of Nea, of House Pearson rather well and so would comfortably say that he was just as reluctant as Barrat was to invade. What some of you may not know is that, without Barrat, a lot of innocent people of the South would have lost their lives. Catar, whom I won't honour with her title, planned on invading without sending word - an honourless act from an honourless woman. But Barrat opted against her order and sent word so that the elderly, the vulnerable, and the children, who are the future of our land, could get to a safe place during the battle. The pain that Barrat brought to our family meant that he deserved his punishment but, as far as I am concerned, that punishment is now served. Many of you will know of his previous success in leadership and honour during his tenure as Head of Trade throughout many years of the Prosperity Era, and so will know of his vast wisdom despite his tender age. For that reason, I would like him to come forward now."

I did what he said and made my way in front of his throne, kneeling before him as was customary. He smiled as I looked onto his face.

"I, King Bruk, son of Betra, of House Northorpe, hereby reinstate your titles, making you Lord Barrat, son of Nea, of House Pearson, once again. You shall take a seat upon my council and act not as a servant who cleans my sheets but as one that cleanses our kingdom from conflict and greed. Rise to your feet, Lord Barrat."

As I rose, the crowd applauded. Even Lord Robt and Lord Neman applauded, although rather half-heartedly. Those from the High North even cheered for me.

"Thank you, My King," I said, with earnestness.

He spoke only to me, maintaining privacy through the continuing applause.

"I need you to start drafting a plan to maintain peace. Do whatever needs to be done. I worry for the future of this kingdom if conflict were to arise again."

I accepted his order and bowed in front of him.

"Yes, My King. I shall begin right away."

****

"I told him it was a bad idea," moaned Lord Robt.

Before returning to the Midlands, Lord Robt was asked by his king to travel to the North with those who came down for the royal address in order to accompany Lady Oline back to the capital. This group included Lady Daid, of course, as well as a good friend of mine who I met when I was only of fifteen years. They gave me this account.

"The kid is good and you know it," disagreed Lady Daid, who was less concerned with the king's decision to reinstate me.

"The kid killed my brother."

"That's not what I meant."

I never trusted Lady Daid, but she did have a good eye for what was best for the kingdom.

She continued, "He's a smart man and certainly has the charisma to convince the king that whatever he says should go."

"Does that not concern you?" asked Lord Robt.

It clearly concerned him. Before I was told of this conversation by my aforementioned friend, I genuinely thought I had won Lord Robt over. I suppose I was fallible afterall.

"I would trust Lord Barrat's mind more than yours, my old friend," Lady Daid admitted with a loaded laugh.

Lord Robt didn't find humour in her words.

She continued once more."The king has been preparing him for this since he was just a boy. I know because I was there to see it. He's smug, but Lord Barrat has a greater mind than any other patrician that I've met. For that, I will say that I trust him, as foolish as that may prove to be."

Lord Robt was keen on changing her opinion about me.

"You know that it was Barrat who suggested that your sister should become queen, right?" he provoked.

She didn't wait to see if Lord Robt wished to continue.

"I do know, and I think it's a good idea. She is the most beautiful girl in all the land and a true symbol of kindness. If anyone should take up the job of looking pretty and making the people smile, it's Lady Oline."

"Of course you'd like someone from your house being queen," Lord Robt responded, slightly unimpressed by Lady Daid.

Lord Robt was a proud man, and stubborn too. I am also proud and stubborn, but I actually make useful suggestions and have knowledge to offer, something that he lacked.

"Tell me, how does that differ from what Breck could do?" he asked.

"Breck's not as pretty," she provocatively replied.

I would have to disagree with the leader of the North, but that may be ever so slightly biased. Of course, Lady Breck will always be the most beautiful to me.

"Oline is not as popular. The only reason Breck won't be queen is because of her love for Barrat. Do you not find it bizarre how Breck was all set to be queen before Lord Barrat was reinstated as a patrician?"

That was an easy assumption to make but it was somewhat fair. I would've hated to see Lady Breck marry someone else, especially someone who wouldn't have made her happy, but I was a servant when I advised against their marriage. There was no hope of Lady Breck and I marrying at that point, so there was no real benefit for us either way.

"We are both too biased to have this conversation properly. Either way, it doesn't matter now. Lady Oline is to be queen and that is final."

"Yes, she will be, and I imagine she will be a fine queen."

"And I imagine that Lady Breck will be very happy once she marries Lord Barrat."

Teasing the king's chief advisor brought much joy to Lady Daid, especially when she was there to see his face drop at the thought.

She continued, "What? He's a lord again now. As far as I can tell she can have her way with him."

****

On my way to pay a visit to my love, Lord Neman stopped me in the corridor. Now that she wasn't to be queen and I was a lord again, there was no reason why a visit between two old friends and lovers should cause any stir within Castle Eli, especially before one was set to leave. But still, bumping into Lord Neman put me slightly on edge, perhaps because of how accustomed I was to being trapped. I smiled, hoping not to aggravate him.

"Lord Neman, how can I help you?"

"You can cheer that sister of mine up for one," he suggested with a sort of comforting laugh.

It was nice to feel accepted.

He continued, "She is slightly annoyed that she's being sent away as soon as you can be together again."

"That annoyance is very much mutual, I can assure you. But I understand that she is needed in the High North."

I missed her so much and so the thought of being away from her once more made me feel slightly sick.

"She is indeed," Lord Neman confirmed.

I'm not sure he understood why she was needed, in all honesty, but I just smiled.

He continued, "I shan't keep you for long, I promise. I just wanted to congratulate you on your new position on the King's Council. I'm sure you will be of great service to the king and his kingdom."

I could tell that he was commanded to have this conversation with me by the king, but I told myself that there was some truth hidden within Lord Neman's words.

"Thank you for your kindness, My Lord."

"You are climbing up the ranks rather quickly. From servant to advisor. A lackey to a lord. At this rate, you'll be king by the end of the year."

He looked smug. I didn't like it.

"I hope not," I admitted with a laugh, mainly to match his chuckle.

"Wouldn't you want to be king, Lord Barrat?"

An interesting question posed by a far less interesting man. The answer itself was not too interesting either. No, I never wanted to be king. I lack intimidation and poise. I was the most intelligent man on the council. In fact, I was possibly the most intelligent man on the isle. Yet, intelligent men shouldn't face power head on but rather pull the strings from behind the scenes instead, as I was now set to do. Besides, I had no desire for that throne. By all accounts it was rather uncomfortable - unfit for a king. It had the finest cushion in all the land placed upon it and yet always remained uncomfortable. Having a crown placed on your head is always coupled with a big target on your back, and a meek man like myself would get shot at from all angles if I were to wear both crown and target. But that's beside the point. I had no desire for that throne because I had found something much more valuable. I had the woman that I loved in arm's reach, and my arms are where she belonged. Since I was of six years I wanted to spend my life with her. That was before I knew of marriage, or sex, or love. I just liked having a friend. I suppose that's where all true love starts, friendship. And now it was so much more than that. You see, whenever I'm with her I'm not Lord Barrat, son of Nea, of House Pearson. I'm not the Bastard of Saddle Isle, either. I'm not a bastard son of King William II of England, or any other unnecessary title or name. No, I am simply hers, but that's all I ever wanted to be.

"No, My Lord, I don't think I would."

The Sacred Vows

After what I imagine was a rather tedious journey from the North in the company of Lord Robt, Lady Oline had been welcomed into the capital with great excitement, which was lovely to see. She seemed rather optimistic for her future as queen. Whether or not she was happy to be marrying King Bruk remained unknown to me for a long while, but I don't suppose that really mattered. She stayed in Castle Eli for a few months before eventually agreeing to the marriage officially. Within that period, I got to know her well and we became rather good friends. I had met her before, of course, but was never allowed to speak with her for long durations. Lady Daid treated her like the jewel of the North - too precious to be involved in anything of real importance within the province. So, with me being a man of real importance, whenever I visited the North in my trading days she was often encouraged to scuttle back to her chamber once any welcome gathering had come to a natural conclusion. Those welcome gatherings consisted of a small conversation with each of the provinces' patricians and nothing more.

Within these two or so months in which she had been learning of the role of queen, I was reassured about the decision to marry her off to King Bruk. She seemed born for the role, so kind and loving to all that she met and certainly calm and understanding enough to accept that she wouldn't see her husband all too much, as he often had many important things to attend to. After the proposal was accepted, plans for the wedding could commence properly and that's exactly how things panned out. Lady Oline was then invited to join the King's Council, which she refused in the end after a rather lengthy conversation with Lady Breck. It was never fully revealed to me exactly what was said during that discussion and so I cannot say for sure what her reason for declining was exactly. I found it a real shame that she turned down the opportunity. It would have been nice to have someone alongside the king and myself who wasn't a complete incompetent fool. It was, instead, suggested that Lady Daid take up the role on her behalf, but that didn't exactly go down well with the king. King Bruk very much blamed Lady Daid and my sister for the war breaking out in the first place and, considering that many of his loved ones died because of that (which I too am to blame for, although he never spoke about it with me after my reinstatement), he was less than keen on the idea of Lady Daid having such a prominent role in the kingdom.

Contrastingly, I rather liked the idea and expressed to the king himself my thoughts on the matter. I never trusted her, as I've said before, but that is no reason to prevent her from being close. I was taught to keep a close eye on those I did not trust, and I believed that this was the perfect excuse to get some much needed surveillance on the woman before she had any stupid ideas. The king, on listening to my proposal, said that he needed time to think and so time he got. Despite what I had said, I was rather glad that Lady Daid hadn't been added to the King's Council before my plan for peace was presented. I had finished my proposal and something told me that the provincial leader of the North was not going to be too pleased with my plans for her, so perhaps a compromise in which she received her coveted seat on the council in exchange for her cooperation with my plan could be arranged to aid us with her temper.

****

As the wedding day came upon us, the doors to the Great Hall opened. King Bruk and Lady Oline walked past their people and their fellow patricians, who were all in attendance, and made their way to the rear of the hall to stand in front of the throne. This was excluding Lady Wonin and Lord Kinby of House Wharram, of course, as they were still in hiding. Both the bride and groom looked incredibly regal in their linen clothing and seemed rather pleased with how everything had turned out. Linen was a fine choice as it opposed the customary wool worn by most on the average day. We were lucky enough to have the climate to produce linen on the isle, but finding those with the skills to utilise it was a trickier task. It was certainly a luxury.

Technically, marriage was considered a lawful act as opposed to one of religion, mainly because the majority of patricians generally didn't partake in Leonism. However, to please the Leonist common folk, their gods did get mentioned in what were known as the sacred vows - the lawful words that tied two people together in marriage. This was the way during the Prosperity Era but was open for change going into the Autocracy Era. As it happened, King Bruk was a believer in the gods and so the mention of them remained in the sacred vows after his coronation, despite their trivial nature, however they were made an optional addition to a couple's vows. There were no priests, as such, on the isle. Because of this, the marriage officiator was often an elder of the land, who generally wasn't all that elderly, or a man of great nobility who the wedded deemed suitable. In this case, Sir Rufus, son of Brant, was named officiator - a great personal honour.

"Please be seated," requested Sir Rufus.

Like most addresses, there were actually very few in the room who were given a seat. I, along with my fellow patricians, was one of the more fortunate people. The seats were located towards the front, as you'd expect, and so the further back you were the less likely you were to be seated.

Sir Rufus continued, "We are gathered here on this fine day to see the bonding of these two servants of our land in front of the people and the gods. Through these sacred vows, you: King Bruk, son of Betra, of House Northorpe and you: Lady Oline, daughter of Mar, of House Matfen pledge yourselves to the gods and to each other for eternity. And so, to show the unity in which you pledge, please say the sacred vows."

The vows were written by a group of elders when we first arrived on the isle all those thirteen years ago and have been a staple of lawful love throughout our land ever since - not that this was a marriage of love. Not yet.

In unison, the two spoke the vows:

"In the eyes of the gods, we, servants to their power, become united.

In the eyes of each other, we become united.

We pledge to be faithful to each other,

To love and respect each other,

And to never break the bond we have formed."

Not the greatest of words in my opinion, but I suppose it does the job.

"To symbolise your union, King Bruk, please take this unity pendant and place it around your beloved's neck."

He handed a pendant to his king, who did as he said.

He turned to King Bruk's bride, "And, Lady Oline, please take this unity pendant and place it around Your King's neck."

Again, Sir Rufus handed her a pendant. She placed it around King Bruk's neck, before curtseying before him.

"Under the protection of the gods, I now pronounce you husband and wife. Please give a round of applause to King Bruk, son of Betra, of House Northorpe and his new wife: Queen Oline, daughter of Mar, of House Matfen and House Northorpe."

I should probably point out that, in noble marriages, only the one being added to the house was given the extended title to their name. That person was the one deemed lesser by society. This depended on who held the power in the marriage, so all of House Northorpe were deemed to be higher as they were connected to the Crown. To the sound of applause, they made their way back through the crowd and headed straight for their chambers. I was pleased to have been given some time off due to the wedding, which I spent with Lady Breck, of course. My mind was, admittedly, elsewhere at times, though. I grew rather worried about offering the proposal for peace that I was due to present to the King's Council once we reconvened.

*** * * ***

Eventually, the time did come for me to present my plan for the future to the King's Council. As nervous as I was, which wasn't like me at all, I knew that this plan had the potential of working and so wasn't specifically nervous about that. What I was nervous about was how my fellow council members would react considering their seemingly selfish approach to power up to that point. It is quite unfair of me to call both Lord Neman and Lord Robt selfish considering that my plan allowed me to have the one thing that I'd ever wanted, but I'm sure we can look past that detail considering that it does, technically, make sense within the plan itself.

"Thank you all for attending today. I know that the king has had his new marriage to occupy himself with, so thank you specifically for your presence today, King Bruk."

I was granted leadership for this particular meeting. I should point out that on the very rare occasions when we had council meetings without the king, they were poorly led by the chief advisor, Lord Robt.

"I have finished my plan for peace and would like to present my ideas today, as long as the king doesn't have more urgent matters."

"I do not, Lord Barrat. Please, do continue," King Bruk confirmed.

"Now, the king has led by example by marrying for the benefit of peace and so I implore my fellow lords to consider doing the same. This is to be considered as part of our duty in protecting our people."

"That doesn't sound too promising," Lord Neman remarked with a nervous laugh.

I didn't appreciate his interruption.

"I assure you, My Lord, it's not as bad as you'd think. My plan centres around marriage to bond potential enemies to the Crown."

"That seems sensible," commented King Bruk.

"I shall tell of my plan for ourselves specifically in due course, but first I would like to ask Lord Robt how his search for Lady Wonin and Lord Kinby is going."

The annoyed look on his face told me that he had been unsuccessful thus far, which I already knew, of course. I couldn't pass up the chance to somewhat embarrass him in front of his brothers.

"We have not yet found them, My Lord," he responded, reluctantly.

I could see in his eyes how his anger grew. It was delicious.

"Well, that's a real shame," I provocatively remarked. "But I believe that my proposal could help us to find some success in that regard."

"How, exactly?" asked the king, who seemed equally concerned by my suggestion as I was for his reaction.

"By not punishing them, as such, My King," I nervously answered.

This didn't exactly go down too well, so I was forced to explain my thinking further. I had expected this, admittedly.

"Look, we don't have them in captivity at the moment. We don't even know where they are and so they have the upper hand. For all we know, they could be planning a vengeful attack right now. If we can get them on our side then we can ensure that the people of this kingdom don't have to go through any more pain and suffering unnecessarily. I know Wonin rather well from my time as Head of Trade and she is a lovely person, I assure you. I know that she wouldn't have opposed the laws that we asked Eli to implement and so she can be trusted with some semblance of power. As for Kinby, well, we know he's a ratty man but one that can certainly be controlled."

After a pause, King Bruk nodded for me to proceed.

"Thank you, My King. I mean no offence by this, Lord Robt, but your lack of control over the Midlands is causing me great concern."

I meant offence, the guy was a fool.

"It is causing me great concern, also," seconded the king, who shot his brother with a disappointed look.

"I believe that the Midland Savages are more likely to accept you if someone they know and appreciate also resided in the castle. Besides, we need to solidify the bond between those who remain of House Wharram and the Crown. For those reasons, I propose a marriage between yourself and Wonin, making her a lady of the Midlands once more."

"No way," was not the answer from Lord Robt that I had hoped for.

"Please, Lord Robt, consider it."

I was practically begging, which he enjoyed more than I'd have liked.

I continued, "Maintaining order in the Midlands is of paramount importance and you need all the help you can get. You are failing, Lord Robt, respectfully. She's a woman of much beauty and she is a kind soul. I'm sure that you can find a way to make it work."

After a pause, Lord Robt agreed to consider it.

"Now, Lord Neman, we have a similar scenario with you. The people of the Deep South are peaceful, as I'm sure you've noticed. Lady Anto, daughter of Elan, of House Hepston has been nothing but respectful since the king took to his throne but has since received no reward for her continued cooperation. Her sister and herself both live outside of castle walls and I for one see that as a mistake on our part. Because of this, I propose that you, Lord Neman, wed Lady Anto and allow her to take her place back in the castle in which she grew up."

I knew of his attraction to her, and now she had fully blossomed into a beautiful woman so I was not too worried about his answer.

"I shall agree to that proposal, for the benefit of our kingdom," was his noble response.

I'm sure I wasn't the only one who could sense his lustful satisfaction at the prospect, but it was still nice to have some support for my plan.

"You do us a kind deed, My Lord," I respectfully replied.

It was safe to say that my time as a servant was the only reason why I was so good with all the unnecessary niceties.

I continued, "As well as this, I plan on rewarding the selflessness of Lord Neman's sister-in-law to be with a marriage to the fine Lord Angull, son of Limo, of House Matfen. Because Queen Oline, daughter of Mar, of House Matfen and House Northorpe is bonded to the Crown by law, House Matfen are sworn to support the Crown. These marriages will solidify the bond with those of House Hepston, which may not seem necessary now but may well be in the future."

"But Lady Aott is still just a girl," complained Lord Robt.

"I'm sure she shall bleed soon. We shall just have to hope that Lord Angull is more patient than his sister. I refer to Lady Daid, of course."

There wasn't much else I could say about that matter.

"Speaking of," began King Bruk.

The king seemed pleased with my plan but was worried about what was to follow.

"What are your plans with our potential new council member?"

I was most worried about this proposal, to be frank.

"I'm glad you asked, My King. I'm not sure you'll be too glad of my answer, though. We still have the rather difficult issue of dealing with Kinby. Wonin is manageable and I do hope that you, Lord Robt, see her fit to be your bride. But Kinby is less desirable as a partner. Unfortunately, the only suitors left are Lady Daid and your sister, My King."

"I refuse to let him marry Breck," King Bruk insisted with real fury in his voice.

"And I would never ask you to curse her with such a marriage, My King. But that just leaves us with Lady Daid, who will definitely refuse to marry Kinby. He did attack her province, if you remember."

"So your plan doesn't work then, Lord Barrat?" smirked Lord Robt.

"Well, it might yet, My Lord. I don't worry about convincing Kinby to marry the brute. The promise of a full royal pardon and the chance to stop fleeing from place to place should be enough. But Lady Daid is more difficult, as I've said. However, if we were to strike a deal with her then we may be in luck."

The king predicted my suggestion.

"Ah, I see. You propose that, rather than letting her join the council on the merit of my wife, we trade her a seat on the council for a marriage to Kinby."

"Yes, that is my proposal, My King," I confirmed.

King Bruk stopped to think for a while.

I added to my point, "My King, the only reason you are still considering giving her a position in the first place is because of what I said about keeping our enemies close. She is currently our biggest threat, but Kinby is our second. If they both reside here then we can keep an eye on them at all times. It's the best place for them."

"But what about the North?" asked Lord Neman, rather reasonably for a change.

"The North shall be led by Lord Angull. Perhaps that would be enough to convince him that marrying the young Hepston lady whilst she remains unbled, isn't all that bad."

The king took some more time.

"You're right," King Bruk eventually said, confirming what I already knew. "It is the only way to convince Lady Daid, if it is even enough. I shall allow you to try to convince her that the marriage is for the best."

I nodded with appreciation at his understanding. It was going to be tough to convince the brute that this was beneficial but I was certain that the allure of some remnant of power would be enough to sway her into agreement. Having said that, I was keen on sorting out my other arrangements before tackling hers so that she had very little room for negotiation.

"That conveniently leaves just yourself and Lady Breck," Lord Robt added.

He certainly wasn't too impressed by this.

Lord Robt continued to moan, "I suppose you are going to suggest some elaborate reason as to why your marriage to our sister is paramount for the kingdom."

That was a rather petty response to the situation, I thought.

"Well, if I were to devise a reason for our marriage, it would be that I'm the only remaining member of House Pearson and so to ensure full loyalty from my house to the Crown, a marriage between myself and Lady Breck would be a suitable solution."

I turned to face King Bruk directly.

I continued, "But I would like to request, My King, your blessing for me to ask your sister to marry me, not because it is necessary to the kingdom or because it works in a plan, but because I love her and marrying her is all I could ever want in my lifetime."

The king smiled proudly, which was a good sign.

"You have my blessing, Lord Barrat. Of course you do! You do not know how many times Breck has told me of her wish to marry you. There might as well be one noble wedding where the two patricians in question are, indeed, in love. I know that the two of you will make each other very happy."

Lord Neman stood and congratulated me and, to be fair to him, so did Lord Robt, but I assume that he thought it would result in me leaving the King's Council given that I would be in the High North once more. But his opinion didn't matter. I was granted the permission needed to marry the love of my life and I could not wait to tell her our great news.

Connected Somehow

After the royal wedding between King Bruk, son of Betra, of House Northorpe and the beautiful Queen Oline, daughter of Mar, of House Matfen and House Northorpe, my beloved Lady Breck returned to the High North before I had the chance to present my proposal for peace. This meant that, despite my excitement, it was some time before I could break the news of our marriage to Lady Breck, as my duties in the capital prevented my long travel and it was hardly something that I wanted to just throw into a letter. I wanted to tell her in person so I could see her beautiful beaming smile. By the end of the season, King Bruk requested that we meet alone and told me that it was time to head up to my home in the High North to inform my beloved of our marriage. He gave me two options, the first being to go to the High North and tell her of the news before travelling straight back to the capital. Then we would wait for an opportunity when Lady Breck, who would be too busy to drop everything and leave, could afford to travel to the capital for a big wedding. The second option was to have a small wedding in the High North on my arrival. I, as I rightly thought she would want, opted for the second option. I set off on my journey from the capital in the knowledge that, by the time I arrived back, I would be lawfully bonded to the only woman I have ever loved. That was a thought that made the day-long trip, which often felt neverending, float seamlessly past my consciousness. Before I knew it, I was at the gates of Castle Catar. I had decided to imagine my former home was named after my fallen sister out of respect rather than the truthful meaning behind its rebranding.

****

"Oh, my love! It is so late. You must be bitterly cold."

"I'm fine, Breck," I assured my beloved as I held her in my arms in an embrace.

"I did not know you were coming. I would have ridden out to meet you part way."

She kissed my cheek softly.

"I wanted it to be a surprise. I did intend to stop and camp part way but my mind was so adrift that I rode through the dark."

I looked into her beautiful deep, brown eyes as she shivered slightly in the cold wind. Her shudders caused us to move inside the castle -a more sensible place to reconnect in the circumstances of the weather. She seemed annoyed at my action, more out of worry than anything else.

"As dangerous as that is, I am certainly glad you did, just for the extra time that I get to spend with you."

She hugged me again before her face shifted from happiness to concern.

"I am worried about your reason to visit, I must admit - as happy as I am to see you. Is there something wrong in the capital? Are my brothers okay?"

"Your brothers are fine. In fact, they are more than fine. They are all set to be married."

"Married!" Lady Breck exclaimed, pleasantly shocked. "But they haven't even been courting, as far as I'm aware."

"Well, I slightly sped up the process."

This was perhaps an understatement.

She looked confused, so I continued, "As part of our attempt at retaining as much peace as possible, your brothers are to connect houses together through marriage. Lord Neman is set to wed Lady Anto, daughter of Elan, of House Hepston."

"Oh, he has been fond of her for a while now."

"And Lord Robt is to marry Lady Wonin."

"Lady Wonin! Of House Wharram?" she exclaimed in shock.

It seemed she wasn't as pleased with that suggestion, probably due to misconceptions about the woman.

"I know it seems bizarre," I admitted.

"Isn't she in hiding at the moment, awaiting punishment?"

I didn't realise that my wife-to-be would need more convincing than the man set to actually partake in the bonding.

"Not anymore. The king has stated that those of House Wharram shall both be pardoned in a sort of olive-branch gesture."

"I suppose that makes some sense."

I reached out and took her hands as I explained my thinking.

"Look, I know that Wonin isn't exactly the name you wanted to hear but you don't know her as I do. I assure you that she is a kind and honest woman. Even you must admit of her beauty and grace."

Lady Wonin, daughter of Manty, of House Wharram was not like the rest of her siblings. She did not shave her head to her scalp or go out hunting. Instead, she was eager to gain knowledge and spent most of her days learning how to read and write. She had beauty that her siblings did not possess. She looked well protected and was actually rather kind in her nature, despite her upbringing. Of course, she was the blood-sibling of Lord Eli and so her protection was his biggest concern. I think that slightly contradicted his entire philosophy, but what do I know? Her long, dark hair was always washed and neat whenever I saw her, and she had full, plump, naturally pink lips that many in the kingdom admired. She was truly beautiful - although I must admit, I may have slightly oversold the prospect to my beloved. She let go of my hands in mild fury, taking up a mocking tone as she spoke.

"Well, if she's so beautiful, graceful, kind, and honest, then maybe you should marry her instead of Robt."

Her jealousy made me smile, only due to the news I had for us.

"I don't want to marry Wonin! I would much rather marry you."

She blushed and pulled me in for a hug.

"I know you would, but my brothers wouldn't allow it."

She kissed my cheek again as I realised that she hadn't quite understood.

"Oh, wouldn't they?" I asked, provocatively. She looked into my eyes from our position of embrace with a glimpse of what she considered to be momentary hope. "Then why is it that King Bruk gave me his blessing?"

"To marry me?" she asked.

She jumped away from me in excitement and continued to jump again and again. It was a similar routine to how she reacted to good news as a child, which I hadn't seen for many years.

"Of course to marry you! That is, if you'll have me."

She ran up to me and locked her lips onto mine, which was answer enough for me who, in that moment, knew that I was truly the luckiest man in the Kingdom of Saddle Isle.

****

We didn't wait long to marry, only a night's sleep. It was mainly down to our sheer excitement, although a part of me still wonders if our haste was partially down to my beloved's fear of her brothers changing their minds. I had told her of the two options that King Bruk had given us and she was more than happy with the one that I picked, as I knew she would be. She did, however, say that she would feel unworthy of a grand wedding, not dissimilar from her brother's to Queen Oline, on the basis that she didn't possess the same beauty that she felt necessary for such an occasion. I, of course, assured her that she had never been more wrong and that her beauty was spoken of fondly across the kingdom, which was the truth. We both agreed, considering her prominence in our love through the years as an observer over our safety as children, that Miss Norma would be the perfect person to conduct the ceremony, despite her lowly status. On asking if she was willing, her reaction of bursting into prideful tears only assured us that we had made a perfectly sound choice.

We waited until nightfall, when the province was still and quiet, and headed out into the very fields in which we had shared our first kiss all those years before. The servants, who all admired Lady Breck's approach to leadership and were much more grateful to be under her command than her predecessor, had gone out of their way to form an archway of flowers and completed the scene with candles, which shone brightly in the darkness. Miss Celie had also decorated my beloved's hair with flowers once more, as she did on her very first springtime visit in 1102. And so, with Lady Breck looking as stunning as she always did but magnified with her glow of happiness and love, we stood in the presence of only Miss Norma and Miss Celie and made our vows to the gods. Despite my disbelief, I knew it meant a lot to Lady Breck to say the sacred vows and so that is what we did, in unison:

"In the eyes of the gods, we, servants to their power, become united.

In the eyes of each other, we become united.

We pledge to be faithful to each other,

To love and respect each other,

And to never break the bond we have formed."

After the vows were made, Miss Norma instructed us both to place the unity pendants around each other's necks, which we did. Then she proclaimed the binding words, although slightly altered.

"Under the protection of the gods, and the watchful eyes of your fallen siblings, I pronounce you husband and wife."

I took in her beaming smile, which brought me such pride and joy whenever I saw it, and pulled my wife closer and kissed her to the applause of our observers. At last, my Lady Breck was my wife. It was a relatively short horse ride back to the castle - a ride that was made all the shorter by our eagerness to get there.

After thanking our officiator and seeing her off to her chamber we, like the giddy teenagers that we were only a few years before, quickly made haste to the chamber of our own to celebrate our love in the way that we had longed to do for quite some time. It was in that celebration where our daughter first came to be.

The King's Council

I mentioned it during my proposal for peace, but I never did fully explain the issues that Lord Robt was having regarding control in the Midlands. In his defence, it was always going to be a difficult task to regain order in what was a substantially poorly governed province, so it was something that the King's Council expected. Considering that the Midland Savages were still prominent in the province and remained incredibly loyal to their former leader, we always knew that adding laws that coincide with the rest of the kingdom was going to be a big ask and that proved to be the case. The reign of King Bruk was meant to maintain peace in the land and, on the whole, he was being effective in that regard. However, the conflict in the Midlands was detrimental to the overall atmosphere of the kingdom and so needed to be resolved quickly. This wasn't helped by the further reluctance of Lord Robt to marry Lady Wonin, which would have added some House Wharram blood back into the Midland leadership. I could never understand what Lord Robt's initial objection was. This was only furthered when I saw them get along just fine after he eventually agreed to marry her a few seasons after the events of this account. I was pleased, however, by the overall response to the other marriages that I had arranged. My marriage to my beloved was met with great appreciation in the High North, who seemed pleased to have me back in the fold in my home province. Similarly, the two marriages for the Hepston sisters seemed to also run smoothly, especially the one between Lord Neman and Lady Anto. The Deep South, in similar fashion to the High North, was pleased with Lady Anto's return and, although the feelings within the marriage were rather one sided, the two patricians seemed to get along just fine. It was just the House Wharram marriages that proved difficult, but that stress was soon to be halved due to the arrival of Lady Daid in the capital.

****

King Bruk greeted his sister-in-law at the castle gates.

"Lady Daid. Thank you for making the trip on such short notice."

"Well, you didn't give me much choice, My King," she sternly remarked.

She was never one to address her fellow patricians properly but you would have thought that even she would address her king with at least a curtsy.

She continued, "Sending a pigeon up to the North demanding my presence without any specific reason mentioned. You must know, as a brother with a little sister situated far away from home, how the mind does wonder in worriment when a letter such as yours arrives at the castle gate."

Despite her rudeness, King Bruk understood why she was so angry. He often worried about how dear Lady Breck was coping in the High North but never did want to bother her with regular queries about her wellbeing. She was a woman, after all, and often did complain when she was treated like a child by her eldest brother.

"I am sorry that our diction caused you distress. I can assure you that Oline is perfectly well and is rather looking forward to seeing you later on."

She, against protocol, reached out her hand for the king to shake, which was accepted by King Bruk purely based on his knowledge of her tendencies.

"Well, that is a relief. Now, if Oline is perfectly fine then what is the purpose of my visit to the capital?"

"Actually, Lady Daid, the Council and I have a proposition for you, if you would follow this way."

The king led her into the small room in which the King's Council met where myself, Lord Neman, and Lord Robt waited in anticipation.

****

"You want me to do what?" Lady Daid screamed.

I expected her to be less than pleased but her shouting did seem somewhat unnecessary. Even though she had lost some of her seemingly unshakeable might after being forced into submission during the war, I remained slightly apprehensive of her temper when she was as frustrated as on this occasion.

"I know it sounds like an incredibly bad deal," Lord Neman naively commented.

I knew of his incompetence but this lack of initiative even shocked me.

He stupidly continued, "But it's for the good of the kingdom, and so you have a duty to serve. I am amongst many others who have done our part for the kingdom and so should you."

"But your pretty little wife isn't a ratty Savage," Lady Daid aggressively pointed out.

She had a point. Lord Neman's insistence to make out like his perfectly comfortable marriage was an act of heroism on his part was incredibly annoying and certainly wasn't helping our situation. I had lost all patience with my fellow councillors so I butted in.

"Look, Lady Daid. Do you want to be a member of the King's Council or not?"

"You know I do, but I think it's rather shallow of you to assume that I would give up my dignity in this way all for a seat on the council! Does my sister know of this?"

"Yes, she does."

I was shocked by Lord Robt's interruption, although was impressed by his willingness to support my proposal in this regard. Having said that, it did seem rather contradictory considering his reluctance to marry Lady Wonin, which was a much better option than the one we had to sell to Lady Daid.

He continued, "And she understands the necessity of your union."

"How exactly is the union necessary?" she asked, baffled by the request.

Her unimpressed expression deemed it suitable for me to regain control.

"Kinby is the biggest threat to the peace in our kingdom, Lady Daid. If we can trick him into thinking that he's a valued member of our society by allowing for him to have a noble marriage then perhaps his threat will decrease."

"I understand that! But I don't see why that has to be me," she established.

King Bruk, who had been relatively quiet at the head of the table, asserted his calm authority as he often did. He too was fed up with the seemingly never ending back and forth.

"Enough of this! Lady Daid, we have granted you a great honour here! Being a member of the King's Council brings pride to your family's name and to your province. We have identified you as a suitable addition to our council but that does not come without its sacrifices! Just look at Lord Barrat, a married man miles away from a wife whom he loves. A wife who is with child. He sacrifices an easy life in the High North in order to better our kingdom, and I for one am grateful for his sacrifice and acknowledge the pride in which he can claim."

"Thank you, My King," I said with gratitude.

It was a rather touching sentiment from my friend, but the deal had not yet been sealed.

I continued, "I understand, Lady Daid, that this seems foolish. But I know that you feel deserving of your seat, which you are. Marrying Kinby is just a formality in order to gain control over him, which is vital to the kingdom's survival. You can be part of that survival, Lady Daid."

She took a moment to consider what had been said. She knew that she craved power more than anything else. She was intelligent enough to know that those on the King's Council are the most powerful in the kingdom, even more so than simply being a provincial leader.

"What of my post in the North?" she eventually asked. "You gave me the reason of distance as an excuse to prevent my presence on the King's Council in the past. What has changed?"

Despite her response being a further question, this was promising. I continued to butter her up as best I could.

"I know that you pride your position as leader in the North, but your intelligence and skill is worth much more in the capital. Your brother: Lord Angull, son of Limo, of House Matfen, has shown great promise and giving him an opportunity to lead, alongside his wife, will be great for his progression. You must admit that he is developing into quite the capable lad."

"He is indeed. He has made great progress under my guidance."

She was, to give her credit, proud to admit it.

I continued, "We propose that he take over as leader in the North and that you reside here, as I do, in the capital."

Again, she paused for contemplation. Having power in the capital was a steep upgrade on her current position, but the North was her home. She knew nothing else and was proud of the work she had done to aid their success.

"It would be a great change," she admitted, sounding rather concerned.

King Bruk intervened, "I know, Lady Daid, but change offers opportunity. You know as well as us that peace is of paramount importance, and I am telling you now that your contribution through this marriage is vital to peace being maintained. The Midlands are rioting and you know how dangerous that may be. Seeing Kinby respected will act as a great contribution to their cooperation when aiming to secure peace in our kingdom. Besides, my wife misses her sister and I know you care about her deeply. You only showed me that concern this very morning. Lord

Angull is a strong lad who has a wife to keep him company. Even you know that he'll thrive up in the North with his new role. What do you say?"

After a brief pause for consideration, she gave her answer.

"Fine, I shall marry that rat for the good of the kingdom."

King Bruk stood and presented her with his hand to shake.

"Thank you, Lady Daid. I am pleased to have you as a member of the King's Council. Your knowledge and experience shall be of great importance for a long while to come."

We had a brief celebration to honour Lady Daid's sacrifice and our new addition to the King's Council. We also celebrated, despite her lack of knowledge of it, that we had managed to secure the entrapment within the castle walls of the kingdom's two greatest threats to the king's reign. Overall, a rather successful meeting.

* * * *

After the celebrations continued, and Queen Oline had joined in with the festivities that praised her sister and their reuniting, we drew a close on procedures and were set to call it a day. Before we could leave, King Bruk asked for Lord Robt and myself to remain in the room with him, which came as a shock to the pair of us. We retook our seats at the Council table.

"My brothers, it is time that we reconsider the nature of our duty."

"Are you sure, brother, that you don't wish to wait until the morrow?" Lord Robt asked. "It is rather late and wine has been drunk."

He seemed rather nervous. The king was keen to continue.

"Wine has always been drunk, my dear brother! It has never stopped us before."

"Very true, very true."

With that, the king was granted his unwarranted permission to continue. He regained his typical professional tone.

"The Midlands is still a great worry of mine and we seem to be getting no closer to resolving our problem. Hopefully the marriage between Kinby and Lady Daid will decrease the chaos, but that cannot be guaranteed. I also, dear brother, hope that you have given more consideration to the marriage proposal of your own."

"I have, My King, and I am still rather conflicted," Lord Robt replied, looking at me.

"Conflict seems to be inescapable for you, my friend," I commented, unable to hide my frustration at his reluctance.

"Now, now, let's not have another one of your fights. This does not need to be so tense."

He took a pause to sip some wine before continuing.

"Please, brother, do consider it further. I would like a solid answer by the time of our next meeting."

"Yes, My King."

"Now, we must discuss my reconsideration of our duty, seeing that is why you are here," King Bruk continued.

He poured out some wine for the two of us, since the servants had all gone to their chambers.

"Currently, as king, I am doing the job of two men. I have to cater for the needs of the wider kingdom as well as the capital itself. In other terms, I act as both King of Saddle Isle and provincial leader of the South simultaneously."

"And what a fine job you do, brother," exclaimed Lord Robt in a rather conspicuous attempt to kiss the king's arse.

"Well, that's the thing, Robt. The job is seemingly getting out of my reach, which hasn't been helped by the constant noise coming from your province."

Lord Robt sat back slightly, embarrassed by this comment.

The king continued, "It has come to my attention that, since my coronation, we have never addressed the role of chief advisor. Robt has had the title for some time but the job has never had much substance to it other than it falling to you to lead the meetings when I am not present. But since my load has become too much, and it is important for one to admit when one is struggling, I have decided to alter the role ever so slightly."

"And how much of an impact will this alteration have on my workload?" asked Lord Robt, concerned as to whether he would be able to cope.

"None, dear brother. I have decided that Lord Barrat is to take over as chief advisor from henceforth."

"What?" exclaimed Lord Robt, momentarily forgetting who he was addressing.

King Bruk wasn't too happy with the raising of Lord Robt's voice.

"Excuse me? A reaction like that is both unprofessional and out of place here. My proposal is that my chief advisor is to act akin to a provincial leader. You can barely cope with your own province, nevermind a second on top!"

He had a point. Lord Robt definitely wouldn't have been able to cope with leading two provinces and I never had much to do, despite my powerful position. It made sense to put some of the king's overbearing load onto his chief advisor and so giving me the role was the most sensible thing.

"Do you understand my decision, Lord Robt?"

"Yes, My King," was his rather reluctant answer.

With that, King Bruk dismissed us both, which saw Lord Robt quickly skuttle out of the room in a state of both rage and embarrassment.

"My King, this is a great honour. Thank you."

"You deserve it, Lord Barrat," he said, patting me on the back as we exited the room.

The Lucky Lord

Sharp in pitch, high in volume, the truly unique experience of the most intrinsic alarm - yet the cry of your own baby holds such strong connotations of love, promise, and hope that it manages to turn the most horrible of sounds into something that fills up your heart in a way that has never been achieved before. Such a small thing, so light to hold, and yet the weight of responsibility made her feel so heavy. In my arms, I held an amalgamation of myself and the one person whom I have always loved above all others. A baby girl who was the most beautiful, intricately detailed blank canvas in our lives. A child who acted as a chance for us to be so much more than we had been previously. Our miracle in a form that was the most common and natural connection between people, no matter ethnicity, background, or status. Our baby girl had been born and there was nothing but joy in existence on that day.

I never truly knew my father. Of course, I knew of him, which arguably made things much worse. I often wondered what our relationship would have been like if the circumstances of my own existence had played out in a more favourable manner. When I was a child, I used to sit at my window in Castle Gelid and watch as the butcher taught his son how to use a sword. I watched that butcher's boy die and knew that his father was proud of him. I wondered if my father would've been proud of me whenever I made a block or managed to, on what I imagine would be the rarest of occasion, strike him in a training duel. It was my own lack of experience that motivated me to ensure that my daughter would never feel as unwanted and irrelevant as my situation made me feel, along with the rest of my patricians. Of course, her sweet nature made that very easy for me. I had always focused all my attention on protecting myself but I would give my own life in an instant in order to protect our precious little miracle. My love for her remains endless and so it is still, to this day, impossible for me not to be obsessed with her.

Similarly, but definitely not the exact same, I didn't get to spend as much time as I'd hoped with my mother. She was such a loving person, so protective and brave during the hardest of times. I often wondered if my mother's strength influenced how my sister acted when she was alive. I wondered whether she acted in the way she did, trying to be strong, ambitious and brave, because she too fantasised about what life would've been like otherwise. There was no way for Lady Catar to know if our mother would be proud of her, so she overcompensated in an attempt to ensure, in her own mind, that our mother would be proud. What my sister never realised was that our mother only ever wanted us to be happy and safe. If she didn't think that her children were at risk then she would never have sent us away, especially considering the role we had to play in the development of our new home. Family was always my mother's number one priority and, between the three of us, we lost that ideology. I don't like to think about it but, on the occasions when my mind doesn't let me choose, I always thought that Mother would be so ashamed and distraught if she knew how we treated one another. Growing up, it was Lord Shay that was most like her. He had her natural gift of compassion and he spread that gift all around our province. That's why he was always the people's favourite, because he didn't try too hard and yet still managed to put the people's needs and worries before his own. After my little girl was born, the time I spent thinking about Lord Shay increased massively. It was the first time that I ever felt as though I wasn't able to do something. I felt like I was going to struggle with the responsibility. I thought, even before his death, that Lord Shay would be a great father. He was, of course, the closest thing I had to one for a long while. There are many things that, despite the tragedies I've endured, I am incredibly proud of. Yet the biggest pride of mine by far is that my little girl grew to be like her Uncle Shay.

*** * * ***

Two weeks before her birth, I was sent a letter from the lovely Miss Norma, who had been looking after my pregnant wife with great affection whilst I was doing my duty in the capital. It is only in the times of reflection that I have realised just how superior the common servants were to us patricians. The letter told me that my daughter's birth was imminent and so I was allowed to travel back to the High North to be with my beloved in preparation to welcome our baby into the world. King Bruk, who was very excited about the prospect of becoming an uncle, was very understanding and allowed for me to leave with very little notice to be with Lady Breck, something that we both expected but still appreciated massively. I set off the next day and made it to the High North, not long after dark, to the delight of my beloved who was starting to worry that I would miss it. Those two weeks with Lady Breck were actually some of the best we shared on the isle. It was the first time in many years that we both had the freedom to just spend time together without having to conform to our duties. Of course, she was struggling slightly with the physical constraints of pregnancy, but just spending a few days in bed having time to ourselves was a suitable way to start off a lifetime of joy. The labour was tough - an event of beautiful agony. Possibly the only pain that causes more happiness than trouble and that gives more than it takes away. After all of Lady Breck's enduring, and the great work of Miss Norma, we were left as the new three of us: myself, my beloved, and the best thing that ever happened to us. My wife was unable to take her eyes from her and I couldn't take my eyes from Lady Breck.

"She doesn't seem real. She's too perfect."

"I know," I agreed, kissing Lady Breck's forehead.

"She looks like you."

"At least I know she's mine," I joked, chuckling to myself.

My beloved hit me playfully in response.

"Have you heard what the people have been saying?" she asked as she sank into me.

In truth, I hadn't heard what my wife referred to. I had been so busy that I hadn't been amongst the people for quite some time. It was quite sad actually as I always gained from their experiences. Of course, Lady Breck had been stuck in her bed for a few weeks but Miss Norma always filled her in on what was being said around the province.

"No," I admitted. "I hope it's not anything too bad."

For the first time, Lady Breck took her eyes off of our daughter to look into mine.

"Of course it's not! They've just come up with a new name for you, that's all."

"Oh, really? What is it?"

"The Lucky Lord."

It was the first time that the people had referred to me as something that was quite nice, and they were right. I was by far the luckiest man in the kingdom, especially when I compared myself to the other people I knew on the isle.

"I like it," I smugly admitted.

"Me too. Do you know why they say you're lucky?"

There were so many possible reasons, but I wanted to hear them from someone other than myself.

"No, but I would like to."

"It's a three pronged reason. The first is this beautiful little girl right here. Our daughter is the first of the second generation of patricians and so, considering that monarchs are chosen and not appointed through succession, she has a great chance of being queen one day."

"That's a lot of pressure for a baby," I quipped.

"Yes, I know. We'll have to wait until she's a bit older to tell her about it."

"Definitely. Let's wait until she's of five years, at least. What are the other reasons?"

"Well, the second reason is that you should be dead."

This one wasn't quite as sweet.

She continued, "Obviously, you weren't meant to be punished at all, but there was a point when you had a death sentence to your name. They say that you're very lucky that you had such a good relationship with me."

"Well, I am most certainly lucky to have you," I said, kissing her again.

"Actually, that is sort of the third reason. They say that you are the Lucky Lord because you are the only married patrician who is actually in love with his wife."

"Then you must be a lucky lady. I'm certainly very happy that everyone can see how lucky I am. Although, I don't think that we are going to be the only ones in love for much longer."

"Oh, really?" she asked, intrigued. "What makes you think that?"

After being trapped in bed for so long, she was rather excited at some news.

"Well, your brother becomes closer to Queen Oline by the day. They are spending more and more time together and their conversations have become informal and even somewhat romantic. It's nice to see them so happy," I disclosed.

She, expectedly, seemed happy about it.

"I imagine it is. Hopefully everyone else can become like that."

I stroked her hair as we spoke.

"That was the hope from the start, but not everyone is as lucky as us."

We lay together some more, still amazed by the miracle that had been gifted. I took my daughter from Lady Breck's arms and held her for the first time. After a while longer, she said something that reaffirmed, despite there being no doubt at all, that she was perfect.

"She has your eyes," Lady Breck pointed out as I continued to stroke her hair.

"She really does. I haven't looked into eyes like these since I was in my mother's arms. I really miss her."

We paused, thinking about how proud our mothers would have been to see that our little baby girl was healthy and safe.

"Well, I think that we've found our name. We should call her Nea, because of her pretty, green eyes."

I beamed and couldn't seem to stop crying.

"Thank you. I love you so much."

"I love you too."

And so, Lady Nea, daughter of Breck, of House Northorpe and House Pearson, was born. A day in which my beloved and I were blessed with the sweetest, most loving person to ever walk the perfectly uneven cobbles of Saddle Isle.

The Nursemaid

There is nothing, in my humble opinion, more satisfying than a good cut of beef accompanied by a large, hearty serving of wine. Being from the High North, this calming and delectable delight was one that was very rarely experienced throughout my childhood. I suppose that is a rather selfish positive outcome spawned by the transition between the Prosperity Era and the Autocracy Era that followed, but I should be allowed to be selfish at times. I was never one for the drinking game until the dawn of the Great Packsaddle War. Since that fateful time, I often need a rather generous helping of the liquid of the vine in order to get any sleep at all. This only increased as I began to worry for my Little Lady, whom I saw a lot less frequently than I wished. I should also note that, as the years seemingly grew longer and all the more chaotic - which one may assume would create a sense of fast passing but rather seemed to have the opposite effect on time itself - my rather unselfish acceptance of spending the majority of my time away from my beloved wife became a much more difficult sacrifice to make. This was heightened when the relationship between my great king and his queen transitioned from one of convenience to one of love, as happy as I was for my dear friend. Looking back to the past, there were many aspects of myself that caused me to feel a separation from my own house - when my siblings were alive, of course. I have an understandable regret towards how I naturally was with them, as the best memories I have was when we argued and I was victorious. But anyway, those many separations between myself and my house seemed strangely but significantly magnified by my love for beef, which was a meat never associated with our own province. I will be open and honest with you, as I constantly have been thus far, I only talk of my love for the great dining provided in the capital to create some sympathy towards myself. I am sure that you have that one thing, as big or small as it may seem, that brings you great enjoyment in an otherwise distressing reality. And so, I am sure that you will pity me as I tell you that this somewhat blissful meal was abruptly interrupted with what I considered, and still consider with less disdain than previously in the knowledge of what did follow, to be a rather ridiculous quibble for me to have to see to.

*** * * ***

"Do I disturb thee, Lord Barrat?" Queen Oline asked.

The queen was never one to unnecessarily interrupt anyone. She was brought up by her brute of a sister to please everyone around her, no matter how that impacted her personal mental state. I had the pleasure of many encounters with the beautiful queen and, in all the conversations we shared, she possessed such grace and kindness. I stood up to respect her entrance into my room and dropped down to one knee to enhance that esteem before quickly hopping back to two feet, reminded of my injured knee by the pain that shot through my leg. The genuflect was a custom that never sat well with me, mainly as I could rarely just remain seated.

"Of course not, My Queen. How may I assist you?"

I lied to cover up my disappointment. If this conversation was lengthy, my beef would go cold and my appetite would fade, but this was the reality of my job and so I was forcibly happy to help, always. She sat in a chair in the corner of my chamber, looking rather distressed.

"It's my brother, My Lord. He, under the reminders that I have given him on behalf of the king, understands that his marriage to Lady Aott is one of importance for the kingdom, but he is unhappy with his situation."

"Well, I am sorry to hear that, My Queen."

My sorrow was, in fact, genuine. This was due to two main reasons. Lord Angull had recently taken over as the provincial leader in the North, as Lady Daid now permanently lived in the capital to take her seat on the King's Council. Thus, the young lord had power in the kingdom and so his cooperation was important. The other reason for my sympathy was simply aimed towards Queen Oline herself. Despite being happy with King Bruk, I had to acknowledge the sacrifices she made for the kingdom and I related to her worry for her loved one, who resided many miles away similarly to mine.

"Thank you for your sympathy. I have expressed these worries with the king and he sent me to you for assistance."

That doesn't surprise me. He was never keen on tackling interpersonal issues.

"Of course," I answered, trying to further the disclosure of my disappointment.

Despite my great admiration for the queen, I didn't appreciate the added workload.

"The king has deemed it suitable for you to travel to the North to hold discussions with my brother in an attempt to resolve this issue. I do hope you don't mind."

"Of course not, My Queen. I shall prepare for travel."

"Oh, thank you, good lord," she said with a look of relief plastered across her beautiful face, which slightly diminished my disappointment.

I had a lot of issues to resolve a little closer to the capital that I was forced to put aside for this venture north but the rather nostalgic trip, that mimicked my days as Head of Trade, wouldn't be the worst thing I could waste my time doing.

"There is one more thing, Lord Barrat, if you don't mind," Queen Oline continued.

"Yes, My Queen. Whatever you need."

I continued to hide my discontent but only had one thought: "Great, another task to add to the neverending list".

"Do go and spend some time with your family," she suggested.

This was not expected but was met with much gratitude from myself, who regretted making such a hasty judgement on what the queen's request would consist of.

"You and your wife have been nothing but accepting of my entering into your extended family and I really do appreciate your kindness. I have arranged for Lord Robt, despite his reluctance, to deal with some of the issues that you were set to sort before this change of plan. The king has also personally requested that you give his beautiful niece an embrace from her favourite uncle, which I second as her favourite aunt."

I rushed to hug her, which was against protocol. Luckily, as my friend, she didn't mind.

"Thank you, My Queen. You don't understand the joy that I feel right now. Thank you! Thank you ever so much!"

After what was a rather sweet moment between my sister-in-law and myself, things calmed down and returned to the usual professional tone.

"May I ask something, My Queen?"

"I believe you just have," she joked. "Go on. Ask away, good lord."

"You said that Lord Robt was to take over my duty whilst I'm away."

"That is correct, although he's not happy about it."

"I didn't think he would be, in all honesty, My Queen," I admitted.

He never did like conversing with commoners so I didn't have much hope for any quality in his work.

"I was just wondering if you know any reason why your sister isn't taking my load instead?"

Her expression suddenly altered from a smile to a look of shock, which wasn't the best of signs.

"I'm afraid I'm not allowed to mention it, on orders of the king," she replied.

That seemed odd but I didn't question it, out of respect.

"Right, well, of course."

She nodded her head towards me before heading for the door.

"Well, goodnight, dear friend."

As she reached the door, she turned and softly smiled.

"Do tell my brother that I miss him, and I hope he gains happiness."

"Of course, My Queen. Goodnight."

My beef was now cold but I didn't care. I was going to see my precious daughter again and I could barely sleep due to my excitement.

*** * * ***

"Are you ready to depart, Lord Barrat?"

After what the queen had said the previous night, I was quite shocked to be greeted in the early dawn by Lady Daid, who was dressed for travel. I had assumed that there had been some trouble, as there often was with her. She found it hard to push through her fits of temper and so often was taken away from public duties for a short while for her own good. I smiled at her, sympathetically, assuming that something was the matter.

"Yes, indeed I am. I have to say, this time yesterday I didn't think I'd be forced to act as the crux in your brother's marriage."

"Life does come at us fast, doesn't it?" she said with a chuckle, seeming to be in a surprisingly good mood. "Shall we set off, then? It is a rather long journey, as you know."

"'We,' My Lady?"

I was startled by that word we. I didn't like the prospect.

"Yes 'we,' Lord Barrat. I too am to head north in order to get some quality time away. Did my sister not tell you about this?"

"Clearly not," was my abrupt response.

And for good reason. I committed myself to the aid of the king, and subsequently his wife, but even I would have flirted with the chance of upsetting the monarchs if I had known that I was to travel with a companion such as Lady Daid. Other than my distrust of the woman, her constant moaning was enough to make the poorest person grateful to be poor if being rich forced them to be in her presence.

"Well, what a lovely surprise for you on this fine morning, My Lord."

****

We had not yet reached the border that separated the capital from the Midlands, which was a short ride compared to the rest of the journey, when the brute from the North began to complain about her marital situation. Despite her annoyance, I couldn't help but feel the smallest of sympathy towards my fellow member of the King's Council. I certainly wasn't free from guilt in the knowledge that it was in fact I who damned her to such an inconvenience, which I was assured many a time was known by Lady Daid herself. She wasn't shy to throw direct blame at me in her discussion.

"I just need to know, Lord Barrat, why a man who I formerly respected would do such a thing?"

Her passive aggressive approach did diminish my sympathy ever so slightly.

Unfortunately, she continued, "I mean, Kinby is a slimy man. A ratty creature with not an ounce of respect or any reason to be respected. Yet you chose to dump him onto me."

It was predicaments like these which made me wonder why I didn't just give it all up. I could have been sat by a roaring fire on what was a rather cold dawn for travelling, snuggled with my beautiful wife as our miracle of a daughter told us her stories and her learnings from the prior day. Instead, I was cold to the bone listening to a woman, who I neither liked nor respected, continuously moaning about a situation that I couldn't have helped, expecting me to provide answers that she would respect. That was never going to happen. If I told her the truth - being that

I tricked her into marrying the worst of the remaining patricians because I knew that the allure of power, as fabricated and false as her position of power actually was in the grand scheme of society, would be too desirable for her to refuse - I was sure that it wouldn't go down well at all.

"Tell me, Lady Daid, what is it that you pride yourself on?"

Despite her initial disdain for my apparent alteration of topic, she did love talking about how great she was in power, as deluded as her notions made her.

"In terms of my leadership?" she asked.

"If you want."

"I will happily tell you about my leadership ability. I pride myself on compromise."

"Why's that?"

"What do you mean 'why's that?' I have to listen to King Bruk bang on about what a great man you are and how gifted you are as a leader, yet you don't even know the importance of compromise."

I decided to keep my ambitions quiet, mainly to avoid an argument - a compromise of my own, if you will

"Well, do enlighten me with your wisdom."

At least when she spoke of her wisdom she managed not to moan.

"Well, Lord Barrat, compromise is the most important aspect of leadership. You see, many believe that power results in complete satisfaction and that the person in power has full contentment always. But that's not the case at all. It is the responsibility of those in power to make compromises so that everyone is as comfortable as possible, yet there will always be hard times and moments when people struggle. That's unavoidable. But it's how a leader can push the kingdom forward so that no one gets left behind that is most important, and compromise is how that progression can come to be."

I was relatively impressed with her analysis. She was right, from what I could tell. But that wasn't going to stop me from using her own advice against her.

"Well, you married Kinby as a compromise."

Her smug face dropped slightly as I switched the emphasis to her.

I continued, "You wanted a position of high power - power that was higher than what you already had. You put your initial position of the provincial leader on the line when you strove for war, and you crumbled under the pressure. Eli and my sister lost the war and their lives, but you only lost your power - something that you should have seen as a minor victory. Instead, you were keen to do whatever it took to claw back any remnant of power that you could because you are obsessed. That is why you are married to that ratty man. That is why you are unhappy in your marriage, because you placed unnecessary power above the happiness of yourself. And fair enough, compromise is an important aspect of power. But your compromise wasn't for the benefit of your people, it was solely for yourself. So you can stop moaning at me about your position when you were given the option to turn it down!"

I was, perhaps, slightly harsh. As I said my piece, I could hear myself getting more and more frustrated at the injustice of her placing all blame on me, especially when I recalled her choice in the matter. Did I anticipate her thirst for power? Yes. But that, surely, was the fault of her ways rather than mine. Lady Daid decided to remain in a silent sulk for the majority of the journey from that point, presumably as punishment. Obviously, I rather enjoyed her silence, although I felt slightly guilty for raising my voice. As we approached the North, darkness started to set in. We were met by some of the locals who brought torches to light our path. They rather kindly led us from the border to the gates of Castle Kezi. The castle, formally known as (and should've still been known as) Castle Massif always made me feel rather on edge.

It was, like my home, one of the pre-existing builds and was mostly formed from dark coloured bricks. Whether that was due to weathering over time or not I have no idea, but either way I always found it rather sinister looking. Inside, however, was rather more appealing. Much of the furniture, including the large table and chairs in the meeting room, was constructed from slate from the mountains rather than the traditional wood and, unlike the worn-out slate table in what was Castle Gelid, their furniture was rather slick. We were greeted by Lord Angull and Lady Aott at the gate. I allowed for my travel companion to reacquaint herself with her brother and so conversed with the young Lady Aott. She seemed rather happy to see me after such a long time, despite us not knowing each other all too well.

"It's good to see you, Lord Barrat. How was your journey?"

She greeted me with a rather unnecessary curtsy, which I altered to a hug.

"Relatively peaceful, in the end," I smugly replied.

She smiled, taking note of who I travelled with.

"How have you been?" I asked.

"I have been okay, on the whole," She moved closer and lowered her voice to avoid eavesdroppers. "But Angull has been rather distant of late. I fear that my late bloom has caused him to hate me. That is the reason for your visit, is it not?"

The anxious look on her face made me almost compelled to lie, but I eventually determined that lying in that scenario wouldn't be helpful and so I maintained on the pathway of truth.

"I am sure we will find a suitable conclusion," I said, trying to avoid being too direct. "Please, try not to worry."

My words didn't fill her with much hope.

"I'll try," she said with a disheartened smile.

"I hope you don't mind me saying, My Lady, but you have bloomed into a beautiful young woman. I still remember when you were but a babe on that voyage over. Your flourishment has deemed those nights where your crying kept the entire ship awake worthwhile."

"You're too kind, Lord Barrat," she said, blushing slightly. "Although I am still a child in my husband's eyes."

"Patience, My Lady. Soon enough you will bleed and all of this unnecessary confusion will be over. Don't worry."

"Thank you, Lord Barrat. You are a good man."

*** * * ***

Lord Angull, after deeming his short time engaging with Lady Daid a suitable amount, called over to his wife as his sister departed for her chamber.

"Would you do me the honour of allowing for my guest and I to converse in private? That is, if Lord Barrat feels up to a conversation after his long travel from the capital."

"I am rather tired but I do wish to see my wife and daughter as soon as possible tomorrow, so we can talk now," was my answer.

"Then I shall retire," Lady Aott said.

With that, she hugged me goodbye and followed her sister-in-law's departure.

"Would you like to go somewhere a little warmer?" Lord Angull asked.

He gestured for me to follow him into a small room to the left, which I did.

He continued, "I have had a fire burning in this room since the skies grew dark."

We both sat down on slate chairs, which initially felt rather cold but soon warmed up. I promised I would send him the queen's love, and so I did.

"Our queen, your sister, asked after you. She is rather worried - out of love, of course."

"That's very kind of her. I miss her, truly."

Just the mention of Queen Oline brought a smile to his face.

"That's a mutual feeling," I assured him.

"Thank you for delivering her words to me."

After a smile, I proceeded to lead the dreaded conversation that served some purpose, although ultimately secondary, to my travel north.

"What is all this talk of unhappiness, my friend? You are married to a kind and caring young girl who has never done anything to disrespect you."

I was blunt in my approach and wanted to skip the awkward small talk. I was tired and quite frankly confused as to what the problem was.

"I know that, but..."

I refused to hear him out until I had finished my initial argument.

"... Just look at your sister," I interrupted. "She has spent the vast majority of our journey moaning about her husband, who you know is a nasty piece of work. Your wife is a fine woman and does not deserve your bratty attitude towards her."

"But she's a child, Barrat!" he moaned. "In my own marriage, I am a glorified nursemaid."

He wasn't best pleased with my disapproval but a part of me believes that he understood my point of view. I had to try something and so I put my beliefs aside momentarily.

"She is your wife, Angull. You were bonded together under the watchful eyes of the gods and so you have no reason to quibble about your situation."

"I understand that. I'm just... frustrated."

He slumped in his seat and sighed. It was then, when he was honest, that I realised that there was no issue here at all. Lord Angull was simply impatient. He was desperate for his wife to bleed so that he could feel that they were truly man and wife. I stood and moved to a chair that was closer to him.

"You are a leader now, Lord Angull, and, as a leader, patience is a key quality. I understand that you have your needs and I understand that you have your pride, but you need to realise that you are a fortunate man. You are married to a beautiful woman, who is admittedly very late with her bleeding but is also committed to you and has great care for you. I saw, even in this short time, that she respects you and you respect her in return. There is no shame in your attraction to her. I know that she is still a child by our tradition but we both know that she is blossoming into a fine woman. Soon enough, she will bleed and you will have the marriage that you desire. Be grateful. Be kind. Be patient, and all will be well, I assure you."

He pondered on my words momentarily. I sat looking on, hopeful that I had spoken some sense into the young lord, which I had.

"Thank you, Lord Barrat. She is a kind soul and I am certainly more lucky than my weeping sister."

"That is for sure. Now please, go and give that poor girl some reassurance."

"I will, I will."

Lord Angull poured us both a cup of wine.

He continued, "It is a shame about my sister, though. I wish her misfortune could be solved in a conversation like this. She hasn't been the same since the war."

"I don't think any of us have, if truth be told."

We paused momentarily in nostalgic contemplation.

"She's a strong woman, my sister. How she can remain so strong, so tough, after what she has been through is beyond me."

Lord Angull choked up slightly, showing immense pride in his words. It was rare that I felt lost in a conversation, but this was one of those occasions where ignorance was not a stranger but rather a companion.

"I'm sorry, Lord Angull. I don't know of what you speak."

I placed my cup down on the table and leant forward. Lord Angull, in realising that he had let the cat out of the bag, reluctantly began to tell me of his meaning.

"Of course. You wouldn't have known," he began.

Similarly to me, he placed his cup down before explaining.

"During the Prosperity Era, there was a lot of stability and so we were given a lot more freedom in what we did. There seemed to be a sort of grey area surrounding marriage and, considering that things were often turbulent between ourselves of House Matfen and those of House Wharram, we decided to keep the marriage between Lady Daid and Mister Marn a secret from other provinces."

"Hold on a moment."

I was in shock at this news, mainly because neither Lady Daid nor Queen Oline, who I lived with in Castle Eli for many years, had ever hinted at this possibility.

"You mean to say that Lady Daid was previously married?"

"Ay! And she was the mother to two strapping young lords too."

I smiled in a sort of glee before realising that this tale had a solemn twist ahead.

"Oh, what happened to them?"

"War, Lord Barrat. War happened to them," was his answer.

He took a quick sip of wine before continuing.

"Mister Marn, despite my sister's wishes, was eager to fight. He had very little training, you see, as he was merely a farm lad. Eli made easy work of him in the end."

"Such a tragedy," I remarked.

As tradition, we both raised our cups in the air as a mark of respect for the fallen.

"And what of the boys?"

"They were initially safe within the keep but we were rather unsure of the situation at hand. If Eli had won, then he would have killed all in the keep. We had written to King Bruk for assistance and were granted that request, but there was no guarantee that those of House Northorpe would keep to their word to be civil. Daid was scared that, if the king was to turn, he would kill those in the keep as well."

"He would never do that, not Bruk."

He shifted slightly in a failed attempt to inconspicuously wipe away a tear that had fallen for his fallen nephews.

"You forget, Lord Barrat, we did not know those of House Northorpe in the way that you did. We could not afford to trust them. Daid had already lost her husband and our brother, so she was determined not to lose her two boys. She ordered them to be moved to an inconspicuous hut on the edge of the province for their safety, but that ended up being their demise. As some Savages retreated, they raided the hut where the boys were hiding. By the time we reached them, they had been dead for some time."

We paused for a moment out of shock, regret and respect. After a while, Lord Angull led us in lifting our cups once more for those poor boys.

"I am so sorry for your loss."

I was less keen to hide my tears, which flowed freely down both cheeks. As a father, Lady Daid had experienced my worst fear and kept that pain a secret to most whom she knew. Lord Angull, in seeing my tears, allowed his to flow too.

"It wasn't your doing, my friend. You're one of the good ones. I've heard stories of how you strove for peace. I can only respect that."

After a few more cups, a few more toasts of respect, and a lot more tears, Lord Angull returned to his chamber to relieve his wife of her anxieties. I followed him up the stairs to bid him and his wife farewell, as it was unlikely that I would remain in the castle for his awakening the next day. I needed to hold my wife and daughter more than ever before. I felt incredible guilt towards what happened between Lady Daid and myself. I shouldn't have let my opinions on the matter spew out in such an outburst as it did - not in my ignorance. Now, even in a remarriage, she remained alone. This guilt took me past my chamber and led me to hers, at which I knocked and was allowed entrance.

*** * * ***

"Lord Barrat," a confused Lady Daid began. "Is something the matter?"

Her hair was down and her eyes were weary. She obviously was not expecting visitors at this hour, and had perhaps been asleep for some time before my intrusion. I took a seat in a chair that sat opposite the bed in which she lay.

"I'm afraid it is, My Lady. I believe I owe you an apology for my words today."

She looked down in sadness but insisted that my apology was unnecessary.

"No, you were right. I made that choice for myself. I chose power over potential happiness and so I have no right to blame you."

I wouldn't be able to rest until I knew that she understood.

"Nonsense. I was too hasty and failed to see the bigger picture. The knowledge of your previous trauma was a mystery to me and so I was an ignorant fool to claim that your loss was a small one. I know that, had I lost my dear Breck and my precious Nea, I would not be able to continue. I find you remarkably brave and I must state that I understand your choice to marry for power, as that love that you lost can never be replaced."

"That is very kind of you, Lord Barrat. Knowing of your own losses during that fateful time only adds truth to your word. Although, I'm not all too happy about my brother letting my private secrets slip."

Her words were kind but her eyes were sad, which upset me further.

"I'm sure he meant no harm, My Lady. I assure you that, after my return to the capital, I will do all I can to make your circumstances as comfortable as possible."

"Thank you, my friend, but I assure you that all is as well as it can be."

That was the first time, after so many years, that I had seen Lady Daid vulnerable. For the first time, I saw the emotion in her eyes that accentuated their aqua nature. I saw not a brute but a grieving mother who had lost all of her hope and love. That broke a father's heart. After wishing each other a peaceful sleep, I headed to the guest chamber and rested. If the travel hadn't been so arduous, and the events of the day so emotionally turbulent, then my eagerness for seeing my beloved girls would've kept me up all night long.

Lady Nea, daughter of Breck, of House Northorpe and House Pearson

When my Little Lady was born, I remember discussing how lucky my beloved Lady Breck and I were to have all that we did. I am sure you recall my telling of my favourite of many nicknames that I've been branded with over my lifetime: the Lucky Lord. But what I hadn't anticipated at that moment, as I held onto Lady Nea for the first time, was exactly how much she would change me as a person. I have always loved Lady Breck and a lot of my past decisions were based around her. I always put her safety before my own, and I'm sure she did the same in regard to me, but neither of us were as careful or considerate back then compared to when Lady Nea came along. She made every little scenario hold so much more weight than even necessary, but the thought of anything hindering her happiness was one that kept me up at night. It wasn't even the fact that she was my child that made me love her as strongly as I did. Obviously, as her father I loved her unconditionally but there was so much more to her character that stood out. She was just so full of light and joy. She brought a smile to all who met her and, as the daughter of Lady Breck, who was a favourite throughout the land, she met a lot of people and so was the cause of many smiles. For the first few years of her life I didn't see much of her at all, which was a very difficult reality for me to deal with. With Lady Breck in charge of the High North, it wasn't feasible for me to travel forwards and backwards between home and the capital and so I spent a fair amount of time away. I was used to separation with Lady Breck. We had been coping with separation since we were children ourselves and even after we married that continued for a while. But with Lady Nea now born, it became much harder for me to be away from her, especially as I missed many key moments in her life: her first words, her first walk, and even her first laugh that has always been the cutest of things. I still wish that I could go back in time to be there for those moments but they are the sacrifices that I had to make for the king and his kingdom.

Of course, Lady Breck never complained of me being away. She knew how important I was to her brother and so understood his need to have me with him to help him to make the tough decisions necessary to keep our kingdom going. That didn't mean that Lady Breck found it easy though. She still often jokes with me when I mention missing Lady Nea's first words, saying that she'd have given up hearing those words if it meant she didn't have to potty train. She never meant it, of course. Lady Breck loves Lady Nea more than anything and cherishes every moment they have together. She helped Lady Breck during those times when I was away by giving her a bit of company and love. By the time she was of five years, Lady Nea was at a maturity level where her mother could travel more to visit me and her brother down south. After a few trips, we even allowed for Sir Rufus to safely transport her across the kingdom when she wanted to visit me when Lady Breck was too busy. I was skeptical at first, but I have to admit that seeing her more often seemed to dissipate my worry. Besides, I trusted Sir Rufus with my life, and so did the king, so I trusted him with my little daughter. King Bruk, being Lady Nea's uncle, was incredibly supportive and understanding towards my family and would often encourage me to go home or for his sister to come down to visit, which were always lovely experiences. Despite my discontent for their abilities, I have to say that Lord Neman and Lord Robt were also both great with my baby on the whole. It was, in fact, a time when Lady Breck's remaining family were all within the capital that sticks in my mind the most, even all these years later.

****

"Is everything ready, Lord Barrat?" asked the king.

It was the seven year anniversary of King Bruk's coronation, and normally he remained his humble self and didn't do much in regard to celebration. However, this particular year was a little bit different. With the anniversary landing on a Quillian Day, most of the servants and guards were allowed time to reflect. This meant that the king opted to hold a small familial celebration, as work was always difficult to complete when the castle was void of servants.

"I am still waiting on Lord Robt to give me an update," was my response.

In all honesty, I was still waiting for Lord Robt to become even somewhat competent.

"I am sure he'll give you one soon. I know he is very excited for our guests' arrival."

The king had very kindly arranged for Lady Daid, who had become somewhat of a friend to me since our visit north a few months earlier, to take another brief break back in the North on the arrangement that she would keep an eye on the High North whilst she was there. This was reasonable considering that the North was led by Lord Angull, who was now overcome with joy at Lady Aott's first bleed. I have to admit, knowing that Lady Daid was not going to be present whilst my wife and daughter visited brought me some comfort. At least she wouldn't be reminded of her loss - an act so tragic that it felt unfair to even talk of Lady Nea in her presence, particularly in a castle stupidly named after the catalyst for her broken family. I still haven't quite forgiven my foolish brothers-in-law for that blunder.

"He has made that quite clear. Although I'm sure he's nowhere near as excited as me."

I wasn't lying. I hadn't had a night's sleep in days in anticipation of the arrival of my wife and daughter. It had been a couple of seasons since I had last seen them and, although receiving updates via letter was always uplifting, having them both in my arms was a feeling that could never be replicated.

*** * * ***

"Daddy!" exclaimed my daughter.

Her excited shout, met with a bounding run and a hit straight into my chest for the biggest hug to have ever been given, was the greatest sound a pining father could ever wish to hear. It had only been around two seasons since I had seen her and yet so much had changed. She now wore her flaxen hair in the same half up, half down style that her mother had worn since she was the same age, and she was missing a few teeth that she'd grown out of.

"Hello, gorgeous girl," I kissed her cheek and lifted her up into the air and she held on as tight as she could. I held her in my arms and was prepared to never let her go again. "I can't tell you how much I've missed you, Little Lady."

"I've missed you, Daddy," she admitted with a broken but adorable smile.

She reached into her pocket and pulled out a crumpled piece of paper, handing it to me whilst speaking with great pride.

"I have written you a poem!"

"A poem?"

She smiled brightly at me.

"Yes! Miss Norma has been teaching me how to read and write."

"That's very kind of her," I responded.

Miss Norma had taught me to do the same so this news didn't surprise me.

"Can I read it?"

"Yes, of course, Daddy," she said, as if I were stupid for asking such a question.

With her still in my arms, I read her poem:

'If I put a smile on my face, it will help me through the day,

But to put a smile upon my face, I have to find a way.

So I smell the flowers, hear the birds, and help my mother out,

Because that will surely bring a smile, of that I have no doubt.

But there's one thing better than the rest, that makes the rest seem bad,

That is, of course, a massive hug from my oh so loving Dad!'

"Wow, Little Lady!" I kissed her again, tearing up at her sweetness. "You are amazing!"

"You really think so?" she asked.

I could see a real sparkle in her eye as her excitement built.

"I really do."

She squealed with joy before wrapping her arms around the back of my neck in a tight but wholesome hug.

"I know you've missed your dad, my darling, but I would love to have a go at some point," said a voice that I loved so much.

My beautiful Lady Breck, who had been reconnecting with her brothers whilst Lady Nea and I were reuniting ourselves, couldn't wait anymore.

"Sorry, Mummy! Here, have your turn."

She seemed to genuinely feel guilty. Lady Breck smiled softly as Lady Nea climbed down from my arms.

"Does this mean that it's my turn to have a hug from my favourite niece?" King Bruk called over, to Lady Nea's delight.

He was definitely her favourite uncle too.

"I'm your only niece, silly," she pointed out, laughing in her cute way as she ran over to the king.

As our daughter ran off, Lady Breck gave me a long awaited kiss. As I wrapped my arms around her waist, she rested her head on my shoulder as we watched the three uncles make a big deal out of our baby.

"How are you?" I asked my beloved.

She seemed tired, but I didn't want to say anything. Of course, that fatigue didn't take away from her endless beauty.

"I'm good. Things have been busy, but it's all good. I'm so grateful for this, though."

"Oh, me too. I've missed you so much."

"I've missed you too."

For a short while, we just stood in content quietness, appreciating the presence of each other and the gift that was our beautiful daughter.

"How's he been?" she asked, gesturing to her eldest brother.

"Who, Bruk?"

"Yes."

"He's been alright, on the whole."

It was strange to me that on the day of his coronation anniversary, this familial encounter was the furthest away from a king he had ever seemed to me. On that day, he was simply my brother. Simply my family.

"There have been a few cold interactions with a certain brute from the North, but he seems the happiest he's been for a long while, which is good. I genuinely think that Oline and himself have fallen in love, you know."

"Oh, wow!" she happily exclaimed.

It was nice to see her comforted by this. She did worry about the king an awful lot, as any good sister would worry for her brother.

She continued, "That is such great news! I guess we're not the only lucky ones anymore."

"We're still the luckiest."

I smiled as I watched Lady Nea pulling on Lord Robt's hair as he lifted her up towards the sky.

"Did she give you her poem?"

"Oh, yes. It was so lovely."

"She has been so excited to give it to you for weeks. Of course, Norma gave her some help."

"But it is still great. I mean, she just gets more and more amazing every time I see her."

Just hearing her laughter in the short distance meant that my smile was impossible to fade.

"She really does. She obviously gets that from me."

It was nice to hear Lady Breck laugh again as well.

"Of course," I responded, chuckling too.

"She's very intelligent, though. She definitely gets that from you."

"Well, if she has to get something from me, that is definitely the best outcome."

We both laughed before embracing once more and heading over to our daughter and her uncles, who had been joined by a similarly gleeful Queen Oline. For the first time in a few months, I turned off my advisory brain for long enough to be reminded of the reality of our situation: we were genuinely happy.

Lord Kinby, son of Stanp, of House Wharram and House Matfen

There have been many an occasion where myself or someone else has referred to Lord Kinby as a 'ratty man'. I understand that this might be a cause for slight imprecision on my part and I aim to resolve this as I further explain why Lord Kinby is, and I don't say this lightly, the only man of whom I have ever had full contempt. Despite having no hair at all due to his customary shaven head, there were some obvious reasons as to why Lord Kinby was described to be rat-like. He had a slender face, with a pointed nose and long, sharp teeth that were accompanied by ears that ventured away from his head, almost as if he couldn't bear to hear the lies that spouted from his mouth. He moved abruptly and was always looking over his shoulder, mainly due to the vast number of enemies that he procured. I suppose to truly understand what made Lord Kinby a ratty man, one must have at least a vague understanding as to why exactly rats have such a bad reputation. Rats have a scavenger quality and can often be found around waste, where they pick up whatever they can no matter how disgusting the scene may be in the eyes of a human. They are also a diseased rodent who carry and spread said disease to the detriment of those around them. Rats are nocturnal and so scuttle around at night, sneaky and suspicious, as Lord Kinby often did within the castle.

Lord Kinby spent five years on the run, mainly hiding out in secret bunkers within the woodland located in the Midlands which, of course, was his home during the Prosperity Era. This was a clever move, in fairness, as the woodland was inhabited by the most deadly of Savages that created a small community with each other once Lord Robt moved in. Being from House Wharram, he was guaranteed protection and so he was rather hard to draw out. He would only leave the woodlands at night with the sole aim of hunting to procure food for himself and his sister, Lady Wonin, who slightly deteriorated in decorum during her time in hiding but always maintained some of her class. That is perhaps how she found it so easy to settle back into the routine needed as a patrician after her marriage to Lord Robt. I mentioned previously the impact that Lord Eli had had on Lord Kinby, which played a part in his nature. Lord Eli was a big brute of a man and was the topic of much fear and admiration across the land. Lord Kinby was always scrawny in comparison but certainly had a similar mentality to his brother. They both valued the aspect of freedom and only saw freedom in the ability to survive without the conventional, restricting laws that the rest of the land implemented. This meant that the transition back into civilisation after his eventual marriage to Lady Daid, which took place in the year 1112, was a rather tough one for the rat. Despite his initial optimism towards my proposal, it quickly became clear that Lord Kinby's vision of his own future didn't necessarily coincide with reality. He believed that he would return to a high position in the Midlands, as his sister did, and that things across the land would be more similar to how it originally was.

That was not the case. After a long battle, the Midlands eventually became more civilised, forcing the Midland Savages to choose between death or transitioning towards the more traditional way of life in the kingdom. This caused Lord Kinby great distress. He was also rather unhappy about his living situation. Everyone, including both Lord Kinby and Lady Daid, knew that the marriage was never going to transition into a love-fuelled union, but he never anticipated his lack of power and freedom. I'm sure that even someone as historically naive as Lord Kinby couldn't have expected to be welcomed back into the fray with open arms, but I can understand why spending three years unable to venture out of Castle Eli without constant guard supervision could be frustrating. I suppose the name of his new home failed to help the situation. Due to this sympathy, I had pitched giving him a bit more trust many times to the King's Council. Lady Daid, who hadn't spoken to the man since they married, was always dead against it. That is understandable considering he had spent the majority of his life supporting the Savages who killed her two boys. King Bruk was never too keen either, although understood that my concern for his cooperation was valid.

We went through a three season period where there was no trouble from the man at all, which resulted in the relaxing of his security. He was granted visits to his sister and was allowed to wander around the capital unguarded. Although, we did employ spies who reported back to the council with an account of his activities whenever he did venture out. These spies included my old friend, Miss Aton, who had served her time and was reunited with her sister and niece. For those wondering, I did supply her sister with coin after I was reinstated, as I had promised. We thought that all was going well until one day he came to see me in my chamber to speak his mind. I would have been happy to speak with him, but my darling Lady Nea was visiting and so I was rather apprehensive throughout our conversation.

*** * * ***

"Barrat!" Lord Kinby bellowed.

He didn't bother to knock. Instead, he just stormed into the room, shouting whilst knocking over a pile of letters that were stacked by the door in preparation for the king to look over. I had been going through them with Lady Nea, who sat with me on the bed. I ushered her behind me on account of the aggression which Lord Kinby entered with. She grabbed hold of my arm in fear.

"I demand to speak with you."

"Lord Kinby, I'm afraid now is not the best time. Can this wait until the morning?"

"I plan on leaving in the morning, so no!"

I wasn't quite sure where he was planning to go, but I did think that there was nothing I could say to get him to respect my request.

"Okay then. What is it that you would like to talk to me about?"

I gestured for him to take a seat in the corner of the room but he opted to pace around instead, which put me on edge.

"I need to leave!"

There were times when talking to some of my fellow patricians felt as though I was trying to converse with a pig.

"You said you were planning on leaving tomorrow."

"I am leaving tomorrow!"

"Then what is the purpose of this conversation?" I asked, in a rather frustrated tone.

"Oh, you shrew! I need to leave permanently!"

"Please, Lord Kinby, I am the chief advisor to the king. Try to control your anger in front of my daughter," I calmly requested.

"I will do whatever I like! You're the one who trapped me in a marriage to a woman who despises me, and who forces me to remain in a castle that is named after my dead brother - who was killed by the king!"

Lady Nea gasped. I took some time to compose myself. How could I expect her to act with dignity and decorum if she saw me lose my temper?

"Nea, my love."

"Yes, Daddy," she said, shaking slightly.

"Go and see your Auntie Oline. I'm sure she'll love to hear all about what you've done today."

I helped her get down off the bed.

"Yes, Daddy. I would love to."

She gave me a hug before running out of the room, making sure to avoid Lord Kinby as best as she could. After she left, I turned my attention back to the ratty man, who had just disrespected me in front of my daughter. Knowing she was out of earshot, I moved towards Lord Kinby until my face was against his, which he found incredibly uncomfortable. The heat of the moment removed all professionalism from the situation.

"Don't you talk to me like that in front of my little girl again! If it weren't for me, your scatty little head would be on a stick on the castle walls. There are plenty of common folk out there in the capital alone who would give anything to have a grand chamber in a castle! Stop being so ungrateful for our mercy."

"Barrat, how dare you..."

"... Lord Barrat," I interrupted, now more calm than before. I was keen to request some respect from the rude lord, but that didn't stop me from ensuring that he knew his place. "You address me as Lord Barrat! And you certainly don't get to question any rule or command that is implemented by me. I can say whatever I like to you because I am above you, Lord Kinby. That is how this system works. And I find it suitable to point out that I am only in a higher position than you because I worked hard enough to earn it. I didn't mope about the castle, hoping that my fortune would improve. Instead, I did my work and was rewarded for doing so. Perhaps you should consider doing something similar, Lord Kinby. Did you notice what I did?"

He pulled a face at my pedantic tone but I didn't care.

I continued, "I addressed you with the respect of your title. I expect you to do the same."

"I don't have to listen to this," Lord Kinby said as he turned to leave.

I hadn't finished.

"No, no, Lord Kinby, you are not to go anywhere tomorrow."

"You don't have that authority!"

"Yes I do! In fact, I also have the authority to reintroduce your security when leaving the castle walls. I'm sure that, once I've explained this inappropriate occurrence on your part, the king will be more than happy to support my notion. Now, Lord Kinby, I suggest that you retreat to your chamber and cease to bother me further until you have learned how to address me properly and to talk to me with respect."

He didn't say another word but stormed out to his chamber, leaving me alone in mine feeling a strong sense of anger and a simultaneous regret at how unprofessionally I had acted.

*** * * ***

After a short while, Queen Oline knocked on my door and brought my beautiful daughter back to me, carrying Lady Nea in her arms. I knelt down out of respect.

"My Queen, I am sorry for sending Nea to interrupt you so late in the evening."

"Oh, Lord Barrat, don't be silly. I always love a visit from this little angel."

Queen Oline passed Lady Nea over, kissing her head as she did. I placed her down on the bed.

"Well, thank you either way, My Queen."

The queen sat on the chair that I had previously offered to Lord Kinby and waited for me to preoccupy Lady Nea with quill and parchment before speaking. She leant close to me in an attempt to stop my little girl from hearing.

"Nea said that a strange man came in. I hope there was no trouble."

I felt like she could sense my embarrassment.

"Actually, My Queen, I'm afraid I have made a fool of myself. I let my frustration get the better of me and gave Kinby a real piece of my mind. I have told him that he is no longer allowed to leave the castle without security."

"I shall inform the king of your decision. What was the meaning behind Kinby's visit?"

"He said that he planned on leaving," I explained before turning briefly to check on my daughter, who was enthralled with her writing.

She later informed me that she had written a letter to Lady Breck to tell her of the adventures she had whilst in the capital.

"He said he feels trapped here, which I understand, but he also made some inappropriate remarks in front of Nea. That's what made me lose my professionalism."

She paused briefly in order to absorb the information.

"Well, kind friend, that is very much understandable. I am sure that, once you have both calmed down, we will be able to sort out an apology to you from Lord Kinby."

"Thank you, My Queen."

"You don't have to address me so formally, you know. I really don't mind."

"You always do me the honour of addressing me properly," I pointed out, feeling a weird sense to justify myself. "It is only right that I give you the respect that you deserve."

She stood in preparation to retire to her chamber.

"Well, brother, I do appreciate that but it is truly unnecessary. We are family at the end of the day and I do hope that you consider me as a friend also, Barrat."

"Of course. You're one of the best friends I have, Oline."

She sweetly smiled. Before heading to the door, she gave me a friendly embrace and smothered Lady Nea with many kisses, which my Little Lady was highly appreciative of.

"It will all be okay with Lord Kinby, you know. Try not to worry too much."

"Thank you for your concern."

"Anytime, my friend."

With that, she headed to the king's chamber and left me and my daughter to have a peaceful sleep that would've only been improved by the presence of my beloved.

****

It would turn out that, despite the kindness that she showed to me that night, Queen Oline was naive to think that Kinby - who, from this moment, lost his right to be respected with a title - was able to be reasoned with. Her telling that all would be fine gave me comfort, but was a notion that I shouldn't have believed to be entirely accurate considering who it was that we were talking in reference to. A wiser man than me would've taken Kinby's aggressive nature that night to be a sign of deterioration and would've most likely sent the ratty man to the dungeons for the night to teach him a lesson. Perhaps, if he was not of noble title, that would have been where he ended up after our encounter. But I sent him to his chamber and allowed for him to have the freedoms that no hateful man should ever be entitled to.

As the kingdom slept, Kinby sneaked out of his chamber - something that he had been doing for some time in preparation. If he had attempted to leave the castle then he would have been stopped by guards. Even Kinby was too intelligent to try that. Instead, he made his way to the library where he examined our collection of maps that had been transported as part of our land's collection in 1096. This was, to quote what King Bruk had once told me when I was a boy, to give us means to escape if ever an invasion was to occur in the many years to come which, of course, would require a lot more ships than we possessed on the isle. Kinby had derived, over a three season long period, the direction a pigeon would need to be sent in order to make it back to Mainland England. He felt like a prisoner in his own land and so decided that it was his right to take back his freedom. And so, he waited for the next Quillian Day to arrive and utilised the brief decrease in guards to acquire a bird to send his carefully worded plea for freedom. He was successful in his quest and sent word to our hateful uncle, Henry, in England that disclosed our location and informed him that we had adopted a monarchy of our own. He had bargained for his own protection in the letter in exchange for his information and felt no guilt towards the thousands who would die as a consequence. Of course, Kinby believed that he would have to wait for our father to die before an invasion was to occur, and he heavily relied on the message not being intercepted or lost on its way. Birds making long journeys didn't always make it to their destination but there was nothing anyone could do but hope that the creature survived. What Kinby wasn't to know was that his wait would be much shorter than he had anticipated. Our father, King William II, was dead and King Henry now sat on the throne, bitterly thirsting for the blood of any bastard he could get his hands on.

The New King of England

Up until this point, I have been able to give accounts of the events on Saddle Isle based on my personal experience, or at least based on the experiences of some of my closest friends. However, considering that I was not in England as Kinby's letter arrived to King Henry, I can only speculate what occurred when our location was revealed. This presented me with a few options. I could have carried on with this format of writing where I could explore many variations of my own guesses as to how the events leading up to the invasion panned out. However, I feel as though it would be more useful for me to present the events in a way that, despite not necessarily representing the truth, may allow for you, the reader, to fully understand the impacts that this invasion had on the kingdom.

It was King Henry who initially sparked the fear that all bastards endured whilst in England and so the new king was already a figure for whom we had much contempt. The Great Voyage of 1096 not only created separation between Henry and ourselves but it also separated us from that aforementioned fear. This sense of security meant that the news of King Henry discovering Saddle Isle created only the darkest of thoughts, which resulted in many horrific speculations in regard to what was to come. It was obvious that the invasion would be a negative thing. Even now that feels stupid of me to write, but we could only imagine the most horrific and evil of outcomes for our kingdom. This is based on the knowledge that they would have a significant numerical advantage on us and so we would not stand a chance, like a pride of lions hunting wounded prey. We were destined to be the victims of an onslaught and so the man behind the attack must have been the worst possible person that we could ever imagine. With that in mind, my account here will present the King of England to be as such.

****

Before my speculative account, it may be useful to know some historical information about England and their monarchs - something that I only learned recently but did help me to answer questions I had about our fate. In the summer of 1100, King William II of England, father to all patricians of Saddle Isle, was shot and killed by an arrow in the New Forest. Folklore hails any royal death in the New Forest as karma for the destruction of parishes because of its creation by the preceding monarch, King William I, or William the Conqueror, or (more relevant to Saddle Isle history) William the Bastard. Our father died having been unmarried and so left behind no legitimate heir. It was King William II's older brother, Robert Curthose, who aimed to take the throne based on a short lived agreement made in 1087. After his father's death, Robert Curthose was granted the Duchy of Normandy and my father was granted the kingdom of England, which was why Curthose wasn't king in the first place. However, considering that he had already been overlooked once, it was always thought that the youngest of the brothers, Henry, would prevail to the throne instead of Curthose. He seized the Crown from his older brother, whose journey back from the First Crusade delayed him from making his own claim for the throne. Curthose wasn't helped by his shortage of money. This resulted in the title Duchy of Normandy being mortgaged to King William II in order to fund the First Crusade - something that he later unsuccessfully tried to buy back. This ultimately led to England being in possession of Normandy, which only made King Henry stronger in his fight against Saddle Isle. Curthose did attempt an invasion in 1101, but that was a failure. Henry subsequently drafted the Treaty of Alton, which forced his older brother to forfeit his claim to England's throne. After that, King Henry made it that Curthose would remain in captivity for the rest of his life. If Curthose had been successful, it is likely that our fear for Saddle

Isle's safety would have been pointless. Of course, that is all a moot point now.

****

"My King," said a nervous voice.

After receiving a pigeon from an unknown land, by chance rather than design, a young and common man rode to the New Forest from Clapton after being informed that King Henry was on a hunt. He eventually found his king and looked to deliver some news.

"I have some important news from a place called Saddle Isle."

"Never heard of it," said the king bluntly, not looking up from his crossbow to address the man who had travelled to see him.

"Your Majesty, I must admit that I have never heard of such a place either," the young man nervously added.

"Then why have you interrupted my hunt with all this talk of such a place that no one has heard of! If no one has heard of it then it can't be important!"

The king gestured for his entourage to follow him as he aimed to move deeper into the forest after his attempt was foiled by this unknown man. Interruption was something that always made the king rather annoyed on his hunts.

"But, Your Majesty, I feel as though you may be rather interested to read what the letter says."

"Well, if you feel as though I will, then I shall read it. But if I find these words to disinterest me then you shall be the next beast I hunt. Do you hear me?"

"Yes, Your Majesty," he said, gulping with anxiety.

"Good."

The king took the letter and read it, altering his disinterested look with one of great wonderment and intrigue.

"Where did you get this?"

"It landed by my hut, My King. A rather tired pigeon had collapsed on my land. Attached to its foot was this letter."

King Henry was concerned about the validity of the man's claims.

"Tell me, boy, this is not some joke? Because if it is, there will be severe consequences for what you have done!"

The boy began to sweat.

"I swear, Your Majesty, I would never lie to any man, never mind a man who was chosen by God to lead us."

"Yes, yes, okay. You can go now."

In a rather confused state, the young man left Kinby's letter with King Henry and rode back home somewhat dissatisfied with what was his one and only interaction with his king. The king waited for the young man to ride off before showing his utter delight at the discovery.

"Oh this is brilliant! This letter is the miracle I've been waiting for!"

The king's chief advisor, who spent more time at brothels than doing his duty for the country, was intrigued as to what was making his king so happy.

"Your Majesty, what news has brought you such joy?"

"This is a letter from a man named Kinby from a place named Saddle Isle. He claims to be William's bastard son and that the patricians, as he calls his siblings, and their people have elected a bastard named Bruk to be King."

"Are you saying, Your Majesty, that the island that King William II sent the bastards of England to - the isle that was once unknown to us after all evidence of its existence had been destroyed by your brother - has been found?"

"Exactly, my good sir," King Henry confirmed with an evil chuckle. "The bastard boy has provided knowledge of a land they call Saddle Isle, all in exchange for the preservation of his own life."

"Will that request be met?" the chief advisor asked, with a smirk that suggested he knew the answer already.

"Of course not! All those illegitimate demons shall burn at my command! For too long my father has been tarnished by the branding of 'bastard', but my brother was too sensitive to his own bastards to do anything to restore our father's pride and dignity. And now his bastards and their contaminated community have committed treason, a fine excuse for me to finally deal with them! Once the world finds out what happens when you insult my family, and when you tarnish a great man's legacy by banding him in with abominations, no one shall call my father a bastard again."

The king demanded his chief advisor quickly ride back to the castle. He was to order a fleet to prepare to set sail on the rather arduous journey from England to Saddle Isle and to kill every last citizen that they come across, all in the name of treason with the secret aim of 'purification'. They were to burn the isle to ash and tear down every hut, farm and castle until they were sure that every living thing was dead. After a quick season-long preparation, they headed our way. The chief advisor did this immediately, thinking of the grand story he could tell whilst interacting with his most favourable prostitute. As he left, the king remained with his entourage in the New Forest, now imagining that every deer, bird or fox that he killed was a bastard from our most cherished home.

Persephone

It terrifies me how quickly the disparity between peace and turmoil can be altered. It was only a few seasons prior to the King of England discovering our location that the Kingdom of Saddle Isle was running as smoothly as ever. It was arguably an even greater period of time than there ever had been during the Prosperity Era, a state we had been fighting so hard to return to. The crime rates were down and the relationships between provinces were better than they had ever been before. The marriages that caused some real outrage when I initially suggested them were, on the whole, working out. Lady Breck and myself had always been strong and the monarchs had been blossoming for many years, but I didn't expect some of the other positive results. After Lady Aott finally bloomed, Lord Angull truly came to terms with his attraction to her and their relationship only grew stronger. Lord Neman had always loved Lady Anto but it appeared that, perhaps only down to sheer persistence, those feelings had begun to be reciprocated. Of course, Lady Daid and Kinby didn't have a marriage quite like the others and so that was an expected failure, but it was nice to see that, despite the initial reluctance from Lord Robt, Lady Wonin had managed to win his heart and their love also grew relatively strong. With Lord Robt finally grasping tight control over the Midlands, the Savages seemed to just disappear. As mentioned, they were given a choice to change or die, and it seemed as though most of them opened their minds to the possibility of civilised life. The lack of fear allowed for people to feel comfortable moving across the kingdom, only increasing the unity and prosperity of the land.

Lord Angull was beginning to impress as well. He developed the idea for a reconstruction program that really helped to shape the justice system in the kingdom. Instead of simply sentencing people to serve time as servants, Lord Angull rightfully pointed out that the context of each case should be examined more thoroughly so that more lenient matters could be implemented if necessary. This meant that people, like my friend Miss Aton, weren't punished for desperately struggling but were given the option to take an apprenticeship in order to fix what society had broken. Of course, there were still many cases where it was necessary for people to serve, and other cases where murders still led to death sentences, but it really did seem like we were moving healthily forward in the development of our kingdom's approaches to crime.

Despite our initial doubts, Lady Daid acted as a great asset to the King's Council. I had taken up the role of provincial leader in the South, leaving the king to be able to focus on the more important aspects of his job, such as visiting provinces, sorting accounts, re-evaluating the army system, and many more duties. With Lord Robt, Lord Neman and myself all having provincial leadership duties, it was good to have an extra body to pick up the load that was left behind. This was similar to the job I was doing before being promoted to chief advisor. Lady Daid assisted in many developing projects across the land, the most notable being the redevelopment of bridges, which was way overdue after damages caused during the Great Packsaddle War. Lady Daid also provided me with much needed assistance in presiding over the proposed alterations within the structure of the capital. After the Battle of Midland Bay, most villages had been destroyed. For a few years afterwards, temporary fixes were put in place but the South did not return to its former glory. To make amends, having felt guilty about the matter, I made it a goal of mine to rebuild and improve the South once I became the provincial leader.

We both felt as though the capital province should be somewhat different to the rest and so we devised a change in structure. Rather than the numerous circular villages, we wanted to create a more vibrant province and so we rebuilt housing to be lined in streets that surrounded various large squares for a much larger number of citizens to make use of. After the construction was finally completed in 1114, each of the squares were often full of music and celebration, with the capital province feeling warmer and more united than it ever had before. Unfortunately, the cobbled streets remained uneven, despite my best efforts. I suppose it added some character, in a way. For the first time, the patricians had seemingly come to terms with their roles and happily dedicated their time towards what was best for the people rather than what was best for their own self-interest. Then there was Kinby, who somehow had acquired the power to make all of our previous problems reappear in an instant.

****

"Ah, Lord Barrat, I hope I am not disturbing you," said an intruding King Bruk.

The king, who I had begun to see less and less of since taking up the role of provincial leader in the South, was at my door. It was rare that he would come to me. It was normally a servant who would inform me that the king needed me and so I would go to him.

"No, My King, of course not."

I lied, bowing respectfully from a seated position at my desk.

"You are meant to stand," he said, with a smile that told me not to bother.

"I am sorry, My King."

"I am just coming to deliver a letter. It is from your wife."

He pulled it from his back pocket and handed it to me.

"Isn't letter delivery normally the job of a servant? It's nice to see you finally becoming a man of the people," I commented with a jovial chuckle, opening it as I spoke.

"Watch your tongue! It was just mixed up with all of mine. Did I not tell you how much harder I have to work than everyone else? People assume that I have it easy, but that is nonsense!"

"We all know how hard you work. Isn't that all that matters?"

"I suppose. Anyway, I thought I'd deliver it myself so I could hear what my wonderful sister is getting up to in the High North."

"That's fair enough."

My smile faded as I read the letter.

"What is it?" the king asked, concerned.

"It's the fishing ships, My King. Lady Breck says that there was an attack on the dock last night. All the boats have been burned."

"Who would do such a thing?"

We both paused momentarily to see if any suspects came to mind. It seemed such an anomaly of an event, considering how peaceful things had been for some time. Maybe it was just some scoundrels, bored of the lack of executions, trying to make life more exciting. I had settled on that being the case, when I remembered a certain absentee from my recent memory.

"My King, when was the last time you saw Kinby?"

He took a moment to think thoroughly.

"Not for a day or so. Although, I don't tend to check up on him personally."

I stopped a servant boy who was passing my open door.

"You, young boy. Run down to Kinby's chamber, see if he is there. If he is, return here. If not, head straight to Sir Rufus and tell him that we fear he is missing."

"Yes, My Lord."

The young boy ran off, as instructed. He got to Kinby's chamber, which was located on the far west wing of the castle (far away from mine, thankfully) and found it was locked. He knocked a few times to no avail. Eventually, he took the initiative to ask a nearby guard to unlock the door. The two of them found nothing but a broken window. Kinby was gone. The boy rushed to tell Sir Rufus as instructed. The great sir admitted to not hearing much of him and ordered his guards to begin a search. He came to my chamber, along with the boy, to speak to the king and I. Once he caught his breath, the old man spoke. He got down on one knee out of respect, causing the king to glance at me as I still hadn't stood up.

"My King, My Lord, there has been nothing found but a broken window. We fear he has gone."

"How could he have escaped?" asked King Bruk, flabbergasted that one of the most recognisable men in the kingdom had escaped the most guarded castle of them all.

"There must have been an inside man."

"I don't mean to interrupt, my great king, and I don't mean to be a tattletale but this seems like a serious circumstance," said the boy, rather nervously.

"What is it, boy?" asked King Bruk, trying to appear kinder to calm him down.

"Well, My King, I heard a few men say that they had come into a fair amount of coin. Said they were to lead a rat away from its trap and back to its home."

"My boy, are you sure?"

The boy insisted he was positive. Sir Rufus hurried back towards the door.

He set out a plan, "Then I must ride to the Deep South. They'll have led him through the back streets towards Lord Neman's province and will pass through there to the Midlands. The South has twice the guards of any other province. The sooner they get out of the capital, the safer they are. I'll round up as many Southern guards as I can to accompany me."

"I will come with you," insisted King Bruk. "Barrat, go and inform Neman. He may want to ride that way too."

Lord Neman, who had been in the capital to address a few provincial matters with myself, was thankful for the words of warning. He rushed off towards his home by a horse of his own, but was set to arrive some time after his brother.

****

As the king and Sir Rufus arrived in the Deep South with seven Southern guards that had followed them on command, they soon found out that Kinby had already infiltrated the castle. The Midland Savages, whom we thought had integrated into society but were actually waiting for a prominent moment to rise once more, had crossed the border into the Deep South as Kinby made his way from the capital. Kinby was sure that he could recruit more sentenced servants from Castle Shay (which is painful, even now, to name) whilst on his way to his home province.

"My King!" shouted the chief guard, wanting to ensure he could be heard clearly. "If my men attack the hooligans at the front gate, you will be able to sneak in through the trade gate at the east side undetected."

They did as Sir Rufus planned and, sure enough, Kinby had forgotten to man the trade gate and so the two men could ride in through there. They dismounted their horses and entered the main body of the castle. A rather elderly female servant, who seemed understandably traumatised by the events, ran to them.

"My King, My King! It's the lady, My King. She is hurt," she squealed in blind panic.

The servant, who turned out to be Lady Anto's personal aide, led the two great men towards her chamber, where the young patrician was laying on the floor, holding her pierced side. Her thin, woollen dress was stained with blood, which trickled across the stone tiles and down the room's steps into the corridor. King Bruk rushed over to her and applied pressure to the wound with his hands. Lady Anto turned to face her king as he assisted her.

"Bruk, I'm sorry," she said, so weak that she couldn't speak with any real volume.

"What are you sorry for? You have been brave today."

"He has only just gone," she slowly said, trying to point in the direction.

"My King, I shall go," Sir Rufus insisted, standing up. "You stay with the lady."

Sir Rufus left and continued the horse chase that had been started by Kinby, who had fled back towards the capital once more guards from the Midlands made their way south. Lord Robt had received word from a villager that the Savages were back, so he sent some of his own guards down to their aid. It wasn't long after Sir Rufus and his following guards left that Lord Neman made it to his wife, whose pain had only increased. With each passing second she edged ever so closer to her death, and everyone in the room knew it. He wailed, seeing the blood run along the floor.

"My beloved! Oh, my beloved! I am sorry that I wasn't here in your place."

Lord Neman took King Bruk's position in supporting Lady Anto's body, and the king quickly left to locate some clean cloths, which he found in a room not too far away.

"I love you, Anto. Do you know that? Do you know that I have loved you since the days before wars? I hope that you do know it. You have always had my heart and you always will."

By that point, Lady Anto could barely speak. She had lost too much blood and her eyes were starting to roll to the back of her head. Despite this, she made an effort to turn slightly towards her husband. She couldn't muster enough strength to tell him of her love. Instead, she simply reached out her frail arm to place her hand softly on his chest, feeling the rushing beat of her husband's panicked heart as she continued, hopelessly, to hold on. Not long after, she stopped her struggle, content to die with her husband's loving heartbeat playing to her as she passed on. King Bruk came back with the cloths, but it was too late. Instead of reinforcing pressure on the wound, he was tasked with holding his weeping brother who had lost the one love he had ever had.

＊＊＊＊

I had been left as the only patrician in Castle Eli, meaning that I was in charge of any issues that would come to our gates. Of course, I hadn't yet heard of the tragedy in the Deep South and so remained somewhat at peace. I had remained in my chamber to use the time to complete some plans that I had started to draw up, but was interrupted by the young boy again. I thought he would bear some news in light of the chase, but he had other matters for me to attend to. He dropped down on one knee,

"My Lord, I hope I don't disturb you too greatly."

"As much as I appreciate this respect, you only should do that for the king. A simple address will suffice for me."

He seemed rather embarrassed.

"I'm sorry, My Lord. There is a man from the province who has requested to see you. He says he has urgent news."

"Who is this man?"

"He didn't say, My Lord, but he claims that he has received word about an imminent danger."

I had many people come to me with warnings. Most of them were devout Leonists and seemed to be convinced that the gods had some sort of earthly realignment to perform, which begins to lose impact when they are scheduled twice a season but never seem to occur.

"I suppose you should let him in, then."

I was expecting one of my regulars and so was rather surprised when an old friend of mine from the High North entered my chamber. It was Mister Dearil, an old mate on the fishing vessel that Lord Shay and I would accompany. It turned out that after the Battle of Midland Bay, Mister Dearil had become acquainted with a Southern woman. Not long after King Bruk's coronation, the two got married, solidifying Mister Dearil's move from the High North to the South. He was certainly more rotund than he had been and had lost the majority of his hair, which had been in the process of giving up on him all those years ago, but I was more than happy to see him.

"My Lord, it has been some time," he said, slightly out of breath.

I stood and greeted him with a hug, offering him a seat, which he took.

"It most certainly has, good man. What have I done to deserve such a visit after all these years?"

"I'm afraid my visit is not in positive spirits, My Lord. I have received some terrible news."

"What is it? I'm sure we can help."

"I'm not convinced anyone could." He pulled out a letter from his pocket. "As you know, I am no stranger to map readings, My Lord. Skipper, who I'm sure you fondly remember, always had maps with him from his time in England and so I was given many an opportunity to study them. I soon worked out the direction in order to keep in contact with the mainland. I know we were forbidden, and I hope you can forgive me, but I left my poor mother and sister behind in England and needed them to know I was safe."

Sending letters across that distance was more about luck than anything else. I'm sure that there had been many occasions when their letters didn't arrive, going both ways, but I'm glad that some did arrive for my old friend. I couldn't slate a man for doing something that I would've done if I had the skill.

"That's understandable. Please, continue."

He handed the letter to me as he explained further.

"Well, my family and I have been sending letters back and forth for many years, and my sister and I continue now, even after my mother's death. My sister, to make her way, has turned to prostitution - something steady that she can live on now that she's alone. She is a particular favourite of the new King of England's chief advisor. When he... you know... he likes to tell her of his power and influence, and so he told my sister... that."

He gestured to the letter that I had been reading as he spoke. Mister Dearil's sister had written to warn her brother of an imminent invasion on Saddle Isle, the place where the bastards went, which had been revealed to them by a man named Kinby who had demanded his own survival as a reward for his information.

"And your sister, she is to be trusted?"

"I would trust her with my life, My Lord. She is an honest woman."

"And her source?"

"That one is harder to say, but he has told her of things prior to their occurrences, like of altercations set between King Henry and his brother that always did come to be. She said that she would send more information if she got it, which leads me to believe that she believes her source."

I sat in silence for a while, which must have been quite unsettling for my old friend. I desperately tried to find holes in the information. I thought that there must be something that didn't add up, but with Kinby's escape and this information coming forward, it was hard to deny what Mister Dearil was saying, especially considering that I trusted the man greatly. Besides, how would either the sister or the aide know of Kinby's name? I eventually spoke again.

"Thank you for this information. I hope you don't mind but I would like to keep this letter to show to the king, dear friend. Is that okay?"

"Of course, My Lord. If she sends further word then I will come straight here."

"Thank you. Your loyalty is greatly appreciated."

I smiled as he turned to leave.

"Oh, and Dearil. Please keep this to yourself. We don't want to cause any premature panic."

"Yes, My Lord. Of course."

****

I mentioned that I was the only patrician left in the Castle, which was true. That was because Queen Oline, who would have held more authority than myself if she were present, was visiting the nearby orphanage for the day. Only months before the Great Voyage of 1096, Queen Oline's mother died giving birth to a stillborn sibling, obviously causing the queen great distress. Because of this, she had real sympathy for all those unfortunate few children who lost their mothers in birth and now resided parentless in the isle's only orphanage.

Kinby was gaining separation from Sir Rufus on the chase, mainly due to the many sacrifices made by his bandits that slowed the king's guards down significantly. The rat had decided to abandon his horse in an attempt to blend in with the Southern crowd, admittedly a clever strategic move. He was alone and saw an opportunity for him to make his way to the Midlands from the South-Midlands border, which was his greatest chance of escape now as most guards in the chase for him were coming from the Deep South. He happened to pass the orphanage along a narrow back street that Queen Oline was also walking along after taking a stroll with a small girl named Greta, who had been at the orphanage for five years. Queen Oline had taken the more secluded roads to avoid creating a crowd - something she knew Greta was quite afraid of, from past experience. The sight of the queen, who was unaware of the havoc caused by the ratty man across the day, caused Kinby to panic. He could have passed her undetected, especially as she was completely unaware that he was even out of the castle, but his panic lured him towards threats, not disguise.

"My Queen, I'm going to need you to come with me."

He removed his cape to reveal his scabbard, from which he pulled a stolen sword from the Deep South. The queen urged Greta to stay behind her before answering. They both shuddered slightly in fear - even a fool is intimidating with a sword.

"Lord Kinby, I will do as you say, but please let this innocent child go."

"How can I? She is a witness, so she must die."

He spoke with a chuckle brought on either by his evil nature or, more likely, his own nerves.

"Run!" the queen commanded, pushing Greta in the opposite direction as she stepped before Kinby to block him off from the girl.

The queen put faith in the assumption that she was worth more to Kinby alive than dead, but Kinby was too panicked to think that logically. As she stepped in his way, the rat pierced his sword into her stomach and watched as she fell to the ground with a painful scream. I can only speculate but, having known the man, I believe that he was not a natural killer like his brothers were. I can imagine the act itself caused a similar strand of emotion to how I felt when I killed, which was only ever during the Battle of Midland Bay. I feel qualified to assume that, in the most horrible of moments that happened too quickly for rational thinking to possibly set in, the whole world slowed down to almost a halt. As the beautiful, innocent, kindest of women slowly fell, with the look of excruciating pain reddening her usually delicate face, Kinby thought of everything in that moment. He would've remembered being taught to use a sword as a child by his brother, Lord Eli, whom he looked up to with such awe. He would've remembered being taught by his siblings what power truly meant, and that killing is just a natural aspect of power.

But he would have also remembered the kindness that Queen Oline showed to him over the years. She, unlike most, never judged him for his brother's actions. She, unlike most, treated him as if he were a person on equal ground as the people around him. She, unlike most, did so many loving things for her adopted people without being required to. He would've surely acknowledged that she was partaking in an act of kindness at the very moment that he killed her, and he wouldn't have been able to persist indifferently with that knowledge. As she continued to slowly fall, now with tears flowing from those usually striking, bright green eyes, he would have felt the sweat begin to form as his body heated up from the anxiety and guilt caused by his foolish actions. He would have wanted to reach out and catch her in his arms to help her to survive his evil act, but would have found his mobility frozen like a corpse. He couldn't move. He couldn't help. He couldn't take back what he'd done. And then, as time returned to normality, she walloped against the cobbled ground and lay there at his feet, moaning loudly at the pain. He would have felt considerable regret, but still, he needed to shut her up. If he didn't, he would be caught, and if he was caught then he would have a similar fate to his victim. He closed his eyes and slit her throat, ending her suffering and cementing his error. She was dead. He turned to run but stopped for a moment. He was still panicked; half because of his guilt, half because of his damned fate. Perhaps if he used this as a message, he could strike enough fear to bide himself some time. He bent down to her corpse and, taking two fingers, scooped up some of her blood and turned to the wall to his left. He ran his fingers across the hard surface, writing: 'Kinby is king.' With a stomach churning from his wrongdoing and sweat still streaming from his brow, he wiped his bloody hands on his abandoned cape and fled the scene, trying to walk to avoid drawing any more attention to himself but finding that his anxiety made that much more difficult than he'd have hoped.

And there she was left, the first Queen of Saddle Isle, dead at the hands of a rat. And there was no husband by her side. No friend to hold her hand to ease the pain. No feeling of hope, just the cold stone on her cheek and the sweat from Kinby's hands dripping on her neck as he slit her throat as if she was a mere sheep. As if she was bred to die, not alive to serve in the selfless way that she always did, without needing to be prompted. And what did she die for? It wasn't out of necessity but out of the fear of a coward, and no one should have to die because of a coward's fear. Greta, who owed her life to the bravery of Queen Oline, quickly made it to the orphanage and told the women of the events that had happened. The women headed to the village centre where Sir Rufus continued to look for Kinby, who would have been halfway to the border on the far west of the isle by that point. They led the chief guard to the scene and told him what, to their assumption, had happened. He lifted Queen Oline's lifeless body onto the rear of his horse and brought her back to Castle Eli where she would be buried in ceremony with the honour that she deserved. Saddle Isle lost a great lady and a great queen on that fateful day.

As King Bruk began his ride back to the capital, leaving his mourning brother behind, he thought of how horrible it must be to lose the one person whom you love more than any other. What he didn't know was that, when he arrived home, he was set to feel that pain firsthand. As I anticipated the king's arrival back in the capital, I feared that Queen Oline's death and the impending doom of the kingdom would be too much for my friend.

The Brute's Eunuch

Kinby's escape didn't last for much longer after the murder of Queen Oline. On hearing of the events that occurred in the Deep South, Lord Robt prepared for the rat's re-entrance into the Midlands. Kinby was met by a mixture of Midland guards and loyal citizens when he attempted to cross the South-Midland border. He was quickly taken to Lord Robt and Lady Wonin, the latter of whom was particularly outraged by her brother's actions. After a brutal beating from Lord Robt, Kinby was tied to a horse and forced to shamefully walk back to the capital, where a grieving husband and sister were waiting.

King Bruk broke down in tears as he looked over his dead wife's body. For the Leonists, including the king himself, Sir Rufus had placed her on a bed in preparation for some of the female servants to tend to her. It was important that the dead, especially patricians, were sent to the gods looking respectfully beautiful. She was dressed in fine linen clothes and decorated with flowers. The king had not known romantic love before Queen Oline and this empty feeling was one that he would only wish on Kinby, if the rat were ever able to love another. The king's pain after losing his wife completely overshadowed the threat of doom from King Henry, which certainly had me, among others, rather concerned about what was to come. Having said that, I couldn't fathom a single idea to save our people and on so many occasions, as great as King Bruk was, the king had turned to me for answers.

Lady Daid, who had made a hasty return to Castle Eli after hearing the tragic news, wept too. She had never been close with Queen Oline in the way that King Bruk was with his brothers, but she had much affection for her sister, who became another addition to her rather long list of losses. The fact that it was her husband, whom she hated as much as the rest of us even before these horrific events, made the whole ordeal much worse. Perhaps if she had put more effort into what was essentially a sham marriage then he may have felt less trapped and her sister may have still been alive. Of course, it was incredibly unfair for Lady Daid to blame herself. She was married to a maniac who needed to be removed from society. I too was devastated as I had lost a very close friend. She and I had much in common and her kind nature made every moment in her presence feel warm and full of comfort. We had both grown up with older sisters who attempted to hide us away, for different reasons. We were both the newest additions to the family of those of House Northorpe and had to put in the necessary effort to be accepted. I had the utmost respect for Queen Oline and I still miss her deeply.

****

Soon enough, Lord Robt arrived in the capital with his captive murderer. He was shamefully paraded into the Great Hall, where King Bruk sat on his throne awaiting for an easy judgement to be made. He didn't appear to be outwardly angry. King Bruk sat in silence, failing to move, as if his soul had left his body in a motionless state. Lady Daid wasn't as inactive. She stormed over to Kinby as soon as he entered, screaming abuse in his face, aggressively spitting on him, forcing him down to the ground to kneel before his grieving king as soldiers held the prisoner's arms extended behind his back with rope. For a long while, King Bruk remained his frozen self, just looking down on the man who killed his wife. Not once did King Bruk take his eyes from the rat and not once did Kinby look upon his king's face, opting to keep his gaze on the stone floor instead. The rest of the room, which consisted of many guards, Sir Rufus, Lord Robt, Lady Wonin, myself and Lady Daid, started to become quite unsettled as we eagerly awaited for King Bruk's further instruction. Eventually, Lady Daid became too impatient. She approached the throne and quietly spoke to him.

"My King, what are you doing?"

The king remained silent.

She added to her argument, "He clearly must be punished for his actions. Why haven't you sentenced him to death yet?"

He ignored Lady Daid for a while, not taking his eyes away from his wife's killer. Eventually, he began to calmly address the criminal. His nature turned as if he suddenly became someone else, a man no one in the Great Hall could recognise.

"You are just a man. Just a pathetic, weak man. Who do you think you are? Who are you to take her life? Did it make you feel powerful? Did it make you feel big, make you feel strong? Did it give you the validation that you never got from your brother?"

The rat didn't answer. The king became increasingly and, uncharacteristically, angry.

"Did it make up for the lack of love in your life? Did killing two innocent wives of your enemies feel like justice for you? She was unarmed! They were unarmed!"

Again, the rat was silent. Again, the king raised his aggression.

"Do you know what you are? You're a coward! Come after me if you have an issue! Come after me if you feel any injustice has occurred! If you had any strength whatsoever, then you would have come for me, but you didn't. You ran around scared like the rat that we all know you to be, scuttering about, trying to make an escape, because you know that you are hated and you know that you are vermin!"

For the first time, King Bruk stood. He walked down the steps that lead to the throne and knelt down to get on Kinby's level, lifting his prisoner's head to meet his eyes.

"I know what you're thinking. You think you know everything. You think that I'm just going to slit your throat and be done with it, don't you? But you are wrong, boy!"

Kinby didn't say a word but instead spat in King Bruk's face, which was met by a firm punch from the king, drawing blood from the rat's cheek.

"Touch me again and I will rip your skin from your body!" King Bruk exclaimed, hitting him once more.

King Bruk stood and paced around the hall. He muttered to himself, but it was incredibly difficult to catch any of what he was saying. A few more minutes of pacing passed before he stopped. He stood still and looked around the room until he caught the eye of Sir Rufus, who was beckoned over by his king. King Bruk whispered in his ear and Sir Rufus left the room, before coming back with a small but sharp dagger, which was one of King Bruk's personal favourites. He took the dagger from his chief guard and once more knelt in front of Kinby. He stared at him intently again as he thought of what he was going to do. But then he didn't do anything. Instead, he stood back up and moved to the back of the hall and eventually exited. We looked at each other in confusion, wondering when he'd come back or if he'd come back at all. Our thoughts were interrupted as he re-entered the hall with a bowl and took his place next to Kinby's right arm, which was still being pulled back by a guard with rope. The rat's hand was clenched in a fist, but a few twirls of the dagger into the flesh made his fingers spread. King Bruk gestured for a guard to come and hold his hand open and one eagerly stepped up to assist. As she maintained Kinby's open hand, King Bruk applied the dagger under each one of his fingernails, ripping them off one by one to the sound of painful screams. Each nail was long, curled, sharp and as dirty as a servant's foot, but King Bruk didn't care. He went about his business as if he had done it a thousand times before. I can assure you, he hadn't. No matter how much he struggled, Kinby couldn't break free of this torture and so the pain simply continued.

Once King Bruk had de-nailed one hand, he moved onto the next, following the exact same procedure as before. Each nail that he took was placed in the bowl, along with countless drops of blood that spewed from Kinby's fingers as the echoed sound of his screams filled the room. The king was quickly done with the second hand and stood up and moved back to kneel in front of his prisoner once more. Kinby remained looking at the ground to hide his tears. King Bruk placed the bowl under the rat's face so that he could look at his work. Sir Rufus looked to me from across the room with an expression that highlighted his concern for the king, which emulated my own feelings. I have stated before that Kinby is the only man I have ever hated. Even so, what I was seeing from King Bruk was a truly disturbing display, one which made me feel incredibly uncomfortable.

"Eat them," King Bruk demanded, with no emotion in his voice whatsoever. He lifted the bowl to Kinby's mouth. "You're going to swallow them whole. Let's hope that you choke on one, for your own sake. If I see you chewing, I will hit you twice as hard as I did before. Then, I will hit you harder again, and again, and again! Do you understand?"

There was no response from the now broken rat, who quickly placed his face in the bloody bowl and consumed all ten of his fingernails. Based on the disgruntled expression, they seemed to scratch the inside of his throat as they went down but didn't make him choke. King Bruk looked on, still emotionless in expression, patiently waiting for Kinby to finish. As Kinby swallowed his last nail, he spat the blood from his scratched throat into the bowl, which King Bruk then made him drink again and again, until Kinby spat onto the floor instead. King Bruk, dissatisfied with this avoidance, pushed the rat's face onto the cold floor and demanded he lick the blood clean from the stone. Kinby obeyed as he started to cry. It wasn't a subtle, hidden cry, but a cry like a child missing their mother. King Bruk stood once more and handed the dagger to Lady Daid, who was watching on with a smile on her face. She enjoyed seeing this wicked rat suffer and was proud to show that joy to all in attendance. Lady Daid took the dagger from her king and listened as he whispered his request into her ear. I knew the next act would be disturbing simply based on the look on Lady Daid's face, as even she seemed slightly shocked by his request.

"Are you sure, My King?"

She didn't seem unwilling to do what he wanted but was unsure as to whether it truly matched the king's character.

"You want him to die, right? Then that is how he shall die."

"Yes, My King."

Lady Daid moved to kneel in front of her husband, as the king had done before her. She whispered into his ear - again, something that I couldn't quite make out. Then, she took the dagger in her dominant right hand and stuck her left hand down into his torn trousers. After creating enough separation between Kinby and the fabric, she followed suit with her dagger-filled right hand and began to slice away at his cock. I thought his screams during King Bruk's manic display were harrowing, but they were nothing compared to this. His body completely spasmed as he squirmed in pain, causing the necessity for more guards to hold onto the ropes that kept his arms in position. Eventually, Lady Daid pulled his severed cock from his pants and held it in front of Kinby's face. As blood dripped from his genital area onto the floor, and a mixture of sweat and tears streamed down his agonised face, Lady Daid pulled his head up with her free hand so he looked into her eyes.

"Open wide," she demanded, with a menacing grin.

Kinby refused to open his mouth, so King Bruk got involved. He tipped the rat's head back and, taking the bloody dagger, pierced its tip into the side of Kinby's neck, forcing him to let out another scream. As he did, King Bruk grabbed his mouth and kept it open, allowing Lady Daid to shove his cock straight down his throat, keeping as much of her hand as she could in his mouth. He was choking and, as much as his body naturally attempted to force the phallus back up, Lady Daid's hand constantly remained to stop any refuge. I turned away. I could not watch this scene any longer. I understood that King Bruk and Lady Daid were hurting, but this was too much, even as punishment for a man like Kinby. After a while, I heard King

Bruk and Lady Daid both walk away: he to his throne and she to her chamber. As the Great Hall silently emptied, I turned to see Kinby's corpse be dragged away, not to be buried in honour, but to be dumped.

It was left to be consumed by the capital's rats. I watched King Bruk, my leader and my friend, sit silently on his throne for a while, unable to recognise him as the man I had admired so abundantly as a child. I eventually left him alone in the Great Hall, where he remained staring at the pool of blood that Kinby left behind.

No one who witnessed that day spoke of the event afterwards. It was an unanimous decision that an extreme punishment was necessary for a man such as Kinby, but what happened to him was too much for most to stomach. It seemed the best thing, considering our impending doom, to try to forget that it ever happened. But something like that is hard to forget. I won't mention details of Kinby's execution again past this account. I won't pass judgement on what happened. I will continue on as if the event was the most average of executions there has ever been, which is how the kingdom was told the day panned out. King Bruk was a kind man who fought for equality and peace, but on that day he let anger get the better of him. He was never the same after that.

King Bruk sat on his throne for a few hours before heading to his chamber. He remained isolated in that small room from then on, causing much distress for myself as I had to take over his duties for a while whilst maintaining my role as provincial leader in the South, but I will come onto that soon enough. For now, I want you, the reader, to contemplate grief, blame and anger, and to think about what you would do in the same situation. I have been critical of King Bruk's actions but who's to say that, if it were Lady Breck and Lady Nea that Kinby had killed, I wouldn't have been driven to do the same.

A Broken Man, A Broken King

Grief is an all encompassing thing. It surrounds you until you feel trapped. Until you can't breathe. That can cause a person to fall into one of many seriously dangerous states with a varying range of forms. The scope of how different people deal with grief was highlighted by the reactions of both King Bruk and Lord Neman after the equally tragic deaths of their respective wives. Unfortunately, Kinby had created a situation where there was serious turmoil across the kingdom. This was something that I'm not fully convinced that he intended to do, certainly not with the intellectual foresight that some gave him credit for. I would say that his victims, particularly Queen Oline, were simply in the wrong place at the wrong time. Either way, his actions did cause significant turbulence as the majority of the kingdom's most powerful people were now, for lack of a better term, all over the place. Of course, that was understandable. I couldn't imagine the insufferable pain of losing Lady Breck, or Lady Nea for that matter, and so seeing these tragic losses from the sideline brought out a further sympathetic side to myself. Sympathy towards King Bruk and Lord Neman was the prominent feeling across the kingdom, a fair and kind response from the people. But I felt an equal sympathy for Lady Daid, as her track record of losses was now beyond heartbreaking.

*** * * ***

"Are you sure you don't want some company?" I asked.

After Queen Oline's funeral and the execution of Kinby, Lady Daid decided that it was best for her to go back to the North to be with her brother, Lord Angull. It came to me, because of circumstances surrounding King Bruk's state, to give her the permission to return home. I obviously granted this based on my knowledge of her past, and the small fact that we were all going to die soon anyway. She wore a slight smile, which I imagine was at the thought of being with her remaining family for a while.

"Barrat, I've told you, I will be fine."

"I know."

I didn't really know what to say, in all honesty. Death is such an abstruse topic, and I found it awkward and difficult to be supportive without overdoing it. After all, how can one truly express something that was difficult to understand?

"Are you going to be okay?" she asked, shocking me slightly.

I hadn't really thought about my own feelings towards the deaths. I had always been a great admirer of Lady Anto but never did have a close relationship with her. I should say, of course, that I still understood that her death was a great loss to the kingdom. Queen Oline was different. She was my dear friend and I had much affection for her. I suppose the sight of other people struggling, like King Bruk in particular, undermined my own feelings and distracted me from my own pain. My thoughts stopped me from giving an answer as my impromptu reflection had brought about some sadness.

Lady Daid interrupted my thoughts, "Death is a demon. It doesn't matter if it's your partner, your child, your sibling, or your friend, it always hurts. Don't let the notion that other people are 'hurting more' take away from how you feel. You deserve to grieve just as much as anyone else."

"Thanks, Daid. You're right."

"She loved you, you know. You were her closest friend and she cared about you deeply."

"I know. I loved her too."

Lady Daid gave me a rare hug, something that acted as a comfort for the both of us. She followed it up with a reassuring smile. Then she wiped her tears away and mounted her horse, which was prepared for the journey she had ahead.

"Go and enjoy being with your family," I suggested, smiling back.

"You should go and enjoy being with yours. You might not get many more chances."

****

Lord Neman had been too busy with his own grief to attend the execution of Kinby. He also missed the queen's funeral as Lady Anto was to be buried only a few days after and the provincial leader of the Deep South wanted to make sure that everything was perfect, which was what his wife rightfully deserved after such a cruel and undignified death. Not that death is ever too dignified in general. Similarly, despite the support he had given at the scene of Lady Anto's death, King Bruk was not in attendance for his sister-in-law's funeral as he had locked himself away from all outside life after losing his beloved. Lord Neman understood, but was disappointed that his brother wasn't there. Of course, King Bruk felt rather similar himself when the roles were reversed a few days prior. I, too, was absent from Lady Anto's ceremony due to the king's hiatus from duty. Again, I had the utmost sympathy for them both and so didn't mind bringing order, as best I could, to the kingdom after the mess caused by the king's isolation. Two people who were in attendance, however, were Lord Robt and Lady Wonin, who travelled down to the Deep South from the capital, where the two had been supporting the king after his loss. Lady Wonin felt awful because of the events and felt a sense of guilt considering it was her only remaining brother who was responsible for all of the kingdom's carnage. Of course, one should never be judged for the actions of a family member, but all sound logic can seemingly abandon a person when grief has its tight grip around them.

On the day that followed Lady Anto's funeral, Lord Robt needed to return to the Midlands as he was still the provincial leader and had been absent for a number of days, something that worried him slightly based on the province's tendency to cause problems. Being a loving brother, he made sure to personally visit Lord Neman before his departure. The leader of the Deep South had demanded to be left completely alone, in a similar vein to King Bruk, to the point where he ordered his guards and servants away from the castle completely. Some servants, however, went against their provincial leader's wishes. Those were the servants who had lived in the castle for their entire time on Saddle Isle and so had nowhere else to go. It was from those long serving citizens that the rumours of the events I will now describe were spread. How accurate they are I do not know for sure but, based on my knowledge of what followed these events, I believe the rumours to be sound.

****

"Brother," Lord Robt began. "Again, my deepest thoughts and prayers to the gods go out to you. Unfortunately, we must leave to return to our posts in the Midlands but urge you to stay with us whenever you feel it necessary."

He embraced Lord Neman as he was let into his chamber, shortly followed by his wife, who felt it necessary to show her support too. His brother didn't say anything, which slightly offended the provincial leader of the Midlands.

"Neman, my brother, I know that this is a very difficult time for you, but this behaviour is disrespectful."

"You are the disrespectful one!"

His shouting caused Lady Wonin to startle, which was only increased as Lord Neman threw a table onto the floor, smashing an empty glass vase in the process.

"In coming here with her, all you have done is remind me of the rat who killed my beloved!"

"Brother, that is unfair!" Lord Robt shouted back, defending his wife. "You cannot blame my wife for the actions of her brother. The demon that killed your beloved wife, who I had much love for myself, is no brother of Lady Wonin's, I assure you."

"If that be the case, then why do the words exit your mouth and not hers?"

Lord Robt turned to Lady Wonin sharply and encouraged her to reaffirm what he had said, but his wife was so startled by Lord Neman's aggressive state that she struggled with her words.

"Ne... Neman, m... m... my br... brother..." she timidly said, reluctantly shuffling forward as she spoke in a nervous stutter.

"... I am no brother of yours!" Lord Neman bellowed, interrupting.

"I'm sorry, I'm sorry!"

Lady Wonin dropped to the floor, now in floods of tears at his aggressive nature, pleading for the large patrician's mercy. Lord Robt, incredibly offended at his brother's treatment of his wife, stepped in and pushed Lord Neman back. He ushered his younger brother to move away from Lady Wonin, who refused to open her eyes in fear of what may happen if she stepped out of line in the eyes of her brother-in-law. Lord Robt grew furious.

"Neman! I will forgive you of these vile actions on the basis of your trauma, but please do treat my innocent wife with more respect than this."

"She is not innocent! Ever since we met the rats from the Midlands, we've known of their evil tendencies! They are not people but demons! We have always known! And here you are, brother, trapped under her wicked sorcery. They plague us with their immoral ways. Well, no longer shall we be plagued!"

In all his rage, Lord Neman bundled his brother to the ground, causing Lord Robt to roll through the glass shards, cutting his exposed arms and face. Lady Wonin continued to scream as she tried to crawl away from Lord Neman in pathetic distress, but was soon silenced by the hands of the deranged lord, who tightly gripped her throat. She desperately grasped for breath, struggling and wriggling in a last ditch attempt to create separation, but Lord

Neman's blind rage created an unhinged monster whose necessity for some personal vengeance against those of House Wharram somehow made him more able and determined to keep his grasp. Lord Robt, who rushed back to his feet in as quick a manner as possible despite the pain he felt from the heavy fall, grabbed at his brother's arms after surveying the surroundings and seeing no weapon to use against him. He attempted to rip Lord Neman's hands from his wife's neck, but his brother was too broad shouldered for Lord Robt to overcome. It was only when Lady Wonin's eyes rolled to the back of her head that Lord Neman let go of his grip, brushing his brother away as he made his exit, walking down the three steps at the entrance of the chamber.

On seeing his wife's lifeless body on the floor and being filled with a rage of his own, Lord Robt rushed after his brother and met the middle of his shoulder blades with a strike from his knee. Lord Neman thumped heavily to the ground, dislocating his right shoulder in the process. Lord Robt pinned him down as best as he could, lodging both knees into Lord Neman's back. He hit his younger brother with consistent blows, mostly to the back of the head. Blow after blow after blow, Lord Neman's head continuously bounced off the stone flooring, causing blood to flow once more down the corridors of Castle Shay. Lord Robt continued to attack his brother's dead body for a few moments before eventually tending to his wife's corpse. He closed her eyes, kissed her lips, and then carried her to the trade gate where their horses were ready for departure. On returning to Castle Bennk, he laid his wife on a bed and uncorked a barrel of Southern wine.

****

It had been a few days and King Bruk had still not exited his chamber and, with the impending doom of the isle, it looked even less likely that he was going to re-emerge. Food was brought to his door every day, and every day that food was left untouched and replaced by a new plate doomed to the same fate. The news of his brother's death only had the potential to make his mental state deteriorate further, if that were even possible, and it was for that reason that I decided not to tell him of the news, even though that was the primary reason why I was going against his wish to be left alone. I did, however, feel the need to check on him considering that he was my friend before my king.

"Bruk."

I knocked on his door. There was no answer.

"Bruk, it's Barrat. Can you please let me in?"

After a rather long wait, he eventually unlocked the door, not saying a word. I looked around a completely trashed room, with tables on the floor, curtains pulled down, and a broken chair looking rather sad in the corner. The one thing that remained intact was a small table housing only a bouquet of flowers placed upon it. He sat down in front of an open window and looked out over the onlooking field.

"It is quite the mess in here, my friend. You know that Oline always liked to keep things clean. She wouldn't be happy with this."

It was a desperate attempt to be somewhat comforting to my brother.

"I know."

He didn't turn around to acknowledge me but remained looking out of the window, not moving a single muscle. I started to move towards him but he raised his arm to tell me to stop.

"Bruk, I'm worried about you. I fear that the longer you stay here in the darkness, the further you slip away from sanity. As your chief advisor, I can only give you my opinion. But as your brother and friend, I am telling you that you need to get out of this chamber and get back into the normal world."

"The world can never be normal without her," was his response as he ignored my advice completely.

"Look, I know that what you're going through is difficult..."

"... No you don't," he interrupted. "If I'm not mistaken, your wife is sitting safely in the High North with your beautiful daughter, happy. My wife has been brutally killed in the back alleys like a common whore. No pride. No honour. No dignity. So no, you don't know anything about what I'm going through, Barrat."

I felt slightly attacked, which I could forgive based on the circumstances, but felt it was unfair.

"Okay, I understand that, but you're not the only one who is struggling with this loss, Bruk. Oline was my friend, and I know it's not the same but I do know how grief can take its hold on you. When I was in this very castle's dungeon, constantly stuck in the same environment and dealing with the grief and guilt I felt towards the loss of my family, not being able to leave made things so much worse. Please Bruk, come out of here. Go to the High North and visit Breck, or at least get back to some sort of normality. I am worried about you. Too many of us have fallen victim to grief recently."

"I'm not going anywhere," he insisted after a long pause. "I don't want things to go back to normal because I don't want to live in the same way as before. Not when Oline isn't here by my side."

I didn't know what I could do to change his state. I was clueless, guilty for not being good enough to help him. I turned to leave.

"Okay, but I hope you change your mind."

"Wait!"

I halted. He still refused to turn around.

"I need to tell you something important. Barrat, there's a ship. A few years ago, I commissioned the build of a ship to be stored by the Southern docks in case of a need for us to flee. It wasn't attacked by Kinby and still sits at the dock now. You and my sister must use it to take Nea away from the danger. You owe it to my niece to give her a life."

This caught me off guard. I was baffled at how I didn't know of this.

"Are you serious? Is this true?"

"Of course it's true, Barrat. You'll need food supplies and sailors, but then you can bring whomever you like."

He spoke in a frustrated tone, still with his back to me.

"Well, you'll be coming with us, of course," I said, somewhat optimistically.

"No, I will not."

The understated tone remained, but the strangeness of his choices became more and more alarming,

"I can't live on... I can't." He paused to compose himself, knowing that he could not appear so vulnerable to me as I would not leave him alone. "I can't leave. My people are going to die because of me. I should at least give them enough respect to die as well."

"None of this is your fault, Bruk."

"Isn't it? Because I feel as though everyone deflects blame away from us just because of who we are. I am responsible for this kingdom and I let Kinby run wild. I should've killed him when I had the chance."

We both remained silent for a moment; me not knowing what I should say and him preferring I didn't say anything at all.

"Barrat, I appreciate what you're doing, but can you please just leave me alone."

"Yes, of course," I replied, not knowing that I would never see him again.

★ ★ ★ ★

An open window. The sound of birds chirping from the nearby trees swiftly gliding through the chamber, only interrupted, every so often, by the far off noise of everyday life in the capital just beyond the castle walls. The smell of freshly cut grass overpowering the faint remnants of a queen's scent that a king was so desperate to maintain. The bouquet of flowers - that represented not just a lost beauty but the sorrow of a tragic end - standing proud, with honour and dignity, on the only remaining upright table in the room. A soft spring breeze, not strong enough to cause havoc, yet with enough strength to lightly sway King Bruk's lifeless body that swung from the wooden beam on which he tied his own noose. At peace, at last.

The Fleeing Bastard - I

In a relatively short period of time marked the Autocracy Era, the entire shape of our existence had changed. After the Great Packsaddle War, we appeared to grow as a kingdom through the movement and fight for peace, something that King Bruk had made a priority from the very moment he was crowned. In fact, he was still on the battlefield after the Battle of the Brutes when he initially made his views clear. Yet, in a similar way to how the initial format of leadership during the Prosperity Era crumbled, it only took the bitterness and contempt of one person to cause a ripple of hatred and violence to spread across Saddle Isle once more. That person, of course, was Kinby, whose execution failed to bring the closure that people needed in order for us to carry on in as similar a manner as we had been in regard to comradery.

Now, I am not foolish enough to believe that the inevitable genocide, caused by the English invasion, could have been stopped if Kinby's death would have failed to divide, but the people of the isle needed a sense of hope. They had been encouraged for two decades to look to their patricians during times of distress and need, as we were meant to have knowledge and superiority. Yet we were in tatters. The invasion was the biggest distress of these people's lives, and would result in the end of their lives too, yet the patricians were too busy hating each other and feeling sorry for themselves to give the people the aid that they needed. Instead of support, we showed to our people that all was to remain hopeless. The tragic murders of Queen Oline and Lady Anto, and the subsequent acts of violence that followed between two previously loving brothers, hit too hard for us to recover from. To make matters worse, the death of our queen led to the king's suicide and eventually led to me being named king, something that I had never hoped for, especially not in those circumstances. Either way, it wasn't something that I could turn down, not even if I wanted to. When King Bruk was crowned, he was told to keep an updated letter that stated what should happen to the kingdom on account of his death. Initially, he had stated that Lord Robt would become king after his passing, but later altered that statement after his brother's struggle with leading the Midlands. When he died, his letter stated that Queen Oline would rule after himself if that were a possibility. If not, then I was to become king.

I know I have slandered the feeble attempts at comforting our citizens, but it was very difficult for any of the patricians to provide the people with a sense of hope when our own hope had been completely shattered. My poor Lady Breck had essentially lost three brothers in a day and so fell into a sadness that didn't help the people of the High North, who were still shaken by the image of fiery doom caused by Kinby's vandals at the docks. She did, however, insist on remaining in the High North to show her unity with her people, which I respected. It was, perhaps, slightly harsh to consider Lord Robt as a loss based on the information I have given so far. I know that, if he had been alive, I would have killed Lord Shay without question if he had done anything to harm Lady Breck, and so I understood why Lord Neman's violence caused Lord Robt to strike back. However, Lord Robt's loss of his wife caused him to lose more sense than initially thought. His grief led him on an anger-fuelled march to take what he deemed was rightfully his, which is really where Lady Breck lost all respect for him, especially during a time of mourning.

It was King Bruk's suicide that hit everyone the hardest. He had been such an influential leader, whose reign had led to the development of the kingdom and forged many years of happiness for the vast majority of citizens. It was strange to think back to his coronation, a turbulent time for myself but one of pride for those of House Northorpe, and to compare that day to the way in which his reign ended. I would say that, despite his tragic end, King Bruk should be primarily remembered for his great leadership that led to great development across the kingdom for many years. My coronation was as non-existent as my desire to rule, which was the most befitting way to respect King Bruk. It did cause me some great personal distress, however, when my first official day as king was greeted with a letter from a ship - or ships, to be more accurate - that were headed our way.

*** * * ***

"My King," said a servant who had come to my chamber.

I was rather upset not to see Sir Rufus at my door. I could've done with his support when reading that letter but he was busy dealing with a matter that I was not yet aware of.

"This has arrived by a bird I do not recognise."

"Do you know the birds personally?" I asked, trying to be jovial in such a depressed time.

He didn't seem to appreciate my humour.

"I'm sorry, My King. I mean to say that the black nature of the bird has made me quite confused."

"A black bird, you say?"

"Yes, My King," he quickly answered.

"Well, that must be a raven," I speculated, rather confused myself.

We sent messages by pigeon, mainly because there were no ravens on the isle and pigeons were relatively domestic birds. My initial confusion became a realisation that death for us all was imminent.

"Can you read, good man?"

I never normally asked but was unsure if I could bring myself to read this letter after all the distress that had been caused by these murderous Englishmen, some of which this young man did not know of.

"Yes, My King. My father taught me," he said, with a comforting sense of pride.

"Your father must be a good man to teach you such a great skill. Would you read it to me? If you feel too distressed, don't worry."

"No, no, My King. I'll read it."

He opened it and initially read it in his head. This was against protocol, but I always thought that protocol was rather pretentious and, considering the circumstances, allowed this occasion to pass by.

"You can paraphrase, if it's easier," I suggested, aware that he was taking some time - something we didn't have much left of.

He seemed slightly embarrassed.

"I'm sorry, My King, but I don't know what you mean."

"One should never apologise for not yet knowing something. To paraphrase means to simplify the letter. Tell me the details that I need to know."

"Yes, My King," his face dropped slightly. It wasn't particularly perky to begin with, but there was a real fear in his eyes now. "It's from the Admiral of the British Fleet. He writes to inform you that they are but days away."

I sat down in my chair, leaning forwards, resting my elbows on my knees and twiddling my thumbs in anxiety. I thought that I should say something to the boy to try to make him feel better if I could, but no words came out. After a while, he spoke with sadness.

"I fear that we are all going to die."

I paused, wondering if false hope was even worth selling.

"Go home, boy."

I looked up at him for the first time since he read that damned letter.

"I can't, My King. I'm serving a sentence."

I stood up and faced him, gesturing for him to look at me,

"Right, well, I suppose I should give you something to do then."

"Anything, My King."

I shot him a melancholy smile.

"Here we are. I want you to go to the servant's chambers, then all throughout the castle. Tell all servants that you come across, paid or not, that they can all leave now and go to their homes to be with their families, if they so wish. You are right, young man. We are all going to die, so you might as well spend your final days with people whom you love rather than reading letters for a man who is quite capable of reading them for himself."

"Thank you, My King."

"Don't thank me, boy. I'm part of the reason they're coming."

"Aren't we all?"

I suppose, in a way, he had a point.

****

I am not going to pretend like I am a kind man. A lot of my motives are completely selfish and aim to bring what is best for my family, but sending the servants home gave me a real sense of pride. I hadn't felt this way for a number of weeks. It felt rewarding to do something that benefited others rather than myself, for once. Of course, it was all rather superficial considering that death was sailing just a few hundred miles off shore, but at least it cheered me up ever so slightly. Having said that, in the scope of how our universe seems to work, bright moments in dark times are not designed to last very long. That proved to be the case. I hinted before at the absence of Sir Rufus in the castle and that he was dealing with a matter that was occurring nearby in the province. This occurrence was the doing of a rather intoxicated Lord Robt, who had made his way from the Midlands, with his brother's blood now stained on his clothes, to congratulate me on becoming king. I was still working in my chamber when I heard the commotion down the stairs and felt it necessary, although rather inconvenient, for me to see what was going on. When I made it to the grand doors, Lord Robt was standing there in the grasp of Sir Rufus, who looked rather disappointed in his old patrician companion. Sir Rufus greeted me with a description of the day's events,

"My King, we seem to have an untimely visitor."

"We do indeed. What are you doing, Robt?"

I faced up to Lord Robt, whose breath stank of wine, in an attempt to get some words out of him. Instead, he just maniacally smiled at me.

Sir Rufus, who I had never seen this disappointed before, was keen to fill me in and so I let him proceed.

"My King, may I enlighten you with what has occurred? After what can only be described as carnage in the Midlands between Robt and his now deceased brother, your brother-in-law decided that it was unjust for you to have been named king and so, with the assistance of a few bounders from the Midlands and the South, who posed very little threat to our guards and now lie dead on the streets, Robt thought..."

"... That's Lord Robt to you, you ancient shrew!" interrupted Lord Robt, who was slurring every word.

I was impressed with Sir Rufus' calm nature.

He continued, "Lord Robt, then, thought it wise to come here to take the Crown away from you. So, what would you like me to do with this treasonous scum?"

"Just take him to the dungeons," I ordered, with little conviction. "I'm sure that death is as likely to find him there as it is on a throne."

I had grown tired and, as poor as it is for me to say, slightly disinterested in all of the petty chaos. Sir Rufus attempted to move him away but Lord Robt resisted.

"How dare you, Barrat! How dare you, a bastard who should be long gone, disrespect me with a cell. Give me my chamber and that shall be the last!"

Lord Robt hurled a previously hidden dagger in my direction, which didn't get anywhere close to me. His words caused some of the pent up frustration that had been vigorously bubbling under my rather worn-out surface to rise. I got right in his face but tried my best not to shout. Shouting never seems to get anyone very far.

"It was 'the last' when I, the king, said that you shall be put in a cell. You are lucky that I am not taking your head for treason! If my Breck hadn't already lost two brothers this week, I might have done you that service!"

I turned to walk back to my chamber but he chose to speak further.

"I should have killed you as soon as you put that arrow in Suln's head."

That hit a nerve.

"And I should kill you right now for your inability to realise the irony behind that statement! Is that not Lord Neman's blood on your clothes? You are just as much the monster that I am."

I began to turn once more towards the stairs when I heard him start to weep. His tears caused the dried blood on his face to flow again.

"Please, Barrat, I have nothing left. Please just give me my chamber."

If my life had been different by just one night, I would have caved and let him sleep in his old chamber for the sake of it. But my frustrations were high and my mind could only transport me, not to the times when Lord Robt, despite his flaws, had shown me mercy, but to that fateful day when I let Kinby walk back to his chamber when he should've been locked up like any other rat.

"The last time that a lord deserving of the dungeon was given refuge in a chamber, he went and condemned our isle to death. An armoured fleet with the sole aim of burning our kingdom to the ground is headed our way, and all you can think about is the throne! Have you lost your mind? If I didn't have a wife and a daughter, who mean the world to me, I would let you slit my throat right now if the poisoned chalice of the throne could be passed from me to you."

There was a brief moment of calm. I'm not too sure that Lord Robt believed what I said, especially in regard to not wanting to be king, but it became a moot point. We both seemed to realise in this moment, with death looming over us, how ridiculous this all was becoming. Lord Robt, welling up as he spoke, pulled me to look into his eyes.

"In the dying embers of our existence, you would let me, your own brother, rot alone in a cell."

"Your selfishness outweighs my pity on you. You are no brother to me, Robt. Sir Rufus, take him away."

I pushed him back into the arms of Sir Rufus before turning my back on him.

*** * * ***

On the third attempt, I had managed to ignore Lord Robt's mixture of cries and insults hurled in my direction and made it back to my chamber. I have to admit, I wasn't really doing anything of merit in that room. There were the normal disputes and problems to attend to, but the motivation to attend to them was lacking. Of course, there was no point whatsoever in feeling guilty about my lack of work ethic. There were so many more things to feel guilty about. My rather melancholy thoughts were interrupted as Sir Rufus headed to my chamber and asked if he could speak with me.

"Of course, Sir Rufus. Come in. I hope that Robt has settled well in his new room."

I offered him a chair, which he took.

"Yes, My King," he said, still showing his disappointment regarding Lord Robt's actions.

I remembered that I had sent all the servants away.

"You can go, if you'd like. In fact, tell the guards that they are entitled to leave as well."

"I will inform my men, but I would rather stay here, My King. I have spent the last two decades here. I might as well die here too."

"That makes sense," I responded, with an unexpected laugh.

"It seems to be the only thing that does at the moment," he wisely commented.

I offered him some wine, which he refused.

"Is it true that they are a few days away?" he asked after a while.

I enhanced his knowledge.

"Six, to be exact. I imagine it's closer to five now."

"Yes, especially with that favourable wind. Well, favourable to them."

"I fear it might be favourable to us as well," I sighed. He was confused by my remark, so I elaborated. "If they don't get here soon, we might have all killed each other before they get the chance. They are already coming to kill the wrong king."

"In a way, they have already killed Bruk. Poor lad. I know what it's like to lose a loved one."

His tone got sadder with every word. Perhaps that was why he changed his mind and reached for the wine.

"Me too."

We both held our cups in the air out of respect for our fallen king. He turned to face me.

"My King, why haven't you gone to be with Lady Breck? The days are numbered now, and if the servants deserve it then so do you."

"Breck has deemed it necessary to help her citizens. It would be wrong for me not to do the same, especially now that I'm king."

He chuckled at my expense.

"Oh, My King, you cannot see it. Lady Breck, or should I say Queen Breck now, has hated it here since she was a child. She would tell me how lucky you were to live in the beauty of the High North and how she wished to be there constantly. The South was her house but the High North has always been her home. And then there is you. You have spent just as many years here as you did up there so I see why you have appreciation for this place. But you were a prisoner here before you were king. The people of the High North love you more than these Southerners ever could. You may be their king, but you will always be an outsider here - no disrespect intended, of course, My King."

"No, Sir Rufus, you are right," I stood immediately, "I need to go home."

*** * * ***

Sir Rufus enhanced his wisdom further by reminding me that the journey was too far to take as I would barely make it to the Midlands before darkness crept in. I waited until the next morning to ride up to the High North. I must admit, the joy on the faces of my wife and daughter made me feel foolish for even considering not seeing them before death arrived. We spent the night pretending as if nothing was wrong, mostly for Lady Nea's sake. The meal we shared was a triumph and it was so lovely to hear my little girl's excited tales of her discoveries once more, as well as to hold my dear Queen Breck in my arms again. She had heard all, even about Lord Robt's attempt, as pitiful as it was, to become king. She was just happy to see a face that she loved. Once Lady Nea had gone to bed, Queen Breck and I were left to contemplate the reality of what was to come. I handed her the letter, which she intently read.

"Oh, Barrat, how has this happened? How can they take away our baby's life so soon? She has done no wrong and is so pure of heart. We all have our sins, but she has none at all."

My beloved rested her head on my chest as we lay in bed. Her tears rolled down my stomach.

"I know," I said as I kissed her forehead.

"I wish there was a way for us to escape. Just one last hope of giving our precious little girl a future. Why did those traitors have to burn all the ships?"

We lay in silence, briefly. It was the first time that I had thought of escape. Queen Breck's mentioning of ships reminded me of what King Bruk had said before he died, something that had been cloudy due to my melancholic emotion and attempt to cast that failure of a conversation out of my weeping mind.

"Not all the boats."

I sat up, forcing Queen Breck to do the same.

"I'm sorry to mention the travesty, but in my last conversation with Bruk he told me that there is a fleeing ship still intact."

"Seriously? Then we must go! We must head to the South at first sunrise so we arrive in the dead of night."

Queen Breck jumped up with glee, having completely forgotten that everyone else, including her own people, would still be damned. She paused in her excitement to see me, who hadn't gotten as gleeful as her, still remaining on the bed.

"What's wrong?"

"Nothing. It's a miracle that we have found a way to protect Nea. I couldn't be more pleased."

"Then why do you look so miserable?" she queried in anger.

"You know that I have to stay. I am the king. I'm now the whole reason they are coming to burn the isle. I am the one who let Kinby go. I am the one who has caused all of this. I cannot abandon the people that I have damned, not even if it means that I would get to see my Little Lady grow up."

I started to cry, and so did she. She pulled my face towards her and kissed my lips, which tasted salty with the tears. She was in disbelief that I would even consider staying.

"You aren't going to stay! You can't stay! I can't do it without you. I can't carry on if I know that you're dead and we could have stopped it. I mean, Nea is the image of you! How can I look at my girl, our girl, if all she does is remind me that you're not there anymore."

Her hysterics were stopping her from breathing so I tried to calm her down the best I could. Eventually, she did. I kissed her head again as she cradled in my arms.

"It's my job to stay. It's my job to lead them. How can I lead them when I've selfishly left them all behind?"

"You are so brilliant, you know. Even in this time you still think of the people. But what is the point? They are going to die whether you stay or not. The kingdom knows that you have made your mistakes, but the kingdom also knows what you have given up. All of those people know that you have been the reason for so many great developments and forward steps in this land, and they know that you are responsible for making their lives safer and better. Barrat, there are thousands of people who would be willing to die for you all because of the impact you've made on their lives. And those that wouldn't? Well, they don't deserve you or your loyalty in the slightest! But now there is nothing you can do to make their lives any better. You have done your part. You have earned the right to be with your family. Please, for once, don't do the right thing, because being right sometimes makes you a fool."

She was right. My family is my reward for all those years of service. I deserved to see my little girl grow up and I had the chance to make that a reality. I jumped up, now as excited as my wife had previously been, and kissed Queen Breck's beautiful lips once more.

"I'll go and tell Miss Norma the plan. We can't afford to lose a step."

The Fleeing Bastard - II

After being convinced by my beloved Queen Breck that it was indeed best for me to abandon my duty as king in order to leave the isle for the sake of our beautiful daughter, we weren't blessed with having a copious amount of time and we needed to be particularly careful about how we handled the forthcoming events. We quickly travelled back from the High North to the capital, something that Lady Nea, who had no idea of the severity of the situation in the slightest, was rather excited about. We knew that the fleeing ship was relatively small - it only had around six cabins in total - so we needed to be inconspicuous about our actions. The knowledge of our plans may have caused a riot from our subjects and we needed to avoid that. We had our reasons to flee but it was unfair to expect the damned to see us leave without a sense of injustice. As well as this, if our fellow patricians, who now were all located in the North, caught word of our escape then they too would wish to join. We would have wished for them to come, of course, but a ship needs cooks and sailors. We had no room for them, considering that I had already planned to bring Miss Norma, Miss Celie and, although I hadn't told my angry wife about it, Lord Robt on our excursion. We knew that we needed staff but opted not to acquire them until the ship was ready to sail. That way we could leave the isle with very little suspicion on the part of the people. The ship was located in a hidden boat house at the Southern Dock. Although we were the only people who knew of the ship, the dock was very much in sight from the nearby villages. It was a small dock with very little space, to the point where only one vessel could sit there at a time. This meant that we had to work at night and we had to work quickly.

I had spent the majority of the journey from the High North to the capital contemplating what to do about Sir Rufus. Despite my kindness in allowing servants to leave, I knew that there were still many of them who remained in the castle. They too had lived there all their lives and saw it fit to die there too. This meant that informing Sir Rufus of our voyage would have meant risking other servants discovering our plans. On further contemplation, I regretfully decided that I would not risk discovery on the basis that the man was very old and would probably disapprove of my fleeing. And so, by the time we reached the capital, it was only myself, Queen Breck, Miss Norma, Miss Celie, and the old fisherman Skipper who knew of the planned voyage. Skipper had worked with Lord Shay and I all those years ago and had come into some bother, losing both his wife and his daughter to illness just a few seasons prior to our escape. I was happy that I could provide the man that my brother admired a fresh start. We had many maps, but none of them stretched further than the Mediterranean. It was unknown what, if anything, was out there, but we needed to rely on the assumption that there was something beyond our shores. I had decided with Skipper that we were to sail south until we felt as though we could sail south no more. Then we would head east until we were in sight of land. After that, it was down to the acceptance and kindness of others. If we were to survive we would need kindness, which is never a guarantee.

* * * *

Eventually, I had to tell my beloved of my wish to bring Lord Robt along with us. I knew that he had killed one of her brothers, but in fairness so had I. I thought that we could put his attempted mutiny behind us in favour of allowing our daughter to grow up with at least one uncle. She, as I suspected, fought rather hard against my request.

"Are you sure you don't want me to get Robt from the dungeon?"

I felt much disappointment for Lord Robt after his selfishness and I had told him that he was no brother of mine, but I didn't want my wife to live on with regret.

311

"No! He is to remain in that cell! If I had been there when he rioted, I would have killed him on the spot."

"But he is your brother, Breck."

I thought emotionally manipulating her was my best chance, as wrong as it may be. I didn't want her to condemn her own brother to death. I know the feeling is a bad one.

"Not anymore he isn't! I suggest that you drop it now."

I deemed it suitable to follow her request. Perhaps if it were King Bruk or Lord Neman, or dare I say Lord Suln, I would've made a greater effort to fight the cause. Considering Lord Robt had tried to get rid of me since the Great Packsaddle War had concluded, I decided that it was in fact fate that meant he would be staying behind.

"We need to find some sailors, my love," I reminded her, cautious of our lack of time. "I know every sailor from the High North but fear that my lack of knowledge on the matter down here may hinder us."

"What are we to do, Barrat?"

In her distress, she took a moment to cuddle into me for some reassurance despite that my words brought only fear, not comfort.

"Why don't you go to the castle and wake the cook."

I thought keeping her preoccupied would help.

The cooks shared different quarters to other servants due to their rather early start to the day, and I knew that only one of the seven cooks had decided to stay within the walls of Castle Eli.

"I know that Miss Celie is a cook's daughter but I would like to have some greater experience on board. Whilst you do that, I'll have a little think about our sailor conundrum."

She kissed my lips before quietly rushing into the castle to acquire the cook, whom she had known since she was Lady Nea's age. Whilst she was gone, Skipper, Miss Celie and myself finished loading the ship with the clothes and the food store that I had been acquiring for the past few days in preparation for a possible barricade in the keep. This included cured meats, vegetables, and plenty of grain, flour, salt, cheese and yeast.

"Daddy, where are we?" asked a very soft voice.

After a relatively loud crash was caused by the dropping of a box, Lady Nea awoke from her slumber that had been taking place in the arms of her Auntie Norma.

"We are at the docks, my gorgeous girl," I told her before taking her from Miss Norma's arms and kissing her head.

"Are we going fishing?" she asked, perking up. It was slightly unfortunate as I had hoped that she would quickly drift off back to sleep. "Mummy says that fishing is too dangerous but I have always wanted to go!"

I couldn't help but smile at her enthusiasm, despite the bleak circumstances.

"No, we are not going fishing, but I will take you fishing one day, when you are ready."

"Really Daddy?" she asked, with a sparkle in her eye.

"Of course!"

She giggled with excitement before abruptly pausing.

"Where's Mummy gone?"

Her eyes darted around in search of her mother, who was still inside the castle. I kissed her head, in an attempt to reassure her that everything was okay.

"She'll be back soon, my love. Don't you worry. Why don't you try to get some more sleep?"

"How could I possibly sleep when Mummy is missing?" she asked, concerned. Her sweetness made it hard to be angry. "Mummy!"

Her shout startled our crew and I was forced to quickly cover her mouth with my hand to prevent her from shouting further.

"No, my love. You cannot shout. Not today. Mummy has just gone to find an old friend. She'll be back before you know it."

I took my hand away.

"Your hand was very sweaty, Daddy. Are you okay?" she asked me as she wiped her mouth, giggling.

I found her comment rather amusing.

"Yes, I'm fine, I've just been lifting some heavy boxes, that's all."

"Well, you should've asked me to help. I am getting very strong, you know."

"Are you now?"

"Yes!" she exclaimed, simultaneously flexing her muscles. "Mummy says that one day she'll teach me to be an archer. She says that I'll be better than you."

She bopped my nose with her finger to emphasise her point.

"Well, Mummy is the best archer I know, so you'll be in good hands."

Almost as soon as we finished talking about her superior ability, Queen Breck came from the castle with the old cook, who walked rather slowly towards the dock. She approached and kissed my lips once more and, after the demand of Lady Nea who was reaching her arms out in a plea to be held, took our girl into her arms and led the old cook to meet her fellow passengers. As I continued to contemplate where to acquire some sailors which, thanks to Lady Nea, I hadn't had much of a chance to do with any real conviction, I was startled by the appearance of Sir Rufus.

*** * * ***

"Oh, Sir Rufus, you gave me quite the scare," I admitted, unable to make eye contact with him out of my shame.

Even in his old age, and despite my insistence that he shouldn't, he knelt down to honour me.

"I'm sorry, My King. I heard rumours of your departure and wanted to see if they were true. People saw you with cured meats and flour the other day and questioned whether you were planning on fleeing."

This was annoying considering that the food store was, in fact, not for this voyage. However, we were almost fully loaded and so I wasn't too worried about causing a stir. I helped him get to his feet but very much remained embarrassed.

"Oh, Sir Rufus, you must think so little of me."

"Of course not, My King. The suspicion doesn't seem too high, though a few are labelling you the Fleeing Bastard, amongst the rumours. I can charge them with treason if it suits."

I was already being rather contradictory in my actions so punishing anyone for such a small disservice seemed unfair.

"No, no. Just leave them be. They mustn't have much pride left in their patricians anymore."

"So you are leaving then, My King?"

"Yes, my beloved and I can't stand here and let our little Nea burn in the flames. Not when we have the chance to prevent it, as selfish as that may be."

He looked at me sympathetically.

"My King, may I have your permission, considering the circumstances, to speak to you not as a sir to a king but as an old man to a young one?"

"Of course."

He sat down on nearby steps and gestured for me to follow suit, which I did. The noble man looked at me with such kindness in his weary eyes.

"I know that you are having trouble coming to terms with what you are doing. Being a king is very tough and demands a lot of sacrifices, as you well know. I note that you have not acted as king for all that long but you served your brother with great loyalty for many a year and so you know, more than most, the weight of the task at hand."

I nodded to confirm my agreement with his words.

He continued, "I, as the old man that I am, have made many mistakes in my lifetime and feel as though each mistake has brought me a great deal of knowledge and experience. Bearing that in mind, young Barrat, I implore you to feel no guilt at this decision. You have dedicated so much to this kingdom and made so many sacrifices, but there's no point in making any more. I remember delivering a letter, written by you, to the family during the war. You had gone against your sister's wicked demand not to send word of the imminent attack because you knew that innocent people would die if you didn't. You saved thousands that day, and you lost your only full-blooded family in order to save those innocent people. But this is different. You can't save these people now. You owe it to yourself to leave. Do you know what a miracle is, Barrat?"

"Why yes, Rufus, I do. A miracle is an ineffable event that creates happiness."

"A fair answer, but the best definitions aren't always expressed with words."

He reached across to point to my Little Lady who, still being very tired, was falling asleep in Queen Breck's arms as my wife carried her on board.

He continued, "Your daughter, Barrat, is the closest thing to a miracle I have ever seen. The girl has brought so much joy to your family since the moment of her birth and is the most loved person in all the kingdom. Every day since her birth, I have walked the capital's uneven cobbles and heard the people rave about that girl. If they could know that she is the only reason for your departure, they would wave you off as you drifted away."

I stood, helped him up, and then shook his hand - he never was a fan of a hug.

"Thank you for your kind words, Sir Rufus. I don't think our kingdom has ever seen a man as noble and kind as you. You must come with us. After all of your service to myself and my wife, you have earnt some rest."

He softly smiled at me before bowing his head in appreciation for my offer.

"Thank you, My King, but my rest is on its way from the Mainland. I have had my time. I am ready to sit at the grand table with the gods, and if I can slice a few more enemies to death in the process then I can die a truly happy man. One last hurrah for an old man can do no harm."

I was disappointed to hear that he wasn't coming, but I understood. I pulled him in for an unappreciated hug.

"That is fair. I can't thank you enough for all you have done."

"My King, let me do you one more service, for old times sake, for an old man. I know some fine sailors, which you seem to be lacking. You cannot go on a voyage without them. I hope there is enough room on the ship."

"Yes, I believe there is. It's a kindness that you suggested it, good man."

"I shall be back before the sun rises, My King."

He rushed away to do his final duty, but I felt the need to ask for one more thing from the great Sir. I conservatively called after him and he turned back.

"Oh, Sir Rufus! Do you know of Miss Aton by any chance? She was once a fellow servant in Castle Eli. I believe she lives with her sister and niece."

"Why, of course, My King," he seemed to find the thought of her rather nostalgic. "She is a funny little thing, that niece of hers!"

"I have heard many stories, kind Sir. Could you wake them and bring them here, please? Tell them to pack all that they own."

Those many stories made me think that she would get along with my daughter rather swimmingly, which added to my eagerness to bring them along in Lord Robt's place. I thought that I should try to save at least one of my subjects and I couldn't think of anyone who deserved it more.

"Of course."

With that added task, he picked up the pace. Sure enough, he had delivered the sailors and my guests all before the sun rose. So, as my kingdom was trapped in their slumber, we set off and left our doomed land and our remaining patricians, who all held a great place in our hearts despite our differences over many a year, behind in a mixture of relief, regret, and immense sorrow.

The Voyage of 1116

Something about Saddle Isle that has always frustrated me was our obsession with branding tragic events with the adjective 'great.' It was King Bruk who insisted on such a thing, so he explained to me, on many occasions, the rationale behind the names. I always understood that it is meant in the context of size and significance, but I can't express the difficulty I have endured in relaying our history and being forced to refer to some of the most traumatising experiences of my life as great. I say this because, in the natural cycle of life, I was on yet another voyage fleeing away from my home, twenty years after the first. With that initial voyage being referred to, in true Saddle Isle form, as the Great Voyage of 1096, I am making it clear that the second one is never to be referred to as great no matter the meaning and context behind it.

We had sailed far enough for Saddle Isle to be out of sight. More importantly, we had fled the kingdom in enough time not to see the carnage of the invasion from afar, something that was crucial for the benefit of my little girl who seemingly wasn't aware of the severity of our journey or the permanence of our voyage. For me, however, I am unsure what would be worse: seeing the damnation of my people or being left to only imagine it. I spent many nights unable to sleep after I left my kingdom behind to burn, and so was left with the cruel partnership of time and a lack of distraction - a rather similar experience to when I was in the dungeons of Castle Sear, as it was called at the time, all those years before. It was impossible for me to ignore the tragedy but I had to try to manipulate my thoughts to develop the most positive assumptions about the events, as paradoxical as that seems. I may not have been able to escape the thoughts of their demise, but I could hope that their deaths were as quick and painless as possible. I like to imagine that Lady Daid died in the company of her loving brother and his wife. I like to imagine that Sir Rufus died content with his many achievements and, perhaps, having killed a few more enemies before his death. I like to imagine that Mister Dearil, who warned me of the impending doom, died holding his wife dearly. It doesn't make it much better but it helps me to find some sleep every once in a while, which is what I need to look after my family.

****

I held tightly onto Lady Nea as the winds grew sharper. She was now of six years, the same age as Queen Breck and myself were during the Great Voyage of 1096. It was always going to be a difficult venture but I never imagined that freezing would be a possibility. We had been sailing for almost three seasons and the initial warm weather had quickly shifted. The bannister on the ship deck that supported stairs leading up to the helm was decorated with icicles, causing me great distress for my family's welfare. I spent my early years in the cold of the English north but it was never as cold as this was. We had sailed south, as we had decided. Skipper advised that we should sail south until we can no longer cope with the unpredictable climate and then head east, then slightly to the north, until we find land. We had plenty of supplies as well as our two cooks, so we could sail for as long as we felt necessary. My beloved wife was no better on the waves than she was when we took our voyage from England to the isle. She spent large periods of time in an isolated cabin and didn't improve as the waves grew rougher as we got further south. Lady Nea would visit her daily, as would I, which was necessary for her wellbeing. The waves wouldn't kill her, but the lack of her food intake worried me greatly.

"Will you eat for me please, my love?" I asked, hopefully.

I knew that she was trying, but I wasn't going to stand there and silently watch the one woman I'd ever loved die. Not after the effort we had put in to ensure that our family could stay together. She looked up at me and reached her arm out. I took it. She pulled me to sit on the bed beside her as she remained too weak to sit up.

"I am trying, Barrat, but I can't."

She gestured to the bucket that was set on the floor. Every time she tried to eat, her food would return to the surface and take its place in the bucket. I knew that wasn't her fault, even Lady Nea knew that, but it was difficult to just accept that she was going. I didn't leave my people behind to lose my family at sea. Plus, as much as I loved Lady Nea, I was so used to Queen Breck being her primary carer that I knew I wouldn't be able to cope without her. I couldn't afford to lose my wife.

"Please keep trying," I pleaded as I kissed her sweaty forehead.

✱ ✱ ✱ ✱

"It's getting pretty cold, My King," Skipper pointed out in an attempt to begin a necessary conversation.

Skipper made a great effort to maintain noble courtesy, despite the fact that my kingdom no longer stood.

"Barrat is just fine. I don't deserve the respect of being called king."

I looked down at the deck, ashamed.

"You did what was best for your family, My King, and you allowed me to fill the hole that losing mine had left behind. That deserves my respect."

His acceptance forced me to raise my eyes to meet his.

One minor positive outcome of the voyage was that Skipper and my friend Miss Aton, who was correct when she claimed of her beauty when clean, quickly started to grow close after their introduction to each other. Skipper had quickly become a great paternal figure to Miss Aton's niece and appreciated feeling like a father once more. Of course, she could never be a replacement but his new niece brought back many happy memories of his own daughter, whom he missed so deeply.

"What about those that weren't granted that chance?" I rather unfairly asked.

He didn't answer. For a short while we stood in silence in an almost reflective manner, as if we stood and mourned for all that we left behind to be slaughtered by the genocidal King of England. But my mourning was rather superficial, considering that I was now the Fleeing Bastard of Saddle Isle. I needed to break this silence.

"You're right, it is getting rather cold. How many men have we lost?"

It was Skipper's turn to look at the deck floor.

"Three, My King, all to the frost."

"Start heading east, to the north. We must avoid as much exposure to this frost as we can. I can't be responsible for any more deaths."

"Yes, My King."

He headed to the helm and ordered for the change in direction. For that brief moment I had alone, I simply looked out to the sea. I still remember the sadness of leaving my mother behind. That is a pain that will never leave me. Now I had the sadness of leaving thousands to burn at the hands of King Henry of England - a man who, whether he liked it or not, was my very own uncle. He was given too much power considering his vile tendencies. I do understand the pride that one can have for a parent, though. I felt nothing for my father, despite the fact that he was a king, but my mother was never to be disrespected. Even so, I wouldn't kill thousands of whores just because my mother was wrongly labelled as one.

****

"Daddy, I'm cold," said that soft voice again.

Lady Nea had been with her mother all morning. To my delight, Queen Breck was beginning to get better in a miraculous turn of events. We were owed a miracle, I suppose. She had started to stomach her food and was strong enough to sit up now, which I was ever so thankful for. Not only was I relieved that my love was going to be okay but it somewhat justified the decision for us to leave.

"What are you doing out on the deck, Little Lady?" I asked, picking her up into my arms.

I watched her emerald green eyes examine the sea.

"I came looking for you, Daddy," was her excuse for breaking the rules.

"Well, that is very kind of you."

She shivered in my arms so I carried her towards the doors to the cabins.

"What is this?"

She looked up to the sky as snowflakes slowly drifted down and landed on her cloak. It was then that I realised that all the winters since her birth had been without snow. Granted, some were rather cold, but never as cold as this. Her eyes widened and her smile broadened as she stared in awe at the snow that danced down. I stretched out my finger to catch a snowflake on my nail.

"This is snow, my dear. When I was your age and was living in England, it used to snow quite often."

"It's so pretty, Daddy."

I looked at my daughter and couldn't help but smile. She, at this moment, reminded me exactly why I had to flee the isle. The precious gem that I held in my arms deserved the chance to live and so I did my duty as a father to give her that chance. Her reaching for the falling flakes was interrupted by a rather large yawn for someone so small.

"I think you need to have a nap, Little Lady."

"I want to watch the snow, Daddy. Please can I stay and watch?"

Since it was her first experience of it, I allowed her to enjoy the moment. I asked for a member of the crew to find me a blanket, which he quickly did. I wrapped her up and took a seat on the cold steps that led up to the helm, cradling my precious little girl in my arms.

"I suppose we can stay here until you drift off to sleep."

"Thank you, Daddy," she said as she burrowed herself into my chest. After a pause, she made an odd request. "Will you sing for me, please?"

"Sing for you?" I asked.

This was the first time she'd ever requested this from me.

"Yes, sing for me. Whenever I can't get to sleep, Mummy always sings for me."

I thought for a moment. I did not know of many songs, but I only needed to know one. I sang the only song that had ever meant anything to me:

> "Hush, the wind blows wildly,
> And all the stars shine low,
> But I will be beside ye',
> From now until I go.
> Let all the earthly wonder,
> Close ye' eyes so wide,
> To let ye' see and ponder,
> What lurks on the other side."

As she closed her eyes and drifted into sleep, I looked to the snow and continued to think of my mother for a while.